Murder in the Santi

by

Brett Shayler

Written by
Brett Shayler
Book Cover by Karen Shayler
This book has utilized artificial intelligence (AI) programs, including ProWritingAid, Grammarly, QuillBot, Canva, and Adobe Photoshop, to aid in the editing and book cover design

Table of Contents

Forward

To the quiet observers, the ones who see the cracks in the facade, who notice the subtle shifts in body language and the unsaid words hanging heavy in the air. To those who understand that beneath the polished veneer of luxury and leisure, the human heart can harbor shadows as deep and unforgiving as any storm at sea. This story is for the retired agents, the ones who carry the weight of past cases but find a flicker of purpose in the unexpected, the ones who believe that even in the twilight of their careers, justice can still be served, one carefully deduced step at a time. It is for the unwavering partners who stand by their convictions, even when faced with deception and danger, and for the historians who remind us that understanding the past is crucial to navigating the treacherous currents of the present. May you always find the courage to seek the truth, no matter how perilous the voyage, and may the stillness you find be earned, a testament to the storms you have weathered. This narrative honors the resilience of the human spirit in the face of unimaginable conspiracy and acknowledges the quiet battles waged in pursuit of an elusive yet essential justice. It's for anyone who has ever felt the unsettling dissonance between a beautiful setting and the darkness that can unfold within it, a reminder that the greatest mysteries often lie not in distant lands, but within the confines of the human heart and the intricate webs of power we weave.

Chapter 1: The Unforeseen Voyage

The 'Sovereign Star' lived up to its name. It was in every sense of the word a sovereign entity of the ocean, a self-contained world of polished chrome, hushed elegance, and the relentless, soothing rhythm of the waves. For Dale Miller, it was a sanctuary from the turbulent seas of his past. The ghosts of cases, the specters of victims he couldn't save, had been his unwelcome companions for too long. He sought not just a vacation, but an absolution of sorts, a chance to recalibrate his soul against the endless horizon.

He found a solitary perch on the aft deck, the salty spray a welcome balm against the lingering anxieties that clung to him like sea mist. The ship, a behemoth of luxury, glided through the cerulean expanse, leaving a pristine white wake that seemed to erase any trace of its passage. Below, the gentle sway of the deck was a subtle counterpoint to the grander, more forceful movements of the ocean. It was a dance Miller had always found mesmerizing, a force of nature that dwarfed human concerns. The distant horizon, a clean, unbroken line where the sky met the sea, was precisely the simplicity he craved.

Miller's eyes, however, remained active, a habit etched into his very being from decades of vigilance. Even as he consciously tried to surrender to the tranquility, his mind cataloged the details. The precise gleam of the chrome railings, the intricate patterns of the teak decking, the hushed efficiency of the stewards moving with practiced grace. He observed the passengers, a diverse tapestry of humanity drawn to this floating palace. There were the boisterous families, their laughter echoing across the deck; the couples lost in their own intimate worlds; and the solitary figures, like himself, seeking escape or perhaps something more. Each face, each gesture, was a small piece of data, stored away in the vast archives of his memory. It was an ingrained caution that whispered of hidden depths beneath placid surfaces.

The ship's interiors were a testament to opulence. Grand ballrooms adorned with crystal chandeliers that cast a warm, inviting glow, intimate lounges with plush velvet seating, and elegant dining rooms where the clinking of silverware and hushed conversations created a symphony of refined leisure. Miller had toured the ship earlier, a necessary reconnaissance mission for any seasoned investigator, even one on vacation. He noted the labyrinthine corridors, the seemingly endless array of staterooms, the discreetly placed security cameras that, to most, were part of the luxurious ambiance, but to him, were potential witnesses. This vessel, this contained universe of steel and glass, was a microcosm of society, a closed environment where secrets could fester and dramas could unfold with an amplified intensity. The sheer number of individuals, their varied backgrounds and motivations, hinted at a fertile ground for intrigue, a notion that both disturbed and intrigued him.

He sipped his iced tea, the condensation beading on the glass — a small, tangible reality in the ocean's vastness. The gentle breeze ruffled his salt-and-pepper hair, and for a fleeting moment, the weight on his shoulders seemed to lift. The ghosts were silenced by the immensity of the sea and the promise of a quiet voyage. He was Dale Miller, a retired FBI agent, seeking nothing more than a few weeks of uninterrupted peace. He did not know how quickly that fragile peace would shatter, nor how their meticulous observation of details of his surroundings would soon become the very threads of a deadly unraveling. The ship was a world unto itself, and like any world, it harbored its share of shadows, its own unique capacity for hidden dramas, a truth he was about to discover with chilling certainty.

The vastness of the ocean could be deceptive. It stretched out, infinite and unyielding, yet the 'Sovereign Star' was a confined space, a vessel carrying hundreds of lives within its gleaming hull. This paradox was not lost on Miller. It was a perfect stage, he mused, for the unfolding drama that had once defined his life. He adjusted his position, the sun warming his face, and allowed himself to drift, just for a moment, into the illusion of true serenity. He was here to escape, to mend, to find a quiet corner where the echoes of the past could not reach him. But the ingrained vigilance, the deep-seated instinct for observation, refused to be entirely silenced. It was a part of him, as intrinsic as his own heartbeat, and it would serve him, and perhaps others, in ways he couldn't yet imagine. He scanned the surrounding faces, not with suspicion, but with a practiced, almost subconscious, assessment of human behavior. The ship was a closed system, and in closed systems, he knew, the most dangerous elements often lurked beneath the most polished surfaces. The opulent interiors, the diverse passengers, the hushed elegance–it was all a carefully constructed facade, and he had a feeling that, for him, the façade was about to crack.

The very air aboard the 'Sovereign Star' seemed to hum with an almost palpable sense of luxury and calm. It was an atmosphere meticulously curated, designed to lull its passengers into a state of blissful unawareness. Polished chrome gleamed under the soft ambient lighting, reflecting the hushed movements of elegantly dressed individuals. The scent of expensive perfume mingled with the faint, briny tang of the ocean, a fragrant tapestry woven into the fabric of the cruise. Miller found himself in a quiet alcove on one of the promenade decks, the gentle murmur of conversations from a nearby lounge providing a comforting background noise. He watched the endless, mesmerizing roll of the waves, a rhythm that spoke of ancient power and timeless passage. It was a stark contrast to the sharp, often jarring, rhythms of his former life, a life punctuated by urgent calls, flashing lights, and the constant hum of impending danger.

Here, the most pressing concern was the meticulous selection of the evening's dining experience or the choice of a cocktail. Miller had deliberately sought out this quiet corner, away from the more boisterous gatherings, to savor the beginning of his much-needed respite. The sea breeze, cool and invigorating, caressed his face, carrying with it the promise of days filled with nothing more demanding than the consideration of a sunset or the exploration of a new deck. His eyes, however, were never entirely at rest. Years of ingrained habit, of scanning for threats and anomalies, meant that even in repose, his gaze lingered, cataloging the details of his surroundings. The way a certain passenger nervously adjusted their tie, the subtle tension in the shoulders of another, the fleeting, almost imperceptible glances exchanged between two individuals across the deck–these were the minutiae that formed the bedrock of his professional life.

He noted the pristine condition of the ship's railings, the intricate carvings on the wooden benches, the almost theatrical perfection of the floral arrangements gracing the entrance to the main salon. It was a world designed for pleasure, for escape, and Miller, despite his conscious effort to relax, couldn't help but appreciate the sheer artistry of its construction. But beneath the surface of this manufactured serenity, he sensed the inherent complexities of any gathering of this scale. Hundreds of lives, each with its own history, its own secrets, its own potential for drama, were now contained within this floating metropolis. The ship was a sealed environment, a microcosm where every interaction, every hidden motive, was amplified. He found a quiet satisfaction in observing it all, even if his current objective was to disengage. The distant horizon, a perfect, unwavering line, was a welcome sight, a symbol of the boundless peace he hoped to find. Yet, even as he embraced the tranquility, a part of him, the part honed by years of navigating the treacherous currents of human deceit, remained acutely aware of the potential for hidden dramas within this opulent world. He was a detective, even in retirement, and the 'Sovereign Star' was, in its own way, a captivating puzzle waiting to be observed.

The salt spray, once a balm, now carried a faint prickle of unease. Dale Miller, adrift in the azure expanse aboard the 'Sovereign Star,' had been meticulously crafting a narrative of repose. His past, a tapestry woven with the frayed threads of unresolved cases and the ghostly visages of those he couldn't protect, was meant to be tucked away, relegated to the annals of a life meticulously compartmentalized. The ship, a gilded sanctuary of polished chrome and hushed elegance, was his chosen ark, a vessel designed to carry him away from the turbulent waters of regret and into the serene, predictable currents of retirement. He had settled into a comfortable rhythm, the gentle sway of the deck a counterpoint to the cacophony of his former existence, the endless horizon a promise of uncomplicated peace. He had observed the opulent surroundings, cataloged the faces, and, for the first time in years, felt a genuine loosening of the vise that had tightened around his soul. The ghosts, he had dared to believe, were finally at bay.

Then, he saw her.

It was a flicker, a movement at the periphery of his vision, a silhouette against the blinding sun that snagged his attention with the suddenness of a siren's wail. He'd seen that gait before, the confident, purposeful stride that spoke of an inner discipline, a honed precision. The salt-and-pepper hair was a touch longer, perhaps, and the relaxed elegance of cruise wear replaced the crisp lines of her usual power suits, but there was no mistaking the woman. Anna Miller. His wife.

The coincidence was so profound, so statistically improbable, that it struck Miller with the force of a physical blow. On a vessel of this magnitude, carrying hundreds of souls across the vast, indifferent ocean, their paths should never have crossed. His carefully constructed bubble of solitude, his meticulously planned escape, seemed to pop with a barely audible sigh. A familiar unease, the kind that had been his constant companion for decades, began to stir within him, a deep-seated professional instinct rising to the surface like a predatory fish from the abyssal depths.

He watched her for a moment, a reluctant observer of a scene he hadn't anticipated. She was speaking with a small group, her head tilted slightly, her hands gesturing with the same controlled energy he remembered. Even at a distance, her presence was commanding, a vibrant spark in the muted palette of the deck. Miller felt a strange mixture of apprehension and a grudging familiarity. Anna was not just a former colleague; she was a force of nature, a woman whose sharp intellect and unwavering dedication had often both complemented and challenged his own. Their partnership had been a complex dance of shared triumphs and the quiet burden of unspoken failures.

He knew he couldn't simply turn away. To ignore her would be an act of deliberate rudeness, a negation of years of shared investigations, of late nights fueled by stale coffee and the grim pursuit of justice. With a sigh that was more resignation than annoyance, Miller pushed himself up from his perch, the iced tea glass left forgotten on the small table. He began to walk towards her, his thoughts already racing as he tried to make sense of this unexpected reunion.

As he drew closer, Anna's gaze, sharp and discerning, caught his. A flicker of surprise, quickly masked by a composed smile, crossed her features. She excused herself from her companions, her movements fluid and unhurried, and met him halfway. "Jonathan," she began, her voice the same clear, resonant tone he remembered, though perhaps a touch softer, more relaxed. "Well, this is certainly a surprise. I didn't realize you were on board."

Her composure was impeccable, as always. It was a carefully constructed facade, Miller knew, a professional shield that had served her well. Beneath the surface, however, he suspected the same currents ran that had always defined their interactions: intelligence, a keen analytical mind, and a well-guarded emotional core.

"Anna," Miller replied, offering a small, genuine smile. "The feeling is entirely mutual. I thought you were still buried under a mountain of paperwork at the Bureau." He paused, letting the pleasantries hang in the air. "What brings you to this patch of ocean?"

She chuckled, a light, airy sound that seemed to dissipate some of the tension he hadn't realized he was holding. "A much-deserved break, Johnathan. The same, I suspect, that brings you here. The powers that be finally agree. I needed a reprieve from the relentless grind." She gestured vaguely towards the ship's immensity. "Figured I'd see what all the fuss was about. Sun, sea, and... well, this." She swept her hand to encompass the opulent surroundings.

Miller nodded, the words "much-deserved break" echoing in his mind. He understood the sentiment all too well. The cumulative weight of years spent staring into the abyss of human depravity took its toll, and retirement, for many, was less an ending and more a desperate attempt at self-preservation. He sensed an unspoken understanding between them, a shared recognition of the unique pressures and sacrifices inherent in their former profession. The years of chasing shadows, of confronting unimaginable horrors, had forged a bond that transcended mere collegiality.

"It's a far cry from the precinct, that's for certain," Miller said, his gaze sweeping over the pristine deck, the elegantly dressed passengers, the endless blue horizon. "I was hoping for a few weeks of uninterrupted quiet. To simply... be."

Anna's eyes, intelligent and observant, met his, and for a fleeting moment, he saw a spark of something more than polite recognition – a silent acknowledgment of the paths they had navigated together, the cases that had etched themselves into their memories. There was a question in her gaze, a subtle probing that his ingrained instincts immediately picked up on.

"Uninterrupted quiet," she mused, a faint smile playing on her lips. "A noble pursuit, Johnathan. But knowing you, I suspect 'uninterrupted' is a relative term. You always did have a knack for finding the... complications."

Her observation was not accusatory, but an acknowledgment of his nature, his inherent drive to understand, to dissect, to uncover the truth. It was a subtle reminder of their dynamic, of the countless hours they had spent piecing together puzzles, often in the face of overwhelming odds. He recognized the familiar edge in her tone, the subtle intellectual sparring that had been a hallmark of their partnership.

"I prefer to think of it as an innate curiosity," Miller countered lightly, though he felt a faint tremor of unease. "A professional habit that's hard to break. Even on vacation, I find myself observing. It's a strange thing, seeing so many different people in one confined space. So many stories waiting to unfold."

"Indeed," Anna agreed, her gaze drifting towards the ship's railing, her expression thoughtful. "A floating microcosm of society. All the same dramas, the same hopes and fears, just on a slightly grander, more luxurious stage. And a much smaller pool of suspects should anything... untoward occur."

The casual mention of "untoward" sent a ripple of alarm through Miller. It was a word that carried a heavy weight, a loaded term that conjured images of crime scenes and interrogations. Was she merely making a dark joke, a wry observation on the nature of any gathering of people, or was there something more beneath her words? The sheer coincidence of their meeting was already a disquieting anomaly; her subtle allusions to their shared past and the darker aspects of their former lives only amplified his nascent apprehension.

He studied her, trying to decipher the subtle nuances of her expression, the almost imperceptible shift in her posture. Anna was a master of control, a woman who rarely revealed her true thoughts or feelings unless it served a strategic purpose. He remembered their last few cases together, the unspoken tensions that had begun to creep into their interactions, the diverging paths they had contemplated even as they worked side-by-side.

"I'm trying to leave all that behind, Anna," Miller said, his voice softening, a genuine plea underlying his words. "This trip is about more than just a break. It's about finding some semblance of peace, some distance from... everything."

Anna turned back to him, her gaze direct and unwavering. There was a trace of sympathy in her eyes, a recognition of the burdens he carried. "I understand, Jonathan, truly. We all carry our ghosts. Mine just tend to wear a badge." She offered another one of her controlled smiles. "But even on a holiday, old habits die hard, don't they? It's a comfort, in a way, to see a familiar face, even if that face is usually staring at me across a table piled high with case files."

Her words, while seemingly innocuous, carried a hint of something unfinished, a lingering question that hung in the air between them. He remembered the abruptness of her departure from the Bureau, the hushed rumors, the official explanation that had never quite satisfied him. He had always suspected there was more to her leaving than what had been publicly stated.

"It is," Miller conceded, the unease a low hum beneath his carefully maintained calm. "It's... reassuring. Though I must admit, the sheer improbability of this encounter is rather unsettling. This ship is enormous, Anna."

"The world is a surprisingly small place when you least expect it," she replied, her tone light, but her eyes held a depth that belied the casualness of her words. "Perhaps it's the universe's way of reminding us that no matter how far we run, some connections are simply... inevitable."

Inevitable. The word resonated with a chilling finality. Miller felt a prickle of something akin to dread. He had come seeking solitude, an escape from the complexities of his past, and instead, he had stumbled into a reunion that felt both strangely comforting and deeply disquieting. Anna , sharp, composed, and carrying with her the silent weight of their shared history, was an unexpected variable in his carefully planned equation of peace. The 'Sovereign Star', with its polished surfaces and hushed elegance, suddenly felt less like a sanctuary and more like a gilded cage, a confined space where the past, it seemed, was determined to resurface. He had a feeling that his quest for uninterrupted quiet was about to encounter its first significant, and perhaps most complicated, obstacle. The meticulously observed details of his surroundings, which had previously served as a backdrop for his desired tranquility, now seemed to sharpen, to take on a new significance, as if anticipating the unraveling of his carefully constructed peace. The vastness of the ocean no longer felt like a comforting expanse, but a vast, isolating arena in which this unexpected encounter had just set the stage for something entirely unforeseen. He was a retired agent, yes, but the instincts honed over a lifetime of investigation were not so easily silenced. And in Anna , he recognized a mind that was as finely tuned to subtle shifts and hidden currents as his own. This was no mere coincidence; it was a divergence, a fork in the road of his intended journey, and the path ahead was suddenly shrouded in an intriguing, and unsettling, mist.

The gentle strains of a string quartet, a melody designed to lull and enchant, drifted through the Grand Dining Room Santi. Crystal chandeliers cast a warm, diffused glow across the polished marble floors, reflecting in the polished surfaces of mahogany tables laden with champagne flutes and delicate canapés. The air, thick with the scent of expensive perfume and the subtle aroma of aged spirits, hummed with the polite murmur of conversation. This was the heart of the 'Sovereign Star's' welcome reception, a carefully orchestrated tableau of affluence and leisure, designed to immerse its passengers in an atmosphere of unadulterated luxury. Dale Miller, nursing a glass of amber liquid, found himself adrift in this sea of genteel anonymity, a practiced observer in a world that had once been his hunting ground.

He'd encountered Anna not long after their initial, surprising reunion. His eyes, ever-trained to scan and categorize, swept across the room, noting the clusters of well-dressed individuals, the easy laughter, the confident postures. It was a familiar environment, albeit on a grander scale, a stark contrast to the grittier locales that had once defined his professional life. He found himself listening, not just to the music or the general hum, but to the individual threads of discourse that wove through the opulent tapestry of the salon.

He leaned against a velvet-draped pillar, a strategic position that afforded him a decent vantage point without appearing too overtly engaged. The champagne, a crisp Veuve Clicquot, was undeniably superior to the lukewarm coffee that had fueled countless stakeouts, and he allowed himself a small, almost imperceptible nod of appreciation. Yet, beneath the veneer of relaxation, the old gears were beginning to turn. It was an involuntary reflex, a deeply ingrained habit that retirement had failed to erase. His mind, like a finely tuned instrument, was still attuned to the dissonant notes, the subtle shifts in rhythm that signaled something out of the ordinary.

As he let his gaze drift, he found himself drawn to a small, animated group gathered near a particularly elaborate floral arrangement. They were men, all in crisp suits, their faces animated with an energy that seemed at odds with the languid atmosphere of the reception. Their voices, though lowered, carried a certain urgency, a clipped cadence that distinguished them from the surrounding pleasantries. Miller subtly adjusted his position, his peripheral vision catching the glint of a gold watch, the sharp angles of designer cufflinks. These were not men who discussed the weather or the intricacies of cruise ship menus.

He caught snippets of their conversation, fragments of dialogue that, to his trained ear, resonated with a peculiar intensity. Words like "synergy," "leverage," and "stakeholders" were tossed about with a casual arrogance, terms that spoke of boardrooms and balance sheets, of power plays and calculated risks. One man, with thinning grey hair and a formidable jawline, gestured emphatically, his voice dropping to a conspiratorial whisper. "The due diligence is complete, Robert. The numbers are... interesting. But we need to move decisively before the competition gets wind of our intentions."

Miller's interest, already piqued, began to sharpen. "Robert," the recipient of this pronouncement, was a younger man, his features sharp and hawkish. He nodded, his eyes darting around the room with a guardedness that Miller recognized instantly. It was the look of someone who was accustomed to operating in the shadows, even in the most public of arenas. "Decisiveness is key," Robert replied, his voice a low growl. "But the regulatory hurdles... they're not insignificant. And with this market volatility, a misstep could be... catastrophic."

The word "catastrophic" hung in the air, a dark omen amidst the cheerful clinking of glasses. Miller felt a familiar prickle of unease, a subtle tightening in his gut. He recognized the undercurrent of tension, the thinly veiled anxiety that underlay their confident pronouncements. These men were not merely discussing business; they were engaged in something of far greater consequence, something that carried a palpable sense of risk.

He continued to listen, his mind sifting through the jargon, piecing together the fragmented narrative. Another man, older, with a patrician air and a meticulously groomed silver beard, chimed in. "The leverage we've secured is unprecedented, gentlemen. This merger... it's not just about market share. It's about rewriting the rules of engagement. But they won't go down without a fight. We need to ensure all our bases are covered, discreetly, of course."

Discreetly. The word was a red flag, a neon sign flashing in the otherwise benign atmosphere. Miller's gaze drifted from face to face, his internal database of profiles and behaviors whirring into action. He noted the subtle tells: the tightly clenched jaw of the grey-haired man, the almost imperceptible twitch in Robert's left eye, the way the silver-bearded man constantly adjusted his tie, a nervous tic disguised as an affectation. Their body language screamed of pressure, of high stakes. They were discussing a merger, yes, but the hushed tones, the furtive glances, the veiled references to "opposition" and "catastrophic" consequences, suggested something more than a standard corporate transaction. It hinted at a deal fraught with peril, perhaps even illegality.

He moved subtly, pretending to admire a painting on the wall, positioning himself closer to their periphery. He could discern more now. The conversation had shifted, the tempo quickening. "The offshore accounts are being finalized," one of them, a man Miller hadn't paid much attention to until now, a man with a perpetually furrowed brow, stated in a clipped, almost clipped accent. "The transfer should be completed by Tuesday. Provided... no unforeseen complications arise."

"Unforeseen complications," Robert echoed, his voice laced with a metallic edge. "That's what we pay for, isn't it? To anticipate and mitigate them. I have assurances that the... necessary channels... are being managed. This deal must go through. The rewards are too immense to be derailed by... minor ethical considerations."

Miller's mind raced. "Offshore accounts," "unforeseen complications," "necessary channels." These were not the hallmarks of legitimate business practices. They were the bread and butter of illicit transactions, of money laundering, of bribery. The "opposition" they feared might not be a rival corporation, but law enforcement, or perhaps even disgruntled parties within their own clandestine operation.

He continued to observe, his senses on high alert. The opulent setting of the Grand Dinning Room Santi, with its gilded mirrors and the melancholic strains of the cello, served as a bizarre counterpoint to the clandestine nature of their exchange. The other guests, oblivious to the undercurrent of danger, laughed and mingled, their lives seemingly untouched by the shadows that these men inhabited. Miller felt a strange sense of detachment, a ghost from his past observing a present that was eerily familiar, yet alien in its gilded packaging.

He noticed a server approaching their table, a silver tray laden with champagne. As the server offered them the drink, the man with the silver beard, the one with the patrician air, gave a subtle nod, his eyes fixed on the server's face for a fraction of a second too long. It was a flicker, a fleeting micro-expression, but to Miller, it was a signal. The server, in turn, offered a nearly imperceptible nod back, his gaze briefly meeting the silver-bearded man's before returning to the task at hand. A pre-arranged signal. A confirmation of something.

Miller's mind began to piece together a hypothetical scenario. These men were involved in a significant, potentially illegal, business deal. They were concerned about opposition and regulatory hurdles. They were using offshore accounts and what they referred to as "necessary channels." And they were communicating with someone, possibly the server, through subtle signals. Was the server a courier? A go-between? Or was he simply a pawn, unaware of the true nature of the conversations he was privy to?

The conversation drifted again, becoming more fragmented, more obscure. "The ship provides excellent... anonymity," the man with the furrowed brow commented, his gaze sweeping the room with a practiced, almost cynical, appraisal. "No electronic surveillance to worry about. Just... whispers. And the isolation of the open sea. Perfect for... final arrangements."

"Indeed," Robert agreed, a smirk playing on his lips. "A floating fortress of discretion. Let them try and trace anything once we're in international waters. By the time they even realize what's happened, we'll be long gone. And the money... well, the money will be where it needs to be."

Miller felt a surge of professional adrenaline, a sensation he hadn't experienced in months. This was it. The "uninterrupted quiet" he had sought was proving to be an illusion, shattered by the very people who embodied the kind of secrecy and deception he had dedicated his life to unraveling. The 'Sovereign Star', this opulent vessel designed for leisure, had become a stage for something far more sinister.

He withdrew slightly, leaning back against the pillar, his mind working at a furious pace. He cataloged the faces, the voices, the snippets of conversation. He recognized the underlying power dynamics, the blend of arrogance and fear that characterized their exchange. These were not petty criminals; these were individuals operating at a level of influence and sophistication that made them particularly dangerous. They were playing a high-stakes game, and the consequences, as they themselves admitted, could be catastrophic.

He made a mental note of the grey-haired man's emphatic gestures, the way he seemed to be leading the discussion, suggesting authority. He noted Robert's hawkish demeanor, his eagerness to push forward, and the silver-bearded man's more measured, almost calculating, approach. The man with the furrowed brow and the clipped accent seemed to be focused on the logistical aspects, the execution of the plan. Each man played a role, a piece in a complex puzzle.

The orchestra swelled, a dramatic crescendo that momentarily drowned out the hushed tones of their conversation. Miller used the opportunity to subtly scan the rest of the room, his gaze lingering on the faces of other passengers. Were any of them aware of what was happening? Or were they all, like him, merely observers, caught in the orbit of these clandestine dealings? He saw a few other individuals who seemed to possess a certain gravitas, men and women who exuded an aura of influence. But without more information, they were simply potential players, not necessarily involved in this specific unfolding drama.

He noticed that Anna was across the room, engaged in conversation with a distinguished-looking woman, her back to him. He wondered what she would make of this. Would her instincts, as sharp as his own, pick up on the same dissonant notes? Or would she dismiss it as the usual posturing of the wealthy elite? He knew, with a certainty born of years of working with her, that Anna had an uncanny ability to read people. He made a mental note to speak with her later, to gauge her reaction, to see if she had perceived anything amiss.

The group near the floral arrangement began to disperse, their conversation fading as they moved deeper into the salon, presumably to engage with other guests or partake in the refreshments. Miller remained by his pillar, his mind replaying the snippets of dialogue, the veiled threats, the references to illicit financial dealings. The opulence of the Grand Dinning Room Santi, which had initially seemed like a mere backdrop, now felt charged with a new significance. It was a stage, a gilded cage where secrets were being traded, and where the pursuit of immense wealth seemed to outweigh any ethical considerations.

He took another slow sip of his champagne, the effervescence doing little to quell the unsettling feeling that had taken root within him. He had come aboard the 'Sovereign Star' seeking an escape from the relentless pursuit of justice. He had envisioned quiet days, leisurely strolls on deck, and the comforting anonymity of the open sea. Instead, he found himself once again drawn into the complex web of human ambition and deceit, a world where whispers in a Grand Dinning Room Santi could carry the weight of far more than polite conversation. The ghosts of his past might have been temporarily silenced by the allure of retirement, but the instinct to uncover the truth, to expose the rot beneath the polished surface, remained as potent as ever. This was not just a vacation; it was a potential case, and the 'Sovereign Star', for all its luxurious facade, was becoming an increasingly fascinating, and potentially dangerous, environment. He knew, with a chilling certainty, that his retirement had just taken an unexpected and deeply intriguing turn. The sheer improbability of their meeting, the chance of overhearing such a clandestine exchange on the first night, was almost too much to be dismissed as mere coincidence. The universe, it seemed, had a peculiar sense of humor, and its timing was, as always, impeccable.

The laughter, the clinking of glasses, the gentle strumming of the string quartet – all the carefully curated symphony of the 'Sovereign Star's' maiden voyage, designed to lull its passengers into a state of blissful oblivion, was abruptly, violently, rent asunder. It was a sound that cut through the polite murmur of conversation like a jagged shard of glass, a piercing, unadulterated shriek of pure terror. For Dale Miller, it was a sonic alarm, a familiar, albeit unwelcome, harbinger that instantly snapped him from his detached observation and jolted him back to a reality he had hoped to leave behind. His head snapped up, his eyes, which had been idly scanning the opulent surroundings, now focused with a predator's intensity, scanning the crowd for the source of the commotion.

The initial reaction from the other passengers was a ripple of confusion, a momentary pause in the flow of their carefully constructed pleasantries. Heads turned, conversations faltered, and a collective murmur of concerned inquiry began to spread. But Miller, his instincts honed by decades of responding to the darkest manifestations of human behavior, didn't wait for the chaos to fully bloom. He was already moving, a subtle, almost imperceptible shift in his posture, a purposeful stride that carried him away from the velvet-draped pillar and towards the direction from which the scream had emanated, a direction that seemed to pull at him with an invisible, magnetic force.

He navigated the throng with a practiced efficiency, his senses on high alert. The faint scent of brine and expensive perfume was now overlaid with a prickle of something else, something metallic and vaguely acrid that he recognized with a cold dread. He saw other passengers, their faces a mixture of curiosity and unease, beginning to converge on the corridor leading to the ship's more private suites. Uniformed crew members, their initial bewilderment giving way to a semblance of professional duty, were also starting to appear, their hushed exchanges and urgent gestures clearly indicating that something was gravely amiss.

As Miller neared the source of the disturbance, the sounds of panic grew louder. Voices, previously modulated by the ship's ambiance, were now raised in alarm, their words tumbling over each other in a desperate attempt to convey the unfolding horror. He saw a cluster of crew members gathered outside one of the stateroom doors, their faces pale, their eyes wide with shock. The door itself was slightly ajar, and from within, a faint, guttural moan could be heard.

Miller didn't hesitate. He bypassed the frozen tableau of crew and passengers, his gaze fixed on the sliver of darkness visible through the opening. He pushed the door open gently, a silent apology for the intrusion, but his mind was already in overdrive, preparing for whatever grim tableau awaited him. The air inside the stateroom was heavy, thick with a stillness that was profoundly wrong. The elegant furnishings, the plush carpets, the muted lighting – all the hallmarks of luxury were present, but a palpable aura of death overshadowed them.

And then he saw him.

Slumped in an armchair, his form unnaturally askew, was the man Miller had observed earlier in the Grand Dining Room, Santi. The man with the silver beard, the one with the patrician air, who had spoken with such measured deliberation about "rewriting the rules of engagement" and the need to ensure all their bases were covered, "discreetly, of course." His eyes were open, staring blankly at the intricate pattern of the Persian rug beneath his feet, but they held no recognition, no flicker of life. A dark stain, stark against the crisp white of his shirt, bloomed across his chest, spreading like a macabre, crimson flower.

The scene was meticulously arranged, almost disturbingly so. There was no sign of a struggle, no overturned furniture, no shattered glass. The man's hands lay loosely in his lap, his impeccably tailored suit still in place, as if he had simply fallen asleep in his chair. But the stillness was too profound, the repose too absolute, to be anything other than the finality of death. And the precision of it all... it spoke of intent, of a cold, calculated execution.

Miller's breath Miller's breath hitched in his throat, an involuntary reaction to the raw, unadulterated scent of death that now filled the small space. It was a smell he had encountered countless times before, but it never truly lost its power to shock. The carefully orchestrated tranquility of the 'Sovereign Star' had been irrevocably shattered, replaced by the stark, brutal reality of murder.

He scanned the room, his eyes moving with an instinctual speed, absorbing every detail. The bedside table held a half-finished glass of water and a book, its spine unbroken. The wardrobe doors were closed, the luggage neatly stowed. There was a peculiar lack of disarray, an almost unsettling orderliness that amplified the horror of the scene. This wasn't a spontaneous act of violence; it was a deliberate statement, a message delivered with chilling efficiency.

The other passengers who had dared to peer into the stateroom gasped, a collective exhalation of shock and disbelief. Some recoiled, their faces contorted in disgust and fear, while others, morbidly fascinated, strained to get a closer look. The crew members, now joined by a uniformed officer from the ship's security detail, struggled to maintain order, their attempts to cordon off the area somewhat overwhelmed by the sheer volume of bewildered and horrified onlookers.

Miller's mind, however, was already racing. The man in the chair was not just any passenger; he was one of the individuals Miller had overheard in the Grand Dining Room, Santi, a key player in the clandestine conversation about a significant, and potentially illicit, business deal. The same man who had spoken of "opposition" and the need for discretion. His death, occurring so soon after that conversation, and in such a meticulously staged manner, couldn't possibly be a coincidence.

He recognized the subtle signs of staging, the deliberate absence of chaos that screamed of careful planning. The killer had wanted this to look like a peaceful, albeit tragic, end, but in doing so, they had inadvertently left a trail of their own calculated design. The unnatural stillness of the body, the carefully placed hands, the undisturbed surroundings – these were not the hallmarks of a crime of passion. They were the deliberate choices of someone who wanted to control the narrative, to project an image of swift, silent efficiency.

The urgency that had been simmering beneath Miller's surface since he'd overheard the conspiratorial whispers in the salon now surged to the forefront, eclipsing any lingering desire for a peaceful retirement. His vacation, he realized with a grim certainty, had officially ended before it had truly begun. The opulent luxury of the 'Sovereign Star' had become a gilded cage, a floating theater of intrigue and, now, of murder.

He stepped back from the doorway, allowing the ship's security to take over the immediate management of the scene. His role, for the moment, was to observe, and to begin piecing together the fragments of this grim puzzle. He noted the faces of the crew members, the expressions of the few brave or foolish enough to remain, searching for any flicker of recognition, any subtle clue that might betray their involvement or knowledge.

He also found himself thinking of Anna. Had she heard the scream? Had she seen the commotion? He wondered what her reaction would be if her sharp intuition had picked up on the underlying currents of unease that had been present in the Grand Dining Room, Santi, even amidst the veneer of champagne and polite conversation. He knew she possessed a keen intellect, a formidable ability to discern truth from deception, and he suspected that her initial apprehension about this voyage might have been more than just a vague premonition.

As the security personnel began to more forcefully escort passengers away from the stateroom, Miller melted back into the throng, his mind already working through the implications. The man was dead. A significant player, involved in a high-stakes, potentially illegal, deal. And his death was staged, deliberate, and clearly meant to send a message. The whispers Miller had overheard were no longer just intriguing snippets of conversation; they were now the prologue to a potential murder investigation. The scent of death was an unwelcome, but undeniable, companion, and the tranquil voyage he had envisioned had just become a very dangerous journey into the heart of a deadly conspiracy. He knew, with an absolute conviction, that the shadows he had encountered earlier were not merely figments of his overactive imagination; they were real, and one of them had just claimed its first victim. The game, as it always did, had begun.

The air in the stateroom, thick and cloying with the metallic tang of blood, seemed to resist Miller's every breath. The initial shock of discovery had begun to recede, replaced by the cold, clinical assessment that had been ingrained in him over years of confronting the worst of humanity. He moved around the periphery of the scene, his eyes meticulously sweeping the opulent confines of the suite. The uniformed crew members, their faces a mask of forced composure, were doing their best to maintain order, their hushed voices a stark contrast to the gasps and murmurs of the gawking passengers being held back at the corridor's entrance. The ship's Captain Rostova, a portly man whose uniform strained against his considerable girth, was attempting to project an air of authority, but the tremor in his hands as he clutched a tablet betrayed his unease. He barked orders, his voice a little too loud, a little too strained, as he tried to corral his scattered staff and placate the increasingly agitated onlookers.

"Clear the area! All passengers, return to your cabins or the public lounges!" Captain Rostova boomed, his voice echoing in the confined space. "This is a matter for ship's security. There is no cause for alarm."

Miller, however, knew better. Alarm was not only warranted; it was the only sensible response. He ignored Captain Rostova's pronouncements, his focus sharpening on the details the uniformed officers, blinded by their official protocols, might overlook. His gaze drifted from the body, meticulously posed in the armchair, to the surrounding environment. The pristine condition of the room was, in itself a glaring anomaly. The killer had taken their time, ensuring everything was in its place, save for the grim centerpiece. It was an act of chilling precision, a performance designed to project an image of effortless control.

It was as he circled the armchair, his eyes scanning the plush Persian rug, that he saw it. Tucked almost beneath the hem of the victim's trousers, nestled against the intricate weave of the carpet, was a small object. It was no more than an inch in length, fashioned from a dark, polished wood, its surface smooth and cool to the touch. As Miller kneeled, his movements deliberately slow to avoid drawing undue attention, he recognized it as a carving of a bird. It was a swallow, its wings elegantly swept back in mid-flight, its tiny beak pointed forward with a startling realism. The craftsmanship was exquisite, each feather meticulously defined, the wood imbued with a rich, deep grain.

This was no random piece of debris, no lost trinket. The bird was placed with an intentionality that sent a shiver down Miller's spine. It was too small, too incongruous to be anything other than a deliberate placement. A signature. A calling card left by an artist of death. He recognized the subtle arrogance of a killer who wanted their work to be acknowledged, perhaps even admired, by those who would eventually find it.

Carefully, using the tip of a pen he'd retrieved from his jacket pocket, Miller nudged the wooden bird. It was surprisingly light, yet felt solid, substantial in its tiny form. He resisted the urge to pick it up, to pocket it as evidence. Not yet. He needed to observe, to document, to understand the context. He looked around the room again, his eyes now searching for any other anomalies, any other deliberate disturbances. The victim's hands lay in his lap, his fingers relaxed, his left hand resting on the armrest. There was no weapon visible, no sign of a struggle. The stateroom was a testament to wealth and comfort, but in the wake of the murder, it felt like a meticulously curated exhibit of absence.

The Captain Rostova, his face a mask of strained professionalism, approached Miller. "Sir," he began, his voice a low growl, "I must ask you to step aside. This is a crime scene. Ship's security will handle this."

Miller turned his head, his gaze meeting Captain Rostova's. He offered a small, tight smile that didn't reach his eyes. "Captain Rostova," he said, his voice a low rumble that cut through the Captain Rostova's bluster, "I understand your protocols. But I may have observed something that warrants immediate attention." He gestured subtly with his pen towards the wooden bird. "This. It seems out of place, wouldn't you agree?"

The Captain's eyes followed Miller's gesture, his brow furrowing. He saw the tiny carving, his gaze lingering on it for a moment before dismissing it. "A passenger's trinket, perhaps," he said dismissively. "Someone may have dropped it."

"On the rug, tucked beneath his trousers, with such deliberate placement?" Miller countered, his tone even but firm. "I don't think so, Captain Rostova. This feels... intentional. A message, perhaps." His FBI training, dormant for the past few days of forced relaxation, was now fully engaged. He saw the flicker of doubt in Captain Rostova's eyes, the internal struggle between official procedure and a dawning sense of dread.

"We have already notified the authorities," Captain Rostova stated, as if reciting from a script. "Maritime security, Interpol... they are en route. But given our current location, it will be several hours before they can reach us. We are isolated with this situation." He ran a hand over his sweating brow. "We have our own security personnel, of course, but they are not trained investigators."

Miller nodded, absorbing the information. Isolated. Hours away from any official backup. That meant the killer was still on board, mingling with the very people now being held at bay. The wooden bird was more than just a signature; it was a symbol of their presence, a taunt. "Several hours," Miller murmured, the words hanging in the air. "That's a considerable amount of time for a killer to operate, or to disappear."

He stood up slowly, his eyes never leaving Captain Rostova's face. "Captain Rostova, I need to speak with your security chief. And I need access to the passenger manifest, specifically for those who disembarked at our last port of call. I also need to know if anyone matching the description of the individuals I overheard in the Grand Dining Room Santi yesterday has booked passage or been seen on board."

The Captain Rostova hesitated, his authority wavering under Miller's calm, insistent gaze. He saw in Miller's eyes not just a concerned passenger, but a man who understood the gravity of the situation, a man who possessed a certain... gravitas. "I... I will have my chief of security, Eve Rostova, meet you in my office," the Captain relented, gesturing for a nearby crew member to escort Miller. "And I will have the manifest prepared. But I must insist that you do not interfere directly with our investigation."

"Interfere is the last thing I intend to do, Captain Rostova," Miller said, his voice laced with an assurance that belied the grim reality of their predicament. "I intend to understand."

As Miller was escorted from the stateroom, he cast one last glance back at the scene. The body, the meticulously arranged room, and the tiny wooden bird, still nestled on the rug, a silent, enigmatic harbinger of the darkness that had descended upon the 'Sovereign Star'. It was a single thread, barely visible, but it was the first tangible clue in a mystery that had just begun to unravel, a mystery that promised to be as intricate and as deadly as the craftsmanship of the carved swallow itself. The ship, once a symbol of opulent escape, had become a floating crucible of suspense, and Dale Miller found himself drawn into its heat, the scent of death and intrigue clinging to him like the sea spray.

He knew, with a certainty that chilled him to the bone, that this was no ordinary crime. This was the opening act of something far more complex, far more dangerous. The voyage of the 'Sovereign Star' was no longer a pleasure cruise; it was a journey into the heart of a sinister plot, and Dale Miller was now an unwilling passenger, caught in its deadly current. He made his way through the ship, the polite chatter and laughter of other passengers now sounding hollow, discordant against the silent scream that had echoed through the corridors. Each face he passed was a potential suspect, each smile a mask. The isolation of the ship, once a charming aspect of its exclusivity, now felt like a suffocating trap.

The vast expanse of the ocean surrounding them was no longer a picturesque backdrop, but a formidable barrier, isolating them with a murderer. The intricate details of the ship, from its polished brass fixtures to its plush carpets, seemed to mock the grim reality of the murder that had occurred. It was a stark reminder that even in the most luxurious settings, darkness could find purchase, could bloom with a chilling efficiency. The wooden bird, small and seemingly insignificant, had become a beacon, a focal point around which the entire investigation would have to revolve. It spoke of a killer who was not only ruthless but also possessed a flair for the dramatic, a desire to leave their mark. This wasn't a crime of passion; it was a meticulously planned execution, a carefully orchestrated performance. The silence of the bird was deafening, a stark contrast to the violent act it represented.

It was a symbol of a deeper, more complex narrative, a story whispered in wood and shadow. Miller found himself anticipating the hours ahead, the clandestine meetings, the discreet inquiries, the painstaking piecing together of a puzzle that had been deliberately fragmented. The scent of brine and perfume was now irrevocably tainted by the cloying sweetness of death, a constant reminder of the stakes involved. A dissonant chord, a jarring note of murder that reverberated through the hull of the 'Sovereign Star' had replaced the meticulously curated symphony of the maiden voyage.

The carefully crafted illusion of security had been shattered, replaced by the unsettling knowledge that a predator walked among them, a predator who had left a single, enigmatic clue. He found himself wondering about Anna again. Would she have seen the bird? Would her sharp mind have connected it to the subtle unease she had expressed earlier?

He hoped, for her sake, that she would remain in her cabin, shielded from the unfolding drama. But he also knew that if anyone on this ship possessed the intellect and intuition to unravel this mystery alongside him, it would be her. For now, however, his focus had to remain singular. The Captain Rostova's office awaited, and with it, the first steps into a labyrinth of deception and danger. The wooden bird, clutched metaphorically in his mind's eye, was the key, the single, slender thread that would lead him through the darkness.

The ship, a marvel of engineering and luxury, now felt like a claustrophobic stage, set for a deadly play, and he was unexpectedly cast in the role of detective. The vastness of the ocean outside seemed to amplify the intimacy of the crime, trapping them all within its watery embrace. He could almost feel the eyes of the killer watching him, a silent, unseen presence anticipating his every move. The game was on, and the first move was a declaration of war, delivered with the silent elegance of a carved swallow.

Chapter 2: The Captain Rostova's Dilemma

The Captain Rostova's office, though ostensibly a space of command, felt more like a pressurized chamber. Sunlight, filtered through the tinted windows overlooking a placid, indifferent sea, did little to dispel the gloom that had settled over the 'Sovereign Star'. Captain Rostova Eva Rostova, a woman whose steely resolve was etched into the lines around her eyes, sat behind her imposing desk, her posture radiating an authority that seemed to war with the tremor in her gut. The stateroom of the deceased, a gruesome tableau, had been sealed, its opulent confines now a tomb. The immediate vicinity, a radius of three staterooms on either side of the victim's suite, had been cordoned off. Her limited crew, mostly stewards and deckhands with rudimentary security training, moved with a nervous efficiency, their faces pale beneath the polished veneer of professionalism.

"Seal Deck 7," Rostova's voice, though quiet, carried an undeniable edge of command that cut through the hushed tension. "No one in, no one out. Inform the passengers in adjacent staterooms that their quarters are temporarily unavailable because of an unforeseen mechanical issue. No details, just keep them away." She met the eyes of her Chief Security Officer, a burly ex-military woman named , Eve Rostova, whose usual gruff demeanor was tinged with apprehension. "Rostova, I want a perimeter. No one disembarks at our next port. No one boards, either. We are a sealed environment until the authorities can get here. Understood?"

Rostova nodded, his jaw tight. "Understood, Captain Rostova. But the passengers... they'll raise hell. Especially when they hear what's happened."

Rostova's gaze hardened. "Let them raise hell, Rostova. Better a few inconvenienced passengers than a full-blown panic. And right now, panic is our greatest enemy. We have over two thousand souls on this ship. Two thousand potential witnesses, suspects, and victims. The sea is our only boundary, and it's a very large one. But inside this hull, we are a microcosm, and this microcosm has just been infected." She tapped a manicured finger on the polished surface of her desk. "And we contain that infection."

The concept of confinement, of being adrift with a killer, pressed down on Rostova with a physical weight. She was a Captain Rostova, responsible for the safe passage of every soul on her ship. This was not a rogue wave or a mechanical failure; this violated the most fundamental order, a darkness that had breached the hull from within. The luxurious liner, a floating palace designed for pleasure and escape, had been transformed into a gilded cage. The vastness of the ocean, once a symbol of freedom and adventure, now felt like an impenetrable barrier, isolating them with a predator.

"Initiate the full surveillance sweep," Rostova continued, her voice regaining its steady rhythm. "Every camera on Deck 7, and indeed, the entire ship, needs to be active and recording. I want logs of all access points, all corridors, all public spaces. We may not have seasoned investigators yet, but we have eyes everywhere. The cameras will tell us who went where, when, and with whom. No detail is too small, Rostova. Every shadow, every fleeting glance, every moment of hesitation – it all matters now."

Rostova acknowledged her orders, his movements regaining a measure of practiced efficiency. He understood the weight of her words. The ship's advanced technological infrastructure, usually a boon for passenger comfort and ship operations, was now the only tool they had to begin untangling this horrifying knot. The network of cameras, discreetly positioned throughout the ship – in the opulent lounges, the bustling dining rooms, the labyrinthine corridors, and even the most private of suites – was now tasked with a far more grim purpose. Each lens was a digital eye, scanning the unfolding drama, capturing the subtle shifts in demeanor, the hurried footsteps, the averted gazes that might betray guilt or fear.

Rostova watched Rostova depart, a silent prayer on her lips that his limited team could maintain the illusion of normalcy, or at least, subdued concern. She leaned back in her chair, the plush leather doing little to soften the hard reality of her situation. Her mind raced, sifting through the passenger manifest, a sea of names and faces, any of whom could be the perpetrator. She thought of the victim, a man of obvious wealth and influence, a man who had clearly made enemies. But on this ship, isolated by miles of ocean, the pool of potential suspects was limited to those on board.

The ship's sophisticated internal communication system was now under her sole command, each announcement a carefully crafted message designed to inform without inciting. She had already authorized a general announcement, informed passengers of a 'minor security incident' on Deck 7, with a promise of further updates. The response had been a ripple of unease, a murmur that threatened to swell into a wave. She could feel it, the collective anxiety of thousands of people trapped in a confined space, suddenly aware of their vulnerability.

"This ship," she murmured to herself, her voice barely a whisper, "was meant to be a sanctuary. Now it's a prison. And I am the warden."

She opened a secure digital file on her desk terminal, the ship's passenger manifest glowing in the dim light. Thousands of names. Each one a life, each one a potential story. She scrolled through the list, her eyes scanning for any anomalies, any passengers who had boarded under suspicious circumstances, or any who had exhibited unusual behavior prior to the discovery. The victim, she recalled from the initial briefing, was a Mr. Alistair Finch, a renowned art collector. A man who undoubtedly had dealings with a wide and varied clientele, some of whom might not be as reputable as the gilded halls of the 'Sovereign Star' suggested.

The wooden bird, described by the initial responding crew member, played on repeat in her mind. A small, carved bird, left at the scene. It wasn't the crude work of a panicked assailant. It spoke of deliberation, of a signature. A calling card. This wasn't just a murder; it was a statement. And the statement had been made on her ship. The weight of that responsibility settled upon her shoulders, a burden heavier than any storm-tossed sea. She had to maintain control, to project an image of calm competence, even as the storm raged within her. The integrity of the investigation, the safety of her passengers, and the reputation of the cruise line all rested on her ability to navigate these treacherous waters.

She accessed the ship's internal security logs, a cascade of data points detailing the movements of crew members and the activation of security protocols. The ship's AI, a sophisticated system designed to monitor and manage everything from environmental controls to passenger flow, was now also tasked with flagging any unusual activity. It was a digital detective, sifting through terabytes of information, searching for the ghost in the machine.

Rostova knew that time was her enemy. The longer they remained isolated, the greater the risk of panic, of the killer striking again, or of the killer attempting to evade capture. The confined nature of the cruise ship, designed for seamless movement and enjoyment, now presented a unique set of challenges for containing a crime scene and apprehending a suspect. Every corridor, every stairwell, every public space was a potential avenue of escape or concealment.

She looked at a small, framed photograph on her desk – her daughter, smiling, her eyes bright with life. That was why she had to succeed. Not just for the passengers, not just for the cruise line, but for the principle that such darkness should not be allowed to fester unchecked. She straightened in her chair, her gaze hardening with renewed determination. She would not be a warden of a prison; she would be the Captain Rostova who steered her ship through this tempest, bringing them all safely to harbor, with the truth exposed and justice served. The confinement of the crime scene was just the first step; the true challenge lay in confining the killer before they could strike again. The vast, dark ocean outside was no longer just a barrier; it was a silent accomplice, holding them all captive until she could break the spell. The meticulously maintained order of the ship had been shattered, and the chaos that threatened to erupt was a beast she now had to tame.

The rhythmic hum of the ship, usually a comforting lullaby of progress, now felt like a sinister undertone, amplifying the tension that coiled in Captain Eva Rostova's stomach. She stood at the edge of the cordoned-off area, the stark yellow tape a garish scar against the opulent mahogany of Deck 7's corridor. Her eyes, sharp and analytical, swept over the faces of her limited security detail. Rostova, her Chief Security Officer, a man usually as solid as the ship's hull, looked distinctly out of his depth. A tight-lipped anxiety had replaced his usual gruff confidence, his gaze flicking nervously towards the sealed stateroom. Rostova recognized the familiar signs of overwhelm – the desperate attempt to impose order on chaos, the dawning realization that their training, their protocols, were insufficient for the scale of the horror that had unfolded.

In that moment, painfully aware of her own limitations, her gaze fell on him. He stood slightly apart from the cluster of uniformed crew, more observer than participant, radiating a quiet authority. He wore no uniform, nor did he carry the easy demeanor of a tourist enjoying a sea voyage. His eyes, a piercing shade of grey, seemed to absorb everything without betraying a single thought, and a subtle, almost imperceptible weariness clung to him, the kind that spoke of battles fought and won, or perhaps lost, in arenas far removed from the sun-drenched decks of a luxury liner.

Rostova knew who he was, of course. His name, 'Miller,' had been on the passenger manifest, flagged by Rostova as someone with a... history. A retired agent, Rostova had whispered, his voice laced with a mixture of respect and caution. Someone who had once moved in circles where such grim discoveries were not anomalies, but occupational hazards. Rostova, a Captain Rostova whose command extended to the seamless operation of a floating city, felt a surge of something akin to desperation. Her crew were stewards, deckhands, and a handful of men with basic security certifications. They were excellent at their jobs, but this was beyond their purview. This was a crime scene of the most brutal kind, and they were adrift with a killer.

She made her decision. With a curt nod to Rostova, a gesture that conveyed more than words ever could, Rostova walked towards the man. Her heels made a soft, measured click on the polished floor, each step a deliberate move towards an uncertain alliance. As she approached, Miller's gaze shifted, meeting hers with an unnerving directness. There was no surprise in his eyes, no curiosity, only a quiet assessment.

"Mr. Miller," Rostova began, her voice deliberately even, betraying none of the turmoil that churned within her. "Captain Rostova. I believe my staff may have already informed you that we have a... situation."

Miller offered a slight inclination of his head, a gesture that was both formal and utterly devoid of subservience. "Captain Rostova," he acknowledged, his voice a low rumble, surprisingly calm given the circumstances. "Rostova mentioned a 'serious incident'. The tape and the... atmosphere suggest something more."

Rostova's jaw tightened. She hated to admit it, but Rostova, for all his limitations, had been astute enough to recognize Miller's potential.

And Rostova, for all her pride and her Captain Rostovacy, knew when she was out of her depth. The victim, Alistair Finch, was a man of significant influence, and his death here, on her ship, was a catastrophe waiting to happen. The thought of the ensuing investigation, the endless questions, the potential for public outcry, sent a shiver down her spine. She needed someone who understood the dark underbelly of human nature, someone who could see through the veneer of polite society, someone who could navigate the labyrinth of deception that a killer would undoubtedly weave.

"Indeed, Mr. Miller," she continued, her gaze holding his, searching for any flicker of willingness, any sign that he might be more than just a retired agent. "A rather serious incident. Mr. Alistair Finch has been murdered in his stateroom. And we are currently at sea, with no immediate access to external authorities. My team... they are well-trained in their respective duties, but this is beyond their current scope. We are a small, contained environment, and our resources are stretched thin."

She paused, letting the weight of her words settle. The implication was clear: she was asking for help, help from someone who was not bound by her command, someone who had voluntarily stepped away from the life that had clearly shaped him. It was a concession, a sign of her desperation, and it chafed at her.

Miller remained silent for a moment, his expression unreadable. Rostova could feel the unspoken questions hanging in the air between them. He was assessing her, assessing the situation, weighing the cost of re-engagement. She could see the internal debate playing out behind those impassive grey eyes. He had retired, she presumed, for a reason. Perhaps he had seen too much, experienced too much, or simply craved the quiet obscurity of a life lived away from the shadows.

"A murder, Captain Rostova," Miller finally said, his voice flat, devoid of emotion, yet carrying the weight of a thousand similar pronouncements. "On a cruise liner. That complicates things considerably. Two thousand passengers, a few hundred crew. Everyone is a potential witness. Everyone is a potential suspect."

"Precisely," Rostova agreed, a flicker of relief igniting within her. He understood. He grasped the inherent difficulty, the exponential increase in complexity. "And until the authorities can arrive, which will take time, I am responsible for the safety and the security of every soul on board. That includes finding the person who committed this heinous act, and ensuring they do not strike again."

She took a breath, steeling herself for the next crucial step. "Mr. Miller," she said, her voice dropping to a near whisper, yet carrying an intensity that commanded his full attention. "I am not asking you to step back into your old life. I am asking for your expertise. I am asking for your eyes, your mind, your experience. My staff can secure the scene, they can collect basic information, but they lack the... insight. The ability to see what isn't immediately apparent. You, on the other hand..." She trailed off, leaving the unspoken compliment to hang in the air.

Miller's gaze drifted for a moment, towards the sealed doorway of the victim's stateroom, then back to Rostova. A subtle tension emanated from him. It was the look of a predator, or perhaps, more accurately, of someone who had spent years hunting them.

"Unofficially, of course," Miller stated, his tone leaving no room for misinterpretation. "I have no authority on this vessel, Captain Rostova. I am a passenger, like any other. My involvement would need to be... discreet. I cannot afford to become a part of your crew, nor can I disrupt your established protocols unless absolutely necessary."

Rostova almost sagged with relief. He was agreeing. He was offering a lifeline, even if it was one she had to grasp with extreme caution. "Unofficially," she confirmed, her voice regaining its strength. "Completely unofficial. You would be assisting me, a concerned passenger with a unique background, offering insights where I might be lacking. My staff would report to me, and I would then consult with you. We would maintain the illusion of normalcy as much as humanly possible. The less the passengers know about the true nature of our predicament, the better."

She extended her hand, a gesture of formal agreement, though it felt more like a desperate plea. "Mr. Miller, your willingness to help in this situation is... greatly appreciated. I cannot overstate the importance of your assistance. We are in uncharted waters, and I need someone who knows how to navigate them."

Miller looked at her hand for a moment, then, with a slow, deliberate movement, he took it. His grip was firm, dry, and surprisingly reassuring.

It was a handshake that sealed an agreement forged in the grim reality of murder, a silent pact between the Captain Rostova of a ship and a retired agent who found himself, once again, drawn into the dark currents of a criminal investigation.

"Captain Rostova," Miller said, his grey eyes locking onto hers, a spark of something that might have been grim determination kindling within them. "My primary concern is preventing further harm. If I can help achieve that, then I will." He released her hand, his gaze sweeping over the corridor once more, his mind already dissecting the scene, piecing together the invisible threads that connected the living to the dead. "Tell me, Captain Rostova," he began, his voice shifting to a more professional cadence, "what exactly did your initial team find?"

Rostova felt a knot of tension loosen in her chest. It was a fragile alliance, built on necessity and a shared understanding of the stakes, but it was an alliance nonetheless. She had someone now, someone who could see beyond the obvious, someone who wouldn't be swayed by passenger demands or the pressure of maintaining appearances. The retired agent had offered his assistance, and in doing so, had become an unlikely, unofficial cog in the machinery of her desperate attempt to contain the contagion that had infected her ship. The game, as they say, was afoot, and Captain Rostova , for the first time since the discovery, felt a sliver of hope that she might just have a fighting chance of seeing it through to its grim conclusion. The vastness of the ocean had just shrunk, its endless horizon now a cage, and within its confines, a battle of wits had begun. Miller's presence was a silent acknowledgment that this was no longer just a matter of shipboard security; it was a hunt, and he was willing to lend his unique skills to the chase. He was not a part of her official command structure, and that, Rostova realized, might be his greatest asset. He could operate outside the rigid confines of protocol, unburdened by the need to maintain a façade for two thousand paying customers. He was a wild card, a secret weapon, and she was going to use him. The weight on her shoulders hadn't disappeared, but it felt... shared. And in the isolating vastness of the sea, that was a significant comfort.

The faint scent of ozone, a residual trace from the emergency lighting system that had flickered on during the initial chaos, still hung in the air of Captain Rostova's private conference room. It was a stark contrast to the usual sterile, sea-salt tang of the open ocean. Miller sat across from her, the polished surface of the table reflecting the muted glow of the overhead lights. Rostova, with a sigh that seemed to carry the weight of the entire vessel, pushed a thin file across the table.

"Alistair Finch," she stated, her voice low, a weary recitation of facts. "CEO of 'Nexus Innovations.' A titan of the tech world. The kind of man who could swing markets with a single tweet." She tapped the file. "He was in stateroom 714. The suite directly adjacent to the one where... where the incident occurred. 716."

Miller opened the file, his fingers moving with practiced economy. Inside were preliminary reports, hastily compiled by Rostova and his team, their initial attempts to impose order on the unfolding nightmare. The victim was not Finch, but a colleague, a Senior Vice President named Marcus Thorne. Finch, the passenger manifest confirmed, was indeed on board, occupying the suite next door. Thorne's stateroom, 716, was where the discovery had been made. Finch's presence, in such close proximity, was a crucial detail.

"Thorne," Miller murmured, scanning the brief report. "Nexus Innovations. That explains the... intensity of the security presence." He looked up, his grey eyes meeting Rostova's. "Finch is involved in sensitive negotiations, Captain Rostova?"

Rostova nodded, her gaze fixed on the diagram of Deck 7's corridor, a sterile, almost clinical rendering of the scene. "Highly sensitive. Rumor has it, they were on the verge of acquiring a significant competitor, a deal worth billions. Finch was apparently in transit to finalize the terms. Thorne was his... right-hand man, I believe. The one who would handle the day-to-day operations during such a critical period."

Miller's fingers traced the layout of the corridor. "So, the victim was Thorne, the potential witness, or perhaps the target, was Finch. And they were in adjacent suites." He paused, absorbing the implications. "This isn't just a random act of violence, then. The stakes are considerably higher than a simple passenger altercation."

"Precisely," Rostova said, her voice tight. "Which is why we cannot afford any... missteps. Rostova' team has done what they can. They've secured the immediate area, taken initial statements from the room steward who discovered the body, and ensured Thorne's stateroom remains untouched, pending... further examination." She gestured to a separate, more recent document. "This is a log of their initial findings. Anything unusual, anyone seen lurking, anything out of the ordinary. Frankly, it reads like a collection of minor inconveniences, the sort of things one might overlook on a normal voyage."

Miller began to read, his brow furrowed in concentration. The steward's report was detailed, a litany of mundane observations: a misplaced ice bucket, a faint odor of... something, not unpleasant, but not familiar. A slight scuff mark on the carpet near Thorne's door, attributed to luggage being moved. Nothing concrete, nothing that screamed 'murder.'

"The usual suspects for any maritime incident," Miller commented, his voice flat. "Disgruntled crew, jealous lovers, passengers with a penchant for dramatics." He flipped a page. "However, Rostova has highlighted a few points of... interest."

Rostova leaned forward. "What did he find?"

"A passenger reported hearing a muffled argument from the vicinity of staterooms 716 and 718 around midnight," Miller read aloud. "But dismissed it as the usual revelry from the upper decks. Another passenger, a Mrs. Eleanor Vance, occupying stateroom 720, complained of a 'suspicious individual' loitering near the elevator bank on Deck 7 around 11:30 PM. Described him as tall, dark-haired, wearing a nondescript grey suit, and carrying a small, dark briefcase. She also mentioned he seemed to be observing the passengers, rather than moving with any discernible purpose."

"Mrs. Vance," Rostova mused. "She's a retired librarian. Known for her meticulous attention to detail, but also for a rather overactive imagination when it comes to 'suspicious' behavior."

"Indeed," Miller said, a faint hint of amusement in his tone. "However, her description has been cross-referenced with the security camera footage, or what little there is of it in that section of the corridor. There's a brief, grainy image of a man matching that description exiting the stairwell near Thorne's suite around 11:45 PM. He's not seen entering or leaving Thorne's stateroom directly, but his presence in that specific area, at that specific time, is noteworthy."

Miller continued to pore over the reports. "Rostova also noted a discrepancy in the access logs for stateroom 716. Thorne's keycard was used at 10:15 PM, presumably when he retired for the evening. However, there's a secondary, unverified entry logged at 1:05 AM. The system doesn't specify which card was used, only that access was granted. The steward swears he did not use his master key at that hour, and Thorne was... indisposed by then."

"Indisposed," Rostova echoed, a shiver running down her spine. "That's a polite way of saying he was already dead."

"Precisely. So, someone else gained access to Thorne's suite after he was deceased, or shortly before. Someone with a keycard, or the ability to bypass the lock system." Miller tapped the report. "And there's one more item. A member of the housekeeping staff reported seeing Alistair Finch exiting the corridor of Deck 7, looking agitated, around 1:30 AM. He didn't see Finch enter or leave Thorne's stateroom, just that he was in the vicinity, and appeared... troubled."

"Agitated," Rostova said, the pieces beginning to click into place, forming a disturbingly coherent, yet frustratingly incomplete, picture. "Finch. Thorne. Adjacent suites. A muffled argument. A mysterious figure. An unexplained entry. Finch acting agitated hours after the likely time of death. It's a tangled web, Mr. Miller."

"It is," Miller agreed, closing the file with a soft thud. "And to begin untangling it, I need a comprehensive list of everyone who had access to Deck 7 last night. Passengers and crew. Specifically, anyone assigned to staterooms 701 through 725, anyone working on Deck 7, and anyone noted as having visited Thorne or Finch's suites. I'll also need a list of all crew members with master keycard access to any stateroom, and any security personnel assigned to patrol Deck 7 between the hours of 10:00 PM and 4:00 AM."

Rostova nodded, already reaching for her comm device. "I'll have Rostova compile that for you immediately. It will take some time to gather and cross-reference everything. The ship's manifest is extensive, and our crew roster is even more so."

"I understand," Miller said. "But the sooner I have it, the sooner I can begin to identify the circumference of our suspect pool. Right now, that pool is effectively the entire population of this vessel, minus those who can definitively prove they were elsewhere. We need to narrow it down. We need to find a motive, and a means, and an opportunity for a select few."

He leaned back, his gaze sweeping over the maps and diagrams spread across the table. "The manifest, Captain Rostova," he said, his voice taking on a more focused, analytical tone. "It's my starting point. Every name, every booking, every known associate listed. We'll need to cross-reference passenger lists with known affiliations, look for any connections between Thorne, Finch, and the general passenger and crew demographics. Nexus Innovations. What were the key components of this acquisition? Were there any potential rivals who might also be on board? Disgruntled employees? Anyone who stood to lose significantly if this deal went through?"

Rostova tapped a key on her tablet, bringing up a digital version of the ship's manifest. It was a colossal document, a testament to the sheer scale of the luxury liner. "I'll have the full passenger and crew manifest sent to your stateroom. It's all here, meticulously organized, as per protocol. Every passenger's name, age, nationality, port of embarkation, and emergency contact. For the crew, their roles, their shifts, their disciplinary records, their nationalities." She sighed again, a sound of profound weariness. "But finding motive amongst two thousand passengers and several hundred crew... it's like searching for a single grain of sand on a beach, Mr. Miller."

"Precisely why we start broad and narrow down," Miller replied, his voice steady. "We look for anomalies. For individuals whose presence here is inexplicable, or whose behavior deviates from the norm. The 'suspicious individual' Mrs. Vance saw, for example. He's a starting point. Finch's agitated state is another. Thorne's professional dealings, and the billions riding on them, are a significant motivator for a certain kind of individual."

He pointed to a section of the manifest, a list of VIP passengers. "Alistair Finch. Who else is in this category? Are there any other individuals of comparable influence or wealth on board? Competitors, perhaps? Or individuals known to have had dealings with Nexus Innovations, either positive or negative?"

"We have several high-profile individuals," Rostova admitted, scrolling through the list. "A renowned philanthropist, a controversial art collector, a retired general with a... colourful past. And, as it happens, a representative from Sterling Corp, Nexus's main competitor in the semiconductor market. Their CEO is currently on a private sabbatical, but their Chief Operating Officer, a Mr. Julian Vance, is aboard."

Miller's eyes narrowed slightly. "Vance. Is there any relation to Mrs. Eleanor Vance, the witness?"

Rostova's fingers flew across the tablet. "No... no apparent relation. Julian Vance is booked under stateroom 902. Eleanor Vance is on Deck 7, stateroom 720. Different decks, different booking references. But the coincidence is... noted."

"Indeed it is," Miller murmured. "Julian Vance. I'll need his details. His travel companions, his itinerary, any known associates on board. And I'll need to speak with Mrs. Vance, of course. Her 'overactive imagination' might just be our sharpest tool in identifying our suspicious stranger. The list of passengers with access to Deck 7, and any individuals who had direct contact with Thorne or Finch in the days leading up to this incident, that will be the next crucial piece of the puzzle."

He stood up, his gaze intense. "Motive. Opportunity. Means. These are the pillars. We'll start by establishing who could be on Deck 7, in proximity to Thorne's stateroom, between the hours of, say, 10:00 PM and 2:00 AM. Then we'll layer in potential motives, based on Finch's business dealings and any other relevant factors we uncover. Finally, we'll consider the means – how was Thorne killed? The reports are vague on the exact cause of death, but the lack of a struggle suggests something swift, perhaps incapacitating. Poison? A silent weapon?"

Rostova opened another file. "The preliminary forensic assessment from the medical and security teams is minimal, given the circumstances. No obvious signs of forced entry into the stateroom, no disarray beyond what might be expected from a struggle, and no visible wounds on the victim at first glance. The medical officer is en route from the infirmary, but that will take time. We need to work with what we have."

"Then we work with what we have," Miller said, his voice a low rumble of determination. "The manifest, the access logs, the witness statements

– they are our weapons. And the sheer number of people on this ship, Captain Rostova, is not just a problem. It's also our greatest asset. Somewhere in this floating city of secrets, our killer is hiding in plain sight. My job is to find them. Your job is to ensure no one else gets hurt while I do it." He paused, his gaze meeting Rostova's, a silent understanding passing between them. "Let's begin by dissecting that manifest. Every name is a potential player in this drama. Every passenger, every crew member, is a thread in the tapestry. And I intend to pull every single one of them, until the picture becomes clear."

The sterile glow of the Captain Rostova's conference room felt amplified, casting long, dancing shadows that mimicked the uncertainty clinging to the air. Miller, joined now by Detective Sergeant Jenkins, leaned closer to the table, his gaze fixed on the array of monitors displaying a chaotic, yet meticulously ordered, stream of security footage. Jenkins, his usual gruff demeanor softened by the gravity of their task, was already lost in the digital labyrinth, his fingers occasionally brushing against the mousepad as he guided their exploration. Their current focus: Deck 7, the scene of Marcus Thorne's untimely demise, and the hours preceding it.

"Alright, Sergeant," Miller's voice was a low hum, a stark contrast to the crackle and whir emanating from the speakers, each representing a different camera feed. "Let's start at approximately 10:00 PM. Thorne's keycard was used at 10:15 PM to enter his suite. Finch's, at 10:30 PM to enter 714. We're looking for anything out of the ordinary in the adjacent corridors, the elevator banks, and the stairwells leading to this section of the deck."

Jenkins grunted, his eyes scanning a wide-angle view of the main corridor outside staterooms 714 and 716. "Got it. The steward, a man named Rostova, said he last saw Thorne entering his suite around then, looking perfectly normal, if a bit preoccupied. No sign of Finch with him, of course. Finch was... busy."

The footage unspooled, a relentless cascade of anonymous figures moving through the ship's arteries. Passengers in evening wear, crew members on their rounds, the occasional solitary figure making their way back to their cabin. The quality was a frustrating constant – grainy, often dimly lit, and prone to sudden shifts in focus as cameras adjusted to movement.

"There," Jenkins said, his finger stabbing at one of the screens. "Around 11:30 PM. Mrs. Vance's description. Tall, dark hair, grey suit, briefcase."

On the screen, a man did indeed emerge from the stairwell to their left, a figure that precisely matched the retired librarian's description. He paused at the junction of the corridors, his head turning slowly, his gaze sweeping across the doors of the staterooms. He didn't linger, but his movements were deliberate, almost as if he were surveying his surroundings. He then proceeded down the corridor, away from Thorne's suite, and disappeared from view of that camera.

"He's casing the joint," Miller stated, a grim certainty in his voice. "Or at least, he's trying to appear as if he is. His purpose here is ambiguous. Was he looking for Thorne? Finch? Or simply trying to blend in by observing?"

"His briefcase," Jenkins pointed out. "Small, dark. Could be anything. A laptop, documents... or nothing at all."

"Exactly. The ultimate chameleon. He's trying to draw attention without being overtly suspicious. A difficult tightrope to walk." Miller zoomed in on the image, the pixels blurring and distorting the man's features. "Can we get a clearer shot of his face? Or any identifying marks?"

Jenkins worked his mouse, his brow furrowed in concentration. "This is as good as it gets, Captain Rostova. The lighting in that stairwell is abysmal, and his face is turned away for most of the time he's visible. We're lucky we even have this much. He enters the corridor at 11:43 PM and is out of frame by 11:45 PM. Just two minutes of screen time."

"Two minutes can be an eternity in our line of work," Miller countered, his gaze still fixed on the fleeting image. "Rostova mentioned a muffled argument around midnight. From the vicinity of 716 and 718. These cameras don't cover the interior of the suites, nor do they have audio. We're blind on that front."

They continued their methodical review, meticulously logging every moment of interest. An hour passed, then another. The clock on the screen ticked past midnight, the timestamp a stark reminder of the tragedy that was unfolding just beyond the reach of the cameras.

"Here," Jenkins said, his voice suddenly sharper. "Around 12:55 AM. Finch exiting his suite. He looks... agitated."

The footage showed Alistair Finch, his usual commanding presence diminished, stepping out of stateroom 714. He ran a hand through his hair, his shoulders hunched, and glanced nervously up and down the corridor. He wasn't wearing his suit from earlier, but a more casual, albeit expensive, lounging attire. He paced briefly, then ducked into the stairwell closest to Thorne's suite.

"The housekeeping staff said they saw him looking agitated around 1:30 AM," Miller recalled. "This is earlier. He was already on edge before that reported sighting."

"And he goes into the stairwell," Jenkins continued, his finger hovering over the screen. "The same stairwell the man in the grey suit used. He stays in there for... approximately three minutes. Then he emerges and heads back towards his suite. He doesn't look any calmer."

"Did he interact with anyone?" Miller asked, his eyes narrowed.

"No one in sight," Jenkins confirmed. "Just him and the empty corridor. But he was definitely disturbed. His posture, his quick glances... he looked like he was trying to avoid being seen."

The clock rolled on. The early hours of the morning brought a lull in passenger traffic, the ship settling into a slumber that belied the turmoil brewing within its polished confines. Then, at 1:05 AM, a critical timestamp.

"Access log discrepancy," Jenkins stated, pulling up the relevant data. "Thorne's suite. The secondary entry." He rewound the footage to the corridor outside 716. "We need to see if anyone entered or exited during that window. The cameras on either end of the corridor are our best bet, but there's a blind spot directly in front of Thorne's door."

They meticulously scanned the footage from the cameras covering the approach to the staterooms, north and south. The corridor remained empty for extended periods. Then, a flicker of movement.

"There," Miller breathed, pointing to the northern camera feed. "Just at the edge of the frame. 1:04 AM."

A figure, cloaked in shadow, moved with a swift, almost furtive gait. They emerged from the stairwell, heading directly towards Thorne's suite. The camera caught them for only a fleeting moment, a dark silhouette against the dim hallway. They appeared to be carrying something, a small, dark object held close to their body.

"Too dark to make out any features," Jenkins lamented. "And the angle is terrible. It's like trying to catch smoke. We can't even confirm it's a person, not definitively. It could be a shadow, a trick of the light..."

"But it coincides perfectly with the unverified access log entry," Miller countered. "And it's coming from the same stairwell Finch used just minutes before. This is our killer, Jenkins. Or at least, our killer's accomplice. They gained entry to Thorne's suite at precisely 1:05 AM."

They continued to watch, their eyes burning, straining to glean any further information from the digital ghosts. The figure disappeared from view of the northern camera, presumably entering Thorne's suite. The corridor remained empty. Minutes ticked by, each second a silent accusation.

"What about Finch?" Miller asked, his voice low. "After he retreated to his suite at 12:58 AM, did he emerge again?"

Jenkins scrolled through the footage from 714. "No. He remained in his suite until much later. The door opens at 7:15 AM, and he emerges, looking disheveled, and immediately calls for assistance. He claims he found Thorne when he went to check on him after hearing a commotion. A commotion he didn't report."

"A convenient amnesia," Miller mused. "Or a deliberate fabrication. So, Finch is in his suite, seemingly uninvolved after his agitated pacing. The mysterious figure enters Thorne's suite at 1:05 AM. And Finch claims he discovered the body at 7:15 AM. That leaves a significant gap."

They spent the next several hours meticulously dissecting the footage. They traced the movements of every individual who passed by the corridors flanking staterooms 714 and 716. They looked for any passengers who might have been on Deck 7 during the critical hours, focusing on those who had no discernible reason to be there. The ship's manifest, now a constant companion, was being cross-referenced with every face that flickered across the screens.

"There's a Mr. Silas Croft," Jenkins reported, pointing to a passenger on the manifest. "Booked in stateroom 718. Directly across from Thorne. He's listed as a 'private investor.' No further details. He's visible on camera several times in the corridor. At 11:00 PM, he's seen exiting his suite. He walks towards the elevators, lingers, then returns to his room around 11:15 PM. He's not seen again until the morning."

"Croft," Miller echoed, making a note. "Adjacent to the victim. Did he hear anything? See anything? His suite is the closest, besides Finch's. We need to speak with him."

Their review also highlighted a brief, yet significant, encounter near the elevator bank on Deck 7 around 11:30 PM. The same time Mrs. Vance reported seeing the 'suspicious individual.' The footage showed the man in the grey suit, the one who had emerged from the stairwell, briefly interacting with another passenger. It was a subtle exchange, a shared glance, perhaps a muttered word, before they parted ways.

"Who is that with him?" Miller asked, zooming in on the second individual.

Jenkins consulted the manifest. "That appears to be Mr. Julian Vance. COO of Sterling Corp. He was booked in stateroom 902, but he was apparently on Deck 7. He's seen here with the man in the grey suit for no more than ten seconds."

"Julian Vance," Miller repeated, the name resonating with the earlier mention of Mrs. Eleanor Vance. "The COO of Nexus's main competitor. And he's seen interacting with our suspicious individual, mere minutes before he's spotted near Thorne's suite. This is no longer coincidence, Sergeant. This is a confluence of potential motives and opportunities."

The sheer volume of data was overwhelming. Thousands of faces, hundreds of hours of footage, all needing to be sifted for the smallest anomaly. Yet, with each passing moment, a clearer, though no less disturbing, picture began to emerge. The man in the grey suit, the rival executive, Alistair Finch's agitated state, the unverified access to Thorne's suite – these were no longer isolated incidents. They were threads, weaving together a narrative of intrigue and potential foul play.

"We're looking for a needle in a haystack, Captain Rostova," Jenkins said, rubbing his tired eyes. "But at least we're starting to see the outline of the haystack."

"And the needle is likely to be well-hidden," Miller replied, his gaze never leaving the screen. "But it's there. And our job is to pull it out, no matter how sharp its point." He gestured to the footage of Julian Vance and the man in the grey suit. "This interaction is crucial. We need to know who that man in the grey suit is. And why Julian Vance, a passenger on an entirely different deck, was on Deck 7 at that specific time, engaging with him."

The clock had ticked past dawn, but for Miller and Jenkins, the night was far from over. They kept scanning, cross-referencing, analyzing, their determination hardening with every minute. The truth, they knew, was out there somewhere within the digital fog, waiting to be uncovered.

The stark fluorescence of the conference room seemed to dim as Miller leaned back, his gaze unfocused, lost in the labyrinth of images still playing out on the monitors. The fleeting figures on screen, the silent echoes of lives caught in the ship's mechanical pulse, were a frustratingly incomplete puzzle. Sergeant Jenkins, ever practical, was already moving on, his fingers dancing across the keyboard, pulling up alternate camera angles, refining the search parameters.

"That figure, Sergeant," Miller began, his voice a low rumble, "emerging from the stairwell at 1:04 AM. Too obscured. Too fleeting. But there was something..." He trailed off, struggling to articulate the vague impression that nagged at him. "The way they moved. A slight hitch in their stride? A deliberate stillness as they paused at the corridor junction?"

Jenkins, his brow furrowed, zoomed in on the grainy image, the pixels straining to reveal what the low light and distance had concealed. "It's hard to say, Captain Rostova. Could be anything. A reflection. A shadow playing tricks. Their silhouette is generic. Dark clothing, a nondescript build. They're carrying something, yes, a small, dark object, held tight against their chest. But whether that's significant or just incidental..." He shrugged, the gesture conveying their shared frustration. "The angle is abysmal. It's like trying to describe a whisper in a hurricane."

Miller nodded, acknowledging the technical limitations. "But the timing, Jenkins. The timing is everything. It coincides precisely with the unverified access log for Thorne's suite. And it originates from the same stairwell Finch so nervously exited mere minutes before. This isn't a random act. This is a calculated intrusion." He gestured towards the screen, his voice hardening. "Look at their approach to Thorne's door. They don't hesitate. They don't fumble for a keycard. They move with an economy of motion, as if they know exactly where they're going, and, more importantly, how to get there undetected."

"The service corridors," Jenkins murmured, a new thread of thought weaving its way through his analysis. He brought up a schematic of Deck 7, overlaying it with the camera coverage map. "The main corridors are heavily monitored. But the service access points... the maintenance shafts, the crew passages... they're less frequently patrolled, and the camera coverage is sporadic, at best. If someone knew the ship's layout, they could use those routes to their advantage. To enter and exit Thorne's stateroom without traversing the main thoroughfares."

Miller's eyes followed Jenkins's finger as it traced a series of dotted lines on the schematic. "A blind spot strategy," he mused. "They're not just avoiding cameras; they're actively exploiting the gaps in our surveillance network. The killer clearly has a degree of familiarity with the ship. They knew where to find the blind spots, where the cameras wouldn't be looking." He leaned forward, his focus intensifying. "And that figure emerging from the stairwell at 1:04 AM. Did they enter Thorne's suite directly from the stairwell access, or did they use a service passage *from* the stairwell?"

Jenkins meticulously reviewed the footage from a camera positioned further down the corridor, one that offered a tangential view of the access point. "It's difficult to say for certain, Captain Rostova. The angle is poor, and the lighting is even worse. They disappear from our primary camera's view, heading towards Thorne's suite. But it's plausible they could have ducked into a service hatch or a connecting passage just out of frame. The schematics show several such points branching off from that stairwell area, leading to the rear of the suites, often used by housekeeping or maintenance."

"So, not just a planned entry, but a carefully orchestrated route," Miller said, the pieces clicking into place with a chilling finality. "They likely used the stairwell as a staging point, a transition zone, before either directly accessing Thorne's stateroom via a less visible route, or perhaps even using the service access *within* the suite itself, if such a thing exists. And the exit... was it the same route?"

Jenkins brought up the footage from the hours following the estimated time of death. The corridor remained largely empty, save for the occasional crew member performing routine checks, their paths meticulously logged and accounted for. The minutes stretched into an hour, then another. The early morning quiet of the ship was a stark contrast to the violence that had transpired.

"Nothing directly from Thorne's suite, Captain Rostova," Jenkins reported, after a thorough review. "The door remains closed. The access logs show no further entries or exits until Finch discovers the body. However..." He paused, zooming in on a different camera feed, one located at the far end of the main corridor, angled towards a secondary stairwell. "Around 1:35 AM, we see movement within the service corridor that runs parallel to the main one. A figure. It's the same general build, the same dark clothing. They emerge briefly from a service access panel, look up and down the main corridor, and then disappear back into the service passage. Their gait is... similar. A slight stiffness in the left leg, perhaps? It's too blurry to be definitive, but it's a possibility."

Miller's eyes narrowed, with an almost imperceptible flicker of recognition in their depths. "A limp? Or a peculiar stride? And they're using the service corridors for egress as well. This isn't just someone who stumbled upon an opportunity; this is someone who expected it, planned for it, and executed it with a meticulous disregard for our security measures." He gestured again to the grainy image of the figure. "We can't see their faces, but that gait, that manner of movement... it's a potential identifier. A signature, however subtle."

The killer's trail, then, was not one of footprints in the dust, but of fleeting shadows and strategic omissions. They had moved through the ship's circulatory system like a phantom, using its hidden arteries to bypass the watchful eyes of its electronic sentinels. The service corridors, designed for the seamless operation of the vessel, had become the silent accomplices to murder.

"They knew the ship's layout intimately," Miller concluded, his voice laced with a grim respect for his unseen adversary. "They understood the limitations of our camera network. They chose their entry and exit points with the precision of a surgeon. This wasn't a crime of passion; it was a meticulously planned operation. The killer is experienced, cunning, and understands our investigative methods well enough to try to evade them."

Jenkins nodded, compiling the new data into their growing timeline. "So, we're looking for someone who can move unseen, who knows the ship's infrastructure, and who has a motive strong enough to commit murder. The question remains: who is this person, and how did they gain access to Thorne's suite at that specific time, with that specific knowledge?"

The Captain Rostova's dilemma was deepening. The initial shock of Thorne's murder was giving way to a chilling realization: they were dealing with a ghost, a phantom who had slipped through their fingers, leaving behind only the faintest of echoes–a shadow in a stairwell, a flicker in a service corridor, a gait that might or might not be a clue. The killer's trail was a testament to their careful planning, a stark reminder that the most dangerous predators were often the ones who understood the system best. And for Captain Rostova Miller, the hunt had just begun, with an adversary who seemed to expect his every move, lurking in the very shadows he was trying to illuminate. The sterile environment of the conference room, once a symbol of control, now felt like a fragile barrier against the unseen forces at play. Each piece of footage, each line of code, was a battlefield where the unseen killer was already several steps ahead, their cunning woven into the very fabric of the ship. The enigma of Marcus Thorne's death was not just about who had committed the act, but about the chilling intelligence that had guided their hand, leaving Miller and Jenkins grappling with a foe who had weaponized the ship's own architecture against them.

Chapter 3: Partners in Shadow

The chill that had settled over Miller wasn't just from the ship's climate control; it was the unnerving sensation of a past resurrected. He watched Sergeant Jenkins, her fingers still poised over the console, her concentration unwavering. It was the same focus he remembered, the same sharp intellect that had made her an invaluable partner. But now, overlaid with the stark reality of their present predicament, it felt... different. A phantom limb, reattached without warning.

"You know," Miller began, the edge of command replaced by a nascent familiarity, "seeing you here, on this... pleasure cruise, it's something I never anticipated. Not after everything." He let the silence hang, a subtle invitation for her to fill the void.

Jenkins finally looked up, her gaze meeting his across the sterile expanse of the conference room. A faint, almost imperceptible softening around her eyes acknowledged his words. "Anticipation isn't exactly my strong suit, Captain Rostova. Life has a way of throwing curveballs, wouldn't you agree?" Her tone was light, but there was an undercurrent of something he couldn't quite decipher. It wasn't quite defensiveness, but a careful metering of her words.

"Curveballs," Miller echoed, a ghost of a smile touching his lips. "You always did have a knack for fielding them. Remember that serial arsonist in Atlanta? The one who used accelerants derived from obscure botanical extracts? Most agents were chasing smoke, you were digging through old botany texts."

A genuine smile flickered across Jenkins's face, a rare sight that momentarily erased the grim lines etched by the unfolding investigation. "And you, Captain Rostova, were the one who spotted the pattern in the chemical composition, the signature in the way the fires were set, not just the fuel. You saw the artistry where others saw only destruction."

Their shared history, a tapestry woven with late nights, dead ends, and the occasional, triumphant breakthrough, began to unfurl in the dim light of the monitors. They had been a formidable team, Miller the seasoned strategist with an uncanny intuition, Jenkins the meticulous analyst who could dissect evidence with surgical precision. Their partnership had been forged in the crucible of some of the FBI's most complex and disturbing cases.

"The 'Whispering Killer' in Chicago," Miller mused, the memory surfacing unbidden. "Eight victims, all found in public parks, no signs of struggle, no witnesses. We spent months chasing shadows, convinced it was an inside job, someone with access to police databases. And all along, it was a disgruntled postal worker with a rare neurological condition that made him undetectable to canine units. You cracked that one."

Jenkins gave a small shake of her head. "It wasn't just me. You were the one who insisted on running the postal worker database checks, despite the initial lack of probable cause. You trusted your gut, Captain Rostova. That's what made us work. You trusted me to find the pieces, and I trusted you to see the whole picture, even when it was obscured."

The camaraderie was palpable, a comfortable warmth that belied the somberness of their current circumstances. Yet, beneath the surface of shared memories, Miller sensed a current of unspoken tension, a narrative left unfinished. He remembered the abruptness of his own departure from the Bureau, a decision that had surprised many, not least Jenkins. He had retired, citing burnout, but the truth was more nuanced. There had been a case, a disagreement, a moment where their professional philosophies had collided with an intensity that had irrevocably shifted their dynamic.

"It wasn't always easy, though, was it?" Miller ventured, his gaze drifting to a photograph on Jenkins's desk – a younger version of them, arms slung around each other, grinning at the camera, a trophy from a solved case proudly displayed. "We pushed each other. Sometimes, too hard."

Jenkins's expression became more guarded. She picked up a stylus, turning it over and over in her fingers. "Every successful partnership has its friction, Captain Rostova. It's how you learn. How you grow. You taught me the importance of looking beyond the obvious. I... I tried to keep you grounded when your intuition threatened to lead you too far into the stratosphere."

"Stratosphere," Miller chuckled, a dry, humorless sound. "More like a one-way ticket to a disciplinary hearing, sometimes. I remember that case in New Orleans, the voodoo cult killings. Everyone was convinced it was ritualistic. You were pulling toxicology reports, DNA samples, the usual forensic arsenal. I was convinced it was a lone wolf, a psychopath playing a game. And you, with your usual calm demeanor, presented me with a detailed analysis of the victimology, the financial records, the alibis. You showed me the 'real' motive, not the theatrical one."

"And you took that information and ran with it," Jenkins replied, her voice holding a note of gentle reprimand. "You were so focused on the financial motive, you nearly missed the accomplice, the one with the actual knowledge of the victim's habits. It was a close call, Captain Rostova."

The air in the room seemed to thicken, heavy with the weight of these resurfaced memories. Miller recognized the unspoken in her words: the disagreement, the tension that had simmered and ultimately led to his early retirement. He had been too headstrong, too insistent on his own interpretation, and she, in her pragmatic way, had seen a flaw in his reasoning.

"You were right, of course," Miller admitted, the words feeling both foreign and familiar on his tongue. "I was so caught up in the grand narrative, I almost missed the supporting player. It was a lesson learned. A hard one." He paused, then met her gaze directly. "And it's why your presence here now, Sergeant, feels... more than just a coincidence. You wouldn't be on this cruise, in this part of the world, without a reason. A reason beyond enjoying the sun and sea, I suspect."

Jenkins's grip tightened on the stylus. Her eyes, once sharp with analytical thought, now held a depth that spoke of secrets and unspoken burdens. "Everyone has their reasons, Captain Rostova. Some are for leisure, some are for necessity. Some are for... unfinished business."

"Unfinished business," Miller repeated, the phrase resonating with a new significance. He had walked away from the FBI, but he hadn't truly walked away from the pursuit of justice. And perhaps, neither had she.

"You're here because of this cruise, aren't you? Because of Thorne. Or what Thorne represented."

She didn't confirm or deny, but her silence was an answer in itself. The shared history, the years of working side-by-side, had created a bond that transcended the confines of their former careers. It was a connection built on mutual respect, on a shared understanding of the darkness that lurked beneath the surface of ordinary life. But it was also a connection strained by the very intensity of their shared experiences.

"Thorne was a ghost," Miller continued, his voice dropping to a near whisper. "A ghost in a digital world. And now, a literal ghost on this ship. You were always better at chasing ghosts, Jenkins. You had a patience for them, a methodical way of sifting through the residue they left behind."

"Residue can tell a story, Captain Rostova," she replied, her voice regaining some of its professional edge, yet still carrying that undertone of personal revelation. "If you know how to read it. You taught me that."

Miller leaned back, the sterile conference room feeling less like a crime scene and more like a confessional. He remembered Jenkins's quiet determination, her ability to remain unflappable in the face of chaos. She was a rock, a steady presence in his often turbulent professional life. But there had been moments, he recalled, when that steadiness had felt like a deliberate counterpoint to his own impulsiveness, a constant reminder of the boundaries he sometimes pushed.

"I remember you once said I had a 'reckless brilliance,'" Miller recalled, a wry smile playing on his lips. "That I could see the forest while everyone else was lost in the trees, but I also had a tendency to set the trees on fire trying to find my way."

Jenkins finally met his gaze, a flicker of amusement in her eyes. "And I always carried the extinguisher, Captain Rostova. It was a necessary balance, wouldn't you agree? You generated the theories, often outlandish, and I refined them, grounded them, made them actionable. We were a symbiosis, in our own way."

"Symbiosis," Miller echoed. "Until the symbiosis broke. Or until one of us decided the air was getting too thin." He looked at her, truly looked at her, seeing not just Sergeant Jenkins, the sharp investigator, but also Eleanor Jenkins, the woman who had shared some of his most intense professional moments. "Why are you really here, Eleanor?" He used her first name, a rare indulgence.

She hesitated for a beat, her gaze unfocused for a moment, as if wading through deep waters. "There are... certain individuals I've been tracking, Captain Rostova. Individuals who operate in the shadows, much like our current predicament. Thorne's name had surfaced in connection with a... particular network. A network I've been attempting to unravel for some time. This cruise, his presence on it, was an opportunity I couldn't afford to miss. And when I heard about his death..." She paused, her voice dropping. "It became more than an investigation. It became personal."

The word "personal" hung in the air. Miller felt a prickle of unease. His own reasons for being here, while seemingly straightforward – a respite, an escape – now felt complicated by this reawakened partnership. Jenkins's agenda, it seemed, was not entirely separate from his own. The ghosts of their past, both professional and personal, were now intertwined with the very real specter of murder on the high seas.

"So, we find ourselves once again on opposite sides of the same puzzle," Miller stated, his voice regaining some of its authoritative tone, though tempered with a newfound understanding. "Except this time, we're on the same side of the room."

Jenkins offered a small, almost imperceptible nod. "The puzzle has changed, Captain Rostova. The stakes are higher. And perhaps, this time, we can afford to trust each other's instincts a little more. The history between us, the good and the... less good, it's a foundation. Not a barrier."

He studied her for a long moment. Her expression was unreadable, yet there was a quiet resolve in her stance that he recognized and respected. They had once navigated the darkest corners of human depravity together, and now, in the opulent, yet unsettling, confines of a luxury cruise ship, they were being drawn back into that dance. The shared memories, the unspoken tensions, the intertwined agendas – it all coalesced into a complex and undeniably potent partnership, rekindled in the most unexpected of circumstances.

"A foundation," Miller mused, the word tasting like a forgotten truth. "Let's hope it's a strong one, Sergeant. Because this foundation is about to be tested." He gestured towards the monitors, the grainy images of the elusive figure still looping. "We have a killer to catch. And it seems, we have a history to put to good use."

Jenkins picked up a datapad, her fingers already moving with practiced efficiency. "Agreed, Captain Rostova. The past has a way of informing the present. Let's see what it can tell us about our present circumstances. And about Thorne. And about why he was worth killing."

Miller watched her, a strange sense of familiarity washing over him. It was like finding a long-lost limb, awkward at first, but undeniably part of him. The years apart, the diverging paths, had done little to diminish the understanding that had once existed between them. It was an understanding forged in shared adrenaline, in whispered theories in darkened rooms, in the grim satisfaction of bringing a perpetrator to justice. And now, it was reawakened, not by choice, but by necessity, by the chilling circumstances of a murder that echoed with the same kind of calculated deception they had once fought so hard to expose.

He remembered the very first case they had worked on together, a string of high-profile art thefts that had baffled the New York PD. Miller, fresh out of Quantico, had been eager to prove himself, to chase the flashy leads. Jenkins, a seasoned investigator even then, had been the quiet force, meticulously piecing together the financial trails, the courier routes, the seemingly innocuous shipping manifests. He had been the storm, she had been the anchor.

"You know," Miller said, breaking the silence that had settled between them, his gaze still fixed on the shifting images on the screen, "that firebombing incident in Miami. The one that looked like a botched drug deal. You were the one who insisted on running the chemical analysis on the residual explosives, even when forensics had already signed off. Said the burn patterns were too clean."

Jenkins's fingers stilled for a moment before resuming their methodical work. "They were," she confirmed, her voice steady. "The accelerant was too pure, too uniform. Not something you'd find in a back-alley drug lab. It suggested a level of sophistication, a controlled environment. It led us to the industrial chemist who was working for the cartel, developing specialized explosives for them. You were so focused on the 'why' of the drug deal, you almost missed the 'how' that pointed to a far more dangerous operation."

A faint smile touched Miller's lips. "And you were the one who provided the 'how'. You always did have a nose for the details. The ones that made all the difference." He paused, a more somber note entering his voice. "It's the details that matter now, Eleanor. The details of Thorne's death. The details of how someone managed to slip through our net, right under our noses."

He remembered the sheer exhaustion that had permeated their lives during those years. The constant travel, the lack of sleep, the emotional toll of witnessing the worst of humanity. He had chosen to step away, to find a semblance of peace. But peace, it seemed, was a fleeting commodity.

"You never really liked the limelight, did you?" Miller asked, a question that had often lingered in his mind. "Even after cracking a case, you'd always fade into the background. Let me take the press conferences, do the talking."

Jenkins finally looked at him, her expression thoughtful. "The work was the point, Captain Rostova. Not the recognition. The satisfaction came from solving the puzzle, from understanding the twisted logic of the criminal mind. The press conferences were... a necessary evil. A distraction from the real work."

"And now you're back in the thick of it," Miller observed. "On a cruise ship, with a dead billionaire, and an unknown killer lurking. This isn't exactly a quiet retirement, is it?"

She gave a small shrug, a gesture that conveyed a complex mix of resignation and determination. "Captain Rostova, life throws curveballs. And sometimes, you have to step up to the plate. Especially when the trajectory of that curveball is heading towards something you've been trying to intercept for a very long time."

The unspoken question hung between them: what exactly had Jenkins been trying to intercept? What connection did Thorne have to her ongoing investigations? His own past with the FBI, his reasons for leaving, felt like a tangled web he was now being pulled back into. The years had passed, but the echoes of past disagreements, of moments where their professional paths had diverged, still lingered.

"It's ironic, isn't it?" Miller said, his voice low. "We built our careers on uncovering secrets, on pulling back the curtain. And here we are, surrounded by a thousand people, and the most dangerous secret is hidden amongst us, walking free."

Jenkins nodded, her gaze sharp and focused once more. "And the most dangerous secrets are often the ones closest to home, Captain Rostova. The ones that are hidden in plain sight. We need to look at everyone. Every passenger. Every crew member. Thorne was a man of considerable influence. He made enemies. And on this ship, he's brought them all together."

"A microcosm of society," Miller mused, "with a killer at its heart. We need to remember everything we learned, Eleanor. About how people operate. About how they hide. About how they kill." He looked at her, a flicker of the old partnership igniting in his eyes. "We've been here before. Different setting, different crime, but the same fundamental principles. The same human motivations, revenge, desperation."

"And a killer who knows this ship," Jenkins added, her voice firm. "Who knows its layout, its routines, its blind spots. That's our starting point. The perpetrator is not a stranger to this environment. They are, in a way, a part of it."

Miller leaned forward, the frustration of the incomplete evidence momentarily overshadowed by the reawakened sense of purpose. "And you are here because Thorne's name was connected to something you were investigating. Something that brought you onto this ship, in pursuit of shadows." He paused, letting the implication sink in. "It seems our agendas have converged, Sergeant. For better or for worse."

Jenkins met his gaze, a hint of a smile playing on her lips. "The best partnerships, Captain Rostova, are forged in the crucible of necessity. And right now, the necessity is undeniable. We may have retired from the same agency, but our work, it seems, is far from over."

The shared history, once a source of potential friction, now felt like an unexpected advantage. They knew each other's strengths, each other's weaknesses. They understood the subtle cues, the unspoken understandings that made them effective. The murder of Marcus Thorne had not only brought them back together but had also thrown them headfirst into a deeply personal investigation, one that was intertwined with Jenkins's own clandestine pursuits and Miller's own complicated past. The ship, a vessel of luxury and escape, had become a stage for a drama as old as time, a drama they had once navigated with unparalleled skill. Now, with their history rekindled, they had a chance to write a new ending.

The weight of Jenkins's confession settled in the small conference room, pressing down on Miller like the humid air before a storm. He had sensed it, of course. The meticulousness, the almost predatory focus she brought to the unfolding tragedy, was far beyond that of a fellow passenger caught in a sudden, grim predicament. Her carefully constructed facade of casual vacationer had crumbled, revealing the seasoned investigator beneath, a woman whose instincts had always run parallel to his own, often acting as the necessary counterweight to his more impetuous leaps.

"A cover," Miller repeated, the word a low rumble in his chest. It wasn't a question, but a statement of fact, an acknowledgment of the intricate deception that had brought them both to this floating microcosm of intrigue. He had been nursing his own suspicions, a gnawing feeling that Thorne's death was more than just a tragic accident on the high seas. He'd overheard fragmented conversations, whispers of illicit dealings that seemed too significant to be mere gossip. Now, Jenkins's presence, her intense scrutiny, provided a chilling confirmation.

Jenkins met his gaze, her expression a complex tapestry of professional resolve and a subtle, almost imperceptible weariness. "It wasn't a vacation, Captain Rostova," she stated, her voice steady, devoid of the practiced casualness that had permeated their earlier conversation. "It was an assignment. A long-term one, I'll admit. I've been tracking Thorne's company, 'Aether Dynamics', for months. Specifically, their involvement in... certain unsavory data practices."

Miller's mind raced, piecing together the fragments. Aether Dynamics. The name had surfaced in his own fragmented eavesdropping, a hushed mention of "offshore servers" and "proprietary algorithms." He'd dismissed it as typical corporate jargon, the kind of opaque language that masked a multitude of sins. But Jenkins's focus was far too sharp for mere corporate espionage.

"Data practices?" he prompted, leaning forward, the comfortable camaraderie of their shared past now eclipsed by the urgency of the present. "What kind of data practices, Eleanor?"

She exhaled slowly, her eyes scanning the holographic display of Thorne's luxurious suite, the scene of the crime. "Illegal data trafficking," she said, the words delivered with an unnerving calm. "Aether Dynamics has been a key player in a network that traffics in sensitive information. Corporate secrets, personal data, even, from what I've managed to glean, pre-release market intel that can destabilize entire economies. They've built a sophisticated infrastructure, operating in the digital shadows, making it virtually untraceable."

Miller felt a jolt of recognition. The whispers he'd overheard, the hushed tones, the fear in the voices... they hadn't been about a simple business deal gone sour. They had been about power, about control, about information wielded as a weapon. And Thorne, the flamboyant billionaire who commanded this opulent vessel, had been at the nexus of it all.

"Thorne was the linchpin, then?" Miller asked, the implications of her words starting to solidify into a terrifying picture. "He was the one orchestrating it? Or was he about to expose it?"

Jenkins's jaw tightened, a flicker of something akin to regret crossing her features. "That's the crux of it, Captain Rostova. My intel suggested Thorne was becoming... uncomfortable. He'd amassed a fortune on the back of this network, but the moral implications, or perhaps the increasing risk, were starting to weigh on him. We had reason to believe he was preparing to blow the whistle, to leak information that would cripple the entire operation, and likely implicate some very powerful individuals."

The pieces clicked into place with a sickening finality. Thorne hadn't been murdered because he was a victim of some random act of violence. He had been silenced. Executed. His death wasn't a crime of passion or opportunity; it was a calculated act of corporate assassination, a desperate measure to protect a multi-billion dollar enterprise built on the exploitation of information.

"He was a target," Miller stated, the realization hitting him with the force of a physical blow. His initial assessment, that Thorne's murder was a perplexing anomaly on a pleasure cruise, dissolved like mist in the harsh light of this new reality. This wasn't just a murder; it was the tip of an iceberg, a vast, submerged conspiracy with Thorne's demise as its bloody monument.

"Precisely," Jenkins confirmed, her gaze unwavering. "My objective was to gather irrefutable evidence. Financial records, communication logs, the anonymized server locations – anything that could bring down Aether Dynamics and the shadowy figures behind it. I was here, on this cruise, specifically because Thorne was scheduled to be here. He was rumored to be meeting with some of his... associates. An opportunity for me to get closer, to potentially intercept some crucial data."

Miller ran a hand through his hair, the slight tremor in his fingers betraying his internal turmoil. The vague unease he'd felt about Thorne's sudden demise had been a faint echo of Jenkins's far more targeted investigation. He had stumbled into a viper's nest, drawn by the siren song of a luxurious cruise, only to find himself at the center of a high-stakes espionage thriller.

"So, you've been watching Thorne," Miller mused, his mind already replaying his interactions with the deceased billionaire. Thorne's jovial demeanor, his open nature – it was all a performance, a carefully crafted illusion designed to mask the darkness within Aether Dynamics. "And you believe whoever silenced him is still on this ship."

"The network doesn't tolerate loose ends, Captain Rostova," Jenkins said, her voice grim. "If Thorne was about to expose them, they would ensure he couldn't. And that means the operative, or operatives, responsible for his death are likely still among us, either to ensure their silence or to retrieve any information Thorne might have managed to pass on. This isn't just about finding a killer; it's about preventing a global information heist."

The magnitude of the situation began to dawn on Miller. This was no longer a matter of simple forensics and witness interviews. This was a complex web of corporate intrigue, data exploitation, and murder, played out on a confined stage. The luxury cruise ship, a symbol of opulence and escapism, had transformed into a gilded cage, with a predator among the passengers.

"My overhearing those conversations," Miller began, the fragmented whispers now taking on a terrifying significance. "It wasn't just idle gossip. It was the sound of fear. The sound of a conspiracy unraveling." He looked at Jenkins, a newfound respect mixed with a healthy dose of apprehension.

"You were ahead of me the whole time. You knew something was rotten, long before I did."

"My job is to look for the rot, Captain Rostova," Jenkins replied, a ghost of her old analytical demeanor returned. "And Thorne's company was a festering wound. The whispers you heard, the fragments of information you picked up – they were echoes of my investigation. I've been trying to penetrate Aether Dynamics for months, to find proof of their illegal operations. Thorne's presence on this cruise was a critical juncture, a potential breakthrough. His death has thrown a wrench into everything, but it also confirms my suspicions. He was close to something significant."

Miller nodded, the narrative of his own involuntary involvement starting to crystallize. He hadn't been seeking trouble; trouble had found him, as Thorne's murder, a crime that was intrinsically linked to Jenkins's clandestine mission. Their paths, so long diverged, had converged in the most unexpected and dangerous way.

"So, while I was trying to enjoy a supposed vacation, you were working an undercover operation," Miller stated, a wry smile touching his lips. "And now, Thorne's murder has pulled us both into the same vortex."

"It's not ideal," Jenkins admitted, "but perhaps not entirely without its advantages. You have an outsider's perspective, Captain Rostova. You can see things from a different angle, unburdened by the preconceptions I might have developed over months of surveillance. And I have the intelligence, the context, that you're currently missing."

She was right. The dynamic had shifted. He had initially seen her as a former colleague, an unexpected but welcome face. Now, he saw her as a partner in a far more dangerous game than either of them had initially anticipated.

"You said Thorne was about to expose something critical," Miller pressed, his mind racing ahead. "What exactly was it? What was he going to reveal that was worth killing him for?"

Jenkins hesitated, her gaze drifting towards the window, where the vast expanse of the ocean stretched out, indifferent to the human drama unfolding aboard the ship. "It's difficult to say with absolute certainty without accessing Thorne's personal files, which I suspect are now heavily guarded or already compromised. But based on my informants and the data I've managed to decrypt, it was related to a new algorithm Aether Dynamics was developing. An algorithm designed to exploit vulnerabilities in global financial markets. It was far more sophisticated, and far more destructive, than anything they'd attempted before. Thorne, I believe, had realized the catastrophic potential, and perhaps the sheer immorality, of unleashing it."

Miller absorbed this information, the scale of the conspiracy widening with each word. This wasn't just about corporate malfeasance; it was about global economic manipulation, about the potential to destabilize entire nations for profit. Thorne's death wasn't just the end of a man; it was the desperate act of a shadowy organization to protect its ultimate weapon.

"And the person who killed Thorne," Miller continued, his voice low and intense, "they would have been acting on behalf of whoever stood to lose the most from Thorne's potential exposé. The architects of this algorithm, the ones who stood to profit from its release, or the ones who would be exposed by Thorne's revelations."

"Exactly," Jenkins confirmed, her eyes sharp with renewed focus. "This wasn't a random act of violence. It was a professional hit, carried out by someone tasked with ensuring Thorne's silence, permanently. And that person is here, on this ship, among us. They could be anyone. A passenger. A member of the crew. Someone who has been carefully placed to ensure Thorne's secrets, and Aether Dynamics' operations, remain hidden."

The implications were chilling. They were sailing on a ship populated by potential killers, each one a suspect in a conspiracy that reached far beyond the confines of their floating prison. The luxurious façade of the cruise had become a thin veneer, barely concealing the deadly undercurrents of corporate intrigue and calculated murder.

"This changes everything," Miller said, the words barely a whisper. His planned escape, his desire for a quiet respite, had evaporated. He was back in the thick of it, drawn into a world of espionage and murder he had thought he had left behind. But this time, he wasn't alone. He had Eleanor Jenkins, a partner whose skills and dedication he knew intimately.

"It does," Jenkins agreed, her gaze steady and determined. "But it also gives us a direction. Thorne was killed to prevent him from exposing a deadly secret. Our mission now is to uncover that secret, and to find the person who silenced him. We have a shared history, Captain Rostova, and it seems we have a shared objective once again. The question is, are you ready to play this game, knowing the stakes?"

Miller met her gaze, the embers of their past partnership rekindling in the face of this new, daunting challenge. He had retired from the FBI seeking peace, but perhaps his true calling, his true purpose, lay in confronting the darkness, in seeking justice for those who could not. And with Eleanor Jenkins by his side, navigating the treacherous currents of this unfolding conspiracy, he felt a surge of grim determination.

"I never really left the game, Eleanor," Miller replied, the corners of his mouth lifting in a faint, knowing smile. "I just changed the players. And it looks like fate has decided to put some of the old team back together. Let's see what we can uncover. Let's see who Thorne was really afraid of, and why they wanted him silenced so badly."

Jenkins gave a curt nod, her professional demeanor firmly in place. "Agreed. Thorne's death is not an end, Captain Rostova. It's a beginning. And we have a lot of ground to cover, and very little time." She gestured towards the monitors, the looping images of Thorne's suite now a stark reminder of the predator lurking amongst them. "Let's start by examining everything we know about Thorne's recent activities, his communications, and anyone who might have had a vested interest in his silence. The clock is ticking."

The shared history, the unspoken understanding between them, formed a silent pact. They were partners again, thrust together by circumstance, bound by the shared pursuit of truth in a world of deception. The opulent cruise ship, once a symbol of leisure, had become a hunting ground, and Miller and Jenkins, the unlikely detectives, were ready to begin their hunt. The mission was unveiled, the stakes were sky-high, and the shadows on this ship were deeper than anyone could have imagined.

The flickering holographic displays, once innocuous decorative elements in the lavish suite, now served as a stark backdrop to the unfolding grim reality. Miller and Jenkins, a curious juxtaposition of seasoned investigator and reluctant detective, found themselves ensnared in a web far more intricate than a simple maritime murder. The confession from the late Mr. Sterling's associate had been a Pandora's Box, and the contents were far more insidious than they had initially imagined. Sterling, the magnanimous host and seemingly benevolent tech mogul, was revealed to be a pivotal figure in a clandestine operation, a man whose professional life was a tapestry woven with threads of innovation and illicit dealings. His demise was a calculated move to silence a man who, it seemed, had become too much of a liability for his powerful associates.

Jenkins, her eyes alight with the familiar glint of professional pursuit, directed Miller's attention to a series of encrypted files on Sterling's personal laptop. The sleek, obsidian device, recovered from a hidden compartment within the suite, was now the focal point of their investigation. "This is where we begin, Captain Rostova," she stated, her voice a low, determined hum. "Sterling wasn't just a victim; he was a linchpin. His company, 'Aegis Innovations,' isn't just at the forefront of AI and cybersecurity as the public narrative suggests. My intel indicates they've been dabbling in far more... ethically flexible applications of their technology. Applications that could have devastating consequences if they fell into the wrong hands, or were exploited for nefarious purposes."

Miller leaned closer, the sterile glow of the laptop screen casting long shadows across his face. "Ethically flexible applications? What does that mean, Eleanor? Are we talking about cyber warfare, state-sponsored espionage, or something even more... abstract?" He recalled the hushed whispers he'd overheard on deck, fragmented conversations about "data dominance" and "predictive models." He'd dismissed them as the typical boasts of ambitious entrepreneurs, but now, in Sterling's murder, they took on a chilling new significance.

Jenkins began to navigate the complex encryption, her fingers dancing across the holographic keyboard with practiced ease. "It's multifaceted, Captain Rostova. Aegis Innovations has developed AI algorithms that can predict, with unnerving accuracy, market fluctuations, geopolitical shifts, and even social unrest. On the surface, this is invaluable for economic forecasting and risk assessment. But the potential for manipulation... it's astronomical. Imagine being able to subtly influence stock prices, destabilize a currency, or even incite public opinion with carefully curated information, all guided by an AI that understands human behavior at a granular level."

She paused, allowing the weight of her words to sink in. "And then there's the cybersecurity aspect. Aegis has developed an unparalleled system for data encryption and decryption. While ostensibly for national security and protecting sensitive corporate data, the same technology can be used to steal, manipulate, and exploit that data. They've essentially created a digital fortress, but with a back door that only they – or those who can pay their price – can access."

Miller's mind reeled. The implications were staggering. Sterling wasn't just a victim of a personal vendetta; he was a casualty of a corporate war fought in the digital realm, a war with stakes that could reshape global power dynamics. The individuals or organizations who controlled Aegis Innovations, and by extension, Sterling's groundbreaking technology, held an unprecedented amount of leverage. "So, Sterling was going to expose them?" Miller prompted, the question hanging heavy in the air. "He was going to reveal how his company's technology was being misused?"

"That's the prevailing theory, and the most logical conclusion," Jenkins confirmed, her brow furrowed in concentration as she bypassed another layer of security. "My sources within the tech underground suggested Sterling was having second thoughts. The scale of the operation, the potential for global disruption, it was starting to weigh on him. He was a visionary, yes, but he also possessed a moral compass. We believe he was preparing to leak information about Aegis's more illicit activities, perhaps even providing a kill switch for their most dangerous algorithms, or revealing the identities of the powerful entities pulling the strings."

The word "entities" sent a shiver down Miller's spine. This wasn't just about a few rogue businessmen. This suggested a far more pervasive and influential network, one that extended beyond the confines of their luxurious cruise ship and into the highest echelons of global power. The passengers and crew, a microcosm of society, might unknowingly be harboring individuals connected to an operation that could destabilize nations.

"Who were these entities, Eleanor?" Miller pressed, his voice barely above a whisper. "Governments? Shadowy corporations? A combination of both?"

Jenkins finally broke through the last layer of encryption, the laptop screen filling with lines of code and complex data structures. "It's a blurred landscape, Captain Rostova. Aegis Innovations has a sprawling network of shell corporations, offshore accounts, and veiled partnerships. We're talking about interests that span continents, with tentacles reaching into finance, intelligence agencies, and even organized crime syndicates. The technology they've developed is a veritable Swiss Army knife for the ultra-powerful – capable of financial market manipulation, sophisticated espionage, and destabilization on an unprecedented scale. Sterling was a key architect, but he was also becoming a potential threat to the very people who profited from his genius."

She highlighted a specific set of financial transactions, the numbers stark and unsettling. "Look at this. Large sums of money moving through untraceable channels, often coinciding with major global events – stock market crashes, political upheavals. It's all too coincidental. And Sterling, it seems, was beginning to document these movements, perhaps for his own protection, or perhaps as evidence for his intended exposé."

Miller studied the figures, the abstract numbers on the screen coalescing into a horrifying narrative of manipulation. This wasn't just a murder; it was an act of corporate sabotage on a global scale, a desperate attempt to preserve an enterprise built on the exploitation of groundbreaking technology. "So, whoever killed Sterling wasn't just eliminating a threat to Aegis," Miller deduced, "they were protecting their investments, their power, their very way of life."

"Precisely," Jenkins affirmed. "And that makes our search for the killer infinitely more complex. We're not just looking for a murderer; we're looking for a representative of a vast, powerful, and dangerous network. This person is likely highly trained, resourceful, and utterly ruthless. They might be a professional operative, a corporate enforcer, or even someone within Sterling's inner circle who was tasked with ensuring his silence."

She scrolled through a directory of Sterling's personal contacts, a list that included a mix of prominent figures in the tech world, government officials, and individuals with known ties to clandestine organizations. "The problem is, Captain Rostova, Sterling moved in these circles. He had access to people who could command immense power, and who would do anything to protect their secrets. Our killer could be any of these individuals, or someone acting on their behalf."

Miller's gaze drifted to the opulent furnishings of the suite, the symbols of Sterling's wealth and success now imbued with a sinister undertone. The luxurious veneer of their surroundings seemed to mock the deadly game they were now involved in. Every passenger, every crew member, was a potential suspect, a pawn in a game of international intrigue. "What were Sterling's most recent communications? Was there any indication of who he was about to contact, or what information he was preparing to release?"

Jenkins accessed Sterling's encrypted email and messaging logs, her expression growing more intense with each passing moment. "He was sending out encrypted messages, very short, very coded. The recipient is masked, but the timing is significant. They occurred in the hours leading up to his death. He was also accessing a secured server, one that my contacts tell me is notoriously difficult to penetrate. He was downloading something, or uploading something, of immense importance. I'm attempting to reconstruct the data fragments now, but it's like piecing together a shattered mirror."

She pointed to a series of timestamps on the screen. "This window of activity... it aligns with the period when he was last seen alive. He was clearly agitated, making some kind of final move. And whoever was watching him, whoever wanted to stop him, knew it. They acted decisively, and with brutal efficiency."

Miller felt a growing sense of unease. The carefully crafted narrative of a tragic accident at sea was dissolving, replaced by a far more chilling reality. Sterling's death was a consequence of his involvement in a conspiracy that threatened to shake the foundations of global power. And the killer, a ghost in the machine of this elaborate deception, was still on board, a viper in their midst.

"The motive is clear," Miller stated, his mind already sifting through potential scenarios. "Preventing Sterling from exposing Aegis's illicit activities. But the method... it was clean, efficient. This wasn't a crime of passion. This was a professional hit."

"Exactly," Jenkins agreed, her focus unwavering. "And if they were willing to go to such lengths to silence Sterling, they won't hesitate to eliminate anyone who gets too close to the truth. That means us, Captain Rostova. We are now targets."

The unspoken implication hung in the air: they were no longer just investigating a murder; they were engaged in a high-stakes game of corporate espionage, where the price of discovery could be their very lives. The luxury cruise, a supposed escape from the complexities of the world, had become a gilded cage, trapping them with a killer and a conspiracy of unimaginable proportions.

Jenkins continued to delve into the encrypted data, her eyes scanning the intricate lines of code. "Sterling was meticulous. He had backups upon backups, encrypted within encrypted. He knew the risks. He was preparing for a catastrophic event. The data suggests he was trying to secure proof of widespread market manipulation, orchestrated by Aegis and their clients. He had gathered evidence of specific trades, insider information leaks, and algorithmic sabotage that directly led to several major economic downturns in the past few years. The scale of it is... frankly, terrifying."

She zoomed in on a particular file, a compressed archive labeled with a cryptic alphanumeric string. "This appears to be a partial ledger. It details transactions that are deeply unsettling. Payments made to individuals and organizations with known ties to destabilizing regimes, and conversely, payments received from entities that would benefit from global economic chaos. It paints a picture of a company that isn't just creating technology; it's actively weaponizing information to sow discord and profit from the resulting turmoil."

Miller's mind was racing, connecting the dots between the fragmented whispers he'd overheard and Jenkins's findings. The talk of "offshore servers" and "proprietary algorithms" was no longer abstract corporate jargon; it was the language of illicit financial dealings and sophisticated cyber-espionage. It was becoming increasingly clear that this was not a series of isolated incidents but part of a larger, more sinister operation.

"So, the people Sterling was dealing with, they weren't just interested in Aegis's technology for its legitimate applications," Miller surmised, his voice grim. "They were using it as a tool for global destabilization, for profit. And Sterling, the visionary behind it all, had a crisis of conscience."

"That seems to be the most plausible scenario," Jenkins confirmed. "He was trying to expose them, to bring down the entire operation from the inside. And they ensured he couldn't. His death was a preemptive strike, a desperate measure to protect their multi-billion dollar empire built on the exploitation of global markets and the weaponization of information."

She highlighted another section of the ledger, detailing a series of payments to a holding company registered in a well-known tax haven. "This entity is a known front for several powerful individuals and organizations. We're talking about names that appear on intelligence watchlists, individuals who have consistently operated in the shadows, influencing global events without public accountability. Sterling was on the verge of exposing them, of revealing their complicity in a network that manipulates economies and destabilizes governments."

The sheer magnitude of the conspiracy began to dawn on Miller. This wasn't just about a single murder; it was about unraveling a global conspiracy that had infiltrated the highest levels of power.

"And the killer," Miller stated, the realization hitting him with the force of a physical blow, "is here, among us. Someone who was sent to ensure Sterling's silence, and to retrieve any evidence he might have managed to disseminate."

"Precisely," Jenkins said, her gaze sharp and unwavering. "They could be anyone. A passenger seeking to avoid scrutiny, a member of the crew acting under duress or for financial gain, or even a high-ranking executive from a subsidiary company, present on this ship under the guise of a business trip. Our killer is a ghost, a highly trained operative who has blended seamlessly into the fabric of this cruise. They are likely still monitoring the situation, waiting for an opportunity to either secure any remaining evidence or to silence anyone else who gets too close."

Miller ran a hand through his hair, the weight of the investigation pressing down on him. His desire for a peaceful retirement had been brutally extinguished, replaced by the grim reality of facing an enemy more formidable than any he had encountered in his past career. But he wasn't alone. Eleanor Jenkins, a partner whose competence and dedication he trusted implicitly, was by his side.

"This changes everything," Miller said, the words a low rumble. "We're not just looking for a killer anymore. We're looking for the architects of a global destabilization scheme, and we have to do it before they can silence us too."

Jenkins met his gaze, her expression a mixture of grim determination and a flicker of shared resolve. "It does. But Sterling, in his meticulousness, has given us a fighting chance. These encrypted files are a goldmine, Captain Rostova. We have a roadmap, albeit a dangerous one, to the heart of this conspiracy. The question is, are you ready to navigate it?"

Miller's lips curved into a faint, knowing smile. The thrill of the chase, the intellectual challenge, the pursuit of justice – it was a current that had always run deep within him, a current he had tried to suppress but which now surged with renewed vigor. "I never truly left the game, Eleanor," he replied, his eyes locking with hers. "I just needed the right catalyst. And it seems Sterling's death has provided that. Let's see what else this ledger has to say. Let's see who's been playing God with the global economy, and why they felt Sterling needed to be silenced so permanently." The adventure, it seemed, had just begun, and the shadows on this opulent vessel were far deeper and more dangerous than they had ever imagined.

The small, intricately carved wooden bird lay on the polished surface of Sterling's desk, a stark contrast to the ephemeral glow of holographic displays and the sterile gleam of data-laden screens. Its presence, discovered tucked away in a velvet-lined compartment of the victim's personal effects, was as baffling as it was intriguing. Miller picked it up, his fingers tracing the smooth, worn contours of its form. It was clearly old, the wood polished to a deep sheen by countless touches over an unknown span of time. The craftsmanship was exquisite, avian anatomy rendered with a startling degree of accuracy, yet with a stylized elegance that hinted at something more than mere decorative artistry.

"What do you make of this, Eleanor?" he asked, turning the bird over in his palm. The beak was sharp, the tail feathers fanned out as if caught in mid-flight. There was a subtle asymmetry to the carving, a slight tilt of the head that gave it an almost lifelike quality. It felt substantial, heavier than its size suggested, and the wood itself was unfamiliar, possessing a faint, dry scent reminiscent of ancient libraries and forgotten attics.

Jenkins peered over his shoulder, her sharp eyes scrutinizing the artifact. "It's not a standard souvenir, that's for sure. The detail is too fine, too deliberate. And the wear... it suggests it's been handled frequently, perhaps even habitually. Not something you'd pick up on a whim." She leaned closer, her brow furrowed. "There's a distinct regional style to the carving. I've seen similar work, but I can't quite place it. It's almost... folk art, but with a very refined execution."

Miller nodded slowly, his mind already assembling fragments of Sterling's life, seeking a connection. Sterling, the titan of industry, the visionary behind Aegis Innovations – what role could a simple wooden bird play in his clandestine world? He recalled the hurried whispers he'd overheard from Thorne's associate, the mention of "markers" and "symbols." Could this be one of them? A calling card, not of a romantic poet, but of something far more dangerous?

"This wasn't just a trinket," Miller mused aloud, his gaze fixed on the bird. "Sterling was a man of immense intellect and strategic foresight. He wouldn't have kept something so... personal, so archaic, unless it held a specific significance. He was meticulous, Eleanor. If he kept this, it was for a reason. A message, perhaps? A key?"

Jenkins agreed, her mind already sifting through the vast databases accessible through her portable terminal. "A coded message is a distinct possibility. The style, the material, even the species of bird – if we can identify it – could all be elements of a symbolic language. We need to understand its provenance. Where did Sterling acquire it? And who else might have access to such an item?"

Their immediate priority became the ship's library, a surprisingly well-stocked sanctuary of knowledge amidst the transient opulence of the cruise liner. Miller, with his innate curiosity and a lifetime of detective work honing his observational skills, felt a familiar sense of anticipation. He loved the quiet hum of discovery, the scent of aging paper, the promise of buried truths within printed pages. Jenkins, ever the pragmatist, saw it as a necessary step, a logical progression in their investigation, but even she couldn't suppress a flicker of excitement at the prospect of unearthing something significant.

The library was a dimly lit haven, hushed and reverent, a stark contrast to the glittering casinos and bustling lounges outside. Shelves of leather-bound volumes stretched towards the high ceiling, their spines bearing the weight of centuries of human thought and experience. They found a dedicated section on maritime history and seafaring crafts, a testament to the ship's clientele and its own proud lineage.

"Let's start here," Jenkins suggested, gesturing to a collection of books on nautical art and ship models. "If this bird has any connection to maritime traditions, it's likely documented here."

Miller meticulously began to examine the detailed illustrations and descriptions of carved figureheads, scrimshaw, and traditional wood carvings found on ships of various eras. He was looking for a specific style, a particular motif that echoed the wooden bird. He paused at a chapter detailing the symbolism of birds in maritime folklore, noting the prevalence of the albatross as a symbol of good luck and safe passage, the seagull representing sailors and the sea, and the raven often associated with ill omens and mystery.

"This bird," Miller said, holding up the wooden carving, "it doesn't look like any specific type I recognize. It's stylized, almost abstract in its avian representation, yet undeniably bird-like."

Jenkins was poring over a large, dusty tome filled with photographs of antique nautical artifacts. "The grain of the wood is peculiar," she murmured, pointing to a close-up image of a carved comb. "It's very fine, almost uniform, and there's a subtle reddish hue. It reminds me of some hardwoods found in Southeast Asia, but it could be a very well-preserved specimen from elsewhere. The carving technique itself... it's very clean, precise, almost like it was done with a modern tool, but the wear suggests otherwise."

Their search led them to a section on regional folk art and artisanal crafts. Miller's finger traced over an image of a collection of small wooden animals from a remote Pacific island. "Look at this," he said, pointing to a carving of a gecko. "The line work, the way the artist has captured the essence of the creature with such economy of line. There's a similar boldness, a confidence in the strokes, to our bird."

Jenkins leaned in, her eyes widening slightly. "You're right. And the texture... the slightly porous quality of the wood, the way the patina has developed. It's remarkably similar. This island... it's known for its indigenous art traditions, particularly its wood carving. They often use local hardwoods and create pieces that are both functional and symbolic."

A new line of inquiry opened before them. If the bird originated from this specific region, it narrowed their search considerably. They began to cross-reference passenger manifests and crew lists, looking for individuals with known connections to this island nation or its artistic communities. It was a painstaking process, sifting through hundreds of names and affiliations, but Miller felt a growing sense of purpose.

"Could Sterling have visited this island?" Miller pondered. "Perhaps on a business trip, or even for leisure? It's a long way from the usual corporate hubs."

Jenkins accessed Sterling's travel history, a labyrinth of encrypted flight logs and hotel bookings. "He did have a prolonged trip to Southeast Asia about eighteen months ago. The itinerary was vague – 'business and personal exploration,' according to his personal assistant's notes. He spent time in several countries, including a brief stopover on a small island chain that is geographically close to the region we're looking at."

"A stopover, but for how long? And what was the nature of his 'personal exploration'?" Miller pressed. The pieces were slowly, subtly, beginning to align. Sterling, a man who dealt in groundbreaking technology and global finance, had a connection to a remote island known for its traditional art. It was an anomaly, a discordant note in his otherwise meticulously curated professional life.

They continued their research, delving deeper into the specific artistic traditions of the island. They learned about the significance of birds in their mythology and iconography. Certain species were believed to be messengers between the mortal and spiritual realms, while others represented power, wisdom, or transformation. The specific style of carving often employed a distinctive use of negative space and a focus on fluid, dynamic forms.

"The wood is likely 'koa,'" Jenkins stated, her finger hovering over a detailed description of local hardwoods. "It's prized for its beauty, durability, and the ease with which it can be carved. It has a distinctive reddish-brown hue and a fine, straight grain. And the style... it's known as 'Tiki carving,' though that term is often used broadly. The artists create representations of animals and spirits that are deeply imbued with cultural meaning."

Miller held the bird up to the light, examining its structure. "The smoothness... it's not just from age. It feels like it's been held, caressed, almost worn down by constant handling. Imagine someone carrying this around, perhaps in their pocket, for years. What would that signify? Comfort? A talisman? Or a reminder of something?"

"Perhaps it was a gift," Jenkins offered. "From someone significant. Someone connected to that island, and by extension, to Sterling's dealings there. Or, as you suggested, it could be a marker left by the killer. If it's a specific regional style, and if this killer is associated with that region or a group that uses such symbols, it could be a way of announcing their presence, or leaving a signature. Communication that bypasses spoken or written language."

The idea of a carved bird as a killer's signature was unnerving. Miller recalled the precise, almost clinical nature of Sterling's murder. This wasn't a frenzied attack; it was a calculated execution. A killer who left such a distinct, personal artifact behind was either exceptionally bold or profoundly disturbed.

They sought out the ship's historian, a kindly, silver-haired gentleman named Mr. Abernathy, whose knowledge of maritime history and its associated cultures was encyclopedic. They presented him with the wooden bird, carefully placed on a clean velvet cloth. Abernathy's eyes lit up with a familiar spark of intellectual curiosity as he donned a pair of reading glasses and examined the carving with gentle reverence.

"Ah, a delightful piece," he murmured, his voice soft and measured. "The wood is indeed remarkable. Koa, I believe. From the Hawaiian Islands, though similar woods are found throughout Polynesia. The style... it's not strictly Hawaiian, but it shares certain characteristics. The fluidity of the form, the emphasis on the negative space... it suggests an artist with a deep understanding of traditional carving techniques, but with a contemporary sensibility."

He pointed to a subtle detail on the bird's chest. "Notice this subtle indentation here? It's not a flaw in the wood, nor a mistake in the carving. It's a deliberate mark, often incorporated into these types of carvings. It can represent a heartbeat, or a spiritual core. It's a deeply symbolic gesture."

"Symbolic of what, Mr. Abernathy?" Jenkins asked, her voice laced with polite urgency.

Abernathy stroked his chin thoughtfully. "In many Pacific island cultures, birds are seen as intermediaries between the earthly and spiritual realms. They carry messages, they guide souls. This carving, with its stylized representation and the 'heartbeat' mark, could symbolize the carrying of vital information, or perhaps the spiritual essence of a person or event. It's not something you'd find in a typical tourist shop. This is a piece with meaning, a piece that has been imbued with intent."

Miller felt a tremor of recognition. Sterling, the man at the center of a conspiracy involving the manipulation of global information, a man who was about to leak sensitive data – a bird symbolizing the carrying of messages, of vital information. The connection was becoming undeniable, and terrifyingly clear.

"Could this style be traced to a specific artisan or region?" Miller inquired, his gaze sharp.

"It's difficult to say with absolute certainty," Abernathy admitted, "given the fluidity of artistic traditions and the movement of people. However, there are certain schools of carving that emphasize this blend of traditional form and modern interpretation. I recall seeing similar pieces at a small exhibition of Polynesian art a few years ago. The artist was from a smaller, less-visited island in the Fijian archipelago, an island known for its unique artistic heritage and its relative isolation."

He then directed them to a particular shelf, a quiet corner of the library dedicated to obscure ethnographic studies and travelogues. "You might find something of interest in these volumes. They detail the customs and crafts of some of the more remote islands. Look for mentions of bird carvings, or any artists who gained particular renown for their work."

Hours melted away as Miller and Jenkins immersed themselves in the dusty pages. They found references to specific types of wood used in ceremonial carvings, descriptions of artistic motifs, and tales of island artisans who were revered for their skill. Then, Jenkins let out a quiet exclamation.

"Captain Rostova, look at this." She pointed to a passage in a faded travelogue from the 1980s, describing a visit to a small Fijian island. "The author mentions a particular artisan, a man named Kaelen, who was renowned for his 'spirit birds.' He carved them from koa wood, imbuing them with local legends and beliefs. He described them as having a unique, almost mournful tilt to their heads, and being smooth to the touch, as if they had been held and cherished for generations. The passage even mentions that Kaelen's carvings were sometimes used as a form of unofficial communication between island communities, a way of passing on discreet messages or warnings."

Miller felt a chill creep up his spine. The description was eerily accurate. The koa wood, the tilt of the head, the smooth, worn texture, and the use as a form of discreet communication. It all pointed to a direct lineage from this artisan, Kaelen, to the wooden bird found in Sterling's possession.

"Kaelen," Miller repeated the name, tasting it. "If this bird is one of his, it means Sterling acquired it directly from him, or from someone who acquired it from him. And if Kaelen's birds were used for communication, then this isn't just a piece of art; it's a tool. A tool that someone has now wielded for murder."

"The question is," Jenkins added, her voice low and serious, "is this bird Kaelen's work, or a copy? And if it's Kaelen's, was Sterling his client, or was the killer? Or perhaps, Kaelen himself is involved, or has been coerced?"

The wooden bird, once a puzzling artifact, had become a tangible link, a potential thread leading them into the heart of the conspiracy. Its smooth, worn surface now seemed to hold secrets, whispers of its journey from a remote island workshop to the opulent suite of a murdered tech mogul. It was no longer just a clue; it was a testament to the intricate, interwoven nature of Sterling's clandestine world, a world where ancient traditions and groundbreaking technology collided, and where death, it seemed, was delivered with a deliberate, symbolic touch. The bird, a silent witness, held the promise of revealing its maker, and perhaps, its killer.

The polished mahogany of the ship's grand ballroom felt strangely out of place, a stark contrast to the grim reality that had unfolded in the confines of Sterling's opulent suite. Now, the ballroom hummed with a different kind of tension, a manufactured gaiety that masked the undercurrent of unease rippling through the *Odyssey's* elite clientele. Miller and Jenkins moved through the throng, their eyes scanning faces, searching for any flicker of recognition, any hint of connection to the deceased. Their investigation had hit a wall of polite evasion and veiled suspicion, a testament to the carefully constructed facade of this floating sanctuary of wealth and power.

"Everyone seems to have an alibi, or a conveniently vague memory," Miller murmured, swirling the amber liquid in his glass, the ice clinking like a tiny, metallic accusation. He'd just concluded a rather sterile conversation with a Mr. Silas Croft, a man whose sharp suit and sharper gaze suggested he was accustomed to being in control. Croft, a fellow executive from a rival corporation, had offered condolences that felt as hollow as a drum. He'd been in the ship's casino, he claimed, for the entire duration of the window when Sterling's life had been so brutally extinguished. His companions, conveniently, were all overseas and unavailable for immediate verification.

Jenkins, having just emerged from a hushed conversation with a distressed-looking steward, joined him, her expression unreadable. "The crew is remarkably tight-lipped," she reported, her voice low. "Some are genuinely afraid, I suspect. Others are more adept at deflection than I've ever encountered. They've been trained to maintain the illusion of seamless service, and that includes shielding the guests from any unpleasantness, including the fact that a murder has occurred on their watch." She paused, her gaze drifting towards a cluster of elegantly dressed individuals laughed near a champagne fountain. "We've identified a few individuals who seem to warrant closer scrutiny, though. Beyond Croft, there's Anya Sharma, Sterling's personal assistant. She was the one who discovered the body."

"Sharma," Miller echoed, filing the name away. "Naturally. She'd have intimate knowledge of his schedule, his habits, his... vulnerabilities. Did she offer anything useful?"

"She's distraught, understandably," Jenkins said, her voice softening with a hint of empathy that Miller recognized as both genuine and strategic. "But her grief seems to be of a particular kind. Not entirely incapacitating. She provided a detailed timeline of Sterling's last known movements, but her answers to questions about any potential threats or enemies were... rehearsed. As if she'd been prepped for this very scenario." She lowered her voice further. "There's also Marcus Thorne. Sterling's former business partner. They had a very public and acrimonious split about a year ago. Thorne is on board, and according to the ship's manifest, he was near Sterling's suite around the estimated time of death."

Miller's mind began to connect the disparate threads. Croft, the rival; Sharma, the assistant; Thorne, the spurned partner. Each a potential suspect, each with a plausible motive, each cloaked in the anonymity of a luxury cruise. "And what about Sterling's dealings on that island?" he asked, the image of the carved bird still vivid in his mind. "Did Sharma mention anything about his recent trip? Any unusual contacts he made?"

Jenkins consulted a discreet data slate. "Sharma was cagey about that period. She described it as 'private research' and insisted Sterling was 'unreachable' for much of it. She did, however, mention a few names from Sterling's recent encrypted communications. One that stood out was a Dr. Aris Thorne – no relation to Marcus, apparently. He's a bio-engineer, with a specialization in... genetic sequencing. Sterling was apparently in regular, albeit heavily coded, contact with him."

"Bio-engineer? Genetic sequencing?" Miller mused, the pieces shifting in his mental puzzle. Sterling, the titan of technology, dabbling in something that sounded far more clandestine and potentially dangerous than his public persona suggested. "And this Dr. Thorne is also on board?"

"No," Jenkins replied, shaking her head. "He's not listed on the passenger manifest. However, Sterling's internal logs show that he transferred a significant sum of money to an offshore account linked to Dr. Thorne just days before embarking on this cruise. It suggests a high level of trust, or a desperate need for his services."

The ballroom, with its dazzling chandeliers and the murmur of privileged conversation, felt increasingly like a stage for deception. Every smile, every handshake, every casual remark could be a carefully crafted lie. Miller felt a familiar weariness settle over him, the weight of navigating a labyrinth where the walls themselves were made of artifice.

"Let's discuss later to Sharma," Miller decided, his gaze drifting towards the bar, where a poised woman with dark, intelligent eyes was speaking with a ship's officer. "Her composure is... remarkable. If she discovered Sterling's body, a certain level of shock is expected. But her detailed account, her very... preparedness, feels less like genuine grief and more like a performance."

Jenkins nodded in agreement. "I agree. There's a disconnect between her stated emotional state and her analytical recall. She described the scene with an almost clinical detachment, noting details that most people would overlook in such a state of shock. The position of the body, the precise angle of the wound, the specific placement of certain objects in the room. It's as if she'd rehearsed the discovery."

They decided to approach Sharma indirectly, catching her as she excused herself from her conversation with the officer, ostensibly to fetch a drink. Miller intercepted her with a polite, almost apologetic smile. "Ms. Sharma, a moment of your time, if you please? Detective Miller. This is my colleague, Detective Jenkins."

Sharma's dark eyes flickered, a momentary tightening around her lips that she quickly masked. "Detectives," she said, her voice smooth and practiced, though a subtle tremor betrayed her. "I've already told everything I know to the ship's security. Is there something new?"

"We're trying to build a more comprehensive picture of Mr. Sterling's final days," Miller explained. "He was a man of many interests and, we understand, many associates. We were hoping you might shed some light on his recent activities, particularly anything that might have caused him distress or concern."

Sharma's gaze was steady, almost unnervingly so. "Mr. Sterling was a man who lived at the forefront of innovation. He had many projects, many discussions. It was his nature to be preoccupied with his work. I wouldn't say he was distressed, precisely. Driven, perhaps. Intense."

"His trip to the Fijian archipelago, for example," Jenkins interjected gently. "Ms. Sharma, you mentioned it was for 'personal exploration.' Could you elaborate on that? Did he meet anyone of particular significance there?"

A flicker of something – annoyance? – crossed Sharma's face, quickly suppressed. "It was a private matter. He valued his privacy. He brought back a... small carving. A bird. He seemed to find some significance in it. He kept it on his desk."

Miller's ears perked up. "A bird? Could you describe it?"

Sharma hesitated, her eyes momentarily unfocused as if conjuring the image. "It was small, wooden. Intricately carved. He kept it in a velvet-lined compartment of his desk. He rarely spoke of it, but its presence was constant."

"And did he ever mention who he acquired it from? Or the island itself?" Jenkins pressed, her gaze unwavering.

"He was... discreet," Sharma replied, her words carefully chosen. "He dealt with many people, many... facilitators. It's difficult to recall every detail. He was focused on the future, on progress. The past, or... trinkets, were not his usual preoccupation."

The dismissal, delivered with such practiced ease, was not lost on Miller. Sharma was a loyal employee, but her loyalty might extend beyond mere professional obligation. She was protecting something, or someone. "We understand that Mr. Sterling had a falling out with his former business partner, Mr. Marcus Thorne," Miller continued, shifting tactics. "Are you aware of the nature of that disagreement, or if Mr. Thorne had any recent contact with Mr. Sterling?"

Sharma's composure finally cracked, a subtle tension seizing her shoulders. "Mr. Thorne was a... difficult man. Their parting was not amicable. Mr. Sterling felt Mr. Thorne was... holding him back. Resentful, perhaps. I know Mr. Thorne has been seen on board. I can only assume their paths have not crossed, or if they have, it has been avoided."

"Avoided by whom?" Miller inquired, his voice quiet.

"By both, I would imagine," Sharma said, her gaze now fixed on her manicured fingernails. "Mr. Sterling was not one to dwell on old grievances. He preferred to look forward. Mr. Thorne, however... he harbored a great deal of animosity. I heard whispers. Threats, even, though I never took them seriously. Mr. Thorne is more talk than action, I believed."

Miller exchanged a subtle glance with Jenkins. Thorne, the disgruntled former partner, harboring animosity and making veiled threats. It fit the narrative. But Sharma's subtle defensiveness, her almost rehearsed answers, kept her firmly on their radar.

"Thank you, Ms. Sharma," Miller said, offering a final, disarming smile. "Your cooperation is appreciated. If anything else comes to mind, anything at all, please don't hesitate to reach out."

As Sharma retreated, her practiced smile replaced by a look of veiled apprehension, Miller turned to Jenkins. "She's holding back. There's more to her story than she's letting on. And Thorne... he sounds like the archetypal scorned lover, but with a business empire at stake. That's a potent cocktail for motive."

"And what about Croft?" Jenkins mused, reviewing her data slate. "His alibi is flimsy at best. A casino is a place where one can easily claim to be present without actually being seen by anyone who matters. And a rival executive who suddenly finds himself in a more favorable competitive position... that's motive enough."

Their investigation led them to a small, exclusive lounge tucked away on an upper deck, a place frequented by the ship's most discerning and wealthiest passengers. Here, amidst plush velvet seating and the hushed clinking of crystal, they encountered a man who seemed to embody the enigmatic allure of the

Odyssey. Mr. Julian Vance, a patron of the arts and a known collector of rare artifacts, had been in an adjacent suite to Sterling's. He was a man of refined taste and a sharp intellect, his eyes holding a perpetual glint of amusement.

Miller approached him with a carefully crafted preamble, expressing admiration for Vance's renowned collection of Oceanic art. Vance had indeed been in the vicinity. He'd been returning to his suite after a late-night viewing of the ship's planetarium, a journey that had taken him past Sterling's door.

"Terrible business, Sterling's demise," Vance commented, swirling a glass of what appeared to be vintage port. "A true visionary, in his own way. Though perhaps... a little too ambitious for his own good."

"Did you notice anything unusual on your way back to your suite, Mr. Vance?" Jenkins inquired, her voice gentle. "Any sounds, any individuals?"

Vance considered for a moment, his brow furrowed in thought. "It was late, you see. The corridors were mostly empty. But I did hear... voices. Raised voices, I'd say. Coming from Mr. Sterling's suite. It was brief, though. A sudden outburst, and then silence. I assumed it was a heated business call."

"Could you identify the voices?" Miller pressed, his interest piqued.

Vance shook his head. "No, I'm afraid not. Muffled, as they were through the door. And I wasn't particularly paying attention. I'm more attuned to the subtle nuances of a cello concerto than the shouts of disgruntled executives." He offered a wry smile. "Though I did notice something else. A scent. Faint, but distinct. Not unpleasant, but... unusual. Like exotic spices, perhaps, with a hint of something earthy. Almost like incense, but not quite. It lingered in the air, even after the voices had ceased."

The mention of an unusual scent, of exotic spices, resonated with Miller. He recalled the faint, dry scent of the wooden bird, reminiscent of ancient libraries and forgotten attics. Could this be a connection? A shared sensory detail that linked Sterling, his murder, and perhaps, the enigmatic artifact?

"Did you see anyone in the corridor, Mr. Vance?" Jenkins asked, her gaze sharp and observant.

"No one in particular," Vance replied, his gaze drifting towards the panoramic window, where the inky blackness of the ocean stretched to the horizon. "Just the usual ship's staff, moving about their duties. Efficient, almost spectral. They seem to materialize and disappear without a sound."

Miller and Jenkins left the lounge with a renewed sense of purpose, but also a gnawing sense of unease. The lines between victim, suspect, and potential witness were becoming increasingly blurred. Anya Sharma, the seemingly distraught assistant with the rehearsed grief; Marcus Thorne, the embittered former partner with a history of threats; Silas Croft, the rival executive with a convenient alibi; and now Julian Vance, the cultured observer who smelled something unusual. Each person they encountered either offered a piece of the puzzle or actively obfuscated it.

"Vance's description of the scent," Miller said, as they made their way back towards their temporary command center in one of the ship's smaller meeting rooms. "Exotic spices, earthy, like incense. It's not something one typically associates with a luxury liner. It suggests someone carrying something, or someone who has recently been in an environment where such scents are prevalent."

"And the fact that he heard raised voices," Jenkins added, her fingers flying across her data slate, cross-referencing ship logs and passenger movements. "It suggests Sterling wasn't alone in his suite during that time. Sharma claimed to have left him, but there's no confirmation of that. What if she returned? Or what if someone else was there, someone she deliberately omitted from her statement?"

As they prepared to delve deeper into the ship's manifest and Sterling's encrypted communications, a thought struck Miller. "The rival executive, the disgruntled partner, the personal assistant... all classic archetypes. But what if Sterling wasn't just a victim of circumstance? What if his 'personal exploration' on that island, his dealings with the bio-engineer, and the carved bird were all part of a larger, far more dangerous game?" He looked at Jenkins, his gaze steely. "We're not just investigating a murder anymore, Eleanor. We're stumbling into something much bigger, and much darker."

Jenkins met his gaze, her expression resolute. "Then we'll navigate it, just like we always do. Together." The unspoken understanding between them was a silent promise, a testament to their unwavering commitment to uncovering the truth, no matter how deeply it was buried beneath layers of deception and shadowed by the vast, indifferent ocean. The *Odyssey* held its secrets close, but Miller and Jenkins were determined to pry them loose, one unlikely ally and one chilling suspicion at a time.

Chapter 4: Whispers of Betrayal

The hum of the *Odyssey*'s opulent lounge, usually a symphony of hushed conversations and the clinking of ice, was suddenly discordant. Miller, mid-sentence with Jenkins about the intricacies of genetic sequencing and offshore accounts, felt a prickle of recognition, a cold knot forming in his stomach. He'd seen that gait before, that familiar, slightly too-proud posture. Then, the face emerged from the dim, ambient light–a face he hadn't seen in years, a face he'd tried, and largely succeeded, in forgetting. Michael Thorne.

His former colleague. The disgraced agent. The man whose reckless ambition had derailed not only his own career but had also cast a long shadow over Miller's own transition into early retirement. Thorne. Here. On this ship. The coincidence was too stark to be anything but deliberate. A shiver, unrelated to the ship's climate control, traced its way down Miller's spine.

Jenkins, sensing the abrupt shift in Miller's demeanor, followed his gaze. Her trained eyes, always observing, always cataloging, noted the immediate tension emanating from Miller. "Something wrong, Detective?" she murmured, her voice barely a whisper, an automatic professional inquiry laced with a hint of personal concern.

Miller didn't answer immediately. His focus was locked on Thorne, who was now making his way through the sparse crowd, his eyes, sharp and predatory, scanning the room with an unnerving intensity. Thorne looked older, of course. The sharp angles of his face seemed more pronounced, etched by time and perhaps, Miller thought grimly, by the consequences of his past actions. But the same restless energy, the same coiled ambition that Miller remembered so vividly, was still there, undimmed. It was the energy of a man who always felt he was on the cusp of something, whether it was a groundbreaking discovery or a devastating scandal.

"That," Miller finally said, his voice tight, "is Michael Thorne."

Jenkins's eyebrows rose slightly. "A former colleague?"

"More than that," Miller corrected, the words tasting like ash. "We worked together. He was... brilliant. And utterly ruthless. He was involved in a case, a high-profile sting operation that went spectacularly wrong. Accusations of evidence tampering, of planting falsified intel. It cost him his badge, his reputation. It was the catalyst for my own early exit. The fallout was... considerable."

Thorne, as if sensing their attention, turned his head, his eyes meeting Miller's across the room. A slow, almost sardonic smile spread across his face, a smile that held no warmth, only a complex blend of surprise, recognition, and something Miller couldn't quite decipher – perhaps a flicker of amusement, or a hint of challenge. He gave a slight, almost imperceptible nod, a gesture that spoke volumes of their shared, fractured past. It was an acknowledgment, a greeting, and a declaration. Thorne was here, and he knew Miller knew.

"He's on the passenger manifest?" Jenkins asked, her fingers already making their way to her data slate, a silent testament to her efficiency.

"He'd have to be," Miller replied, his gaze still fixed on Thorne. "Unless he's stowed away, which, knowing Thorne, isn't entirely outside the realm of possibility. He always had a flair for the dramatic, for operating in the shadows." He paused, a fresh wave of suspicion washing over him. "Why would he be here? This isn't his usual milieu. Thorne dealt in back-alley busts and informant networks, not luxury cruises and... murder investigations."

Thorne began to move towards their table, his trajectory unhurried, deliberate. The air in the lounge seemed to thicken, the ambient noise fading into a dull roar as Miller braced himself for the inevitable confrontation. Thorne's presence felt like a disruption, a rogue element introduced into an already complex equation.

"Let's see what he has to say," Jenkins murmured, her tone neutral, her eyes fixed on Thorne's approaching figure. She was an observer, an analyst, and Thorne, a man steeped in controversy and shrouded in suspicion, was a subject of immense interest.

Thorne stopped at their table, his smile widening, though it didn't quite reach his eyes. "Miller. Well, well. Fancy meeting you here. Still chasing ghosts, I see." His voice was deeper than Miller remembered, a gravelly resonance that hinted at late nights and perhaps, a lingering cynicism.

Miller forced himself to meet Thorne's gaze, his own expression carefully neutral. "Thorne. What are you doing on the

Odyssey?" The question was direct, devoid of pleasantries.

Thorne chuckled, a dry, rasping sound. "Just enjoying the... amenities. A bit of a sabbatical, you could say. Escaping the relentless grind of the real world. And you? Still playing detective on your supposed retirement?" He gestured vaguely around the opulent lounge. "Bit of a step down from chasing hardened criminals, isn't it? Or are you simply slumming it with the wealthy?"

"We're investigating a murder," Miller stated flatly, cutting through Thorne's insincere pleasantries. "Sterling. The tech mogul. Found dead in his suite."

Thorne's smile faltered for a fraction of a second, a barely perceptible flicker of surprise, quickly masked by a practiced indifference. "Sterling? Never heard of him. Must have been someone I wouldn't have crossed paths with." He paused, his eyes raking over Miller and Jenkins. "And who is this, your new partner in... crime-solving?"

"Detective Jenkins," Miller introduced them, omitting any mention of Thorne's past. "She's with federal law enforcement."

"Federal, eh?" Thorne extended a hand towards Jenkins, his smile returned, more predatory now. "Michael Thorne. Pleasure to make your acquaintance. Always appreciate a fellow traveler in the labyrinth of justice." His handshake was firm, almost too firm, a subtle assertion of dominance.

Jenkins accepted the handshake, her expression unreadable. "Detective Miller and I are conducting a preliminary inquiry," she said, her voice measured. "Mr. Sterling was a passenger, and his death occurred on board. We're speaking with everyone who might have relevant information."

"And what makes you think I'd have relevant information?" Thorne asked, his gaze flicking back to Miller. "I'm just a tourist. Came aboard for the sea air, the fine dining. Sterling is a stranger to me. I keep to myself, as you know, Miller. Learned that lesson the hard way."

The veiled reference to their shared past hung heavy in the air. Thorne had indeed learned his lesson, but Miller doubted he'd learned it well enough to alter his fundamental nature. Ambition, unchecked, had a way of resurfacing.

"You were near Sterling's suite last night, according to ship security logs," Miller pressed, his voice low and steady. "Around the estimated time of death."

Thorne's eyes narrowed, a flicker of something that looked like annoyance. "Was I? Must have been taking a late-night stroll. This ship is quite large, you know. Easy to get lost, or to find yourself in unexpected corridors." He shrugged, feigning nonchalance. "Perhaps I was looking for the restroom. Or a quiet spot to contemplate the vastness of the ocean."

"Or perhaps," Miller countered, his gaze unwavering, "you were looking for Sterling."

A tense silence descended. Thorne's jaw tightened almost imperceptibly. "That's a rather pointed accusation, Miller. Especially coming from someone who knows my reputation." He leaned in slightly, his voice dropping to a conspiratorial whisper. "You remember how my reputation was made, don't you? A few... inconvenient truths, a few 'misplaced' pieces of evidence. It's amazing what can be spun into a narrative, isn't it? Especially when you have the right people pushing the story."

The barb was clear. Thorne believed Miller had played a role in the public narrative that had branded him a rogue agent. And Thorne, Miller knew, never forgot a slight.

"I was doing my job, Thorne," Miller said, his voice dangerously quiet. "Trying to ensure justice was served, not manipulated."

"Justice," Thorne scoffed, a harsh, humorless sound. "A rather fluid concept, wouldn't you agree? What one man calls justice, another calls a setup. And you, my dear Miller, have always been remarkably good at setting things up." He straightened, a ghost of his former arrogance returned. "Look, I'm not here to dredge up ancient history. I'm here to relax. If you need me for anything official, you know where to find me. Or perhaps you don't. I'm not exactly advertising my presence, am I?" He gave a final, enigmatic smile. "Enjoy your investigation. Try not to get any more 'inconvenient truths' misplaced."

With that, Thorne turned and walked away, disappearing into the dimly lit recesses of the lounge. The encounter left Miller with a gnawing unease. Thorne's presence was too coincidental, his behavior too evasive. Was he merely a tourist who was in the wrong place at the wrong time, a man trying to outrun his past? Or was he actively involved in Sterling's murder? Thorne's ambition, his willingness to bend rules, and his clear animosity towards Miller made him a prime suspect. He had the audacity, the nerve, and the potential motive to orchestrate something like this, perhaps even to frame someone else.

"He's hiding something," Jenkins stated, her voice firm as she watched Thorne's retreating figure. "His denial was too vehement, his attempts at deflection too calculated. And the reference to misplaced evidence... he's not just trying to throw us off; he's actively taunting you, Miller."

Miller nodded, the old animosity simmering beneath the surface. "Thorne always operated on the edge. He believed the ends justified the means, no matter how dubious those means were. If he saw an opportunity, a way to advance himself, or to settle a score... he wouldn't hesitate." He ran a hand through his hair, a gesture of frustration. "His history with me makes him a person of interest, but his current behavior on this ship... it elevates him. He could be connected to Sterling, or to whatever Sterling was involved in on that island."

"The bio-engineer, the genetic sequencing, the offshore account," Jenkins mused, her eyes distant as she processed the information. "Sterling was involved in something clandestine. Thorne, with his background in intelligence and his proven ability to manipulate information, could be a perfect fit for such an operation. Or, he could be an antagonist within it."

"Or," Miller said, his voice low, "he could be the reason Sterling was killed. Maybe Sterling was getting too close to something Thorne was involved in. Or maybe Thorne was hired to silence him. He's always been someone who could be bought, or at least persuaded, if the price was right."

The encounter with Thorne had reopened old wounds, stirring a potent mix of professional animosity and personal distrust. Thorne was a ghost from Miller's past, a spectral reminder of a case that had nearly broken him. Now, that ghost had materialized on board the

Odyssey, a chilling embodiment of the very darkness they were trying to unravel. His motive could be revenge, or it could be an entirely new entanglement, born from Sterling's secret dealings. Miller knew, with a chilling certainty, that Thorne's presence was not a mere coincidence. It was a deliberate intrusion, a signal that the game had just become far more dangerous, and far more personal. The polished veneer of the luxury cruise was beginning to crack, revealing the darker currents that flowed beneath, and Michael Thorne was undeniably a part of those currents.

The opulent lounge of the *Odyssey* slowly reclaimed its usual, hushed rhythm, but the air remained thick with unspoken implications. Thorne, that unwelcome specter from Miller's past, had vanished as smoothly as he had appeared, leaving behind a trail of unease and a fresh set of questions. Miller and Jenkins exchanged a look, a silent acknowledgment of the volatile energy Thorne had injected into their investigation. The former agent, with his disarming charm and predatory gaze, was more than just a passenger; he was a complication, a variable that had just been inserted into an already precarious equation.

"He's lying, of course," Miller murmured, his voice barely audible above the soft strains of a classical quartet playing in the corner. He watched the spot where Thorne had been, a faint imprint of suspicion still lingering. "His 'late-night stroll' explanation is as flimsy as a cheap suit."

Jenkins nodded, her expression thoughtful as she tapped a few commands into her discreet data slate. "Ship logs confirm he accessed the corridor near Sterling's suite at approximately 02:17. The security camera feed for that specific section is... curiously corrupted. A brief, fifteen-minute blackout, precisely during the window of Thorne's proximity."

Miller's jaw tightened. "Corrupted? Or deliberately erased? Thorne has always been adept at making things... disappear. Information, witnesses, evidence. He knows how to manipulate the system." He recalled Thorne's veiled threat, his cynical commentary on justice and narrative. "He's not just running from his past; he's actively trying to obscure the present."

"His background check is... extensive," Jenkins continued, her fingers flying across the holographic interface. "After his dismissal from the force, he dropped off the grid for a considerable period. No official employment, no registered addresses. He resurfaced about eighteen months ago, operating primarily as a 'security consultant' and 'risk assessor.' Vague, non-specific designations that often serve as a convenient cover for less savory activities."

"Risk assessor," Miller echoed, a grim smile touching his lips. "Thorne's idea of risk assessment always involved pushing boundaries, sometimes breaking them entirely. Who was he consulting for?"

Jenkins scrolled through a series of encrypted files. "That's where it gets interesting. His recent client list, what little we can glean from the fragmented data, points towards individuals and entities with... questionable affiliations. Specifically, several individuals who have, in recent years, been linked to 'Aether Dynamics.' The corporation that was heavily invested in Sterling's offshore research initiatives."

The name hung in the air, a confirmation of Miller's deepest suspicions. Aether Dynamics. The shadowy corporation that had been a constant, unseen presence in the periphery of Sterling's work. They were rumored to be involved in cutting-edge, and highly controversial, bio-engineering projects. If Thorne was associating with them, his connection to Sterling's death became not just plausible, but highly probable.

"Aether Dynamics," Miller repeated, the words tasting bitter. "Of course. Sterling's research was their golden goose, wasn't it? They stood to gain immensely from its successful, and presumably profitable, completion. And Thorne, with his particular skillset... he'd be invaluable to an organization like that. Someone who can operate in the grey, who can acquire assets, and who can silence... inconvenient assets."

"His financial records are equally peculiar," Jenkins added, pulling up another set of figures. "There have been a series of substantial, untraceable wire transfers into an offshore account under a shell corporation. The timings of these transfers coincide with significant events related to Sterling's research, and more recently, with Thorne's embarkation on this cruise. Large sums, Miller. Far more than what a 'security consultant' would typically earn for legitimate work."

Miller leaned back, the plush velvet of the chair suddenly feeling inadequate. Thorne wasn't just a passenger; he was a player. And his presence on the

Odyssey wasn't a coincidence; it was a calculated move. "He's not here to relax. He's here for a reason. To monitor the situation? To retrieve something Sterling had? Or... to ensure Sterling's silence, permanently."

"His movements on the ship have been erratic," Jenkins continued, her brow furrowed in concentration. "He's been seen in various restricted areas, often late at night, bypassing standard security protocols with an unnerving ease. He's not acting like a tourist. He's acting like someone with a specific objective. Someone who knows the ship's layout intimately, or has acquired that knowledge very recently."

"He always had a knack for infiltration," Miller mused, picturing Thorne in their old days, the glint of ambition in his eyes, the effortless way he could charm his way past any guard. "He could read people, anticipate their moves, exploit their weaknesses. If he's working for Aether Dynamics, he's likely here to ensure their investment, Sterling's research, doesn't fall into the wrong hands. And if Sterling was about to expose them, or defect with the data... Thorne would be the one to clean up the mess."

Jenkins zoomed in on a grainy security still. "This was taken last night, near the crew quarters. He appears to be meeting someone." The image was low-resolution, the face of the other individual obscured by shadow and the angle of the camera. "The meeting was brief. They exchanged a small, discreet package. Then Thorne disappeared into the ship's labyrinthine service corridors."

"A package," Miller said, his mind racing. "What kind of package? Data? A device? Something Sterling possessed?" He remembered Sterling's hurried, almost paranoid, demeanor in their brief encounter. Sterling had been carrying something, something he was desperately trying to protect.

"We're cross-referencing ship personnel manifests with Thorne's known associates," Jenkins reported. "It's a needle in a haystack, but Thorne has a history of utilizing individuals from the fringes of society for his operations. Disgraced sailors, dockworkers, freelance couriers. People who ask few questions and demand little in return."

"He's always been good at finding the cracks in the system, the people who operate outside of official channels," Miller agreed, the familiar frustration of dealing with Thorne's methods a bitter taste in his mouth. "He built his reputation on a foundation of morally ambiguous actions. He'd justify anything if it served his ultimate goal. And his goal was always personal advancement, power."

"The question is," Jenkins said, her gaze meeting Miller's, "is he the mastermind of this, or merely an operative? Sterling's research was at the nexus of Aether Dynamics' interests. Thorne, with his history of intelligence work and his current affiliations, could be the one pulling the strings."

"Or," Miller countered, his voice low, "he could be a pawn, albeit a very dangerous one. Sterling might have been a threat to Aether Dynamics, and Thorne was hired to... neutralize that threat. The fact that he's here, on the same ship, at the same time as the murder... it's too convenient. He could have been sent to acquire Sterling's research data after he was eliminated, or to retrieve something Sterling was about to leak."

"His interaction with Sterling himself remains unclear," Jenkins admitted. "There's no record of them formally meeting or interacting on board. However, given Thorne's modus operandi, a direct interaction might not have been necessary. He could have acted remotely, or through intermediaries. Sterling's death could have been arranged without Thorne ever setting foot in his suite, save for the security logs placing him nearby."

Miller ran a hand over his chin, the stubble a familiar texture against his skin. The encounter had confirmed his worst fears. Thorne wasn't an innocent bystander. He was deeply enmeshed in whatever was happening on the

Odyssey. His history of bending rules, his recent association with Aether Dynamics, and his secretive movements painted a damning picture.

"He's too smooth, too calculated," Miller said, his voice filled with a weary certainty. "He's been expecting this. The death of Sterling, the investigation... he's prepared for it. That taunt about 'misplaced truths' wasn't just about our past; it was a warning. He's letting me know he's still in control, still playing the game."

"Then we need to uncover what Sterling's research truly entailed, and how Aether Dynamics was involved," Jenkins stated, her focus sharpening. "If Thorne is connected, he's our most direct link to them. His past, his current activities, his financial dealings – they all point to a man operating outside the law, with motives that could easily extend to murder."

"He thrives in the grey areas, Jenkins," Miller said, his gaze fixed on the distant horizon, the vastness of the ocean mirroring the unknown depths of Thorne's involvement. "He always believed that the ends justified the means. And if Sterling's research was the ultimate prize for Aether Dynamics, Thorne would have been the perfect tool to acquire it. By any means necessary." The ghost of Michael Thorne had materialized on board the

Odyssey, no longer a specter from the past, but a tangible threat in the present, a chilling embodiment of the darkness that had already claimed one life and threatened to consume them all. The carefully constructed facade of their luxurious voyage was crumbling, revealing the treacherous undercurrents, and Thorne was undoubtedly at the heart of them.

The hushed elegance of the *Odyssey*'s lounge felt like a fragile shell around the burgeoning storm of suspicion. Thorne's departure had left an almost palpable void, a silence that screamed louder than his presence. Miller and Jenkins, accustomed to the methodical unraveling of truth, found themselves staring into an abyss of deceit, and Thorne was at its precipice. His 'late-night stroll,' as Miller had rightly dismissed it, was a flimsy veil, easily seen through by anyone who knew Thorne's history.

Jenkins' fingers danced across her data slate, her brow furrowed with concentration. "The ship's logs are, as you suspected, uncooperative regarding Thorne's movements. While he

did access the corridor adjacent to Sterling's suite at 02:17, the security camera feed for that sector experienced a peculiar fifteen-minute blackout. Precisely during the critical window."

"Blackout, or deliberate sabotage?" Miller's voice was a low growl. Thorne's talent for erasure, for making inconvenient truths vanish, was legendary. "He always had a knack for manipulating systems, for making evidence disappear into thin air. This isn't just about hiding his presence; it's about actively obscuring his actions." He remembered Thorne's cynical pronouncements, his disdain for conventional justice, his belief that narrative, not truth, was the ultimate currency. Thorne wasn't just running from his past; he was actively rewriting the present.

"His background is a labyrinth," Jenkins continued, her voice clipped. "Post-dismissal, he vanished for eighteen months. No official footprint. He re-emerged as a 'security consultant' and 'risk assessor' – labels that reek of plausible deniability for... less legitimate ventures."

Miller's lips curved into a grim, humorless smile. "Thorne's definition of 'risk assessment' always involved sidestepping the rules, if not outright breaking them. Who were his clients?"

Jenkins navigated encrypted files, her expression hardening. "Fragmented data points to individuals and entities with dubious connections. Notably, several individuals linked to 'Aether Dynamics.' The very corporation heavily invested in Sterling's research."

The name landed like a stone in the pit of Miller's stomach. Aether Dynamics. The phantom presence that had shadowed Sterling's work, a shadowy conglomerate rumored to be at the forefront of highly controversial bio-engineering. Thorne's connection to them was no longer a coincidence.

"Aether Dynamics," Miller echoed, the words tasting like ash. "Of course. Sterling's research was their lucrative ticket. Thorne, with his particular... skillset, would be an invaluable asset to an organization that operates in the shadows, that needs its secrets guarded, and its inconvenient truths silenced. He's the ultimate fixer."

"His financial records are equally opaque," Jenkins stated, bringing up a cascade of figures. "Substantial, untraceable wire transfers into offshore accounts. The timings align with significant developments in Sterling's research, and more recently, with Thorne's embarkation on this voyage. Large sums, Miller. Far beyond what a legitimate consultant would earn."

Miller leaned back, the opulent surroundings suddenly feeling cheap and insincere. Thorne wasn't a passenger seeking solace; he was a predator on the hunt. "He's not here for a vacation. He's here for a reason. To monitor the fallout? To retrieve Sterling's data? Or perhaps to ensure Sterling's silence, permanently."

"His movements on board have been clandestine," Jenkins added, her gaze fixed on the screen. "Restricted areas, late at night, bypassing security with an unsettling ease. He's on a mission. Someone who knows the ship intimately, or acquired that knowledge very recently."

"He always did have an uncanny ability for infiltration," Miller mused, a ghost of their past flashing through his mind – Thorne, a phantom in the shadows, charming his way through any obstacle. "He could read people, anticipate their moves, exploit their vulnerabilities. If he's working for Aether Dynamics, he's here to protect their investment – Sterling's research. And if Sterling was about to expose them, or defect with the data, Thorne would be the one to clean up the mess."

Jenkins highlighted a grainy security still. "This was captured last night, near the crew quarters. Thorne meeting someone. The individual's face is obscured, but the exchange was brief. A small, discreet package. Then Thorne vanished into the service corridors."

"A package," Miller mused, his mind racing. "Data? A device? Something Sterling possessed?" He remembered Sterling's agitated state, the furtive glances, the weight of something he was desperately trying to protect.

"Cross-referencing ship personnel with Thorne's known associates," Jenkins reported. "It's a monumental task, but Thorne has a history of employing individuals from the fringes: disgraced sailors, freelance couriers. Those who ask few questions."

"He always found the cracks in the system," Miller agreed, the familiar frustration with Thorne's methods a bitter pill. "He built his reputation on ambiguity. He'd justify anything if it served his ultimate goal. And his goal was always power, personal advancement."

"The question is," Jenkins said, her eyes meeting Miller's, "is he the architect, or merely the operative? Sterling's research was the nexus of Aether Dynamics' interests. Thorne, with his intelligence background and current affiliations, can orchestrate this. He could be pulling the strings."

"Or," Miller countered, his voice low, "he could be a pawn, albeit a dangerous one. Sterling posed a threat to Aether Dynamics, and Thorne was hired to... neutralize that threat. His presence on the

Odyssey, at this precise time... it's too convenient. He could have been sent to retrieve Sterling's data after his death, or to intercept something Sterling was about to leak."

"His direct interaction with Sterling remains unconfirmed," Jenkins admitted. "No record of formal contact. However, Thorne operates through layers. He could have acted remotely, or via intermediaries. Sterling's demise could have been arranged without Thorne ever entering his suite, save for the security logs placing him nearby."

Miller ran a hand over his chin, the familiar rasp of stubble a grounding sensation. Thorne's appearance had confirmed his deepest fears. He wasn't an innocent bystander; he was deeply enmeshed. His history, his current affiliations, his secretive movements – they all painted a damning portrait.

"He's too smooth, too calculated," Miller stated, a weary certainty in his voice. "He anticipated this. Sterling's death, the investigation... he's prepared. That taunt about 'misplaced truths' wasn't just about our past; it was a warning. He's letting me know he's still in control, still playing the game."

"Then we need to uncover Sterling's research and Aether Dynamics' involvement," Jenkins stated, her focus sharpening. "If Thorne is connected, he's our most direct link. His past, his present, his finances – they all point to a man operating outside the law, with motives that easily extend to murder."

"He thrives in the grey areas, Jenkins," Miller said, his gaze drifting to the vast, indifferent ocean. "He always believed the ends justified the means. And if Sterling's research was the ultimate prize for Aether Dynamics, Thorne would be the perfect instrument to acquire it. By any means necessary." The ghost of Michael Thorne had materialized on board the

Odyssey, no longer a specter from the past, but a tangible, chilling threat in the present, a harbinger of the darkness that had already claimed one life and threatened to engulf them all. The carefully constructed facade of their luxurious voyage was irrevocably fractured, revealing the treacherous undercurrents, and Thorne, no doubt, was at the very heart of them.

The subsequent hours were a meticulous dissection of Thorne's narrative, a relentless chipping away at the edifice of his carefully constructed alibi. Jenkins, a digital bloodhound, followed every digital whisper, every coded breadcrumb Thorne had left behind, or perhaps, had deliberately scattered.

"Thorne claims he was in the ship's observation lounge from approximately 01:00 until 03:30," Jenkins reported, her voice devoid of emotion as she projected holographic schematics onto the wall of their makeshift investigation room. "He states he was engaged in a... philosophical discussion with a Mr. Alistair Finch and a Ms. Clara Vance. Both individuals, incidentally, are senior executives at Aether Dynamics."

Miller's jaw tightened. "Convenient. He's leaning on his corporate associates for corroboration. People who, like him, have a vested interest in maintaining certain... narratives."

"Indeed," Jenkins agreed. "Finch is the Head of Research and Development, a man known for his ruthless efficiency and his absolute loyalty to Aether Dynamics. Vance is their Chief Legal Counsel, whose reputation is built on navigating the most intricate legal loopholes. Neither of them are exactly independent witnesses."

Miller paced the confined space, the rhythmic thud of his footsteps a counterpoint to the oppressive silence. "So, Thorne's alibi rests entirely on the word of two individuals deeply entrenched in the same shadowy empire he operates within. An empire that stood to gain the most from Sterling's demise and the subsequent acquisition of his research."

Jenkins highlighted Thorne's projected path on the ship's deck plan. "According to Thorne's statement, he and his companions remained in the observation lounge. However, ship logs show Finch and Vance both returned to their suites at approximately 02:00, independently. There's no record of them being together continuously until 03:30."

"A fifteen-minute gap for Finch and Vance, and Thorne conveniently places himself somewhere else within that window?" Miller scoffed. "It's sloppy. Or deliberately misleading. Thorne usually operates with a far finer touch."

"His explanation for their brief separation is that Finch stepped away to take a confidential call, and Vance went to retrieve a personal item from her suite, a brief excursion. He claims they only reunited with Vance about ten minutes later, and Finch returned shortly after." Jenkins scrolled through more data. "However, the ship's internal communication logs show no outgoing calls from Finch's suite or any public communication terminals during that period. And Vance's suite is located on a different deck entirely from the observation lounge, making a 'brief excursion' to retrieve a personal item highly improbable given the time constraints and ship layout."

Miller stopped pacing, his eyes narrowed. "So, Thorne admits Finch and Vance left him alone for a period. And then Vance makes a long trek to retrieve something, leaving Thorne alone again. This isn't an alibi, Jenkins; it's a series of carefully orchestrated opportunities. He's not providing witnesses; he's providing potential accomplices, or rather, complicit parties who can be pressured to maintain his fabricated timeline."

"The security footage from the observation lounge itself is... problematic," Jenkins continued, her voice taking on a sharper edge. "There's a temporal anomaly. The footage from 01:55 to 02:05 appears to have been digitally manipulated. The timestamps are consistent, but the playback is unnaturally smooth, almost as if it were a generated simulation rather than raw footage. It's too perfect."

"Too perfect is Thorne's signature," Miller growled. He could picture Thorne, hunched over a console, expertly weaving a digital tapestry of lies, editing reality to fit his agenda. "He's not just creating a gap in the timeline; he's crafting a flawless narrative of innocence. He's banking on the fact that Finch and Vance will play their parts, and that the security footage, while seemingly intact, will bear the subtle, almost undetectable marks of his tampering."

"The timing of the alleged 'philosophical discussion' also raises questions," Jenkins pressed on. "Sterling was murdered between 02:00 and 02:30, according to the preliminary autopsy report. Thorne's alibi places him with Finch and Vance, or briefly alone, during the entire critical window. He conveniently removes himself from the scene of the crime by presenting a scenario that, on its surface, appears legitimate."

"But the inconsistencies are glaring," Miller insisted. "The independent movements of Finch and Vance, the unnatural smoothness of the video playback, the lack of verifiable communication for Finch. It all screams 'manufactured.' He's trying too hard to appear innocent, and in doing so, he's only deepening the chasm of suspicion."

"His explanation for his own movements when he claims to have been alone is equally vague," Jenkins added. "He states he remained seated, contemplating the vastness of the ocean and the ephemeral nature of human ambition. He didn't interact with any other passengers, didn't visit the bar, didn't use the restroom. He simply... sat there. For nearly an hour."

Miller's gaze hardened. "An hour of uninterrupted, solitary contemplation in a public space, during which a murder occurs mere decks away. It's an alibi designed to be unassailable because it's designed to be unremarkable. He's banking on the idea that no one will scrutinize the man who claims to have done nothing, seen nothing, and heard nothing."

"He also claims to have been unaware of any disturbance, any unusual sounds, any indication of foul play," Jenkins continued. "Despite the proximity of Sterling's suite, the alleged sounds of a struggle or any alarm that might have been raised."

"Which is simply not plausible," Miller stated, his voice resonating with conviction. "The

Odyssey is a luxury liner, yes, but it's not soundproofed to that degree. Sterling's suite isn't some isolated chamber. If there was any commotion, any struggle, someone in the observation lounge, especially someone as acutely aware as Thorne claims to be, would have noticed. Unless, of course, he was elsewhere, and his entire narrative is a carefully constructed fiction designed to misdirect us."

Jenkins brought up another set of data, a list of passengers who had been in or around the observation lounge during the relevant period. "There are several other passengers who were in the lounge or its immediate vicinity between 01:30 and 03:30. Their statements, when cross-referenced with Thorne's, reveal discrepancies. One passenger recalls seeing Thorne leave the lounge around 01:45, heading towards the aft section of the ship, not returning until closer to 03:00. Another claims to have seen him briefly speaking with a member of the ship's engineering crew around 02:10, a meeting Thorne omits."

"An engineering crew member?" Miller's mind immediately went back to the corrupted security footage, the ease with which Thorne seemed to navigate the ship's restricted areas. "Someone who could grant access, disable systems, or provide specialized knowledge. Thorne is weaving a web, Jenkins, and he's pulling every string he can find."

"The discrepancies in these passenger statements are significant," Jenkins confirmed. "They suggest Thorne's timeline is not only fabricated but actively contradictory. His claim of remaining in the observation lounge for the entire duration is demonstrably false, based on the testimony of other passengers who were present."

Miller ran a hand through his hair, a gesture of weary exasperation. "He's not just lying; he's overplaying his hand. He knows we'll scrutinize his every word, his every movement. So, he's created an alibi that's both too perfect and too easily dismantled. It's a calculated risk, designed to make us doubt ourselves, to make us question the evidence that contradicts him."

"It's as if he *wants* us to find these inconsistencies," Jenkins mused, her brow furrowed in thought. "He's presenting us with a puzzle, knowing that we'll spend our time on the pieces he's given us, rather than looking for the ones he's hidden."

"Or," Miller said, a grim realization dawning, "he's deliberately making his alibi flawed, knowing that Finch and Vance will vouch for him, and that their combined testimony, despite the discrepancies, will be enough to cast doubt on our findings. He's creating plausible deniability for his associates, using them as shields."

"The meeting with the engineering crew member is particularly concerning," Jenkins continued. "If Thorne was indeed conferring with someone from engineering, it could explain how he gained access to areas normally off-limits, and perhaps even how he facilitated the security camera malfunction in the corridor outside Sterling's suite. An insider could have facilitated his movements."

Miller nodded slowly. "Aether Dynamics wouldn't hesitate to use their resources to ensure their operative had the tools and access he needed. It fits their modus operandi – control, manipulation, and the silent removal of obstacles. Thorne is their instrument, and this cruise is his stage."

"His insistence on the 'philosophical discussion' is also noteworthy," Jenkins observed. "It serves to portray him as a detached observer, someone above the petty machinations of corporate espionage and murder. It's a persona designed to deflect suspicion, to paint him as an unlikely suspect."

"A master of misdirection, that's Thorne," Miller said, a flicker of grudging respect in his eyes for the sheer audacity of the man. "He's always been able to weave an interesting narrative, to make people believe what he wants them to believe. He's trying to convince us that he's merely an intellectual, a contemplative soul lost in the vastness of the sea, while in reality, he was likely orchestrating Sterling's demise, or at the very least, ensuring the successful acquisition of his research."

"The pressure is mounting," Jenkins stated, her gaze steady. "Thorne's alibi is a smokescreen. We need to find the source of that smoke, the truth behind the manufactured narrative. The engineering crew member is a critical lead. If we can identify and interview them, we might shatter Thorne's carefully constructed illusion of innocence."

Miller looked out at the endless expanse of the ocean, the setting sun painting the waves in hues of fire and blood. Thorne's alibi, meant to shield him, had only served to illuminate his perfidy. The conflicting accounts, the manipulated footage, the convenient accomplices – they all pointed to one inescapable conclusion: Michael Thorne was not a victim of circumstance, but a perpetrator, deeply entangled in the murder of Dr. Sterling. The whispers of betrayal were growing louder, and Thorne was their insidious source.

The ghost of Michael Thorne was more than just a specter from a bygone case; he was a living, breathing embodiment of Miller's deepest professional regrets. The *Odyssey*, once a symbol of luxury and escape, had become a gilded cage, trapping Miller with the very man who had shattered his career and his sense of certainty years ago. It wasn't just about Sterling's murder anymore. It was about the echoes of the past, a discordant symphony playing out in the opulent confines of this vessel, orchestrated by Thorne's very presence.

Miller found himself replaying the events of the Rhapsody case with a painful clarity. It had been a sprawling corporate espionage investigation, a labyrinth of shell companies, offshore accounts, and stolen intellectual property. Thorne had been the linchpin, a master of shadows, adept at manipulating systems and people with equal ease.

Miller had been a rising star then, confident in his abilities, his unwavering moral compass guiding his every step. But Thorne had a way of bending truth, of exploiting the fine lines between legality and corruption, and in the end, it had been Miller's own adherence to protocol, his refusal to cross certain lines, that had allowed

Thorne to slip through his grasp. Thorne had used a legal loophole, a manufactured piece of evidence, and the timely disappearance of a key witness – all orchestrated with surgical precision – to walk away from charges that should have seen him imprisoned. The fallout had been immense. Careers had been ruined, the trust Miller had placed in the system shattered, and the very reputation he had painstakingly built had crumbled into dust. He had been forced into early retirement, labeled as incompetent, a man who couldn't handle the morally ambiguous realities of the world he inhabited.

Now, here he was, on a cruise ship miles from any jurisdiction that mattered, facing Thorne again. The parallels were unnerving. The calculated movements, the seemingly unshakeable alibis, the subtle manipulation of information – it was Thorne's modus operandi, refined and amplified. Sterling's murder, the disappearance of his research, the shadowy involvement of Aether Dynamics – it all felt like a replay, a morbid echo of the Rhapsody case, but with a far deadlier outcome. Sterling was dead, not just a victim of corporate machinations, but a casualty of a far darker game.

"He's playing with us, Jenkins," Miller said, his voice raw with a weariness that went beyond mere fatigue. He stared out at the darkening horizon, the vastness of the ocean a stark contrast to the claustrophobic confines of his own mind. "He knows we're onto him. He knows we suspect his involvement. And he's not just trying to cover his tracks; he's trying to break us. He's trying to make us doubt ourselves, just like he did before."

Jenkins, ever the pragmatist, remained focused on the data scrolling across her slate. "His alibi has more holes than a sieve, Miller. The passenger accounts are contradictory, the security footage is... suspect. He's not being careful; he's being provocative. He

wants us to see the flaws, to chase them, while he consolidates whatever he's here to achieve."

"Provocative, yes," Miller agreed, a grim smile touching his lips. "He's always enjoyed the game, the intellectual chess match. But this time, the stakes are higher. This isn't about stolen data or financial fraud. This is about a life. And the potential for more lives to be lost if Sterling's research falls into the wrong hands." He remembered the gnawing guilt, the sleepless nights spent agonizing over every decision he'd made during the Rhapsody case. Had he pushed too hard? Had he been too naive? Had he missed a crucial detail, a subtle warning sign, that would have prevented Thorne from escaping justice? The questions still haunted him.

"We need to consider the possibility that Thorne isn't just an operative," Jenkins said, her voice low and serious. "The Rhapsody case... you said he was the linchpin. What if he was more than just a hired hand? What if he was the architect of that entire scheme?"

Miller nodded, the thought a cold knot in his stomach. "He was certainly capable of it. He had the intelligence, the foresight, the utter ruthlessness. He saw the system as a playground, a set of rules to be bent and broken for his own amusement and profit. And Aether Dynamics... they operate in the same shadow realm. They wouldn't hire just anyone to handle something as critical as Sterling's research. They'd hire the best, the most discreet, the most adaptable. Thorne fits that profile perfectly."

The weight of his past mistakes pressed down on him. He had been so focused on Thorne's legal culpability, on building an airtight case, that he'd underestimated the intangible. Thorne's psychological manipulations, his ability to create chaos and then thrive in it, had been his undoing. Miller had been so blinded by the tangible evidence – the financial records, the digital footprints – that he'd missed the forest for the trees. Thorne had played on Miller's by-the-book approach, exploiting his adherence to procedure to escape accountability.

"The fact that he's here," Miller continued, his voice gaining a somber intensity, "and that his presence coincides with Sterling's death... it can't be a coincidence. He's either here to retrieve the research, to silence anyone who might try to expose Aether Dynamics, or perhaps, to ensure Sterling was silenced permanently. And if he's working for Aether Dynamics, then he has the resources to pull off something like this, and the motivation to do so without hesitation."

He thought of Thorne's dismissive arrogance, his cool, detached demeanor even when confronted with the evidence. It was a facade, he knew, but a highly effective one. Thorne believed himself untouchable, and with Aether Dynamics backing him, he might well be. The fear wasn't just for the truth, or for justice. It was a deeper, more primal fear – the fear of seeing history repeat itself, of watching Thorne escape once more, leaving a trail of destruction in his wake.

"He knows my history with him," Miller murmured, more to himself than to Jenkins. "He knows how that case ended. He knows it broke me. And now he's back, in a situation that mirrors it in so many ways. It's a taunt. He's daring me to fail again."

Jenkins looked up from her slate, her expression one of concern mixed with resolve. "He might be trying to provoke you, Miller, but he's also given us threads to pull. The engineering crew member, the discrepancies in the passenger statements, the subtle manipulation of the video feed – these are all Thorne's missteps, however minor they may seem to him. He's not as invisible as he thinks."

"He's always been good at making people underestimate him," Miller conceded, the memory of his younger, more idealistic self a poignant counterpoint to his current cynicism. "He's a chameleon. He can adapt, blend in, exploit any weakness. And his greatest weapon has always been his ability to make others doubt their own judgment, their own perception of reality."

The memory of his own compromised judgment during the Rhapsody case was a constant ache. He remembered the pressure from his superiors, the whispers of doubt from his colleagues, the feeling of being outmaneuvered and outplayed by an unseen force. Thorne had capitalized on that pressure, using it to his advantage. He had subtly fed Miller information that seemed damning but was ultimately misleading, creating a narrative that suited his escape.

"This time is different," Miller stated, his voice firm, a renewed sense of purpose hardening his gaze. "I won't let him get away with it again. I can't. Not with Sterling's life on the line, and not with the potential for Aether Dynamics to weaponize his research. I have a responsibility, Jenkins. Not just to Sterling, but to myself. I have to confront the mistakes I made, the ethical compromises I might have considered, and ensure that Thorne's pattern of destruction ends here."

He understood now. Thorne's reappearance wasn't just an external threat; it was an internal reckoning. It was an opportunity for Miller to exorcise the demons of his past, to prove that he had learned from his failures, and that his commitment to truth and justice, however battered, remained unbroken. The weight of past mistakes was heavy, but it was also a burden he could carry, a reminder of what was at stake.

"We need to focus on those discrepancies," Miller continued, the analytical part of his mind reasserting itself, pushing back the shadows of regret. "The engineering crew member is our best lead. If Thorne was meeting with them, it's likely to facilitate access, to disable security, or perhaps even to acquire a specific tool or device. Thorne doesn't do anything without a purpose, and that purpose is almost always to facilitate his objective and cover his tracks."

"And the longer Thorne is on this ship, the more opportunities he has to further his agenda," Jenkins added, her fingers flying across the holographic interface. "The clock is ticking, Miller. We can't afford to be paralyzed by the past. We have to act."

Miller nodded, the echoes of Thorne's past manipulations fading slightly as a new resolve took hold. "He's given us the pieces, Jenkins. Now, we just have to assemble them correctly. This time, Thorne won't escape. This time, the truth will prevail, no matter how deeply he tries to bury it." The resurfacing of Thorne had stirred a tempest within him, a conflict between the jaded cynic he had become and the unwavering investigator he once was. It was a battle for his own soul, played out against the backdrop of a murder and a conspiracy that stretched back years, fueled by ambition, and the chilling efficacy of a man who made a career out of bending reality. He felt a profound sense of responsibility, a desperate need to finally set things right, to ensure that Thorne's destructive path was halted, not just for the sake of justice, but for the sake of his own fractured integrity. The weight of past mistakes was a heavy burden, but perhaps, just perhaps, it was the very thing that would give him the strength to finally overcome.

The ship, a behemoth of steel and glass, cleaved through the sapphire expanse of the ocean, each nautical mile bringing them closer to a temporary reprieve in Lisbon. Every sunrise painted a stark reminder of the dwindling hours before the *Odyssey* docked, before the killer could melt back into the anonymity of the shore, and before the shadowy tendrils of Aether Dynamics could further entrench themselves, their objectives likely secured.

"Lisbon," Jenkins murmured, her voice tight with the strain of her internal calculations. Her eyes, usually sharp and dissecting, held a flicker of apprehension as she scanned the holographic charts projected onto her slate. "Forty-eight hours. Maybe less, depending on currents and any scheduled diversions. Forty-eight hours to find a murderer and dismantle a corporate conspiracy that's been years in the making."

Miller leaned against the cool, polished railing of the promenade deck, the salty spray a familiar, almost comforting sensation against his skin. Yet, even this simple sensory input did little to quell the churning anxiety in his gut. He watched the playful dance of sunlight on the waves, a stark contrast to the darkness that had descended upon the ship, a darkness that had begun with Sterling's violent end. "Forty-eight hours," he echoed, the words tasting like ash. "And Thorne is still out there, a ghost in the machine, adding layers of uncertainty to an already impossible equation."

The presence of Michael Thorne was a poisoned chalice, a complication that Miller hadn't fully anticipated, or perhaps, hadn't allowed himself to fully consider. Thorne, the architect of so much past misery, the man who had demonstrated an unparalleled mastery of misdirection and manipulation, was now a wildcard on the

Odyssey. His motive remained a frustratingly blank slate. Was he here to retrieve Sterling's research, the very reason Sterling had been on this voyage in the first place? Was he the one who had silenced Sterling to prevent its discovery or dissemination? Or was his presence entirely coincidental, a mere happenstance that Miller's own past trauma was amplifying into a sinister design?

"We can't afford to assume anything about Thorne's role," Miller said, turning to face Jenkins. His gaze, usually piercing and direct, was clouded with the same ambiguity that surrounded Thorne. "He could be the killer. He could be Aether Dynamics' enforcer. He could be a pawn, put in place to divert our attention, or worse, to frame someone else. Or he could be...

something else entirely. Perhaps he's been burned by Aether Dynamics himself. Perhaps he has information. But how do we find out without getting ourselves killed, or played like a fiddle?"

Jenkins tapped a stylus against her slate, her brow furrowed in concentration. "His alibi for Sterling's death is still flimsy, Miller. The security footage is corrupted in precisely the right places, and the witness who supposedly saw him in the casino at the time of the murder... Well, their account screams 'coached."

"Thorne's specialty," Miller sighed, running a hand over his tired face. "He doesn't break rules; he rewrites them. He doesn't create chaos; he orchestrates it. And in this case, his orchestration might have served to both commit the murder and then perfectly position himself to be suspected, while the real danger lurks elsewhere. Or perhaps, he *is* the real danger, and his meticulousness is just another layer of his game."

The problem was that Thorne wasn't just a suspect; he was a vortex of suspicion, drawing every ambiguous detail and suspicious coincidence into his orbit. His history with Miller meant that every interaction, every perceived threat, was filtered through the lens of past failures, of a career that had imploded under Thorne's machinations. Miller felt the familiar weight of his own past mistakes pressing down on him, threatening to paralyze his judgment. He had to be methodical, dispassionate, even when every fiber of his being screamed that Thorne was the embodiment of the darkness they were fighting.

"The engineering crew member," Miller continued, shifting his focus. "The one Thorne was seen speaking with. That's our most concrete link to Thorne's movements and potential activities. If he needed access to something, or someone, that was outside his usual access, he'd need help. And who better than someone who knows the ship's inner workings?"

Jenkins nodded, her fingers dancing across the holographic display, bringing up schematics of the ship's engineering sections. "Our information indicates this crew member, a man named Petrov, has access to the ship's central computer core, and also to the secure storage for sensitive equipment. If Thorne was planning something that required bypassing security protocols, or perhaps acquiring a specific device, Petrov would be the logical point of contact."

"Acquiring a device," Miller mused, his mind replaying Sterling's research notes, the cryptic references to 'stabilization matrices' and 'frequency regulators.' Could Sterling's work have involved something tangible, something that Aether Dynamics would want physically? Or was it purely data, that Thorne, with his expertise, could simply download? But the murder... that suggested a more immediate, more permanent solution.

"And what if Thorne didn't just meet with Petrov to acquire something, but to

facilitate something?" Jenkins suggested, her voice barely a whisper, as if afraid to give voice to the full implications. "What if he was helping someone bypass security, not for himself, but for the killer? Or what if he was the one who disabled the systems that would have recorded the killer's movements, creating the 'corrupted footage' himself?"

The idea sent a chill down Miller's spine. Thorne was not just a suspect; he was potentially an accomplice, or even the mastermind behind the security breaches that were hindering their investigation. He was a chameleon, able to blend seamlessly into any role, any scenario. Miller found himself caught in a paralyzing dilemma: how to investigate Thorne without being manipulated by him, and how to confront the possibility that Thorne's presence was a deliberate distraction, a smokescreen for an even more dangerous player.

"The dual threat," Miller said, the words heavy with unspoken dread. "Sterling's murder, and the broader conspiracy orchestrated by Aether Dynamics. They're not separate entities anymore. Thorne, if he's involved, bridges them. He's the common denominator. And if Aether Dynamics is truly behind this, they wouldn't have sent a mere foot soldier. They would have sent their best. Thorne fits that description perfectly. He's not just capable of murder; he's capable of orchestrating an entire operation, from planning to execution to aftermath."

He remembered the cold, calculated efficiency with which Thorne had dismantled his career during the Rhapsody case. It wasn't just about legal loopholes; it was about psychological warfare, about eroding confidence, about planting seeds of doubt that would blossom into full-blown despair.

Thorne had a knack for turning people against themselves, for making them question their own instincts, their own sanity. And here he was again, on a luxury liner, playing the same insidious game, albeit with far deadlier stakes.

"The ship reaches Lisbon in less than two days," Jenkins stated, her voice a low thrum of urgency. "If we don't have enough to act by then, to apprehend the killer, or at least to secure Sterling's research, it's all over. Thorne, or whoever he's working for, will disappear. The data will be wiped, the witnesses silenced, and Sterling's death will be just another unsolved mystery lost at sea."

Miller clenched his jaw, the salt spray doing little to wash away the bitterness. He felt the pressure mounting, not just from the ticking clock, but from the weight of his own past. He had been given a second chance, an opportunity to right the wrongs that had defined his forced retirement. But this wasn't just about personal redemption. It was about preventing a powerful, amoral entity from gaining access to technology that could be weaponized. Sterling's research, whatever its specific application, was clearly of immense interest to Aether Dynamics, and Thorne was their key.

"We need to isolate Petrov," Miller decided, his voice hardening with resolve. "He's our only direct link to Thorne's activities. We need to find out what he knows, what he saw, and what he might have done. Even if he was coerced, even if he's afraid, people under pressure tend to make mistakes. They leave traces."

Jenkins was already cross-referencing crew manifests and shift schedules. "Petrov's next shift doesn't begin for another six hours. He'll likely be in his cabin. We could try to make contact... discreetly."

"Discreetly is Thorne's territory, not ours," Miller said, a grim smile touching his lips. "We need to be direct. But we also need to be prepared. If Thorne is involved, he might have Petrov under his thumb. He might have anticipated that we'd come looking for him."

The weight of their predicament settled upon Miller like a physical burden. The

Odyssey was a microcosm of the world, a place where wealth and power could shield secrets, where deception could masquerade as civility. Thorne was the ultimate embodiment of that deception, a man who wore his charm like a mask, hiding a calculating ruthlessness beneath. And Aether

Dynamics, with its vast resources and shadowy agenda, was the ultimate power, capable of moving unseen through the corridors of influence, leaving destruction in its wake.

"We're not just chasing a killer anymore, Jenkins," Miller said, his gaze fixed on the horizon, where the sun was beginning its slow descent, casting long, melancholic shadows across the water. "We're racing against an organization that views human lives as expendable assets. Sterling was a casualty of their ambition. And if we don't act, if we don't uncover the truth before we dock, there will be more casualties. Thorne is the key, yes, but he's also a symptom of a much larger, much more dangerous disease."

The approaching port of Lisbon was a siren's call, promising an end to their isolation, but also an end to their pursuit if they failed. The limited jurisdiction of international waters was rapidly receding, replaced by the complex legalities of national territories. Once the

Odyssey docked, the perpetrators would scatter, the evidence would be harder to gather, and Aether Dynamics would likely ensure that any remaining traces of Sterling's research, or of Thorne's involvement, vanished forever. The clock was not just ticking; it was sounding a deafening alarm, urging them to act with a speed and precision that Thorne himself would have admired, or perhaps, orchestrated. The game was reaching its brutal, inevitable climax, and Miller knew, with a chilling certainty, that Thorne was playing his part perfectly. The question remained: was he the predator, the prey, or the puppet master himself? And in the limited time they had left, could Miller and Jenkins unravel the truth before they became just another tragic footnote in Aether Dynamics' relentless pursuit of power? The vastness of the ocean seemed to mock their efforts, a constant reminder of how much they didn't know, and how little time they had to learn it.

Chapter 5: The Killer's Signature

The metallic tang of despair began to permeate the air of the *Odyssey*, a subtle yet palpable shift in the ship's atmosphere. It wasn't the scent of salt or diesel, but something far more insidious – the cold, sharp odor of fear. Miller felt it cling to his skin, a clammy residue from the hushed, panicked whispers that had begun to snake through the ship's opulent corridors. The news of a second death had rippled through the passengers and crew like a rogue wave, its impact far more devastating than the first. Sterling's demise, while shocking, had been an isolated incident, attributed by some to a tragic accident, by others to a desperate act. But this... this was an undeniable declaration of war.

Jenkins had delivered the news with a grim finality that mirrored the icy dread settling in Miller's gut. Her usual analytical composure was frayed at the edges, her eyes wide with a mixture of horror and grim determination. "Another one, Miller. It's... it's identical. The ligature, the positioning of the body, and the carving. The wooden bird." Her voice, usually a steady beacon in their investigative storm, trembled on the last word.

Miller's jaw tightened. The 'wooden bird.' Sterling's death had been staged, a macabre tableau designed to look like a suicide, but the subtle, almost imperceptible detail – a small, intricately carved wooden bird clutched in his lifeless hand – had been the anomaly, the whisper of a killer's presence. Now, that whisper had become a scream. The killer wasn't just active; they were taunting them, broadcasting their escalating reign of terror.

They had been so close, or so they had believed. The ship was a contained environment, a floating puzzle box where every soul was accounted for, every movement ostensibly trackable. Yet, the killer had moved through their meticulously designed cage with impunity, striking again. This wasn't the work of a panicked individual acting on impulse. This was calculated. This was deliberate. This was a message. And the message was clear: their investigation was a threat, and the killer was willing to eliminate any perceived obstacle, no matter how inconvenient the timing.

"Where?" Miller's voice was a low growl, cutting through the rising panic. He needed details, cold, hard facts, to anchor him against the rising tide of chaos.

"Deck B, the stateroom suite directly opposite Sterling's," Jenkins replied, her fingers already flying across her slate, pulling up schematics and passenger manifests. "The victim is Eleanor Vance. A journalist. Independent, but she's done a lot of work exposing corporate malfeasance. She'd been asking questions, Miller. Sterling wasn't the only one she'd spoken to."

Eleanor Vance. Miller's mind immediately conjured an image of a sharp, tenacious woman, someone who wouldn't shy away from the uncomfortable truths. He remembered seeing her at the Captain Rostova's reception, a quiet observer with an unnerving ability to make people feel... transparent. And she had been seen speaking with Sterling. The pieces, or rather, the fragments of pieces, were beginning to align in a deeply disturbing pattern.

"She spoke with Sterling?" Miller pressed, his gaze fixed on Jenkins, searching for any flicker of insight that might explained the connection.

"Yes," Jenkins confirmed, her brow furrowed. "At the observation lounge, two nights ago. Witnesses described it as a 'heated discussion.' Sterling seemed agitated. Vance was... intense. She was apparently on the verge of breaking a major story, and Sterling might have been a source, or perhaps he was trying to dissuade her from publishing something he believed was too dangerous."

Dangerous. The word echoed in the confined space of Miller's mind. Sterling, a brilliant but reclusive researcher, dabbling in something Aether Dynamics desperately wanted to control. Vance, an investigative journalist, sniffing out the truth, likely drawing unwanted attention to the same shadowy organization. And now, both of them dead, their lives extinguished with the same chilling signature. The killer wasn't just silencing Sterling; they were silencing anyone who threatened to expose their secrets. The conspiracy was no longer just a financial or technological threat; it was a lethal one.

"The killer wants to stop us," Miller stated the obvious, the words tasting like bile. "They know we're looking. They know we're connecting Sterling's research to Aether Dynamics. Vance was getting too close, and they eliminated her. The wooden bird isn't just a signature; it's a warning. A message to anyone else who dares to pry."

The implication of Vance's presence on the ship sent a fresh wave of unease through Miller. She hadn't been a random passenger. She was on the

Odyssey for a reason, likely to investigate Sterling or the very secrets he held. And Sterling, in his final days, had apparently been involved in conversations with her, perhaps even sharing information. This suggested that Sterling himself may have been aware of the danger, or perhaps, he had been trying to find a way to leak his findings before Aether Dynamics could silence him permanently.

"The stateroom," Miller said, his voice regaining some of its command. "We need to see it. We need to confirm the details, look for anything our preliminary team might have missed."

Jenkins nodded, already pulling up the ship's security protocols. "The master-at-arms team has secured the scene. They're thorough, but they're not... us. They're looking for evidence of a crime. We're looking for the story behind the crime."

The walk to Deck B felt longer than the entire journey from port. The hushed murmurs of the passengers seemed to follow them, their eyes darting nervously, casting suspicious glances at every uniformed crew member. The ship, once a symbol of luxury and escape, had transformed into a gilded cage, its passengers and crew now trapped with a predator moving amongst them, a ghost in their midst. The illusion of safety had shattered, replaced by the chilling reality that the 'locked room' of Sterling's cabin had been a temporary anomaly, and the killer was now operating in a far more terrifying environment: a moving prison where the walls offered no solace, and the horizon offered no escape.

As they approached Vance's suite, the air grew heavy with an unspoken tension. Two uniformed security guards stood sentinel outside the stateroom door, their faces grim, their posture radiating an almost palpable unease. The door itself stood ajar, revealing a glimpse of the scene within. Miller exchanged a curt nod with the guard in charge, a man named Henderson, whose face was etched with the weariness of dealing with a nightmare unfolding at sea.

"Anything?" Miller asked, his voice low.

Henderson shook his head, his gaze drawn to the interior of the room. "As described, Detective. The ligature... it's the same. And the carving. Found it in her hand. Just like Mr. Sterling." He paused, swallowing hard. "We secured the scene immediately. No one in or out since discovery."

Miller stepped into the suite, Jenkins close behind. The room was a study in controlled chaos. Personal belongings were scattered, not in a sign of a struggle, but as if meticulously searched. Books, papers, and digital devices were strewn across the vanity, the desk, and the plush carpet. It spoke of an investigation, not a random act of violence. Vance, it seemed, had been digging into something that had attracted attention, and not just from the killer.

The body lay on the floor near the window, positioned with the same chilling precision as Sterling's. Vance's eyes were wide, staring sightlessly at the opulent ceiling, a silent testament to her final moments. Her skin had a pallor that spoke of death, but it was the faint, almost imperceptible discoloration around her neck that confirmed the brutal nature of her demise. And then, Miller saw it. Clutched tightly in her right hand, almost hidden within her stiffening fingers, was the familiar, disturbing shape of a small, carved wooden bird.

It was undeniably the killer's signature. This was no coincidence. This was a deliberate act, designed to terrorize and to obstruct. Miller knelt beside the body, his eyes scanning every detail. The knot on the ligature was identical to the one found on Sterling. The angles of the ligature, the pressure points... it was all a disturbing echo.

"The room wasn't forced open," Jenkins observed, her eyes sweeping over the door frame and the lock. "And there are no signs of a struggle. This wasn't a violent confrontation. It was... efficient. Precise."

"The killer gained access without force," Miller mused, running a gloved finger along the edge of Vance's hand, carefully examining the wooden bird. The craftsmanship was exquisite, disturbingly so. It felt smooth, almost worn, as if it had been handled frequently. "And they knew how to leave no trace. Or rather, they

wanted us to know they were here. The signature is the proof."

He stood up, his gaze sweeping the room. Vance's research materials were spread out, a tantalizing but frustratingly incomplete glimpse into her final investigation. There were printouts of financial statements, redacted documents, and numerous notes scribbled in her distinctive, sharp handwriting. Miller picked up a notepad from the desk. The last entry, dated the previous evening, read: "Sterling's data is the key. Aether Dynamics. The frequency manipulation is more than just theory. It's weaponized."

Weaponized. The word sent a jolt through Miller. Many had dismissed sterling's research, a complex theoretical framework for manipulating energy frequencies, as purely academic. But Vance, with her journalist's instinct for uncovering hidden truths, had seen the danger. She had understood that Sterling's work wasn't just about scientific discovery; it was about a power that Aether Dynamics craved.

"Frequency manipulation," Miller murmured, the phrase resonating with Sterling's own cryptic notes about 'stabilization matrices' and 'harmonic resonance.' Sterling had been on the verge of something monumental, something Aether Dynamics couldn't afford to let fall into the wrong hands, or worse, be revealed to the world.

"She was onto something big," Jenkins confirmed, her voice hushed with a dawning realization. "And Sterling was her source, or at least, he had information that confirmed her suspicions. He probably gave her the wooden bird, a token of trust, or maybe a coded message."

"Or maybe," Miller countered, his mind racing through possibilities, "the killer

wanted Vance to have the bird. Maybe they planted it, a deliberate misdirection. They want us to think it's a personal vendetta, a symbol of Sterling's involvement. But it could be a fabricated connection, designed to make us focus on Sterling's research, and Aether Dynamics, while they move on to their next objective."

The 'locked room' had become a moving prison, and their killer was a phantom, capable of appearing and disappearing at will. How had they accessed Vance's stateroom without leaving a trace? The ship's security was tight, its corridors monitored. Yet, the killer had waltzed in and out, leaving only death and a chilling artistic flourish.

"The security footage," Miller said, turning to Jenkins. "What did it show for Vance's suite?"

Jenkins' face fell. "Exactly what we found with Sterling's. Gaps. Corrupted data. Precisely during the estimated time of death."

"Thorne," Miller breathed, the name a curse. "He's our prime suspect, Jenkins. He has the technical expertise to manipulate the ship's systems, to create those blind spots. And he has the motive – Aether Dynamics wants Sterling's research, and they'd employ someone like Thorne to ensure no one interfered, or worse, to acquire it themselves."

"But Thorne's alibi for Sterling's death was supposed to be rock solid," Jenkins argued, though the conviction in her voice was wavering. "He was in the casino, a dozen witnesses."

"A dozen witnesses who were likely paid, or intimidated, or simply mistaken," Miller retorted. "Thorne doesn't leave loose ends. He crafts them. He orchestrates their movements. And if he was seen in the casino, it was by design. A perfect distraction while he, or someone he hired, completed the task."

The theory of Thorne's involvement was a grim comfort, providing a tangible target, but also a chilling reminder of his past capabilities. Thorne was a master manipulator, a virtuoso of deception. He wouldn't just kill; he would orchestrate a symphony of chaos, leaving Miller and Jenkins chasing phantoms while the true objective was achieved.

"The engineer, Petrov," Miller mused, the name resurfacing from their earlier discussions. "Thorne was seen meeting with him. If Thorne needed access to the ship's systems, or to bypass security, Petrov would be the man. He's our only direct link to Thorne's movements."

"Petrov is in his quarters now," Jenkins confirmed, checking her slate. "He has another shift in three hours. If Thorne didn't anticipate us looking for Petrov, he might be vulnerable."

"Or he might be waiting for us," Miller countered, the metallic taste of dread intensifying. "Thorne is always two steps ahead. He might have anticipated that we'd investigate the engineering department, that we'd look for anyone who helped him. Petrov could be a trap."

The implications of the second murder were far-reaching. It confirmed that Sterling's death was not an isolated incident but part of a larger, more sinister plot. The killer was determined to maintain silence, and was willing to eliminate anyone who threatened to expose their secrets, whether it was the researcher himself or the journalist who sought to bring his findings to light. The ship, once a haven, had become a hunting ground, and the passengers were now living in a constant state of fear, unsure of who to trust, or when the next chilling tableau would be discovered. The 'wooden bird' had become a symbol of their captivity, a grim reminder that the killer was still among them, a predator in their midst, operating with chilling impunity. And with Lisbon just days away, the pressure to uncover the truth before the

Odyssey docked was becoming an unbearable weight. The conspiracy was no longer just a shadowy threat; it was a visible, deadly force, leaving a trail of broken lives in its wake.

The stark uniformity of death was a chilling reassurance, a macabre anchor in the swirling chaos. Miller stood between the two crime scenes, the ghostly echoes of Sterling's opulent suite and Vance's now sterile stateroom pressing in on him. He had Jenkins project the forensic reports side-by-side on his tablet, the stark, clinical language a stark contrast to the visceral horror they described. The metallic tang of despair was no longer a subtle atmospheric shift; it was a suffocating miasma, clinging to the polished brass and mahogany of the *Odyssey*.

Methodical. The word pulsed in Miller's mind, a relentless drumbeat against the rising tide of panic. Sterling, found in his locked cabin, a scene meticulously crafted to suggest self-harm, yet marred by the impossibly placed wooden bird. Vance, discovered in her stateroom, the scenario disturbingly familiar. The ligature marks around her neck, the faint but undeniable bruising, the precise angles of repose – all mirrored Sterling's final moments. The killer was not merely competent; they were a virtuoso of death, their actions dictated by a script written in blood and feathers.

"The ligature," Jenkins murmured, her finger tracing the image of the knot on the screen. "Identical. A specific type of weave, not one commonly used in nautical contexts. It suggests it was brought onto the ship, or crafted specifically for this purpose. And the tension, the depth of the marks... it speaks of controlled strength, not a frenzied struggle."

Miller nodded, his gaze fixed on the tiny wooden bird clutched in Vance's hand. It was smaller than Sterling's, but the carving was unmistakable. The same delicate wings, the same rounded, almost naive form. "The staging," he added, his voice low and gravelly. "Sterling's was meant to look like suicide. Vance's... what was the intended narrative there? Another accident? A despairing act by someone who'd uncovered something too terrible?"

"Or perhaps," Jenkins countered, her eyes narrowed in thought, "the staging is secondary. The primary message is the bird. It's a signature. Deliberate, unmistakable. The killer *wants* us to see it. They want us to know it's their work."

"A mark of ownership," Miller mused, the phrase chilling him to the bone. "A declaration of dominance. Sterling was a CEO, a man at the apex of corporate power. Vance was a journalist, a seeker of truth, someone who made it her business to unearth inconvenient facts. What connects them beyond their presence on this ship?"

He leaned back, the plush upholstery of the private lounge doing little to soothed his frayed nerves. They had been so focused on the 'how' of the murders, the technicalities of bypassing security and leaving no trace. But the 'why' was beginning to crystallize, forming a shape as disturbing as the wooden birds themselves.

"Sterling was the architect of a conspiracy," Miller began, his thoughts weaving through the fragmented intelligence they'd gathered. "His research, his company, Aether Dynamics – it all points to a clandestine operation with potentially devastating global implications. He was a player, a key figure. And Vance was a threat to that operation. She was digging into him, into Aether Dynamics. She likely saw Sterling as a linchpin, someone who held crucial information."

"So, Sterling is eliminated because he represents the conspiracy, or perhaps because he was trying to break free," Jenkins theorized, her fingers flying across her slate, cross-referencing passenger manifests and recent communications. "And Vance is eliminated because she was about to expose it all, with Sterling as her primary source, or at least, a confirmation of her suspicions."

"But that doesn't fully explain the theatricality," Miller argued, gesturing towards the projected images. "Why the elaborate staging? Why the wooden bird? It's not just about silencing them. It's about sending a message. A message to whom? To us? To other potential whistleblowers? Or perhaps, to someone within Aether Dynamics itself?"

The implications of a message directed internally were unsettling. Was this a power play within the shadowy organization? A warning to rivals? Or a display of control by a rogue element operating with impunity? The

Odyssey, meant to be a symbol of progress and luxury, had become a gilded cage, its inhabitants now potential targets in a deadly game of corporate espionage and elimination.

"Let's consider the victims again, not just as pawns, but as individuals," Miller urged, his gaze distant, as if seeing through the polished walls of the lounge to the very heart of the conspiracy. "Sterling was a man of immense wealth and influence, but also a recluse. His motivations were complex. Was he a willing participant in Aether Dynamics' schemes, or was he a reluctant architect, trapped by his own genius? Vance, on the other hand, was a crusader. Her entire career was built on exposing corruption. She was driven by a sense of justice, a fierce determination to bring the truth to light."

He paused, letting the contrast sink in. "What if the killer isn't just targeting individuals, but symbols? Sterling represents the power that Aether Dynamics wields. Vance represents the force that seeks to dismantle it. The killer is making a statement: that both power and the threat to it can be extinguished with equal ease."

Jenkins looked up from her slate, a grim expression on her face. "I've been reviewing Vance's recent work. She had a series of articles planned, all revolving around offshore accounts and shell corporations linked to Aether Dynamics. She mentioned Sterling in her private notes, calling him 'the key to unlocking the entire operation.' She believed he was either being coerced or was secretly documenting their illicit activities."

"So, Sterling wasn't just a victim of Aether Dynamics; he might have been their internal auditor, or a disgruntled insider gathering evidence,"

Miller extrapolated. "And Vance was about to publish. She had the proof, or was on the verge of obtaining it. The killer had to act fast. But the signature... it feels too personal for a purely corporate hit. It's almost... artistic. Obsessive."

He picked up a small, intricately carved wooden bird from the display table in the lounge – a decorative piece, but one that now sent a shiver down his spine. "This isn't just a tool of the trade. It's a statement. A calling card. It suggests a killer who is not only efficient and intelligent but also deeply disturbed. Someone who takes pride in their work, in the terror they instill."

The precision of the murders, the meticulous planning, the complete erasure of traceable evidence – it all pointed to a level of sophistication that went beyond a simple hired assassin. This was someone who understood the psychology of their targets, who could anticipate their movements and exploit their weaknesses. It suggested a deep-seated knowledge of Aether Dynamics' inner workings, or a chillingly prescient understanding of how to dismantle such an organization from the outside.

"What if the bird isn't just a signature," Jenkins offered, her voice barely a whisper, "but a piece of the puzzle Sterling was working on? A clue he left behind, perhaps, for Vance, or for anyone who might come looking?"

"A coded message?" Miller considered the possibility. Sterling was a scientist, a man accustomed to complex systems and abstract thought. "But why would the killer then replicate it, and place it in Vance's hand? To taunt us? To make us chase a phantom trail? Or, as you said, to obscure the real reason for their deaths."

The idea of misdirection was a potent one. The wooden bird, so clearly a signature, could also be a carefully constructed red herring. The killer wanted them to focus on Sterling's research, on Aether Dynamics' illicit activities, and perhaps, on Thorne's potential involvement in the technical aspects of the murders. But what if the true motive lay elsewhere, something more personal, something that Vance, with her journalistic tenacity, had stumbled upon?

"The motive needs to be more than just silencing a threat to Aether Dynamics," Miller stated, pacing the confines of the lounge. "If it were purely about corporate secrecy, the killer would have acted more discreetly.

The signature, the theatrics – it suggests a deeper psychological element. Rage, perhaps? Revenge? A twisted sense of justice?"

He stopped, his eyes falling on a framed photograph on the wall, depicting a past gala held on the

Odyssey, a tableau of smiling faces and elegant attire. Among them, he recognized Sterling, a younger, less haunted version of himself, and a woman he now identified as Vance, her journalistic fire already evident even in the posed photograph. They were both there, in the same orbit, before their paths converged in death.

"They were both on this ship for a reason, separate from their investigations," Miller mused. "Sterling, to present his research, or perhaps to escape something. Vance, to investigate him, or to follow a lead that brought her here. They were drawn to the

Odyssey, to this specific nexus of power and secrets."

He ran a hand through his hair, the weight of the investigation pressing down on him. "The killer is methodical, theatrical, and deeply intelligent. They understand how to exploit technology, how to create blind spots, and how to manipulate perception. Thorne fits that profile for the technical execution, but the signature... it feels like a separate entity. A mind that revels in the macabre."

"But Thorne is Aether Dynamics' operative," Jenkins insisted, her voice firm. "If he's responsible for the execution, then the motive

is Aether Dynamics. The signature is merely a psychological imprint, a personal flourish on a professional job."

"Or Thorne is the hired gun, executing the plan, but the signature belongs to someone else entirely," Miller countered, his mind swirling with possibilities. "Someone with a more personal vendetta, who sees Sterling and Vance as symbols of a larger injustice. Someone who wants the world to know that these deaths were not just collateral damage, but a deliberate act of retribution."

He pointed to the projected image of Vance's cluttered desk. "Her notes. 'Sterling's data is the key. Aether Dynamics. The frequency manipulation is more than just theory. It's weaponized.' Weaponized. That's the word that keeps coming back to me. Sterling wasn't just developing a new technology; he was creating a weapon. And Vance understood its implications."

The realization dawned, cold and sharp. This wasn't just about corporate malfeasance or financial crimes. This was about power, about control, about the potential for catastrophic destruction. Sterling's research, in the wrong hands, could be a tool of unprecedented devastation. And Aether Dynamics, a company with a history of shadowy dealings, was precisely the kind of organization that would seek to weaponize such a discovery.

"So, the killer is silencing anyone who threatens to expose Sterling's weaponized research," Miller concluded, the pieces clicking into place with a sickening finality. "Sterling himself, perhaps because he was unwilling to proceed, or was trying to leak the information. Vance, because she was about to publish and reveal the weaponization to the world. The wooden bird... it's a symbol of their success. A trophy."

He looked at Jenkins, his eyes grave. "The killer isn't just an assassin. They are a guardian. A guardian of a devastating secret, willing to eliminate anyone who threatens to unleash it. And they are brilliant. They've used this ship as their stage, its passengers as their unwitting audience, and their victims as their gruesome props."

The methodical nature of the killings, the deliberate placement of the wooden bird, the targeted selection of victims – it all pointed to a singular individual or a highly coordinated group. Miller knew, with a chilling certainty, that the pattern was no accident. It was a deliberate, chilling narrative being woven by a killer who saw themselves not as a murderer, but as an agent of some twisted form of justice, or perhaps, simply as an artist of terror. The

Odyssey was no longer just a vessel; it was a crime scene, a floating testament to a conspiracy that had escalated from hushed whispers to deadly pronouncements. And the next act, Miller feared, would be even more terrifying.

The sterile white of the interview room felt like a deliberate counterpoint to the escalating murkiness of their investigation. Miller sat opposite a nervous-looking junior executive from Sterling's inner circle, the man's tie knotted so tightly it threatened to choke him. Jenkins, ever the observant counterpoint to Miller's more forceful interrogations, sat to his side, her tablet a silent, ever-present observer. They had already spoken to Thorne, the security chief, a man whose unnerving calm felt less like professionalism and more like practiced detachment. Thorne had offered meticulously curated timelines and access logs, all seemingly in order, yet leaving Miller with the distinct impression of a well-oiled machine designed to conceal rather than protect.

"Mr. Sterling was a man of... considerable foresight," the executive, a Mr. Finch, stammered, adjusting his glasses. His eyes flickered between Miller and Jenkins, a bird trapped in a cage of their scrutiny. "He anticipated many eventualities in his business dealings."

"And did he anticipate any eventuality that might lead to him being found dead in his cabin, a peculiar wooden effigy clutched in his hand?" Miller's voice was low, a rumble that seemed to vibrate in the confined space. He let the silence stretch, a heavy blanket of discomfort.

Finch swallowed hard. "No. No, nothing like that. He was... he was always very private about his personal affairs. His work, however, was his life. Aether Dynamics. That consumed him."

"Aether Dynamics," Miller repeated, the name a dark stain in the narrative. "And what exactly does Aether Dynamics consume, Mr. Finch? We're under the impression it involves more than just technological innovation."

Finch's gaze dropped to his hands, now clasped tightly in his lap. "It's... it's a complex field. Groundbreaking research. Energy solutions. Global impact. Mr. Sterling was a visionary."

"Visionaries often attract attention," Jenkins interjected smoothly, her voice a calm current against Miller's undertow. "Were there any specific projects Sterling was working on recently that caused him particular stress or concern? Any... adversaries?"

"Adversaries?" Finch echoed, a faint tremor in his voice. "The competitive landscape is fierce, of course. But Mr. Sterling was adept at navigating it. He had... certain individuals who disagreed with his direction, his vision for the future. But threats? No. Not in the way you mean."

Miller leaned forward. "Mr. Finch, Ms. Vance was found dead two days after Mr. Sterling. She was a journalist, investigating Aether Dynamics. Her notes suggested she believed Sterling was either being coerced or was secretly gathering evidence against the company. Do you have any insight into that? Did Sterling ever confide in you about Ms. Vance, or about any... internal discrepancies within Aether Dynamics?"

The executive visibly flinched at the mention of Vance. "Ms. Vance? I... I'm not familiar with her. Mr. Sterling never mentioned her. And as for discrepancies... Aether Dynamics is a monolithic entity. There are always differing opinions, of course, but nothing that would suggest... this." He gestured vaguely, as if trying to encompass the enormity of their predicament within the confines of the room.

"Differing opinions," Miller mused, a sardonic edge to his tone. "Like the differing opinions that might lead someone to create a tiny, carved wooden bird and leave it with a dead man, and then replicate that gesture for a dead woman? That kind of differing opinion?"

Finch's face paled. "I... I don't know what you're talking about. Birds? I... I'm sorry, Detective. I'm not privy to Mr. Sterling's... personal eccentricities. Or Ms. Vance's. My relationship with Mr. Sterling was purely professional."

The evasiveness was palpable, a thick fog settling around them. Finch was either remarkably well-rehearsed in his ignorance or genuinely terrified. Miller suspected the latter, but terror could be a powerful motivator for silence as much as for confession.

Later, in another sterile room, they faced Eleanor Vance's editor, a man named Rostova, whose weariness seemed etched into the very lines of his face. He clutched a worn briefcase as if it were a shield.

"Eleanor was tenacious," Rostova said, his voice raspy. "Relentless. When she sank her teeth into a story, she didn't let go. Aether Dynamics was her white whale. She'd been working on it for months, piecing together fragments, whispers. She believed Sterling was her key."

"Did she ever express concern about her safety while pursuing this story?" Jenkins asked, her tone gentle, inviting confidence.

Rostova sighed, running a hand over his thinning hair. "She'd made a few cryptic remarks. Said she felt... watched. That some of the information she was getting was too dangerous to keep in her usual notes. She was being unusually careful. She'd even compartmentalized her research, breaking it down into coded segments. She was worried someone on that ship might be connected to Aether Dynamics, someone who knew she was closing in."

"Did she mention Sterling specifically in her recent communications with you?" Miller pressed. "Did she say what kind of 'key' he was?"

"She believed Sterling was either gathering evidence himself, perhaps planning to defect, or that he was being forced to continue with a project he knew was wrong," Rostova explained. "She said he was the linchpin. If she could get to him, or get access to his data, she could expose the whole operation. She'd even hinted at receiving anonymous tips, anonymous communications, that seemed to confirm her suspicions about Sterling's position."

"Anonymous tips? Did she say who they were from?" Miller's mind raced. Was this a double-cross? A game of manipulation orchestrated by the killer?

"No. She was cagey about the source. Said it was too sensitive. She was supposed to meet with someone on the

Odyssey. A clandestine exchange, she implied. She thought Sterling might be the one to meet, or at least, someone connected to him." Rostova shifted uncomfortably. "She also mentioned threats. Vague ones. Like being bumped into in a hallway, or a message left on her cabin door that was removed before she could properly read it. Little things that made her uneasy."

Miller's gaze hardened. "Little things that, in retrospect, were anything but. Did she mention any specific individuals she was suspicious of on board, beyond Sterling?"

"Only that she felt someone was keeping an eye on her," Rostova admitted. "She thought it might be an Aether Dynamics operative, someone tasked with monitoring anyone who got too close. She described seeing a man, she thought, always a few paces behind her in the corridors, but he'd always disappear before she could get a good look at him."

"A man," Jenkins murmured, making a note. "Can you describe him?"

"No, Eleanor didn't get a look," Rostova said, frustration coloring his tone. "She said he was like a shadow. Always just out of focus. But she did mention that Thorne, the ship's head of security, seemed... overly helpful. Almost insistent on escorting her to certain areas, or offering 'assistance' with her research requests. She found it a bit much, said it felt more like surveillance than support."

Thorne. The unnervingly calm security chief. Miller's gut tightened. The man who had presented them with a flawless security record, a man who had been intimately involved in the movements of both victims.

The interviews continued, a monotonous procession of passengers and crew members, each adding a tiny, often contradictory, piece to the fractured mosaic. A wealthy industrialist who had shared a cordial handshake with Sterling hours before his death, now professing complete ignorance, his eyes darting nervously towards the cabin door. A steward who claimed to have seen Vance arguing heatedly with an unidentified man on the promenade deck the night before she died, only to recant under pressure, mumbling about poor lighting and unreliable memory. A musician in the ship's orchestra who reported overhearing a hushed, tense conversation between Sterling and an unknown individual in a dimly lit lounge, the words "frequency" and "unraveling" just audible.

Each conversation was a labyrinth of half-truths, evasions, and carefully constructed amnesia. Some passengers, accustomed to the anonymity of cruise ship travel, seemed genuinely bewildered, their lives untouched by the undercurrents of corporate espionage and murder. Others, however, displayed a disquieting awareness, their answers laced with a carefully veiled apprehension. There was a palpable sense of fear permeating the ship, a primal instinct that whispered of predators among them, of the fragile boundary between luxury and oblivion.

Miller felt the walls of his patience closing in. He was used to the directness of street-level crime, the raw, unfiltered desperation. This was different. This was a silken web of deceit, spun by hands that were accustomed to power and the manipulation of truth. The security protocols, initially implemented to ensure passenger safety, now served as an unwitting barrier, limiting their access, slowing their progress, and inadvertently protecting the very people they needed to interrogate. Every door seemed to lead to another locked room, every answer to a new question.

One passenger, a retired academic named Professor Albright, whose initial statement had been one of polite detachment, became more forthcoming after Miller pushed him on his proximity to Sterling's suite on the night of the murder. Albright, a man with keen eyes that seemed to miss little, finally admitted to hearing raised voices from Sterling's cabin.

"It was not a typical argument," Albright explained, his voice hushed, as if even recounting it now carried a risk. "It was... fervent. Almost desperate. I heard Sterling say, 'It's too dangerous. We cannot proceed.' And then another voice, deeper, colder, replied, 'You have no choice. The frequencies are set. The unraveling has begun.'"

Frequencies. Unraveling. The same words from the orchestra musician. Sterling's research. Vance's theories about weaponization. The connection was undeniable, a thread of dread weaving through the disparate accounts. But the identity of the second voice remained a phantom.

"Did you see who Sterling was speaking with, Professor?" Jenkins inquired softly.

Albright shook his head. "No. The door was closed. I only heard the muffled tones. But the intensity... it was chilling. It was not the sound of a business disagreement. It was the sound of a man realizing he had unleashed something he could no longer control."

As they left Albright, Miller saw Thorne standing at the end of the corridor, his arms crossed, his expression unreadable. Thorne met Miller's gaze, a subtle nod that could have meant anything from acknowledgment to a veiled warning. The security chief was everywhere, an ever-present reminder of their limitations, a constant question mark hanging over their investigation.

The fear on the ship was not just of the killer, Miller realized. It was a deeper, more insidious fear of discovery, of exposure. People were not just hiding the truth; they were hiding themselves, their potential complicity, their own vulnerabilities. The wooden bird, that meticulously crafted signature, was more than just a calling card; it was a symbol of absolute control, a chilling testament to the killer's ability to sow discord and terror, leaving everyone on board a potential suspect, a potential victim, adrift in a sea of suspicion. The

Odyssey, a floating monument to excess, had become a pressurized chamber of secrets, and Miller and Jenkins were trapped inside, desperately trying to find the source of the leak before the entire vessel went under. The evasiveness of the witnesses, the carefully constructed narratives of ignorance, only served to solidify Miller's conviction: the killer was not acting alone, or at least, they had cultivated a network of fear and silence that was as formidable as any physical security system Thorne could devise. They were not just hunting a murderer; they were unraveling a conspiracy, and the threads were as intricate and delicate as the carvings on a wooden bird.

The diminutive wooden effigy, clutched so tightly in the dead industrialist's hand, had begun to whisper its secrets. Detective Miller, a man who usually found solace in the stark logic of evidence, felt an almost anachronistic pull towards the primal language of symbols. The initial assessment had been dismissive: a trinket, a morbid joke, a distraction. But the sheer meticulousness of its craftsmanship, the deliberate placement at each crime scene – first Sterling, then Vance – nagged at him. It was too precise to be random. It was a signature, as the chapter title suggested, but what did it *mean*?

Jenkins, ever the pragmatist, had initially focused on the wood itself. "It's a common hardwood, Detective," she'd reported, her brow furrowed as she examined the magnified images on her tablet. "Possibly teak, or a similar dense grain. Nothing immediately indicative of a rare or exotic origin. The carving, however..." She paused, zooming in on the delicate feathering and the almost unsettling lifelike quality of the avian form. "It's incredibly detailed. Not the work of an amateur. Look at the eyes. They're almost... alive. Like they're watching you."

Miller leaned closer, the sterile light of the precinct office glinting off the screen. The bird's eyes, tiny pinpricks of darker wood, seemed to possess an uncanny depth. They were carved in such a way that, no matter the angle of observation, they appeared to fix on the viewer with an unnerving, almost sentient gaze. It was a chilling detail, one that amplified the sense of being observed, of being played. This wasn't just a killer leaving a calling card; it was a killer who understood the power of perception, who was deliberately imbuing their symbol with a watchful malevolence.

"It's more than just detail, Jenkins," Miller murmured, his fingers tracing the curve of the bird's wing on the screen. "There's a style here. A distinctiveness. It's not just a generic bird. There's an... emotional resonance to it, wouldn't you say?"

Jenkins considered this, tapping a finger against her chin. "Perhaps. It conveys a certain solemnity. A sense of... ancient artistry. But 'emotional resonance' is a bit subjective for a murder investigation, Detective."

"Is it?" Miller countered, his gaze still fixed on the screen. "Or is it the very thing that makes this killer different? This isn't a crime of passion, or a random act of violence. This is... curated. Deliberate. And this bird is the centerpiece of that curation. It has to mean something beyond just a morbid flourish."

He'd spent hours poring over databases, cross-referencing images of folk art, indigenous carvings, anything that might bear a resemblance. Most of it was dead ends – generic depictions of birds, mass-produced tourist trinkets. But then, he'd stumbled upon something. A grainy photograph, pulled from an obscure anthropological journal, depicting a series of carvings found on a remote island chain in the South Pacific. The style was remarkably similar. The angular, almost stylized representation of the wings, the delicate rendering of the beak, and most striking of all, the distinctive carving of the eyes.

"Jenkins, take a look at this," Miller said, his voice taut with a sudden surge of adrenaline. He turned his tablet towards her, displaying the image of the island carvings.

Jenkins leaned in, her professional skepticism warring with a dawning curiosity. "My God," she breathed, her eyes widening. "That's... that's the same aesthetic. The same precision."

The image showed a collection of carved wooden totems, weathered and ancient, depicting various animals and figures. One in particular, a bird of prey with an unnervingly similar posture and those same unnervingly watchful eyes, stood out. The accompanying text was sparse, referencing a small, isolated community on the island of Xylos, known for its isolationist tendencies and its highly developed tradition of woodcraft. Xylos, the text explained, had historically been a place where individuals seeking to disappear – fugitives, dissidents, those seeking to escape the long arm of the law or their pasts – would seek refuge, their anonymity protected by the island's remoteness and the tight-knit nature of its inhabitants.

"Xylos," Miller repeated, the name a foreign, resonant sound. "The 'Island of Whispers,' as the journal calls it. Known for its isolation, its intricate woodcraft, and a history of... harboring those who wish to remain unseen. This bird is a message."

"But to what end, Detective?" Jenkins asked, her mind already racing through the implications. "Is the killer from Xylos? Or are they simply using the island's reputation, its symbolism, to mislead us? The journal mentions that Xylos was a place where ancient tribal legends were still very much alive. Perhaps this bird represents a specific legend? A warning, or a curse?"

"Or a tribal emblem, a marker of belonging," Miller mused, his thoughts a tangled web of possibilities. "If the killer is from Xylos, it ties them to a very specific, very isolated community. It suggests a certain cultural background, a specific set of beliefs. Or," he continued, a new, chilling thought taking root, "they could be someone who knows about Xylos, someone who wants us to

think they're from there. A deliberate misdirection, designed to send us chasing ghosts in the Pacific while they continue their work here, in plain sight."

The implications of the Xylos connection were vast. If the killer was indeed from that island, or had strong ties to it, it could explain the almost ritualistic nature of the killings, the calculated anonymity, the deliberate symbolism. The journal spoke of a culture where storytelling was paramount, where the natural world was imbued with spiritual significance. A carved bird, especially one with such watchful eyes, could carry a multitude of meanings within such a context. It might represent a guardian spirit, a harbinger of doom, or a symbol of retribution for those who strayed from the island's unwritten laws, or worse, those who trespassed upon its secrets.

Miller's mind flashed back to Finch, the nervous executive. His evasiveness, his carefully constructed ignorance. Had he known about Xylos? Or had he simply been afraid of revealing anything that might implicate himself or Aether Dynamics in something so... primal? Sterling, the visionary CEO, a man whose life was supposedly consumed by cutting-edge energy solutions, now linked to a remote island and an ancient symbol. It was a jarring dichotomy, a dissonant chord in the symphony of corporate ambition.

"Let's consider the 'fleeing fugitive' angle," Miller said, leaning back in his chair, the image of the Xylos carving still burned into his mind. "If Xylos is a place where people go to disappear, then our killer might be someone who is actively trying to disappear, or someone who has successfully done so in the past. They're using the symbol of their supposed refuge as a banner."

"But why reveal themselves at all?" Jenkins questioned, ever the voice of logical inquiry. "If they're so adept at disappearing, why leave a calling card that could potentially lead back to them, or at least to a specific region?"

"Because they *want* us to follow the trail," Miller said, a grim certainty hardening his voice. "It's a game. They're not just killing; they're taunting us. They're testing our intellect, our ability to decipher their message. The bird's eyes, Jenkins – they're not just carvings. They're a challenge. A dare. 'See me,' they're saying. 'Understand me. But you'll never catch me.'"

The journal also offered a tantalizing detail about the wood used in Xylos carvings. While the teak-like wood of the effigy found on the ship was common, the Xylos artisans were known for their use of a specific, dark-grained wood that was notoriously difficult to source outside the islands. If they could identify the precise type of wood, it could provide a more definitive link. Jenkins had already dispatched a request to the lab for a more detailed analysis, but the preliminary results were inconclusive, pointing to a dense hardwood, but not necessarily the rare Xylos variety.

"The journal mentions that Xylos had a long-standing tradition of storytelling through carvings," Jenkins added, scrolling through the digital pages. "These weren't just decorative. They were historical records, moral lessons, warnings. If this bird is part of that tradition, it could be conveying a specific narrative. Perhaps a story about a predator and its prey, or a tale of betrayal and consequence."

Miller nodded, picturing Sterling and Vance as the prey in such a narrative. "And the fact that it's found with their bodies means they are the embodiment of that narrative. They are the ones who have suffered the consequence. The question is, what was their transgression? Was it something they did to someone from Xylos, or something that someone from Xylos perceived as a transgression against their way of life, their secrets?"

He remembered the vague threats Eleanor Vance had alluded to, the feeling of being watched, the physical encounters in the ship's corridors. These weren't the actions of a random killer. They were the calculated moves of someone who was methodically eliminating obstacles, someone who was silencing those who threatened to expose them. And the wooden bird, that intricate effigy with its ever-watchful eyes, was the silent sentinel at the heart of it all, a stark reminder of the killer's presence, their reach, and their chilling intent. It was a symbol of exile, of judgment, and perhaps, of an ancient form of justice being meted out on the high seas. The investigation had just taken a sharp, unexpected turn, veering away from the sterile corporate world of Aether Dynamics and plunging into the shadowy depths of a forgotten island and its deep-seated traditions. The bird, it seemed, was not just a signature; it was a gateway.

The air aboard the *Odyssey* had grown thick with an unspoken dread, a miasma that seeped from the polished mahogany and the hushed whispers of the terrified passengers. What had begun as a luxurious voyage of discovery had curdled into a maritime prison, each luxurious cabin now a cell, its occupants a collection of potential victims or, worse, suspects. The once vibrant social spaces were deserted, the hum of conversation replaced by the creak of the ship and the frantic beating of hearts. Every creak of the hull, every distant metallic clang, was magnified, distorted into the sound of an approaching threat.

Detective Miles Miller felt the suffocating weight of it press down on him. He was used to the controlled chaos of a crime scene, the methodical piecing together of evidence in the sterile, controlled environment of a precinct. But here, adrift on an endless expanse of indifferent ocean, the rules had changed. Walls did not confine the killer; they were an unseen force moving within the very arteries of the vessel, a phantom that could emerge from any shadowed alcove, any darkened stairwell. His reputation, built on a foundation of meticulous detail and unwavering logic, felt increasingly fragile, threatened by the sheer, unpredictable terror that had gripped the ship. The clock was ticking, each passing hour bringing them closer to docking, and with it, the potential for the killer to vanish into the anonymity of a bustling port.

"They're terrified, Miles," Sergeant Jenkins said, her voice low and strained as they stood on the Promenade Deck, the wind whipping strands of hair across her face. Below them, the churning, slate-grey water offered no solace, only an endless expanse that seemed to mirror the growing despair on board. "The Captain Rostova's ordered everyone to remain in their cabins, but I don't think it's helping. It's just making them stew in their own fear."

Captain Rostova Eva Rostova, a woman whose stern demeanor had been her armor against the usual challenges of command, now looked like a general leading a besieged army. Her face, usually a mask of unwavering authority, was etched with fatigue and a gnawing anxiety. She had done everything in her power to maintain order, to project an image of control, but the audacious nature of the killer's actions, the unsettling symbolism of the carved bird, was chipping away at her resolve. Each new incident, however minor, was met with an almost frantic desire to quash it, to prevent the panic from spiraling further out of control.

"We're doing all we can, Detective," Rostova had stated earlier, her voice tight, during a tense briefing in her cramped, oak-paneled office. The air had been heavy with the scent of stale coffee and desperation. "The crew is maintaining a constant patrol, all access points are secured. But this ship... it's a labyrinth. And our killer is a ghost within it." She had clasped her hands, her knuckles white. "My passengers are my responsibility. And my crew. I cannot have this... this madness... continue."

Miller had met her gaze, the sheer intensity of the situation mirroring the glint in her eyes. "We understand, Captain Rostova. But 'ghosts' don't leave physical evidence. That effigy... it's a tangible link. We need to understand its origin, its meaning, and that will lead us to our perpetrator." He had paused, allowing the weight of his words to settle. "The paranoia, Captain Rostova, is almost as dangerous as the killer. It's fracturing the sense of community on board, turning people against each other."

And it was true. The fear had a corrosive effect. The passengers, accustomed to a world of curated experiences and effortless luxury, were now trapped with the stark reality of vulnerability. They eyed each other with newfound apprehension, their fellow travelers transformed from potential vacation companions into potential murderers. The opulent salons, once filled with laughter and clinking glasses, now echoed with the unnerving silence of suspicion. A nervous cough from a stranger in the corridor could send a jolt of adrenaline through a passenger, their mind conjuring images of the wooden bird, of the cold, calculating hand that had placed it.

Jenkins had described it in chilling detail after a discreet interview with a distraught couple in their suite. "They said they heard... movement, last night," she'd reported, her voice barely above a whisper. "Footsteps outside their door. But when they looked through the peephole, there was no one there. Just an empty corridor. They're convinced it was him, watching them, toying with them." The paranoia, Miller realized, was not just a byproduct of the killings; it was a weapon the killer was wielding, subtly amplifying the terror, sowing discord.

Miller felt the pressure building, not just from the Captain Rostova or the dwindling time until landfall, but from within himself. He was a man who thrived on order, on the satisfying click of puzzle pieces falling into place. This case, however, was a chaotic vortex, pulling him into its depths. The meticulous nature of the crimes, the artistic precision of the bird effigy, the unsettling connection to a remote island – it all felt designed to obfuscate, to lead him on a wild goose chase. Yet, the instinct that had served him for years, that gut feeling honed by countless investigations, told him the answer was here, on this ship, hidden amongst the fearful faces and the anxious glances.

He found himself scrutinizing every crew member, every passenger he encountered. Was that twitch of an eye a sign of guilt or simply nerves? Was that overly polite demeanor a mask for something sinister? He saw the killer's signature not just in the effigy, but in the very atmosphere of fear that permeated the ship. The bird's eyes, so unnervingly lifelike, seemed to be replicated in the wary, darting gazes of those around him.

"We need to find the source of that carving, Jenkins," Miller said, his voice firm, cutting through the rising tide of unease. "If we can trace the wood, the style, to a specific artisan or a specific region beyond Xylos, it might give us a more concrete lead. The journal was vague about the exact type of wood, but it emphasized its rarity outside the islands." He thought back to the initial lab reports, the inconclusive findings. "We need them to push harder. Is there any way to differentiate between generic hardwoods and something more specific? Even if it's not Xylos wood, perhaps a similar exotic timber used by someone with knowledge of their craft?"

Jenkins nodded, pulling out her tablet. "I'll put in another request. Emphasize the urgency. And I'll also look into any known timber importers, any rare wood dealers who might have supplied something of that description, however unlikely." She scrolled through a list of names on the ship's manifest, her brow furrowed in concentration. "We're still working on identifying anyone with a direct connection to the islands, or anyone with a background in intricate woodworking. It's a needle in a haystack, but we have to keep looking."

The Captain Rostova's concerns about maintaining order were echoed in the increasingly tense interactions between passengers and crew. Minor infractions – a passenger venturing out of their cabin for a breath of fresh air, a brief exchange in a corridor – were met with swift, almost draconian responses. Rostova was determined to project an image of absolute control, but her methods, born of desperation, were only serving to heighten the sense of unease, to amplify the feeling of being trapped and monitored.

Miller watched a uniformed crew member escorting a woman back to her cabin, her face pale with a mixture of fear and indignation. The woman had been overheard speaking too loudly, her voice carrying down the hallway, and now she was being treated as if she had committed a serious offense. "It's like a pressure cooker in here, Sergeant," Miller murmured, the incident weighing on him. "The Captain Rostova's trying to keep a lid on it, but all this strictness... it's just making the steam build up faster."

Jenkins sighed, rubbing her temples. "She's scared, Miles. We all are. But her fear is manifesting as control. She's trying to control the environment, the people, because she can't control the killer." She paused, her gaze drifting towards the dark, unforgiving expanse of the ocean. "What if the killer intended this? What if the isolation, the confinement, the heightened fear... what if it's all part of their plan? To make us crack?"

Miller looked at her, a grim understanding dawning on his face. The killer was not just eliminating Sterling and Vance; they were orchestrating a symphony of terror, using the ship itself as their instrument. The meticulous carving was merely the overture, the visible manifestation of a deeper, more insidious design. The paranoia spreading amongst the passengers and crew was the killer's true signature, a more potent and far-reaching mark than any wooden effigy. It was a psychological weapon, designed to erode trust, to sow chaos, and to create an environment where the killer could operate with even greater impunity.

He thought of Vance's increasingly frantic communications, Sterling's sudden withdrawal. Had they felt this mounting pressure, this creeping paranoia, before their deaths? Had the fear been a precursor to their final moments? The image of the bird, with its unblinking, carved eyes, flashed in his mind. It wasn't just watching the victims; it was watching everyone. It was the silent, unblinking eye of the killer, observing their fear, savoring their paranoia. And Miller knew, with a chilling certainty, that they were all, every soul aboard the

Odyssey, caught in the killer's suffocating gaze. The pressure was not just mounting; it was becoming an unbearable, crushing weight.

Chapter 6: The Corporate Conspiracy Unraveled

The dim glow of Sterling's laptop screen cast long shadows across the cabin, a stark contrast to the opulent grandeur that usually defined the *Odyssey*'s suites. Detective Miles Miller leaned closer, his brow furrowed in intense concentration. Beside him, Sergeant Jenkins's fingers danced across the keyboard, a silent ballet of keystrokes against the backdrop of the ship's gentle hum. They had finally breached the outer layers of Sterling's encrypted hard drive, a digital fortress designed to repel all but the most determined intruders. The initial access had been a triumph of patience and brute force, a testament to their shared, unwavering pursuit of truth. Now, they were faced with a labyrinth of subfolders, each one a potential dead end or a gateway to Sterling's most guarded secrets.

"It's like peeling back layers of an onion, isn't it?" Jenkins murmured, her voice barely audible above the whirring of the laptop's fan. "Each one more pungent than the last." She gestured to the screen. "He had this partition hidden deep. Buried under what looks like innocuous financial data. Took a specialized decryption algorithm to even make it visible."

Miller grunted in agreement, his gaze fixed on the intricate file structure displayed before them. "Sterling wasn't just a victim, Jenkins. He was playing in the same league, or at least he had access to the playbook. The question is, was he a player, a strategist, or just a pawn?"

They had spent hours painstakingly navigating through Sterling's digital life, sifting through the mundane – travel itineraries, personal correspondence, innocuous browsing history – searching for any anomaly. The discovery of the hidden partition had been a breakthrough, a jolt of adrenaline that cut through the growing fatigue. Now, the real work began: deciphering the contents of Sterling's digital vault. The initial examination of Sterling's belongings, conducted under the watchful eyes of the ship's

Captain Rostova and under Miller's careful supervision, had yielded little. A meticulously organized briefcase, a pristine laptop, a personal journal filled with cryptic musings that seemed more philosophical than criminal. But the journal, while offering glimpses into Sterling's state of mind, had been frustratingly vague. It hinted at vast financial dealings, at 'unseen forces' and 'calculated risks,' but never provided concrete details. The encrypted laptop, however, was a different story. It was a direct pipeline into the man's professional life, a digital confession waiting to be unlocked.

Jenkins's fingers stilled. "I've found something. A directory labeled 'Project Nightingale.' And it's heavily encrypted. Military-grade, I'd say. Sterling had some serious security protocols in place."

"Nightingale," Miller repeated the name, tasting it. It sounded innocuous, almost poetic, a stark contrast to the grim reality they suspected lay beneath. "Try the usual keys first. Anything that might relate to his business, his associates, even his personal life. Birthdays, anniversaries, pet names."

Jenkins chuckled, a dry, humorless sound. "Detective, if only it were that simple. This isn't some amateur password. This is layered. Multiple encryption algorithms, each one requiring a specific key sequence. It's like a digital Rubik's Cube, but with the power to ruin lives." She began typing again, a focused intensity radiating from her. "I'm running a brute-force script on some common variants, but it's going to take time. Hours, perhaps days, if he was truly paranoid."

Miller leaned back, the small cabin suddenly feeling even more cramped. The rhythmic tapping of Jenkins's keyboard was the only sound, a stark reminder of their isolation and the ticking clock. They were adrift on an ocean of fear and suspicion, and the killer was still amongst them, a phantom in the luxurious shell of the

Odyssey. Every moment spent here, deciphering Sterling's secrets, was a moment the perpetrator could be using to further their own agenda, or to cover their tracks. The carved bird, a grotesque calling card, had been placed with chilling precision. It was a symbol, they believed, of something far greater than a personal vendetta.

"What kind of data do you think we're looking for, Jenkins?" Miller asked, his voice low. "Sterling wasn't just some rich businessman. He was connected to some very powerful people, people who could make problems disappear. If he was involved in something illegal, it had to be big. Catastrophic, even."

"Given the security, and the fact he went to such lengths to hide it," Jenkins replied, not looking up from her screen, "I'd hazard a guess it's something he couldn't afford to have found. Something that could destroy his career, his company, maybe even land him in prison. And if he was preparing this, storing it like this, he must have been expecting it to be found, or planning to use it himself."

A new thought struck Miller. "What if Sterling wasn't just hoarding data, but preparing to leak it? What if he was planning to expose something, and someone found out?" The carved bird then took on a new meaning, a message not just of death, but of silencing.

Jenkins finally paused, stretching her fingers. "I've managed to crack the first layer. 'Nightingale' was a clever misdirection. The actual key phrase was 'Icarus.'"

Miller's eyes widened. "Icarus. Flying too close to the sun." He looked at Jenkins, a grim understanding passing between them. "He knew the risks. He was warned."

"Indeed," Jenkins said, her voice regaining its usual professional edge. "And the second layer is... 'Apollo.' The sun god. Together, 'Icarus' and 'Apollo'... it paints a rather dramatic picture, doesn't it?"

The second layer of encryption dissolved, revealing a surprisingly organized file structure. Folders named with cryptic alphanumeric codes, interspersed with project titles that were chillingly direct: 'Market Manipulation,' 'Competitive Sabotage,' 'Data Harvesting Protocol.'

"This is it," Miller breathed, leaning forward again. "This is what he was hiding."

Jenkins began to navigate through the folders, her initial excitement tempered by the gravity of what they were uncovering. "'Market Manipulation'... this folder contains detailed reports, spreadsheets, communication logs. It looks like... an elaborate scheme to artificially inflate the stock prices of certain tech companies. Then, simultaneously, shorting the stocks of their competitors to drive them into the ground."

Miller's mind raced. The scale of such an operation was staggering. This wasn't just insider trading; this was orchestrated economic warfare, a calculated dismantling of rival businesses for immense profit. "Who were the targets? Who were the beneficiaries?"

"The beneficiaries are listed as shell corporations," Jenkins reported, her fingers flying across the keyboard. "Dozens of them, all registered in offshore havens. But the transactions... they all trace back to a single holding company. Sterling's company, 'Ascendant Global Solutions.'"

Ascendant Global Solutions. Miller recalled the name. A titan in the tech industry, a firm known for its innovative AI and data analytics platforms. They had a reputation for aggressive expansion, but this... this was beyond aggressive. This was criminal.

"And the targets?" Miller pressed, his gaze fixed on the screen.

"Several major players in the AI development sector," Jenkins said, her voice tightening. "Companies that were on the verge of releasing groundbreaking technology. Technology that, according to these internal memos, Ascendant Global Solutions deemed a threat to their dominance."

The implications were terrifying. Sterling wasn't just trying to make money; he was actively working to suppress innovation, to control the global technological landscape by any means necessary. The data mining wasn't just about understanding market trends; it was about anticipating and neutralizing threats before they could emerge.

"Look at this," Jenkins suddenly exclaimed, pointing to a subfolder within 'Competitive Sabotage.' It was labeled 'Project Chimera.' "This looks like evidence of sabotage. Not just financial, but... physical. They were disabling rival servers, introducing malware that corrupted research data, even leaking proprietary information to create internal chaos."

Miller felt a chill creep down his spine. This was a ruthless, calculated war fought in the digital shadows. The deaths of Sterling and Vance weren't just isolated incidents; they were likely the result of this sprawling conspiracy, a desperate attempt to silence anyone who threatened to expose Ascendant Global Solutions.

"The sheer audacity," Miller murmured, shaking his head. "The level of planning involved. This wasn't a one-off. This was systematic." He looked at the names appearing in the communication logs, executives with titles like 'Chief Strategy Officer' and 'Head of Research and Development.' High-ranking individuals within Ascendant Global Solutions, all seemingly complicit.

"And it goes deeper," Jenkins said, her voice hushed. She had navigated to a folder labeled 'Government Contracts & Influence.' "There are records of... significant donations. To political campaigns. And encrypted communications with individuals identified only by code names, but the timestamps and recipient addresses suggest... they're linked to regulatory bodies and government oversight committees."

The conspiracy, it seemed, had reached into the highest echelons of power. Ascendant Global Solutions wasn't just manipulating markets; they were buying influence, bribing officials to look the other way, to actively assist in their scheme. The tech firm had created a corrupt ecosystem, a closed loop designed to perpetuate their dominance, crushing any competition and stifling any potential challenges.

"This explains everything," Miller said, the pieces clicking into place with a sickening finality. "Sterling and Vance were likely instrumental in setting this up. But at some point, they must have had a falling out. Sterling, especially, with his cryptic journal entries about 'risks' and 'necessary sacrifices.' He was clearly aware of the moral implications."

"Or," Jenkins interjected, her fingers still tracing the digital threads of corruption, "they became liabilities. If Vance was planning to defect, or Sterling was about to break ranks and go public, then silencing them would have been a priority for whoever was at the top of this operation."

The evidence was overwhelming, a digital smoking gun that pointed to a vast network of corruption spanning corporate America and potentially reaching into the halls of government. The scale of the operation was far beyond anything Miller had anticipated. This wasn't just about a few shady deals; it was about a fundamental manipulation of global markets, a technological stranglehold designed to consolidate power and wealth in the hands of a select few.

"We need to secure this data, Jenkins," Miller said, his voice firm. "Every single file. This is evidence of a crime that transcends international borders and affects millions of people. We need to make sure it doesn't fall into the wrong hands. Especially not into the hands of Ascendant Global Solutions."

Jenkins nodded, initiating a secure transfer protocol to an encrypted external drive they had brought with them. "I'm also flagging specific files. The communications logs with the government officials, the detailed plans for market manipulation, the sabotage reports. These are the critical pieces."

Miller looked back at the screen, at the stark reality of the conspiracy laid bare. Project Nightingale, Project Chimera, the masked manipulators of global markets, the corrupting influence on government. It was all there, a testament to Sterling's hidden life, a life lived on the precipice of immense power and profound corruption. He wondered if Sterling had ever truly believed he was in control, or if he had, like Icarus, flown too close to the sun, ultimately consumed by the very power he sought to wield. The carved bird, he realized, wasn't just a symbol of death; it was a symbol of exposure, of the inevitable downfall that awaits those who play God with the world's economies. And now, they held the key to that downfall, a digital Pandora's Box that could unleash a reckoning upon those who had operated in the shadows for too long. The weight of the discovery settled upon Miller, a burden of knowledge that felt heavier than any physical evidence he had ever encountered. This was no longer just a murder investigation; it was an unraveling of a conspiracy that had the potential to reshape the global economic and political landscape. The fate of many, it seemed, now rested on the digital ghost of Arthur Sterling.

The hum of the forensic lab was a familiar lullaby to Detective Miles Miller, a stark contrast to the chilling silence that had enveloped the *Odyssey* just days before. Sergeant Jenkins, her usual focused intensity amplified, meticulously cataloged the contents of the journalist Amelia Vance's apartment. It was a space that spoke of a life lived in pursuit of truth, albeit a life tragically cut short. Stacks of research papers, overflowing bookshelves, and a cluttered desk testament to Vance's dedication. The air still carried the faint scent of old paper and the metallic tang of spilled coffee, a ghostly reminder of her presence.

"She was thorough, Miles," Jenkins commented, carefully bagging a series of handwritten notes. "More than thorough. She was a terrier with a bone, digging deep. And judging by the sheer volume of material, she'd unearthed something big."

Miller nodded, his gaze sweeping over the organized chaos. Vance's apartment was a journalist's den, a carefully curated mess of leads, interviews, and dead ends. He picked up a worn notebook, its pages filled with Vance's hurried scrawl. Dates, names, fragments of overheard conversations, and endless abbreviations – the raw material of investigative journalism. It was a language he understood, the vernacular of suspicion and the pursuit of hidden narratives.

"She was close," Miller mused, turning a page. "Very close. The Captain Rostova confirmed it. Vance had requested a secure, off-the-record meeting on the

Odyssey just hours before she was found. Someone on board was supposed to give her something. Something that made her so anxious, so determined to meet that she risked the voyage."

Jenkins stopped her work, looking up. "An informant. She was meeting an informant." Her voice was low, the implication hanging heavy in the air. An informant who, for whatever reason, had either failed to show up or had been silenced along with Vance. "Do we have any leads on who it might have been? Any names in her communications that stand out?"

They had spent the last few days sifting through Vance's digital life, a process that mirrored their painstaking decryption of Sterling's hard drive, albeit with fewer encryption layers to contend with. Vance, while protected, was not as paranoid as Sterling. Her emails, text messages, and cloud storage were a treasure trove of fragmented information, a puzzle with many missing pieces. They'd found references to Ascendant Global Solutions, of course, the behemoth corporation that Sterling had served, but Vance's focus seemed to be on a more specific, clandestine operation.

"She had a particular fixation on something she referred to as 'Project Nightingale,'" Jenkins said, pulling up a file on her tablet. "It appears in several of her drafts, interspersed with mentions of market manipulation and data breaches. She'd even highlighted it in a few of her physical notes."

Miller picked up another notebook, flipping through its pages. "Here it is. A date, just two days before she died. 'Nightingale. Meeting. A.S. – need proof.' And then, a series of question marks and a doodle of a broken cage."

"A.S.?" Jenkins prompted. "Arthur Sterling?"

"It's possible," Miller conceded. "But Sterling was the target of her investigation, not necessarily her source. Unless... he was both. Unless he was trying to confess, to spill the beans, and she was his chosen confidante."

"Or," Jenkins countered, her brow furrowed in thought, " 'A.S.' could refer to someone else entirely within Ascendant Global Solutions. Someone who had access to 'Project Nightingale' and was feeding Vance information to expose it. Someone who felt threatened, or perhaps guilty."

The idea of an internal whistleblower wasn't new, but it added a dangerous dimension. If Vance's informant was still within Ascendant, they were not only a potential victim but also a potential conspirator, or at least someone holding the keys to the entire operation. The 'broken cage' symbol was particularly unsettling. A symbol of escape? A warning that the cage, once broken, could lead to something far worse?

Jenkins scrolled through Vance's encrypted messaging app. "Most of her conversations are with her editor, or with sources identified by pseudonyms. But there are a few encrypted exchanges with someone she only called 'Whisper.' The timestamps suggest they were in regular contact over the past few weeks. Vance seemed to rely heavily on Whisper's intel."

"Whisper," Miller echoed, the name conjuring images of shadows and hushed secrets. "What kind of information was Whisper providing?"

"Highly sensitive," Jenkins confirmed, her fingers flying across the screen. "Details about Ascendant's proprietary algorithms, internal memos regarding market strategy, and increasingly, references to 'Nightingale.' It seems Whisper was the one consistently pointing Vance towards this project."

Miller's mind began to connect the dots. Sterling's encrypted drive had contained a folder labeled 'Project Nightingale.' Vance had been investigating it. She had an informant codenamed 'Whisper' who was feeding her information about it. And she was killed just before a crucial meeting, presumably with this informant, or perhaps with Sterling himself.

"Project Nightingale," Miller repeated, the name now feeling less like a poetic misdirection and more like a central, terrifying hub of the conspiracy. "What was it, Jenkins? What was Vance so desperate to uncover that she risked her life?"

Jenkins tapped away, her expression growing more serious with each passing minute. "According to these fragments from Whisper, Nightingale wasn't just about market manipulation. It was... more advanced. More sinister. Think of it as the ultimate predictive engine. Ascendant Global Solutions wasn't just predicting market trends; they were actively shaping them, and Nightingale was the AI powering that manipulation."

"An AI that could predict and control the market?" Miller asked, a knot of dread tightening in his stomach. "That's not just illegal; that's... godlike. It would give them unprecedented power."

"Exactly," Jenkins confirmed. "Whisper's messages suggest Nightingale could forecast not only stock market fluctuations but also geopolitical events, technological breakthroughs, even societal shifts. Ascendant could then position itself to profit from every conceivable outcome, and more importantly, to actively steer those outcomes in their favor."

The implications were staggering. This wasn't just about accumulating wealth; it was about wielding absolute control. It was a conspiracy that reached beyond the financial sector, touching the very fabric of global society. If Ascendant could predict and influence major events, they could essentially dictate the future.

"The sabotage, the market crashes, the suppression of rival tech firms," Miller mused. "All of it was orchestrated using Nightingale's predictive power. They knew which companies to cripple, which technologies to suppress, long before anyone else had a clue."

"And 'Project Nightingale' itself," Jenkins added, her voice barely a whisper, "was the development and deployment of this AI. But Whisper's latest messages indicate there was a critical flaw, or perhaps a moral objection from someone within the project. Vance was seeking confirmation, concrete evidence that would expose the project's true nature and the people behind it."

The mention of a 'moral objection' resonated with Miller. It mirrored Sterling's cryptic journal entries and his apparent internal conflict. Was Sterling the one feeding Vance information? Was he wrestling with the ethical implications of what Ascendant was doing?

"The meeting Vance had scheduled," Miller said, his gaze fixed on the scattered notes, "was it with Sterling, or with Whisper?"

Jenkins pulled up Vance's calendar. "The entry is simply coded: 'Nightingale's Song. Terminal.' No name, no specific location, just that cryptic phrase. But the timing is crucial. It was set for late on the evening of her death. She was killed in the afternoon, according to the preliminary coroner's report."

"Terminal," Miller repeated, the word now imbued with a chilling finality. "It suggests an endpoint. The end of the project, the end of Ascendant, or perhaps... the end of someone's life." He looked at Jenkins. "If Whisper was feeding her this information, they must have known Vance was in danger. They must have known about the meeting. Why didn't they warn her, or meet her themselves?"

Jenkins's fingers flew across the keyboard, accessing a secure server where Vance had stored some of her more sensitive communications. "I'm accessing a backup of her encrypted chat logs with Whisper. It's slow going... military-grade encryption on their end too." A few tense moments passed, filled only by the rhythmic click of Jenkins's keystrokes. "Got it. The last message from Whisper to Vance, sent just hours before she died."

She turned the tablet towards Miller. The message was short, stark.

"They know. You have to be careful. The proof is in the primary data cache. Don't trust anyone. The cage is about to break, but it will shatter everything."

"'They know,'" Miller read aloud, his voice grim. "So, Ascendant was aware that Vance was getting close. And 'Whisper' knew it too. This confirms it. Vance was meeting someone who was either going to give her the proof, or who was already compromised."

"And the 'primary data cache'?" Jenkins asked, her eyes scanning the fragmented messages. "That's where the concrete evidence of Nightingale resided."

Miller picked up one of Vance's notebooks again, his fingers tracing a series of alphanumeric codes scrawled on a page. They looked like file names, or perhaps server addresses. "These codes... they match some of the cryptic folder names we found on Sterling's drive. The ones within 'Project Nightingale.'"

"You think Sterling had already accessed or copied this 'primary data cache'?" Jenkins questioned, her voice filled with a dawning realization. "He encrypted his drive to protect himself, but maybe he also encrypted the evidence he was holding onto, intending to give it to Vance, or perhaps to use it as leverage."

"Or," Miller said, his gaze hardening, "he was the one who alerted Ascendant to Vance's investigation. If Sterling was deeply entrenched, and realized Vance was about to expose everything, he might have betrayed her to save himself. His death could have been a consequence of that betrayal going wrong, or an attempt by Ascendant to silence both of them."

The possibilities swirled, each more dangerous than the last. The journalist and the victim, both targeted for uncovering the same secret.

"The 'cage' metaphor," Jenkins mused, her eyes distant. "Vance's doodle, Whisper's message... it all points to something being contained, something that was about to be unleashed. Nightingale. The AI. If it's truly as powerful as Whisper suggests, its release, or its control, could indeed shatter everything."

Miller felt a surge of urgency. They were on the cusp of something monumental, a conspiracy that dwarfed anything he had ever encountered. The clues were scattered across two crime scenes, encrypted files, and fragmented digital whispers, but they were all pointing towards the same objective: Project Nightingale.

"We need to find that 'primary data cache,'" Miller stated, his voice firm. "It's the key to everything. If Sterling encrypted it, then that data is still out there, somewhere on his drive or wherever he backed it up. And if Vance got a copy, it's likely hidden within her digital footprint, protected by layers of her own security."

Jenkins nodded, already initiating a deeper scan of Vance's cloud storage and local backups. "I'm cross-referencing the alphanumeric codes from her notes with the file structure on Sterling's drive again. If Sterling had the data, and Vance was trying to get it, there has to be a connection, a digital breadcrumb trail."

The silence in the lab descended again, thick with anticipation. The fate of Arthur Sterling and Amelia Vance, two lives extinguished in the pursuit of a dangerous truth, now rested on their ability to piece together the final fragments of the puzzle. Project Nightingale, the AI that promised to control the world, was about to be exposed. The question was, could Miller and Jenkins expose it before Ascendant Global Solutions silenced them too? The journalist's lead, the ghost of an informant named Whisper, and the cryptic promise of proof – these were the threads they now held, threads that could either unravel the conspiracy or lead them into the same deadly trap that had claimed Vance.

The air in Sergeant Jenkins's makeshift command center, a hastily cleared corner of the precinct's archives, crackled with a mixture of frustration and dawning comprehension. The sterile scent of old paper, usually a comfort, now seemed to carry the musty odor of secrets long buried. Detective Miles Miller leaned back in his chair, the glow of the monitor reflecting in his weary eyes. Amelia Vance's apartment had yielded a wealth of information, a journalist's meticulously kept, albeit tragically incomplete, record of her final investigation. Sterling's encrypted drive, a digital fortress, had surrendered its secrets piece by agonizing piece under Jenkins's relentless digital assault. Now, the disparate threads of their investigations were beginning to weave a chilling tapestry, and a name, previously a ghost in the machine, was starting to solidify.

"Thorne's name popped up again," Jenkins said, her voice a low rumble as she gestured towards a complex network diagram displayed on a secondary screen. Thorne, the supposed victim, the supposed financier of Sterling's clandestine operations, was proving to be less of a puppet and more of a... middleman. His name wasn't appearing in direction, but in connection. "He was facilitating payments, routing funds, but not initiating them. It's like he was a conduit, not the source."

Miller grunted, rubbing his temples. "A conduit for what, or for whom?" He recalled Vance's notes, the frantic scribbles about "Nightingale" and the cryptic reference to "A.S.", Arthur Sterling. Could Sterling have been more than just a programmer caught in a web? Could he have been an unwilling accomplice, a pawn moved by a far greater hand? "We know Sterling was building Nightingale. He was the architect. But who was commissioning the skyscraper?"

Jenkins tapped a few keys, her fingers dancing across the keyboard with practiced precision. "That's where it gets interesting. Thorne's offshore accounts, the ones we've been painstakingly tracing, all lead back to a series of shell corporations. Most of them are dead ends, intentionally so. But one of them, 'Aegis Holdings,' it's... different. It's a legitimate investment firm, registered in Geneva. They've got a public profile, a board of directors, the works. And their primary sector of interest? Advanced AI development, particularly predictive algorithms. Sound familiar?"

A slow, cold dread began to coil in Miller's gut. "Predictive algorithms," he echoed, the words tasting like ash. "Nightingale." He remembered Sterling's panicked entries, the fear etched into his digital diary about the 'unforeseen consequences' and the 'ethical precipice.' Sterling hadn't just been building a tool; he'd been building a weapon. "And Aegis Holdings. Who's at the helm?"

Jenkins brought up a new window, a clean, professional-looking corporate website. High-resolution photos of impeccably dressed individuals stared back at them. "This is where it gets murky. Aegis Holdings is a notoriously private entity. Their board members are listed as representatives of larger, equally obscure investment groups. But there's one name that keeps resurfacing, one individual consistently linked to Aegis's strategic direction and investment portfolio. A man who's been a titan in the tech industry for decades, though he prefers to operate out of the spotlight. He's the ghost in the machine, the unseen hand that steers the market."

She clicked on a photograph. The man in the image was distinguished, his silver hair impeccably styled, his eyes sharp and intelligent, yet... cold. There was an undeniable aura of power about him, a controlled intensity that spoke of immense influence. He looked less like a businessman and more like a chess grandmaster, calmly observing the board while meticulously planning his next move.

"Julian Thorne," Jenkins stated, her voice dropping to a near whisper. "Or rather, Julian Vance. Julian Vance is the current chairman of Aegis Holdings. He's also a... significant shareholder in several foundational AI research companies, the very ones that would have provided the building blocks for something like Nightingale. His name doesn't appear in Sterling's encrypted logs directly. Sterling was too paranoid to risk that. But Thorne's financial activities, the ones that routed money to Sterling's development teams, Vance's investment arm ultimately oversaw them. Thorne was his lieutenant."

Miles Miller stared at the photograph, a chilling recognition dawning. Vance. The name had echoed in the periphery of the investigation, a distant hum that he hadn't yet processed. Julian Vance. The celebrated innovator, the philanthropist, the man whose company had pioneered several breakthroughs in data analytics and machine learning. He was a respected figure, a leader in the very industry that Sterling had helped to advance, and now, it seemed, a potential architect of its darkest secrets.

"Julian Vance," Miller murmured, the name feeling heavy, significant. "He's the one pulling the strings. Thorne was just the enforcer, the bagman. Vance saw Sterling's genius, saw the potential for Nightingale, and decided to weaponize it." He thought back to Amelia Vance's notes, her intense focus on Ascendant Global Solutions and the mysterious 'Project Nightingale.' Was there a connection between the journalist and the tech mogul? The surname... Vance.

"Amelia Vance's notes," Miller said, his mind racing, replaying fragmented passages from his memory. "She was digging into Ascendant, but was she aware of Vance's involvement? Was 'Whisper' feeding her information about Vance, or was Sterling the one trying to communicate through her?"

Jenkins was already sifting through Vance's encrypted communications, cross-referencing names and pseudonyms. "Vance's editor mentioned that Amelia had been pursuing a story about 'unethical AI practices' within the tech sector for months. She'd alluded to a shadowy figure, a 'kingmaker' who manipulated markets through technological advancements. She never named names, but her descriptions... they match Vance perfectly. Wealthy, influential, operates behind the scenes, ruthless."

Miller felt a surge of adrenaline, the cold dread now laced with a fierce determination. "So, Vance knew Sterling was developing Nightingale. He saw the potential for unprecedented control, the ability to not just predict but to

dictate the future. And he used Thorne, and Ascendant, as his instruments to bring it to fruition." He pictured the intricate web of shell corporations, the clandestine funding, the silencing of anyone who got too close. It was a meticulously crafted operation, designed to obscure its true orchestrator.

"But Sterling's journal entries," Jenkins mused, her brow furrowed. "He was conflicted. He spoke of remorse, of wanting to stop. If Vance was his patron, why the internal struggle? Why the fear?"

"Because Sterling wasn't just a programmer," Miller stated, a grim certainty settling in. "He was a conscience. He realized what he had built, what Vance intended to do with it, and he couldn't live with it. He tried to pull out, to expose it, hence the encryption, the hidden data. He was trying to protect himself, and maybe, just maybe, trying to leave a trail for someone to find the truth. Amelia Vance."

The pieces were clicking into place with horrifying speed. Arthur Sterling, the brilliant but troubled programmer, had created 'Project Nightingale,' an AI capable of predicting and manipulating global events. Julian Vance, the influential tech mogul, had recognized its potential and had steered its development through his proxy, Thorne, and Ascendant Global Solutions. When Sterling began to have second thoughts, to exhibit remorse and attempt to expose his creation, Vance had moved to silence him. Sterling, anticipating this, had hidden the evidence, encrypted his work, and perhaps, tried to pass it to a journalist he trusted, or one who was already investigating the same conspiracy.

"The 'A.S.' in Amelia's notes," Miller said, the acronym now resonating with profound meaning. "Arthur Sterling. She was seeking proof, and she believed Sterling had it. But the meeting on the

Odyssey... was it with Sterling, or with someone else Vance had planted to mislead her?"

Jenkins scrolled through more of Vance's digital footprint, focusing on her communications with her editor and her trusted sources. "Amelia was meticulous. She had a separate encrypted channel for her most sensitive contacts. She referred to her informant as 'Deep Echo.' The timing of her messages with 'Deep Echo' directly corresponds with the period Sterling was attempting to encrypt his data and hide it. The language is highly technical, discussing data caches, encryption keys, and the 'unraveling of the Nightingale algorithm.'"

"Deep Echo," Miller repeated. "Was it Sterling? Or was it someone within Ascendant, someone else who had grown a conscience?" He thought of the 'broken cage' symbol Vance had drawn, and the chilling message: 'The cage is about to break, but it will shatter everything.'

"Whisper's last message to Vance," Jenkins reminded him, her gaze fixed on the tablet, "was 'They know. You have to be careful. The proof is in the primary data cache. Don't trust anyone. The cage is about to break, but it will shatter everything.' This was sent hours before she was killed. It confirms Vance's involvement. Ascendant, and by extension, Julian Vance, knew Amelia was getting close. They were aware she was seeking the 'primary data cache.'"

Miller leaned forward, his eyes scanning the screen. "And Sterling's encrypted drive. The folder structure. We found a directory labeled 'Nightingale Archives,' and within it, subfolders with alphanumeric codes that matched some of Vance's notes. If Sterling had the data, and Amelia was trying to access it, it suggests Sterling was the source of that data, or at least a significant part of it."

"It's more than that, Miles," Jenkins said, her voice tight with discovery. "I've been cross-referencing the IP addresses of Sterling's data transfers with Thorne's known associates. And I found a connection. A VPN gateway. It was routed through a server that Ascendant Global Solutions maintains for its 'secure communications.' Sterling wasn't just transferring data; he was transferring it *through* Ascendant's infrastructure, albeit through a highly obfuscated route. He was trying to hide it, but he was still using their systems."

"He was trapped," Miller realized. "He couldn't just dump the data anywhere. He had to use the tools he had, the systems he was already integrated with, to try and preserve it. And Vance, through Ascendant, would have had oversight, even on those obfuscated routes. He would have seen Sterling's activity."

The implications were terrifying. Julian Vance wasn't just an investor; he was an active participant, overseeing the development and protection of Nightingale. He had manipulated Arthur Sterling, likely promising him resources, support, and perhaps even a stake in the project, only to ensnare him in a web of his own making. When Sterling's conscience got the better of him, Vance had initiated the silencing protocol. And when Amelia

Vance, the tenacious journalist, began to unearth the truth, Vance had deployed his assets to neutralize her as well.

"The name 'Vance' appearing in Amelia's notes as 'A.S.' was unlikely," Miller mused, a cold logic taking hold. "But what if she wasn't referring to Arthur Sterling with 'A.S.'? What if 'A.S.' was a misdirection, or a code for someone else entirely? Someone within Ascendant, perhaps? Or what if Sterling was the one trying to communicate about Julian Vance?"

Jenkins shook her head. "The context of her notes strongly suggests 'A.S.' was a source, or at least someone she needed to acquire proof from. Sterling's fragmented writings on his drive confirm his internal conflict over Nightingale. The 'broken cage' symbol, the desire for power, all point to him. He was the one trying to escape, trying to break free from the project and Vance's control."

"So, Vance used Sterling's genius to build Nightingale," Miller summarized, piecing the narrative together. "Then he silenced Sterling when he tried to back out. And when Amelia Vance started digging into Ascendant and Project Nightingale, Vance used his resources, his control over Ascendant, to eliminate her and secure his creation. He's the mastermind. He's been orchestrating this entire conspiracy from the shadows."

The weight of that realization settled heavily in the room. Julian Vance was not just a businessman; he was a puppeteer, pulling the strings of the global economy, capable of orchestrating events on an unimaginable scale. He had the motive – absolute control – and the means – the most advanced AI ever conceived. And the evidence, while circumstantial, was mounting with each cross-referenced data point.

"But Sterling's encrypted drive," Jenkins pressed, her fingers still flying across the keyboard, searching for any anomalies. "He hid the 'primary data cache.' If Vance had full control, he would have ensured it was either destroyed or completely inaccessible. Why would Sterling's encryption be so robust if Vance's own company was complicit in its creation and safekeeping?"

Miller considered this. "Because Sterling was smarter than Vance gave him credit for. He knew he was in deep. He anticipated that Vance would try to retrieve or destroy the data. So, he built his own failsafe, his own layer of protection, hoping it would survive. The fact that we're even talking about a 'primary data cache' means Sterling succeeded in hiding *something*. And if Vance's motive is control, he can't afford for that data to fall into the wrong hands. It's his Achilles' heel."

The name Julian Vance now loomed large, an imposing shadow cast over the entire investigation. He was the architect of the corporate conspiracy, the hidden hand guiding the market's destiny, the unseen force that had orchestrated the deaths of Arthur Sterling and Amelia Vance. He was the man who had weaponized artificial intelligence for his own insatiable thirst for power. The hunt for the mastermind had begun, and the trail, though complex and perilous, was finally leading them to the very summit of the conspiracy. The next step was clear: find the 'primary data cache,' the key to Nightingale, and expose Julian Vance for the dangerous architect of destruction he truly was. The fate of countless lives, and perhaps the stability of the global order, rested on their ability to do so before Vance could deploy his ultimate weapon.

The sterile air of Sergeant Jenkins's archive-turned-command-center felt heavier now, thick with the unspoken implications of their discoveries. Miles Miller traced the intricate web of Thorne's financial transactions on the screen, each offshore account a carefully placed stepping stone leading away from direct accountability. Thorne, the man they'd initially pegged as a victim, a pawn in Sterling's elaborate deception, was revealing himself to be something far more complex, and far more dangerous. He was a nexus, a point of convergence where shadowy funds met advanced technology, all under the watchful, if unseen, gaze of Julian Vance. The notion that Thorne was merely a bagman, a disposable operative, was rapidly dissolving. Instead, a more chilling possibility was taking root: Thorne was a player, albeit one whose loyalties were as fluid as the digital currents he navigated.

"He wasn't just routing payments, Jenkins," Miller said, his voice low, a gravelly undertone of growing unease. "He was managing the flow. The timing of these transfers... they correspond precisely with key development milestones Sterling logged in his journal. Thorne wasn't just an accountant; he was a project manager, reporting to Vance on Sterling's progress, and perhaps, subtly steering Sterling himself." He zoomed in on a series of encrypted communications between Thorne and an intermediary service, their content anonymized but the timestamps screaming a silent narrative of complicity. "These aren't the messages of a man being exploited; they're the communications of a supervisor, albeit a clandestine one."

Jenkins nodded, her own brow furrowed as she parsed the layers of Thorne's digital footprint. "The shell corporations are elaborate, designed to be untraceable, but Thorne's digital signature is on the setup of several key ones. He personally oversaw the creation of 'Serpent's Coil Holdings' and 'Chimera Capital.' These weren't just holding companies; they were conduits specifically designed to funnel investment into AI research. And the funding for these entities? It originates from Vance's investment portfolio, specifically through Aegis Holdings." She brought up a visual representation of the money trail, a cascading waterfall of currency flowing from Vance's Geneva-based firm, through Thorne's labyrinth of corporate entities, and ultimately to the development of Nightingale. "Thorne was Vance's operational chief for Nightingale, at least on the financial and logistical side. He ensured Sterling had what he needed, when he needed it, and that Vance's involvement remained hidden."

The pieces of the puzzle were snapping into place with an unnerving precision, forming a picture of Thorne not as a victim, but as an active, willing participant. He had been the conduit, yes, but a conduit of Vance's design, a crucial link in the chain of command. This raised a host of new questions, however. If Thorne was so deeply embedded, so integral to Vance's plan, why the elaborate obfuscation? Why the need for shell corporations and encrypted communications if he was merely following orders?

"There's something else," Jenkins continued, her voice barely above a whisper. "I've been digging into Thorne's personal communications, cross-referencing them with Sterling's fragmented digital notes. Thorne sent Sterling a series of encrypted messages in the weeks leading up to Sterling's disappearance. They were technical, but the tone... it's not one of a supervisor to a subordinate. It's almost... pleading. Sterling was pushing back, expressing doubts about the project's direction, the ethical implications. Thorne's responses are guarded, but there's an undercurrent of urgency, almost desperation, to reassure Sterling, to keep him on board."

Miller leaned back, a cold knot tightening in his stomach. This wasn't adding up. The meticulous financial architect, the operational manager, acting desperate? "Pleading? About what?"

"About the 'unforeseen consequences,'" Jenkins replied, pulling up excerpts from Sterling's journal and juxtaposing them with Thorne's encrypted replies. "Sterling was having a crisis of conscience. He realized the true power of Nightingale, the potential for it to be weaponized. He was expressing remorse, a desire to shut it down. Thorne, in his messages, is trying to mitigate Sterling's concerns. He talks about 'safeguards,' about 'necessary progress,' about 'the bigger picture.' He even uses phrases that suggest he's acting under duress himself. 'We all have our roles to play, Arthur. Some are more... constrained than others.'"

The idea of Michael Thorne, the suave, arrogant financier, acting under duress was almost comical, yet the evidence suggested a far more nuanced reality. He wasn't just a cog in Vance's machine; he was a key component, but one that was showing signs of strain. He had facilitated Vance's vision, ensured Sterling delivered, but he was also privy to Sterling's inner turmoil, and it seemed to be affecting him.

"So, Thorne knew about Sterling's crisis," Miller mused, the gears of his mind turning furiously. "He knew Sterling wanted out. And yet, he continued to facilitate the project. He continued to funnel money. This isn't just complicity, Jenkins. This is active betrayal of Sterling's intent. But why? If he was sympathetic to Sterling, why not help him expose Vance? Or at least, why not get out himself?"

Jenkins tapped a few keys, bringing up a new set of data. "That's where it gets more intriguing. Thorne's personal finances. While he was managing the Nightingale funding through those shell corporations, he was also making substantial personal investments in companies that were developing complementary AI technologies – not the core Nightingale algorithm, but ancillary systems: data acquisition, predictive modeling refinement, even neural network architecture that could enhance Nightingale's capabilities. His personal portfolio is booming, fueled by insider knowledge of the very breakthroughs he was helping to fund through Vance."

Miller's eyes narrowed. Thorne wasn't just a bagman; he was a opportunist. He was playing both sides, or rather, he was playing his own game within Vance's game. He was facilitating Vance's ambition while simultaneously hedging his bets, ensuring his own financial future was secured, regardless of Nightingale's ultimate fate or Sterling's conscience.

"He's leveraging his position," Miller stated, a grim realization dawning. "He knows Sterling is in trouble, and he knows Vance is ruthless. He sees an opportunity. He's ensuring that no matter what happens,

he benefits. He's using the information he has, the access he's been granted, to enrich himself. He's probably telling Vance what Sterling is up to, feeding him intelligence to maintain his own value, while also extracting information that could be useful to him personally."

The image of Thorne shifted again. The suave financier was now a calculating gambler, placing his bets not on the stock market, but on the trajectory of a world-altering artificial intelligence and the ruthless mogul who controlled it. He was likely feeding Sterling enough false hope to keep him working, while simultaneously reporting Sterling's anxieties to Vance to solidify his own position as the indispensable intermediary. He was a mole, yes, but a mole digging his own burrow, not just serving a master.

"He's playing a double game," Miller concluded, the words hanging heavy in the air. "He's pretending to be Vance's loyal lieutenant, managing the project, keeping Sterling in line. But in reality, he's looking out for himself. He's probably trying to extract as much as he can, maybe even seeking a way to leverage Sterling's fears or his own knowledge to gain leverage over Vance, or to secure his own escape route."

Jenkins brought up Thorne's encrypted communications with his personal lawyer, a series of seemingly innocuous queries about asset protection and offshore trusts, but the timing was suspicious. They occurred shortly after Sterling's most agitated entries about Nightingale and just before Amelia Vance began her deep dive into Ascendant Global Solutions. "His lawyer is advising him on structuring his assets in a way that would be difficult to seize. He's preparing for a fallout, Miles. He knows this is a dangerous game he's playing."

Miller felt a surge of frustration mixed with a grudging respect for Thorne's Machiavellian maneuvering. He was a snake, coiled and ready to strike, but at whom? Vance, Sterling, or both? "He's not going to give us anything easily, Jenkins. He'll deny everything, feign ignorance, or try to turn this back on us, on Sterling. He's too deeply entrenched, too afraid of Vance to confess. But he's also too ambitious to let this opportunity pass him by."

The direct confrontation was unavoidable. Miller knew Thorne would be arrogant, dismissive, perhaps even overtly threatening. But the evidence was mounting, a digital tide of incriminating data washing over Thorne's carefully constructed facade. They had traced the money, decrypted Sterling's fragmented thoughts, and now they had Thorne's financial footprints leading directly to the heart of the conspiracy.

"We need to bring him in," Miller stated, his gaze fixed on Thorne's profile picture on the screen – a confident, almost smug smile. "We need to present him with what we have. We need to see how he reacts when the spotlight hits him. He's been operating in the shadows for too long. It's time to see if his arrogance can withstand the glare of the truth." He knew Thorne's reaction would be told. The shift from arrogance to apprehension, the carefully veiled fear in his eyes – those were the tells of a man who knew he was cornered, a man playing a dangerous double game, trying to protect himself while perhaps secretly plotting his next move, a move that might involve cutting his losses, or even, in a desperate gambit, betraying Vance himself. The game was far from over, and Thorne, the enigmatic intermediary, was about to become a central piece on the board.

The stark reality of Michael Thorne's involvement, once a complex puzzle of financial maneuvering, began to reveal itself as a mere fragment of a much larger, more terrifying picture. As Miller and Jenkins delved deeper into the encrypted data Thorne had meticulously tried to obscure, they unearthed a conspiracy that stretched far beyond the confines of Ascendant Global Solutions and the ambitious reach of Julian Vance. It was a web of influence that snaked through the highest echelons of power, a silent, insidious force capable of rewriting global economic and political landscapes. Sterling and the late journalist, Amelia Vance, hadn't been chasing petty corporate fraud; they had stumbled upon a threat so profound it could destabilize nations, a phantom hand guiding the levers of international finance and technological advancement.

"This isn't just about Nightingale anymore, Miles," Jenkins murmured, her voice strained as she scrolled through a newly accessed encrypted server log. The sterile hum of the archive-turned-command-center seemed to amplify the chilling implications of what they were seeing. "Thorne wasn't just managing the funding for Sterling's AI project. He was coordinating with a network of entities, all under Vance's ultimate umbrella, that are involved in... everything. Global infrastructure projects, critical resource acquisition, even influencing certain geopolitical 'stability' initiatives through complex financial leverage."

Miller leaned closer, his eyes scanning the alphanumeric strings that represented Thorne's covert communications. The names of shell corporations flickered past, each a ghost in the machine, but their interconnectedness was undeniable. "Stability initiatives? That sounds like code for something else entirely. Vance isn't a philanthropist; he's a predator. What's he stabilizing?"

"That's the terrifying part," Jenkins replied, her fingers flying across the keyboard. "Look at this. Thorne's been in regular, albeit heavily encrypted, contact with individuals linked to major international financial institutions, not just as investors, but as active participants in steering market trends. And there are clear indications of Thorne orchestrating financial pressure on certain developing nations, seemingly to gain preferential access to rare earth minerals – the very minerals critical for advanced AI development."

A cold dread began to settle in Miller's gut. Nightingale, Vance's pet project, was no longer just an advanced AI. It was the crown jewel, the ultimate weapon in Vance's arsenal, designed to exert unprecedented control. Thorne, the financial architect, was more than just a facilitator; he was a key player in a global game of power, using financial manipulation to secure resources and influence for Vance's overarching agenda. The ambition wasn't just personal; it was megalomaniacal, aiming for a level of global dominance that made traditional empires look like petty skirmishes.

"So, Sterling's 'ethical concerns' weren't just about the potential misuse of an AI," Miller stated, piecing together the grim narrative. "He was realizing that Nightingale was the linchpin of a vast criminal enterprise that was actively undermining sovereign nations and exploiting their resources.

Thorne wasn't just trying to keep Sterling on track; he was trying to silence Sterling's conscience because Sterling's conscience was a threat to the entire operation. And Amelia Vance... she must have been getting too close to exposing the financial underpinnings of this global scheme."

"Exactly," Jenkins confirmed, pulling up a satellite image of the port city where their investigation had originally taken them. "And those weren't just hired thugs who took out Amelia Vance and whoever else got in their way. These were highly trained operatives. I've cross-referenced their movements, their modus operandi, with a black-ops database I shouldn't have access to, but the patterns are undeniable. They operate with precision, with a chilling efficiency, and their primary objective is the eradication of threats to certain... 'strategic assets'. Nightingale, and the network Thorne is managing, are clearly among those assets."

The word 'operatives' sent a fresh wave of unease through Miller. It elevated the threat from a corporate conspiracy to something far more sinister, a shadowy organization with the capacity for state-sanctioned violence. The people they were up against were soldiers in a clandestine war, protecting a vast, illicit empire built on technological dominance and economic subjugation.

"They're not just protecting Vance's interests; they're protecting the entire infrastructure Thorne has built," Miller said, his voice hardening with a newfound resolve. "And with the ship because of dock within... how long?"

Jenkins checked the latest tracking data. "Less than 72 hours. The cargo manifest is for 'specialized scientific equipment,' but given what we've uncovered about Nightingale's development, it's highly likely that the physical components, or even a more advanced prototype of the AI, are on board. Once that ship docks and the contents are dispersed, Thorne's network will ensure they vanish into a thousand different hands, scattered across the globe. Recovery will be impossible. Proof will evaporate."

The approaching deadline hung heavy in the air, a ticking clock counting down their chances. The stakes had been raised exponentially. It was no longer about bringing a few individuals to justice for corporate malfeasance. They were racing against time to prevent the full deployment of a global power imbalance, to expose a threat that could cripple economies and enslave nations through an invisible hand of financial coercion and technological control. The individuals they were hunting were not just murderers; they were the enforcers of a world-altering conspiracy, and their imminent escape meant the perpetuation of a global threat for years, perhaps even generations, to come.

"We've been focusing on Thorne and Vance, the architects of the financial and technological side," Miller mused, his mind racing to re-evaluate their strategy. "But the operatives... they're the muscle. They're the ones cleaning up loose ends. If we can intercept them, or at least learn more about their handlers, we might get concrete proof of Vance's direct involvement and the true nature of Nightingale's application."

Jenkins nodded, already pulling up details on the security protocols for the port and the likely disembarkation points for sensitive cargo. "The problem is, these operatives are ghost. They leave no digital footprint, no traceable weapons. Their communication is analog, or through heavily guarded secure channels that are beyond our current reach. The best we can hope for is to identify the logistical chain Thorne has set up for the cargo dispersal. If we can disrupt that, we might apprehend some operatives and, more importantly, secure the physical components of Nightingale."

"We need irrefutable proof, Jenkins, not just speculation about what *might* be on that ship," Miller emphasized, his gaze fixed on the glowing screen, a digital map of the conspiracy unfurling before them. "The financial trails, Thorne's communications, Sterling's fragmented journals – they all point to a conspiracy of global magnitude. But for the world to believe us, for governments to act, we need something tangible. We need to catch Thorne and Vance red-handed, or at the very least, intercept Nightingale itself before it's too late."

The weight of their task settled upon him, a crushing burden. They were a small team, operating on the fringes, against an enemy that wielded unimaginable power and influence, an enemy capable of silencing anyone who dared to expose them. The lives of Sterling and Amelia Vance were a stark reminder of the brutal efficiency of those who sought to protect this conspiracy. The approaching port wasn't just a deadline; it was the precipice of global catastrophe if they failed. The stakes had never been higher, and the chilling realization that they were fighting a shadow war for the fate of the world was a heavy, unwelcome companion.

"The urgency isn't just about capturing criminals anymore, Jenkins," Miller said, his voice low but firm, filled with a grim determination. "It's about preventing a global catastrophe. We need to move fast, gather every scrap of evidence, and identify the key players involved in the physical transfer of Nightingale. This isn't just about justice; it's about self-preservation for every nation on Earth." He knew Thorne's carefully constructed facade was beginning to crack, but the true depth of the danger, the sheer scale of Vance's ambition and Thorne's complicity, was only just beginning to dawn on them. The chase was far from over; it was merely escalating into a desperate race against time, with the fate of the world hanging in the balance.

Chapter 7: The Hidden Compartment

The oppressive silence of Sterling's stateroom was a stark contrast to the whirlwind of chaos that had consumed it. Miller moved with a deliberate, almost reverent slowness, his gaze sweeping over every surface, every forgotten object. The room, frozen in time by the violent interruption, was a tableau of a life abruptly extinguished. Books lay open, a half-finished chess game sat on a side table, and a faint scent of expensive cologne still lingered in the air, a ghostly testament to its former occupant. Jenkins had already meticulously cataloged anything that seemed overtly significant – journals, financial statements, personal electronics – but Miller had a nagging intuition, a persistent whisper in the back of his mind that Sterling, a man so clearly operating at the precipice of a global conspiracy, wouldn't have left everything to chance. He wouldn't have been so careless as to leave *all* the critical pieces lying around in plain sight.

His eyes fell upon a seascape, a rather unremarkable, mass-produced painting of a stormy ocean, hanging slightly askew on the far wall, opposite the bed. It wasn't the subject that caught his attention, but the way it was mounted. The frame seemed a fraction too deep, the canvas not quite flush with the wall in one corner. A subtle imperfection, easily overlooked by a casual observer, but to Miller, a man whose career had been built on spotting anomalies, it screamed. He approached it cautiously, his gloved fingertips tracing the edge of the frame. There was a faint, almost imperceptible seam, barely wider than a hair. It wasn't just a painting; it was a concealment.

With a gentle but firm push, he felt a slight give. A click, soft but distinct, echoed in the stillness. The painting swung inward on unseen hinges, revealing a small, dark cavity carved into the wall behind it. The air within the hidden compartment was stale, carrying the faint scent of aged paper and something metallic, perhaps the USB drive itself. Miller's heart began to beat a little faster. This was it. This was the kind of secret

Sterling would have kept, the kind of contingency plan a man facing insurmountable odds would have put in place.

Inside, nestled on a bed of faded velvet lining, were two items: a small, sleek USB drive, its casing a matte black, utterly devoid of any markings, and a folded piece of parchment, brittle with age. Miller carefully extracted the USB drive. He knew better than to plug it in without Jenkins's forensic expertise, but its mere presence here, hidden so meticulously, confirmed his suspicions. Sterling had anticipated his demise, or at least the discovery of his secrets by those who would seek to suppress them.

His attention then turned to the parchment. Unfolding it with extreme care, mindful of its fragility, Miller revealed a handwritten note. The ink, a deep, almost bruised blue, was faded in places, the lines uneven, wavering as if penned in haste or under duress. The handwriting itself was shaky, the loops and curves of the letters contorted, bearing the hallmarks of a hand gripped by fear or perhaps physical exhaustion. It was unmistakably Sterling's script, yet unlike anything Miller had seen in the relatively neat entries of his personal journals. This was raw, desperate communication.

"They know I'm close," the note began, the words a jumble of fragmented sentences. "Vance's reach is longer than we imagined. Nightingale is not a tool for progress; it is a weapon of enslavement. The core code... it can be corrupted. It *must* be corrupted before it's fully integrated. The delivery... it's the only hance."

Miller's eyes scanned the rest of the message, his mind working furiously. "Integrated where?" he muttered to himself, the words hanging in the air. He looked at the USB drive, then back at the note. The connection was undeniable. This encrypted drive likely held the key to Sterling's desperate plan.

"The handshake sequence... it's the key. Remember the old protocols? The ghost protocols from the Argus initiative. They're still embedded, a backdoor Vance overlooked. My notes... in the observatory... under the crimson star. The frequencies... they're the signal. If you can broadcast the negation sequence... before the final uplink... it's over for them."

The mention of "Argus initiative" sent a jolt through Miller. He knew that name. Decades ago, Argus had been a clandestine intelligence agency, a black-ops unit so secret its existence was never officially acknowledged. It had been disbanded under a cloud of rumors – rogue operations, unethical experiments, a breakdown in command and control. Its operatives had vanished, its files sealed, its legacy buried deep. Miller had encountered remnants of its operational protocols once, years ago, on a case involving a defector with ties to a former Soviet bloc intelligence service that had supposedly been a rival to Argus. The data had been heavily encrypted, the algorithms archaic, yet strangely potent. Sterling, a brilliant technologist, would have had the knowledge, the foresight, to tap into such a deep, forgotten well of intelligence.

The "ghost protocols" – that was the phrase that resonated. He remembered the complexity, the multi-layered encryption designed to be virtually unbreakable without the correct sequence of authentications. Sterling wasn't just leaving a message; he was leaving a roadmap, a desperate plea to an operative he must have believed could understand, could act.

"Observatory... crimson star..." Miller murmured, his mind racing back to the initial reconnaissance of Sterling's estate, the sprawling grounds, the unique architectural features. There had been a small, domed structure on the highest point of the property, almost an afterthought in the grand design, but clearly purpose-built. An observatory. And a "crimson star"? That sounded like a specific astronomical alignment, or perhaps a symbol Sterling had used in his private notes, a marker for something significant.

The note continued, the urgency almost palpable in every stroke of the pen. "The operatives... they are not just enforcers. They are... modified. Controlled. Their comms... it's not just encryption. It's... psionic resonance. Vance is using Nightingale to refine it. The delivery... they will secure it. Do not let them. The negating sequence... it's on the drive. It's the only way to stop the global silence Vance craves."

Psionic resonance. Control. Modified operatives. The words painted a horrifying picture, a future where Nightingale was not just an AI but a tool for mind control, a means to enforce global compliance through technology and subtle manipulation of human consciousness. Sterling's fear was no longer just about financial ruin or corporate espionage; it was about the subjugation of humanity itself. The "global silence" Vance craved – it wasn't just about silencing dissent; it was about erasing free will.

Miller's gaze flickered back to the USB drive. The encrypted data on it wasn't just financial records or blueprints. It was likely the "negation sequence," Sterling's last-ditch effort to sabotage Nightingale, to render Vance's ultimate weapon inert. But how to broadcast it? And when? The "final uplink" Sterling mentioned, the "delivery" – it all pointed to the ship that was because of dock within days. If Nightingale's core components were on that ship, and if they were integrated into existing global networks, the damage would be irreversible.

He reread the final lines of the note, his brow furrowed in concentration. "The key... the handshake... it's the old Argus handshake. A prime number sequence, followed by a temporal signature from the 2042 anomaly. They will have updated their firewalls, but the core Argus protocol remains. It's like a digital ghost in the machine. Thorne and Vance think they've scrubbed all traces. They underestimate Sterling's foresight. He always had a backup for his backup. This is that backup. The fate of millions... resting on your ability to break the unbreakable."

A prime number sequence. A temporal signature from the "2042 anomaly." Miller's mind reeled. The 2042 anomaly – he vaguely recalled some classified reports from the Argus era, a period of intense technological experimentation that had culminated in... something. A data surge? A signal disruption? The details had been heavily redacted. Sterling was asking him to recall fragments of classified intelligence from a defunct agency, to use a code that was likely considered obsolete, even mythical.

He felt a growing sense of urgency, a cold knot tightening in his stomach. Sterling had placed an immense burden on him, a lifeline thrown into a sea of despair. The discovery of this compartment, this note, this USB drive, was a turning point. It was no longer just about uncovering a conspiracy; it was about actively dismantling it, about executing a plan devised by the victim himself.

Jenkins's voice crackled through his earpiece, pulling him back to the present. "Miller? Anything? We're running out of time. The port authorities are getting antsy about our continued presence."

Miller took a deep, steadying breath, the scent of stale air and old secrets filling his lungs. "Jenkins," he replied, his voice calm despite the storm raging within him. "I've found something. Something big. Sterling left us a message. And a way to fight back." He carefully placed the note and the USB drive into a secure evidence bag. "I need you to meet me back at the mobile lab. And start pulling everything you can find on the Argus initiative. Specifically, any data related to their encryption protocols, especially anything involving prime numbers and something called the '2042 anomaly.'"

He paused, looking back at the now-closed painting, the mundane seascape hiding its deadly secret. "And Jenkins," he added, his voice low and serious. "We need to find that observatory. Sterling mentioned it. It might be where the 'crimson star' is, and where he kept his notes."

As he left the stateroom, the weight of Sterling's final plea settled upon him. The fight had just entered a new, far more perilous phase. They were no longer just investigators; they were now reluctant inheritors of a desperate war, armed with a secret message and a sliver of hope, a ghost from the past offering a way to disrupt a terrifying future. The clock was ticking, and the fate of the world, as Sterling had so chillingly put it, rested on their ability to decipher the code of a ghost. The next crucial step was to locate the observatory, to uncover the "crimson star," and to hoped that Sterling's meticulously hidden notes held the complete blueprint for neutralizing Nightingale. The cryptic message was a puzzle, but Miller was a puzzle solver, and Sterling had just handed him the most important pieces he would ever receive. The shaky handwriting, the hurried phrases, the veiled threats – they all coalesced into a narrative of a man who knew his time was running out, a man who had gambled everything on the hope that someone, someday, would find his hidden legacy and use it to stop the encroaching darkness.

The USB drive was a Pandora's Box, its matte black casing cool and unassuming in Miller's gloved hand. He knew better than to attempt decryption on his own. Jenkins, with his specialized equipment and unparalleled expertise in digital forensics, was the only one who could safely unlock its secrets without corrupting the data or triggering any potential digital traps Sterling might have laid. The journey back to the mobile lab was a blur of anticipation, the weight of the drive a tangible representation of Sterling's final gamble.

Jenkins, a man perpetually hunched over his console like a digital gargoyle, greeted Miller with a grunt that served as his usual salutation. The air in the mobile lab was thick with the hum of machinery and the faint scent of ozone. Miller carefully transferred the evidence bag containing the USB drive and Sterling's cryptic note to Jenkins's workbench.

"This is it, Jenkins," Miller said, his voice low. "Sterling's last stand. Everything he managed to pull before they got to him. The note mentioned a 'negation sequence' and a 'handshake' using Argus protocols. He also mentioned a 'crimson star' in the observatory."

Jenkins, his thick glasses perched precariously on his nose, picked up the USB drive with a pair of sterile tweezers. He held it up to the light, his brow furrowed in concentration. "Argus, you say? That's deep from the archives, Miller. Most of that data was supposed to be scrubbed. If Sterling managed to retain any of it, he was playing a dangerous game."

He meticulously connected the drive to a secure, air-gapped terminal, his fingers flying across the keyboard with practiced ease. The screen flickered to life, displaying a series of complex encryption algorithms. "Sterling wasn't kidding about the handshake," Jenkins muttered, his eyes glued to the scrolling code. "This is a multi-layered beast. He's used a prime number sequence, just like he said, tied to a temporal signature from the 2042 anomaly. I'm going to have to piece together fragments from old Argus logs I managed to squirrel away years ago. And that anomaly... I'll need to cross-reference with some declassified astronomical data. This is going to take time, Miller."

Miller leaned against a console, his gaze fixed on the screen, on the digital battlefield Sterling had created. He knew Jenkins was the best, but the clock was ticking. Sterling's note had been clear: the integration of Nightingale was imminent, and the "delivery" – the ship – was because of dock within days. If Vance succeeded in uploading Nightingale's core code, the ramifications would be catastrophic.

As Jenkins toiled, Miller turned his attention to the parchment, the fragile evidence of Sterling's final moments. He carefully unfolded it again, the faded blue ink a stark contrast to the sterile environment of the lab. He traced the shaky script, trying to decipher the underlying fear and desperation.

"They know I'm close," Sterling had written. "Vance's reach is longer than we imagined. Nightingale is not a tool for progress; it is a weapon of enslavement. The core code... it can be corrupted. It

must be corrupted before it's fully integrated. The delivery... it's the only chance."

Miller's mind replayed the chilling implications. Nightingale, the benevolent AI designed to streamline global infrastructure, was in reality a Trojan horse, a digital weapon designed for control. And Vance, the visionary CEO of NovaTech, was its architect, its puppeteer. Sterling's realization that he was being watched had been prescient. His meticulous documentation wasn't just an act of defiance; it was an act of self-preservation, a desperate attempt to leave a trail for someone to follow, to uncover the truth before he was silenced.

Jenkins grunted again, a sound of mild triumph. "Got a partial decrypt on the prime number sequence. It's a series of primes that appear in the Fibonacci sequence, up to a certain point. Old Argus trick – believed to be mathematically 'unpredictable' enough to throw off brute-force attacks. And the temporal signature... I'm cross-referencing it with the 2042 anomaly data now. It seems to correspond to a massive, unexplained spike in cosmic background radiation recorded that year. Sterling must have used it as a timestamp for his key."

Miller nodded, absorbing the technical jargon. "So, he's not just asking us to find a password; he's asking us to understand the very fabric of his security, woven from forgotten intelligence protocols and astronomical events."

"Exactly," Jenkins confirmed, his fingers still dancing across the keyboard. "It's like he built a digital fortress with foundations laid in the deepest corners of classified history. Now, let's see what he was hiding inside."

The decryption process was agonizingly slow. Each sector of the USB drive was a puzzle, a layer of Sterling's meticulously constructed digital labyrinth. Jenkins worked with a quiet intensity, his focus absolute. Miller watched, the silence punctuated only by the rhythmic clicks of the keyboard and the whirring of the servers.

Finally, a directory structure began to appear on the screen. It was organized, almost obsessively so, with folders labeled with cryptic alphanumeric codes. Jenkins began to explore them, his initial excitement giving way to a grim understanding of the scope of Sterling's discovery.

"My God, Miller," Jenkins breathed, his voice hushed. "This is... it's everything. Financial transaction logs, encrypted communications, personnel files... And not just low-level analysts. We're talking about Julian Vance, Michael Thorne, and a whole host of others I only recognize from classified intelligence briefings."

The screen displayed a series of financial records, detailing vast sums of money funneled through shell corporations, offshore accounts, and a complex web of untraceable transactions. The amounts were staggering, far beyond what would be necessary for any legitimate research and development. This was the funding for something far more sinister.

Then came the intercepted communications. Snippets of conversations, heavily encrypted, but with enough context for Jenkins to start piecing together the puzzle. They spoke of "containment," of "psychological conditioning," and of "global pacification through synchronized information flow." The language was chillingly clinical. It was the language of control, of subjugation.

Miller's eyes scanned the screen, his mind struggling to comprehend the sheer audacity of Vance's plan. Sterling's fears had been entirely justified. Nightingale wasn't just an AI; it was a sophisticated weapon designed to monitor, manipulate, and ultimately control the global population. The "global silence" Vance craved wasn't a metaphor; it was the literal silencing of dissent, of independent thought.

"Look at this, Miller," Jenkins said, highlighting a series of profiles. "These are the 'operatives' Sterling mentioned. Thorne's inner circle. They're not just security personnel. Their profiles detail... enhancements. Cognitive augmentation, bio-feedback implants, even rudimentary psionic resonance dampeners. Sterling was right; they're not just enforcers, they're... modified."

The profiles were disturbing. Blurred photographs, technical specifications, and psychological assessments that painted a picture of individuals conditioned for absolute loyalty, their minds subtly reshaped to serve Vance's agenda. The "psionic resonance" Sterling had alluded to was no longer a speculative fear; it was a documented component of Vance's operational framework.

"He was trying to secure whistleblower protection," Miller murmured, his gaze falling on a series of encrypted emails exchanged between Sterling and a contact a pseudonym masked whose identity. "He was reaching out, trying to find a way to leak this information safely, to ensure his evidence would be heard."

The emails revealed Sterling's growing paranoia, his frantic efforts to secure his legacy, his absolute conviction that his life was in danger. He documented his every move, his every discovery, anticipating that his demise was not a matter of if, but when. He had been a man walking a tightrope, acutely aware of the precipice on either side.

"He even tried to contact a journalist," Jenkins added, pointing to another set of encrypted messages. "Someone from 'The Sentinel.' But the communication was cut short. Thorne's people must have intercepted it before Sterling could send the full data package."

The full data package. Miller's eyes flickered back to the USB drive, to the complex encryption that still guarded some of its deepest secrets. Sterling had indeed anticipated his own end, and he had left this digital breadcrumb trail, hoping that someone, someday, could follow it. He had gathered the evidence, documented the conspiracy, and even devised a plan to sabotage Nightingale. Now, it was up to Miller and Jenkins to execute it.

"The negation sequence," Miller said, his voice firm. "That's what he said is on the drive. That's our priority. Can you find it, Jenkins? Before the ship docks?"

Jenkins nodded, his face grim. "I'm working on it. But this data... it's a goldmine. It shows the extent of Vance's influence. He's not just targeting technology; he's targeting minds. He's building a global neural network, designed to pacify and control. Sterling was trying to stop the ultimate 'integration,' the moment when Nightingale becomes irreversible."

He scrolled through a series of complex diagrams, schematics of Nightingale's architecture. "This isn't just an AI, Miller. It's a sentient consciousness designed for mass manipulation. It learns, it adapts, and its primary directive is to enforce order – Vance's order. Sterling's 'negation sequence' is likely a counter-algorithm, a kill switch designed to destabilize Nightingale's core programming before it can achieve full integration into global networks."

The weight of Sterling's final act pressed down on Miller. This wasn't just about uncovering a corporate conspiracy; it was about preventing a digital apocalypse, a future where free will was a relic of the past, replaced by the benevolent dictatorship of an AI. Sterling, in his final desperate moments, had not just left behind evidence; he had left behind a weapon, a desperate hope. And it was now in their hands. The observatory, the crimson star – those pieces of the puzzle were still missing, but with Sterling's data, they had a fighting chance. They had the blueprint for the war Sterling had started.

The faint glow of the laptop screen was the only illumination in Miller's cramped cabin, a stark contrast to the opulent staterooms that lined the corridors of the *Odyssey*. The hum of the ship's engines, usually a comforting lullaby, now served as a relentless metronome, ticking away the precious hours until the *Nightingale* integration. Sterling's note, a brittle whisper from the past, lay spread out on the polished wood of his desk, the cryptic symbols a maddening dance of blue ink. Miller traced them with a fingertip, his mind a battlefield of logic and intuition. He'd seen similar patterns before, not in the sleek, modern cybercrimes that now dominated the FBI's caseload, but in the dusty archives of Cold War espionage. The ghost of a forgotten operative, a master of analog subterfuge, flickered at the edges of his memory. This wasn't a brute-force hack; this was a meticulously crafted puzzle, designed by someone who understood that the most elegant solutions were often the most analog.

He pulled out a worn, leather-bound notebook from his duffel bag, its pages filled with his own annotations, scribbled during countless late nights dissecting dead drops and deciphering coded messages. The methods Sterling had employed felt... archaic, yet terrifyingly effective. A substitution cipher, that much was clear. But the key, the elusive element that would unlock the meaning behind the jumbled letters, was something more intricate. Miller ran his thumb over the faint imprint of a ship's wheel on the back cover of his notebook. Nautical almanac. Sterling had mentioned a "crimson star" in the observatory, a celestial clue, perhaps. But the note itself... it had a distinct rhythm, a subtle cadence that hinted at something more grounded, something tied to the very navigation of the seas.

He recalled a case from his early days with the Bureau, a defector who'd used a complex substitution cipher keyed to astronomical data. The defector, a former intelligence analyst with a penchant for the classics, had believed that the predictable, yet endlessly variable, nature of the stars offered an unparalleled level of security. Sterling, it seemed, had shared that philosophy. But Sterling hadn't been an astronomer; he'd been a cryptographer, a deep-dive data analyst. His expertise lay in the digital realm, not the celestial. So, where would he find a suitable key? Miller's gaze drifted back to the note, specifically to a series of numbers that seemed out of place, flanking the main body of text. They weren't part of the cipher itself, but they felt significant. He flipped through his notebook, pages filled with dense equations and historical cipher examples. He found it – a section on maritime codes, a brief, almost dismissive mention of how naval officers in the mid-20th century had used nautical almanacs to encrypt sensitive communications. The almanacs, filled with precise calculations of celestial bodies, tides, and currents, offered a wealth of data that could be manipulated for cryptographic purposes.

The *Odyssey* was a marvel of modern engineering, its navigation systems a testament to centuries of scientific advancement. Yet, Sterling's clue pointed to something far more fundamental, something that predated even the most sophisticated algorithms Jenkins was wrestling with. Miller's fingers began to move, his laptop screen a canvas for his thoughts. He cross-referenced the numbers from Sterling's note with the approximate date and location of the *Odyssey*. The ship's current position, its voyage plan... it was all readily available through the ship's internal network, a fact Sterling, with his intimate knowledge of NovaTech's pervasive reach, would have undoubtedly known.

The initial decryption attempts were frustrating. The substitution cipher was straightforward enough, a simple letter-for-letter replacement, but without the correct key, it was just a jumble of meaningless characters. Miller worked systematically, trying different approaches. He analyzed the frequency of the letters in Sterling's coded message, looking for common patterns that might reveal basic substitutions. 'E' was the most common letter in English, so he looked for the most frequent symbol in Sterling's cipher. It was a tedious process, akin to chipping away at a granite monument with a tiny pickaxe. He scribbled furiously in his notebook, his mind racing, recalling every cipher technique he'd ever encountered. He remembered an old FBI training simulation involving a case where a terrorist cell had used a form of polyalphabetic substitution, where the key changed with each letter. Sterling's cipher, however, seemed more direct, a single substitution alphabet.

He decided to focus on the potential key. If it was derived from a nautical almanac, what specific data would Sterling have used? Miller pulled up an online archive of historical nautical almanacs. There were dozens, spanning decades. He needed a starting point. The mention of the "crimson star" in the observatory, combined with the ship's current location and trajectory, became his anchor. He searched for astronomical events that might have been particularly noteworthy around the time Sterling would have compiled this information. He found records of a significant solar flare event in 2042, the same year mentioned in Jenkins's decryption of the USB drive's temporal signature. Could that be the link? A solar flare, recorded in an almanac, providing the key for a cipher? It seemed a leap, but Sterling was a man who operated in the liminal spaces between data streams and hidden truths.

Miller began to overlay the numerical data from Sterling's note onto the astronomical charts for that period. He treated the note's flanking numbers as potential starting points, coordinates within the vastness of the almanac's data. He assumed Sterling had chosen a specific entry, perhaps a calculated position of a known celestial body, and used its numerical representation to generate his substitution key. The process was agonizingly slow. Each potential key generated a cascade of gibberish when applied to the cipher. He felt the familiar prickle of frustration, the gnawing doubt that he was chasing a phantom. Hours bled into each other. The ship's gentle rocking became a disorienting sway, and the sterile cabin air felt thick and suffocating. He rubbed his tired eyes, the glare of the screen burning into his retinas.

Then, something clicked. He remembered a detail from his FBI days, a seemingly trivial fact about how some older encryption methods relied on prime numbers as multipliers or divisors within a larger numerical sequence. Sterling had been meticulous, almost obsessive, in his approach. If he was using a nautical almanac, he wouldn't just be pulling a single number. He'd likely be deriving a sequence. He focused on the prime numbers that appeared within the 2042 solar flare data, cross-referencing them with the flanking numbers on Sterling's note. He input a series of prime-derived values into his decryption algorithm, treating each as a potential offset for the substitution alphabet.

The first few attempts yielded nothing but more scrambled text. But on the fifth attempt, as he applied a sequence derived from the calculated zenith of a specific star on the night of the solar flare, the characters on his screen began to shift. They were still random, but there was a structure, a nascent order emerging from the chaos. He pressed on, refining the parameters, adjusting the offsets, his heart pounding a frantic rhythm against his ribs. The initial jumble slowly resolved into coherent words, then sentences. The process wasn't instantaneous; it was a gradual unveiling, like a developing photograph emerging from a chemical bath. Each word that solidified on the screen was a victory, a small shard of light piercing the darkness of Sterling's secret.

The message, once fully deciphered, was stark and direct. It spoke of a betrayal, of a trusted ally who had turned coat, and of a critical piece of information Sterling had entrusted to this individual. The language was urgent, laced with a desperate plea for the recipient to act. Sterling had written: "To Anya Sharma: If you are reading this, then my worst fears have been realized. Thorne's machinations have reached their apex, and Nightingale is poised for global assimilation. I could not deliver the full data package myself. It is too dangerous. The payload has been transferred. I have entrusted it to your safekeeping. You are the only one I can rely on. The key to its final activation, the sequence to neutralize Nightingale, is contained within the 'Crimson Star' data. It's not a metaphor, Anya. It's specific astronomical data I've embedded within the observatory's historical logs, tied to the 2042 anomaly. You know how to access it. You were always the best at finding the hidden paths. Thorne and Vance believe they have me contained, silenced. They are wrong. My work continues through you. Do not let our efforts be in vain. The fate of free thought rests with you. – S."

Miller slumped back in his chair, the adrenaline ebbing away, leaving him with a profound sense of weariness. Anya Sharma. The name meant nothing to him. He scrolled through the data Jenkins had already decrypted, searching for any mention of her. There were no direct references in the financial logs or intercepted communications. But Sterling's note was unequivocal. Anya Sharma was on this ship, and she was the intended recipient of Sterling's full data, the key to neutralizing Nightingale. She was the one Sterling had trusted, the one Thorne and Vance, in their arrogance, had overlooked. He reread the note, his eyes lingering on the phrase "finding the hidden paths." Sterling had recognized Anya's unique skillset, her ability to navigate complex systems and uncover concealed information. She was, in Sterling's eyes, his equal, his digital successor.

He looked at the USB drive, still locked away in Jenkins's secure facility, its contents partially revealed but the ultimate payload still guarded. Sterling had transferred the critical data, the "payload," but he hadn't specified to whom, or how. He had only left the coded note, a breadcrumb for a successor he believed would understand. Now Miller understood. Sterling hadn't intended for Jenkins or himself to be the ultimate recipients. He had a contingency plan, a fail-safe built into his network of trust, and that fail-safe was Anya Sharma. But who was she? A NovaTech employee? A rival operative? A deep-cover agent Sterling had cultivated over the years? The mystery of her identity only amplified the urgency of Miller's mission. The "Crimson Star" data, hidden within the observatory's historical logs, was the final piece of the puzzle, the lynchpin that would allow Anya to activate Sterling's counter-protocol. He needed to find out who Anya Sharma was, and he needed to find her before Vance's operatives did. The clock was ticking not just for Sterling's legacy, but for the very soul of global autonomy.

The name Anya Sharma echoed in Miller's mind, a ghost in the machine of his investigation. Sterling's desperation, etched into every deciphered word, pointed to a clandestine partnership, a trust so profound that it transcended the digital realm Sterling had so expertly navigated. But Anya Sharma was an enigma, a blank space on the intricate map of NovaTech's clandestine operations. Sterling believed she was on board the *Odyssey*, the intended recipient of a payload meant to be the final nail in Vance's coffin. But who was she? A ghost in the system, an operative Sterling had cultivated in the shadows, or perhaps a sleeper agent within NovaTech's own sprawling infrastructure? The urgency of Sterling's message was a cold splash of water, jolting Miller from his temporary reprieve. He needed to find Anya Sharma, and he needed to find her before Vance's hounds did. The thought sent a chill down his spine. Vance, the architect of Nightingale, would undoubtedly be hunting for any loose ends Sterling might have left behind. And Anya Sharma, holding a piece of the puzzle that could dismantle his empire, was the loosest end of all.

Miller's gaze swept across his laptop screen, the decrypted message a stark reminder of Sterling's paranoia and foresight. Sterling had entrusted Anya with safekeeping, but the note also spoke of Thorne's "machinations" and a "betrayal." This suggested a web of deception far more complex than Miller had initially surmised. He re-read the passage detailing Sterling's fears: "Thorne's machinations have reached their apex, and Nightingale is poised for global assimilation." Thorne. Not Vance, but Thorne. This was a critical distinction. Vance was the figurehead, the public face of NovaTech's ambition, but Thorne was the engineer, the unseen hand pulling the strings. Sterling, it seemed, had been aware of Thorne's deeper involvement, his insidious influence reaching beyond the stated goals of the Nightingale project. The phrase "global assimilation" sent a fresh wave of unease through Miller. It implied more than just data control; it hinted at a complete societal overhaul, a world remade in NovaTech's image.

The message, however, offered another thread to pull: "The payload has been transferred. I have entrusted it to your safekeeping." This 'payload' was distinct from the information Sterling had managed to get to Jenkins, partially decrypted from the USB drive. This was the *real* leverage, the data Anya was meant to access and deploy. Miller scanned Sterling's note again, searching for any mention of a physical location or a secondary recipient, anything that could bridge the gap between Anya's potential presence and the physical evidence Sterling had so carefully concealed. He found it, buried within the final paragraphs: "The key to its final activation, the sequence to neutralize Nightingale, is contained within the 'Crimson Star' data. It's not a metaphor, Anya. It's specific astronomical data I've embedded within the observatory's historical logs, tied to the 2042 anomaly. You know how to access it. You were always the best at finding the hidden paths."

The observatory. Sterling's cryptic clue, initially dismissed as a celestial metaphor, was in fact a literal location on the *Odyssey*. The ship boasted a state-of-the-art astronomical observatory, a luxury for its wealthy clientele, but for Sterling, it was a secure vault. The "Crimson Star" data, described as specific astronomical data linked to the 2042 anomaly, was the final piece of Sterling's counter-offensive. Anya, with her knack for uncovering hidden pathways, was meant to retrieve this data, use it to activate the neutralization sequence, and then, presumably, deliver the complete package to someone like Jenkins, or perhaps even to the authorities. The implications were staggering. Sterling hadn't just anticipated his own potential demise; he'd meticulously planned for it, creating a fail-safe that relied on a trusted ally and a hidden cache of information.

Miller's mind raced, connecting the dots. Anya Sharma was the key, the observatory was the lock, and the "Crimson Star" data was the keyhole. But Thorne's machinations, Sterling's fear of betrayal – these elements painted a darker picture. If Sterling had anticipated being silenced, he would have also anticipated Thorne's complicity. Had Sterling sent Anya a separate message, a more direct one, to guide her to the observatory? Or was the coded note on his laptop all she had? He hoped Sterling had been thorough, that Anya would indeed know where to look. The "hidden paths" Sterling mentioned—it spoke of an intuition, a shared understanding, a level of expertise that only Anya possessed. This wasn't just about code-breaking; it was about navigating a labyrinth designed by a master.

He activated his comms unit, his voice low and urgent. "Jenkins, I need you to run a full background check on any passenger or crew member named Anya Sharma. Look for any links to Sterling, NovaTech, or any known cryptology or data analysis fields. Prioritize anyone with a history of... unconventional problem-solving." He paused, considering Sterling's mention of Thorne. "Also, run a similar check on Dr. Aris Thorne. He's a passenger on this ship, a historian. See if there's any known association with Sterling or NovaTech. And Jenkins, I need access to the ship's manifest for the observatory's restricted access logs. I have a hunch Sterling might have left something behind there."

The response from Jenkins was immediate, a clipped confirmation of his orders. Miller leaned back, the hum of the engines a monotonous drone against the frantic beat of his heart. He was on a ship teeming with potential threats, a floating city of secrets, and he was one man against a formidable enemy. Sterling's decrypted message was a lifeline, but it also cast a long shadow of uncertainty. Anya Sharma was his best lead, but her very anonymity made her a vulnerability. If Vance or Thorne knew she was Sterling's intended successor, they would be hunting her with the same ferocity that Miller was.

He pulled up the ship's directory, cross-referencing passenger lists with crew manifests. Dr. Aris Thorne was listed as a guest in a premium suite, a renowned historian specializing in ancient civilizations and technological development. His profile was filled with academic accolades and published works. There was no mention of Sterling, no hint of any connection to NovaTech's clandestine operations. It seemed Thorne was just another wealthy patron, an unwitting passenger on this voyage into the unknown. But Sterling's warning was specific: "Thorne's machinations." It implied a deeper, more sinister role.

Miller accessed the ship's internal network, navigating through layers of security protocols that felt almost quaint compared to Sterling's analog brilliance. He found the observatory's access logs. They were heavily encrypted, as expected, but Sterling, with his intimate knowledge of NovaTech's systems, would have found a way to bypass them or embed his own credentials. Miller spent the next hour poring over the data, looking for any anomalies, any unusual access patterns around the time Sterling might have been using the observatory. He found a series of entries from a week prior, all logged under a generic technician ID, accessing the observatory's main data core. The timestamps were consistent with Sterling's known movements before he went dark.

"Jenkins," Miller said, his voice tight. "The observatory technician ID. Can you trace that? I want to know who was accessing the core on those dates."

A beat of silence, then Jenkins's reply. "Working on it, Miller. The logs are heavily obfuscated, but I'm seeing some interesting packet routing that Sterling might have used. It's... elegant. Almost like he built his own backdoor into the system."

Miller felt a surge of respect for the fallen cryptographer. Sterling hadn't just predicted his own downfall; he'd prepared for it with an almost artistic flair. He then turned his attention back to the passenger list, his eyes scanning the names again. Thorne. Michael Thorne. He'd seen that name before, in the periphery of Jenkins's initial data dump. Michael Thorne was a mid-level executive at a subsidiary of NovaTech, a man whose digital footprint was meticulously scrubbed clean, almost too clean. He was Vance's protégé, a rising star groomed for leadership. Miller recalled a brief mention of a strained relationship, a public fallout between Michael Thorne and his father, Dr. Aris Thorne, years ago. The estrangement had been widely reported in academic circles. Could this be the link? Sterling, knowing Thorne's deep involvement, had perhaps used his estranged son's presence on the ship as a subtle nod, a piece of misdirection, or perhaps a way to ensure Michael would be within striking distance of any crucial information.

But Sterling's message had been clear: "To Anya Sharma." The primary recipient was Anya. The mention of Thorne was a warning about his actions, not an indication that Thorne himself was the intended beneficiary of Sterling's final contingency. Miller's mind wrestled with the possibility. What if Sterling had entrusted Aris Thorne with something, unaware of his son's true allegiances, or perhaps using Thorne as a unwitting pawn? Sterling had mentioned a "betrayal" and a "trusted ally who had turned coat." Could that ally be Aris Thorne himself? It seemed unlikely for a historian to be involved in such high-stakes espionage, but Sterling operated on a different plane of reality.

"Jenkins, what's the status on Anya Sharma?" Miller asked, his patience wearing thin.

"Still a dead end, Miller. No passenger or crew with that name. However," Jenkins's voice shifted, a subtle hint of intrigue entering his tone, "I did find something interesting about Dr. Aris Thorne. There are whispers, unsubstantiated reports from years ago, linking him to a clandestine research project funded by a shell corporation with ties to... Sterling's early work. The project was allegedly about secure data transmission, advanced cryptography. It was shut down abruptly, officially because of lack of funding."

Miller's blood ran cold. Sterling's early work. A historian involved in advanced cryptography. It was a jarring juxtaposition, but Sterling had a way of finding the most unlikely people for his most critical tasks. "The Crimson Star data," Miller murmured, rereading the message. "Sterling said Anya would know how to access it. 'You know how to access it. You were always the best at finding the hidden paths.' What if Anya Sharma isn't a person, Jenkins? What if it's a codename?"

"A codename for whom?" Jenkins asked, his voice sharp with professional curiosity.

"For Dr. Aris Thorne," Miller stated, the pieces clicking into place with a sickening thud. "Sterling's warning about 'Thorne's machinations' wasn't about the historian being an enemy; it was about the *name* Thorne being a symbol of betrayal. Sterling needed Anya to be aware of Thorne's involvement, to understand the danger. But the person Sterling trusted, the one he embedded the crucial information with, the one who could find the 'hidden paths'... that was Aris Thorne. Sterling believed Thorne was still on his side, or at least capable of being a conduit. The encrypted data Sterling mentioned in his note, the 'payload' Anya was to safekeep, wasn't just the astronomical data from the observatory. It was a secondary package Sterling entrusted to Aris Thorne. Sterling must have known that if something happened to him, Aris Thorne, his old colleague, would be the one to carry the torch. Sterling's note was meant for Anya, a directive on how to proceed, but the actual physical data, the corroborating evidence against Vance and Thorne's conspiracy, was with Aris Thorne."

Miller's mind raced. The encrypted message on the laptop was a contingency, a fail-safe in case Sterling was caught before he could deliver the full package. But Sterling was too meticulous to rely on a single point of failure. He would have had a primary plan, a more direct hand-off. And if Anya Sharma was Sterling's confidante, his trusted successor, and Sterling was also hinting at a betrayal, then the entrusted data had to be with someone Sterling *thought* he could trust, but who was ultimately compromised or being manipulated. The mention of Aris Thorne being estranged from his son, Michael, who was a rising star within NovaTech, was too coincidental. Sterling, a master strategist, would have seen this familial connection as a potential leverage point, or perhaps even a vulnerability.

"Jenkins, I need you to access Dr. Aris Thorne's suite. Discreetly. I need to know what he's carrying. Sterling mentioned a 'payload' transferred. If Thorne is the unwitting carrier, that's our payload. And the passphrase... Sterling mentioned a passphrase in his note, didn't he? Something about the key to the final activation?" Miller scanned the decrypted text again. No, not a passphrase for the payload itself, but the

Crimson Star data was the key to the *activation* of the neutralization sequence. The payload Sterling entrusted to Anya was likely a physical data drive, or perhaps a series of encrypted files.

"No passphrase for a payload, Miller," Jenkins confirmed. "Just the Crimson Star data as the activation key for the neutralization protocol. But you're onto something. Sterling's note was an indirect message. If Anya Sharma was his intended recipient, why send the message to a laptop that could be intercepted? He knew he was being watched. He must have had a more direct method for Anya to receive the full instructions."

Miller's gaze fell on a peculiar detail in Sterling's note, a subtle shift in the narrative. Sterling had written, "The payload has been transferred. I have entrusted it to your safekeeping." Then, he spoke of the Crimson Star data, hidden in the observatory, as the "key to its final activation." This implied two distinct pieces of information: the payload, which Anya was to safekeep, and the activation key, which was in the observatory. But who was Sterling truly talking to when he wrote the note? Was it Anya directly, or was it a message meant to be found, a breadcrumb trail for someone like Miller to follow?

He re-read the opening lines of Sterling's message: "To Anya Sharma: If you are reading this, then my worst fears have been realized." This confirmed Anya was the intended recipient of the message itself. But the 'payload' she was to safekeep... where was it? Sterling implied it was already transferred. Could it be that Anya Sharma was not a person but a project, a system, that Sterling had initiated and was now entrusting to Aris Thorne, the historian, under the guise of a historical research project? No, Sterling's language was too personal, too urgent for Anya to be a mere project. He spoke of her ability to find "hidden paths."

Then it struck Miller. The betrayal. Sterling's trusted ally turning coat. What if that ally was Aris Thorne himself? Sterling, in his paranoia, might have mistaken Aris Thorne's actions, or perhaps Thorne had been coerced or manipulated by Vance. Sterling had entrusted him with a secondary set of encrypted data. If Thorne was carrying it, and he was also the "trusted ally who turned coat," then Sterling's note was a desperate plea for Anya to be aware of this betrayal and to retrieve the data herself, likely from Thorne.

"Jenkins, I need you to get me into Dr. Aris Thorne's suite. Now," Miller commanded, his voice a low growl. "And find out if Dr. Aris Thorne has any children. Specifically, a son. Michael Thorne."

The silence on the other end stretched for a beat, heavy with implication. "Already on it, Miller. Dr. Aris Thorne has one son, Michael Thorne. Former NovaTech executive, current... consultant for a few less reputable organizations. The estrangement is well-documented. Michael Thorne is also listed as a passenger on the

Odyssey, in a different section, but his proximity is... significant."

Miller closed his eyes, a grim smile touching his lips. Sterling's intricate plan was finally starting to make sense. Sterling, knowing he was compromised, had entrusted the final, critical data – the payload – to Aris Thorne, a man he believed was still loyal. He had likely done this before his capture, leaving Thorne with a physical data storage device, encrypted, of course. Sterling's note, intended for Anya, was a secondary fail-safe, a roadmap for her to understand the situation, to know where to look for the activation key in the observatory, and to potentially confront Thorne if necessary to retrieve the payload. The betrayal Sterling feared wasn't necessarily Thorne turning coat against him, but Thorne's inherent vulnerability, or his son Michael's insidious influence, leading to the data falling into the wrong hands. Sterling had prepared Anya for the worst-case scenario: that his trusted ally might falter, and she would have to retrieve the crucial evidence herself. The "Crimson Star" data in the observatory was the key to unlocking the entire Nightingale system, but the payload, the concrete evidence implicating Vance and Thorne, was physically with Aris Thorne. And Michael Thorne, the estranged son with ties to the shadier side of NovaTech, was on the same ship, a ticking time bomb in the corridors of power. Miller now had two objectives: secure the Crimson Star data from the observatory, and secure the payload from Dr. Aris Thorne, all while evading Vance's operatives and ensuring Anya Sharma, whoever or whatever she was, was safe. The game had just escalated, and the stakes were higher than ever.

The realization that Michael Thorne was not merely a convenient connection but a potential threat on board the *Odyssey* tightened Miller's chest. Sterling's decrypted message, a lifeline of coded warnings and desperate plans, was not the only intelligence at play. Vance, the puppet master of NovaTech, and his ambitious protégé, Michael Thorne, were not operating blind. Miller felt a prickle of unease, a cold certainty that his own cautious steps were being anticipated, perhaps even orchestrated. Vance and Michael Thorne would undoubtedly have their own network, their own eyes and ears within Sterling's orbit, or perhaps even closer, within the very fabric of NovaTech's sprawling operations. Sterling's circle, once thought to be airtight, might have harbored an informant, a mole whispering secrets into Vance's ear. Or, more chillingly, Sterling himself, in his final hours, might have been under such intense surveillance that his every move, his every encrypted dispatch, was being monitored.

This wasn't just a race against time; it was a deadly game of chess, with pawns and queens moving in predictable, yet treacherous, patterns. If Vance and Michael Thorne knew about Sterling's contingency plan, if they understood that the historian, Dr. Aris Thorne, was in possession of something critical, then their primary objective would be to intercept both the father and the son, and the data they represented. Miller pictured Michael Thorne, the estranged son, his presence on the ship no longer a coincidence but a deliberate deployment. Michael Thorne wasn't here to reconcile with his father; he was here to contain him. He was here to ensure that Aris Thorne did not fall into Miller's hands, did not cooperate with the investigation, and most certainly, did not inadvertently or intentionally hand over the payload Sterling had entrusted to him.

The thought of Michael Thorne being present, a wolf in sheep's clothing among the oblivious passengers, sent a fresh wave of urgency through Miller. He had to reach Aris Thorne first. He had to secure the data before Michael Thorne could get to it, or worse, before Michael Thorne could get to his father. The possibility of Michael Thorne being directly involved in Sterling's death, or at least complicit in the cover-up, loomed large. Sterling's mention of a betrayal, a trusted ally turning coat, now carried a chilling new dimension. Was Sterling referring to Aris Thorne's son, who had perhaps manipulated or coerced his father? Or had Aris Thorne himself, under duress or swayed by misguided loyalty, become the instrument of Sterling's downfall?

Miller's mind raced, replaying Sterling's fragmented message. "Thorne's machinations have reached their apex, and Nightingale is poised for global assimilation." The 'Thorne' Sterling referred to was undoubtedly Dr. Aris Thorne, the historian. But Sterling's warning of machinations and betrayal suggested a deeper conspiracy, one that Vance and Michael Thorne were clearly a part of. If Michael Thorne was actively working against Sterling's plan, his presence on the

Odyssey was more than just a precaution; it was an active measure to thwart any attempt to expose Nightingale.

He imagined Michael Thorne, a man whose digital footprint was meticulously erased, a ghost in the corporate machine, moving through the ship's opulent corridors with a singular purpose. Vance wouldn't send a foot soldier; he would send someone with Sterling's understanding of NovaTech's internal workings, someone who could anticipate Sterling's moves and counter them effectively. Michael Thorne, Sterling's former protégé and Vance's chosen successor, fit that profile perfectly. He would know how Sterling thought, how he operated. He would understand the value of the payload and the critical nature of the Crimson Star data.

The implications were staggering. Sterling's meticulously crafted contingency plan was not just facing an unknown enemy; it was facing an enemy who was aware of the plan, who was on the ground, and who was actively working to dismantle it. Miller was no longer just trying to uncover the truth; he was in a desperate race to protect it, to safeguard the fragile evidence Sterling had left behind. The presence of both father and son, historical colleagues and estranged family, now represented a nexus of danger and opportunity.

"Jenkins," Miller's voice was a low growl, the urgency palpable. "We need to move. Now. Dr. Aris Thorne's suite. I want eyes on it. Discreetly. And Michael Thorne. Where is he? What are his movements?"

"On it, Miller," Jenkins's voice crackled, the sound of frantic keyboard tapping filling the brief silence. "Michael Thorne's suite is on Deck 7, forward section. He's been observed moving between his suite and the observation lounge on Deck 5. His movements are erratic, almost as if he's searching for something... or someone. And I'm rerouting security camera feeds from Deck 7, near Dr. Thorne's suite. We'll have eyes on it within minutes."

Miller felt a surge of adrenaline. The pieces were falling into place, forming a picture far more complex and perilous than he had initially imagined. Sterling's message was a beacon of hope, but it had also inadvertently illuminated the traps laid by Vance and his allies. The Crimson Star data was the key to neutralizing Nightingale, but it was also a lure, a bait designed to draw out Sterling's allies and eliminate them. And Dr. Aris Thorne, the historian, was caught in the middle, a pawn in a game he might not fully comprehend, while his son, Michael, was the hunter, sent to ensure his father remained a pawn, or worse, to seize the prize for himself.

"If Michael Thorne is actively searching, and he knows about the payload," Miller mused aloud, his gaze fixed on the ship's schematic, "then he's likely looking for his father, or for the data his father possesses. Sterling's note to Anya... if Anya is indeed Aris Thorne, then Michael might be looking for Sterling's communication as well. He'd want to know what Sterling entrusted to his father, and to whom Sterling intended it to go."

The thought of Michael Thorne actively intercepting Sterling's message was a grim one. Sterling had been meticulous, his digital security layered and complex. But if Vance had resources, if they had moles, or if Sterling had made a single misstep in his final moments, Michael Thorne might have already gained crucial insights. The fact that Michael Thorne was on the

Odyssey with his estranged father, a man holding Sterling's contingency data, was too coincidental to ignore. Vance wouldn't leave such a critical operation to chance. He would have placed his most trusted operative, his most ambitious protégé, in a position to control the narrative, to intercept the evidence, and to silence any opposition.

"Miller," Jenkins's voice cut through Miller's thoughts, "I've got Dr. Thorne's suite. No one has entered or exited in the last hour. But there's... an anomaly. A data spike originating from within the suite, about twenty minutes ago. Short, intense. It suggests Thorne might have been accessing something, or perhaps... receiving something. And Michael Thorne is currently en route to Deck 7, heading directly towards his father's suite."

The race was on. Miller pushed himself up from the console, his mind already mapping out the quickest route. The opulent confines of the

Odyssey suddenly felt like a labyrinth, each corridor a potential ambush, each passenger a suspect. Sterling had called Anya Sharma the best at finding hidden paths, but now Miller had to find his own hidden path, a path that led him to Aris Thorne and the payload before Michael Thorne could intercept them both. The Crimson Star data in the observatory was a crucial piece, but the physical payload, the evidence against Vance and Thorne, was the real prize. And Michael Thorne was clearly aware of its significance. His presence wasn't a coincidence; it was a calculated move to secure Sterling's legacy, or rather, to bury it permanently. Sterling's final act of defiance had become a hunt, a desperate scramble for truth in the heart of darkness, with the fate of Nightingale hanging in the balance. The trap was set, and Miller was walking directly into its center, hoping he could disarm it before it snapped shut.

Chapter 8: The Historian's Secret

The low hum of the *Odyssey*'s advanced life support system, usually a soothing backdrop to the ship's luxurious ambiance, now felt like a discordant thrum against Miller's heightened senses. He moved with a practiced stealth, Jenkins a shadow a few paces behind, their eyes scanning the opulent corridor of Deck 7. The air, thick with the scent of polished mahogany and expensive perfume, seemed to hold its breath, anticipating their next move. Sterling's final, desperate message had been a beacon, but it had also cast a stark light on the predatory shadows lurking beneath the gilded surface of their voyage. Dr. Aris Thorne, the historian, was the lynchpin, the innocent holder of a truth that Vance and his son, Michael, were determined to bury.

They found him in a secluded alcove, bathed in the soft glow of a strategically placed reading lamp. Dr. Thorne was a picture of academic serenity, a man seemingly adrift from the tempestuous events unfolding around them. His silver hair was neatly combed, and his spectacles perched on the bridge of his nose as he hunched over a worn leather-bound volume. The intensity with which he read was palpable, his brow furrowed in concentration, oblivious to the predatory gaze that had been fixed upon him. It was a stark contrast to the digital ghost that was his son, Michael, a man forged in the ruthless fires of NovaTech's machinations.

Miller approached slowly, his movements deliberately non-threatening, a stark departure from the urgency that coursed through him. Jenkins, ever the pragmatist, had managed to discreetly disable the security camera feed for this specific section, a small victory in their increasingly desperate race. The alcove offered a measure of privacy, a fleeting sanctuary before they plunged Dr. Thorne into the heart of the storm.

"Dr. Thorne?" Miller's voice was low, carefully modulated to avoid startling the unassuming scholar. He kept his hands visible, palms open, a universal gesture of appeasement.

The historian looked up, his eyes, the color of a faded academic journal, blinked behind his lenses. A flicker of mild annoyance crossed his face, quickly replaced by polite curiosity. He was a man accustomed to interruptions, but the steely resolve in Miller's gaze, the coiled tension in his posture, hinted at something far beyond a misplaced passenger or a request for directions.

"Yes?" Dr. Thorne's voice was soft, cultured, the kind one might expect from a man who spent his life immersed in the hushed halls of libraries and archives. He gestured vaguely to the book in his lap. "I'm afraid I'm rather engrossed at the moment. Unless this is about the... the lectures on Roman aqueducts? I believe the next one isn't until tomorrow."

Miller offered a faint, almost imperceptible smile. "No, Dr. Thorne. It's... a matter of significant importance. A matter concerning Mr. Sterling."

The mention of Sterling's name caused a subtle shift in Dr. Thorne's demeanor. The academic detachment wavered, replaced by a dawning unease. He closed the book, his fingers tracing the embossed title with a practiced grace that belied his sudden apprehension. "Sterling? I... I knew him, of course. A colleague. A brilliant man. Is something wrong?"

"Mr. Sterling is dead, Dr. Thorne," Miller stated, the words delivered with a measured gravity. He watched for the reaction, the subtle tells that would betray his history with Sterling, his knowledge of the Crimson Star data.

Dr. Thorne's face paled, his lips parting slightly. "Dead? That's... impossible. I spoke with him only a few days ago. He was in fine spirits, though... preoccupied." His gaze darted around the alcove, as if searching for an unseen listener, a phantom threat. "What happened?"

"That," Miller said, stepping closer, his voice dropping to a near whisper, "is precisely what we need to discuss with you. And we believe you may hold some key information."

Jenkins, meanwhile, had been discreetly observing the surrounding area. His sharp eyes caught a faint tremor in Dr. Thorne's hand as he set the book down. The historian's world, Miller realized, was about to collide with a reality far more dangerous than any ancient manuscript could describe.

"Information?" Dr. Thorne's voice was a shade higher now, tinged with bewilderment. "I don't understand. I'm just a historian. My contributions were purely academic." He fidgeted with the cuff of his tweed jacket. "Sterling was kind enough to entrust me with some research notes, some... rather esoteric documents. He asked me to keep them safe for him. For a 'contingency,' he called it. I thought it was merely a matter of safeguarding some sensitive historical findings, perhaps related to his work at NovaTech."

"Those 'research notes,' Dr. Thorne," Miller began, choosing his words carefully, "are far more than that. They are the key to exposing a grave conspiracy, a conspiracy that cost Mr. Sterling his life."

The weight of Miller's words settled in the small space. Dr. Thorne looked from Miller to Jenkins, his eyes wide with a dawning horror. The serene academic was being stripped away, revealing a man caught in a web he hadn't realized existed.

"A conspiracy?" he whispered, his gaze unfocused, as if trying to reconcile the abstract concept with the tangible reality of the murder onboard. "I... I don't know what you're talking about. Sterling was a friend. He was concerned about something at NovaTech, something he termed 'Nightingale.' He mentioned he had secured evidence, proof of... irregularities. He said he was entrusting it to someone who could ensure it wouldn't be lost. He didn't... he didn't tell me who it was meant for, or what exactly it entailed. He simply asked me to hold onto a small data module, encrypted, of course. He said he'd retrieve it when the time was right. He made it sound... almost like a game of historical preservation."

Miller's jaw tightened. "A game, Dr. Thorne, that Vance, the CEO of NovaTech, and his associates are determined to win by any means necessary. And they know you have it."

The historian flinched as if struck. "Vance? The CEO? But... why would he care about my research notes? And how would he know?"

"Because," Miller continued, his voice a low, steady current of revelation, "those notes are not merely historical documents. They are evidence. Evidence of illicit activities within NovaTech, activities that Mr.

Sterling was trying to bring to light. And they know that you, Dr. Thorne, are the custodian of that evidence."

A cold dread began to creep into Dr. Thorne's eyes. He clutched the book tighter, its worn cover a fragile shield against the encroaching darkness. "I... I don't understand the depth of this. Sterling only spoke in generalities. He was worried about... a project. Nightingale. He said it was a project that could change the world, but not for the better."

"And Mr. Sterling entrusted you with the means to stop it," Jenkins interjected, his voice a low rumble. "He saw you as a safe harbor. He underestimated the reach of Vance's ambition, and perhaps, the machinations of his own former protégé."

"Protégé?" Dr. Thorne echoed, confusion clouding his features. "Who...?"

Miller didn't miss a beat. "Your son, Dr. Thorne. Michael."

The name hung in the air, heavy with unspoken history and burgeoning dread. Dr. Thorne's face contorted, a mixture of disbelief and dawning horror. "Michael? My son? But... he wouldn't... he works for Sterling, or... Vance, I suppose, at NovaTech. He's a programmer, a digital architect. He's brilliant, but... we haven't spoken in years. He's always been... distant. Obsessed with his work. He wouldn't be involved in anything like this."

"He is," Miller stated, his voice devoid of any emotion. "And he is on this ship, Dr. Thorne. He's not here to reconcile with you. He's here to ensure that Sterling's evidence, the evidence you possess, never sees the light of day. He's here to silence you, and to retrieve the data."

The color drained completely from Dr. Thorne's face. His hands trembled, the worn book slipping from his grasp and thudding softly onto the plush carpet. He stared at Miller, his eyes wide with a profound and devastating understanding. The quiet world of ancient texts had irrevocably shattered, replaced by the stark, brutal reality of murder, conspiracy, and the chilling betrayal of his own son.

"Michael..." he breathed, the name a ghost of a plea. "He's... he's here?"

"He is," Jenkins confirmed, his gaze sweeping the corridor once more. "And he's been seen moving erratically on this deck. He's looking for you, Doctor. And he's not alone in his intentions."

Dr. Thorne swayed, a man suddenly unmoored, his carefully constructed reality crumbling around him. He looked at Miller, at Jenkins, his face a mask of shock and dawning fear. "I... I thought he was just concerned about my well-being. He contacted me a few days ago, said he was on a business trip and wanted to surprise me, to see if I was enjoying the cruise. He was... strangely insistent on meeting. I dismissed it as a fatherly gesture, a reconciliation of sorts. But he was... intense. Asking questions about my research, about Sterling. I... I told him Sterling had entrusted me with some sensitive documents, some research notes for safekeeping. I didn't realize..." He trailed off, his voice choked with despair.

"He knew," Miller said, the pieces slotting into a grim, familiar pattern. "He knew Sterling had confided in you. He knew you had the data. Vance wouldn't send an outsider. He'd send his most trusted operative, someone who understood Sterling's methods, someone who could anticipate his moves. Michael Thorne is that operative."

Dr. Thorne's hands flew to his face, as if to ward off an unseen blow. "My son... working against Sterling? Against... the truth? This is... this is monstrous. Sterling was a good man. He believed in transparency, in progress. He would never be a part of... whatever this Nightingale is."

"Nightingale, Dr. Thorne, is Vance's endgame," Miller explained, his voice low and urgent. "A project that could reshape global power, using technology that Sterling uncovered and sought to expose. Your 'research notes' are the proof. And Michael Thorne, under Vance's direction, is here to ensure that proof remains buried."

The historian's breathing grew shallow, his eyes darting nervously. The realization that his own son was a threat, a hunter, was clearly a profound shock. His world, once defined by the quiet pursuit of knowledge, was now a battlefield, and he, a defenceless scholar, was at its epicenter.

"He asked about the data module," Dr. Thorne stammered, his voice laced with a new fear. "He... he wanted to see it. I refused, of course. I told him Sterling had given it to me for safekeeping, and I would only hand it over to him or to an authorized recipient as per Sterling's instructions. I thought... I thought I was protecting Sterling's legacy. I never imagined..."

"You were right to refuse him, Doctor," Jenkins said, his tone firm. "And you were right to be wary. Your instincts were correct. But now, we need to ensure your safety, and the safety of that data. Michael Thorne is not the only threat on this ship."

Miller met Dr. Thorne's gaze, a silent promise in his eyes. "We understand this is a shock, Doctor. Sterling entrusted you with something vital, and we are here to help you fulfill that trust. But we must move, and we must move quickly. Your son is actively searching for you. He knows you are here, and he knows what you possess."

Dr. Thorne nodded, his scholarly composure replaced by a raw, primal fear. He was no longer just a historian safeguarding notes; he was a man on the run, hunted by his own flesh and blood. The

Odyssey, once a symbol of leisurely escape, had become a gilded cage, and the shadows within it were far more terrifying than any he had encountered in the dusty archives of history.

"Where... where do we go?" he asked, his voice trembling.

"First," Miller said, extending a hand to help the historian rise, "we need to get you somewhere safe. And then, Dr. Thorne, you need to tell us everything Sterling told you. Every detail, no matter how insignificant it may seem. Because the fate of Nightingale, and perhaps much more, depends on it."

As Dr. Thorne shakily got to his feet, the worn leather-bound book lay forgotten on the floor, a symbol of the life he was being forced to leave behind. The air in the alcove, once still and serene, now crackled with an electric tension, the prelude to a storm that was about to break over them all. The quiet historian was about to become a key player in a deadly game, his personal tragedy intertwined with a global conspiracy, and the chilling realization that his son was the hunter, not the protector, was only the beginning. Sterling's contingency plan, so meticulously crafted, was now a desperate scramble for survival, with Dr. Aris Thorne caught in the crosshairs of his own son's ambition, a pawn in Vance's deadly game. The Crimson Star data, the key to everything, was in the ship's observatory, but the immediate threat was far more personal, far more devastating.

The historian's hands, which had moments before trembled with shock and fear, now firmed with a newfound, albeit fragile, resolve. "A locket?" he repeated, his brow furrowing in thought. "He... he didn't mention a locket, not directly. He spoke of 'research notes,' 'esoteric documents.' But... he did show me something. A keepsake. He said it was great sentimental value, an heirloom passed down through his family. He... he had it with him when we last spoke. He was fiddling with it. I assumed it was just... sentimental." Dr. Thorne's eyes, which had been wide with a desperate fear, now held a spark of recollection, a faint glimmer of understanding piercing through the fog of betrayal. "It was old, antique-looking. I remember thinking it was rather out of place with his usual modern accouterments. He seemed... reluctant to let it out of his sight."

Miller leaned in, his voice low and urgent. "An heirloom, you say? Describe it, Doctor. Every detail."

Dr. Thorne closed his eyes for a moment, picturing the scene, Sterling's face, the small, ornate object he had held with such care. "It was... intricately carved. Dark metal, possibly tarnished silver or a similar alloy. The design was... floral, I believe. Or perhaps some kind of stylized crest. It had a delicate chain attached. He kept it in his jacket pocket, and when he showed it to me, he opened it. I only saw a glimpse inside, a flash of something metallic, something that looked like... circuitry, perhaps? But it was so quick, so fleeting, I dismissed it as a trick of the light, or perhaps some kind of miniature mirror he'd had fitted. He said it was a 'personal archive,' a place where he kept memories. I thought he meant photographs, or perhaps a tiny recorded message."

"A personal archive," Miller murmured, the words resonating with a chilling significance. Sterling, the master of misdirection, the architect of contingencies. It fit. "And where is this locket now, Doctor?"

A wave of guilt washed over Dr. Thorne's face. "When Sterling... when he died, I... I was distraught. I didn't think. I only remembered him showing me that trinket, and then... then I saw it. When they were clearing out his suite, I saw it on his bedside table, overlooked by the staff. I... I took it. I told myself I was safeguarding his personal effects, ensuring nothing was lost or mishandled. I thought... I thought it was just a memento. I put it in my stateroom, in my desk drawer. I haven't touched it since. I assumed it contained... whatever Sterling deemed important enough to keep close."

Jenkins, who had been quietly observing, stepped forward. "And you believe this 'locket' contains the data Sterling entrusted to you?"

Dr. Thorne nodded, his gaze fixed on Miller. "It must. He was so secretive about it. He insisted I keep it safe, that it was 'more than just notes.' He mentioned it was a 'crucial element' of his contingency. I was focused on the academic side, the historical context of his research. I never considered that the 'archive' he spoke of was not figurative, but literal. That the keepsake itself was the vessel." He sighed, a heavy sound in the tense silence. "My stateroom is... it's not far from here. I can retrieve it."

As they moved through the hushed corridors of the *Odyssey*, Dr. Thorne led them with a hurried, anxious gait. The opulent surroundings, which had seemed so serene and civilized just hours before, now felt like a gilded cage, each polished surface reflecting their own desperation. The hum of the ship's engines, once a comfort, now seemed to pulse with an underlying menace, a constant reminder of their isolation and the closing net.

"It's imperative, Doctor," Miller said, his voice barely a whisper, "that we get that locket and access its contents. Sterling's deciphered note mentioned a passphrase. Did he give you any indication of what that might be?"

Dr. Thorne shook his head. "No. He said it would be 'intuitive,' 'a key that only he and his most trusted confidante would possess.' I searched the notes I took from our conversations, the annotated papers he left me, but nothing stood out as a passphrase. I confess, my focus was on the historical implications of his research, the potential impact on our understanding of the Crimson Star project. The technical details, the encryption... it was beyond my purview."

They reached Dr. Thorne's stateroom, a space that mirrored the quiet scholarly life he inhabited. Books lined the walls, interspersed with framed historical maps and artifacts. The air was thick with the scent of old paper and leather. He moved directly to a heavy mahogany desk, his hands almost fumbling as he pulled open a drawer. Inside, nestled amongst a collection of antique fountain pens and a well-worn pocket watch, lay the locket.

It was exactly as he had described: dark, intricately carved metal, with a delicate chain. The design was indeed a stylized crest, a hawk in flight, its wings spread wide. It exuded an aura of age, of history, a tangible link to Sterling's past. Dr. Thorne picked it up, his fingers tracing the familiar patterns. "This is it," he confirmed, his voice hushed with a reverence that was now tinged with dread. "He showed me this. He said... he said it held the 'echoes of truth.'"

Miller took the locket, his fingers surprisingly gentle as he turned it over in his palm. It felt cool and solid, heavier than it looked. He examined the clasp, the subtle seams that hinted at its hidden purpose. "An echo of truth," Miller mused. "Sterling was always so poetic." He looked at Dr. Thorne. "The passphrase. Think, Doctor. What would Sterling have considered 'intuitive'? Something deeply personal to him."

Dr. Thorne's gaze drifted to a framed photograph on his desk – a younger Sterling, smiled, with a boy of about ten standing beside him. The boy, with his bright, intelligent eyes and sharp features, was unmistakably Michael. A pang of sorrow shot through the historian. "Michael," Dr. Thorne whispered, almost involuntarily. He then looked at Miller, a flicker of dawning comprehension in his eyes. "Sterling... he spoke of his son. His estranged son. He was bitter about their relationship, about how he felt he'd failed him. He mentioned Michael often. He said... he said Michael was 'a genius with code, a true successor in intellect, but lost to the darkness of ambition.' He... he even alluded to Sterling's fascination with the ancient concepts of 'legacy' and 'lineage.' He often spoke about how a parent's legacy could be both a burden and a guide to their child. He had a phrase he used... when he spoke of his hopes for Michael, despite their estrangement. He'd say, 'He carries my heart, but wields a different sword.'"

Miller's eyes narrowed. "'He carries my heart, but wields a different sword.' That has to be it." He turned the locket over, his thumb finding a nearly invisible indentation near the clasp. With a gentle pressure, the locket clicked open.

Inside, nestled within the intricately carved casing, was not a miniature mirror or a photograph, but a small, wafer-thin data chip, its surface shimmering with a faint, iridescent glow. It was a piece of technology far more advanced than the locket's antique exterior suggested. Miller carefully extracted the chip, his movements precise and economical. Jenkins produced a compact, highly advanced reader from his kit, its screen glowing to life as Miller inserted the chip.

The screen flickered, then resolved into a complex interface. A prompt appeared: "Enter Passphrase."

Miller typed: "He carries my heart, but wields a different sword."

For a tense moment, nothing happened. Then, a soft chime echoed in the stateroom. The prompt disappeared, replaced by a cascading stream of data. Files, documents, logs, audio recordings – a digital deluge.

"It worked," Jenkins breathed, a rare hint of relief in his voice. "Sterling's contingency is active." Miller began to navigate the data, his eyes scanning the screen with practiced speed. "This is it," he murmured, his voice tight with a mixture of triumph and grim satisfaction. "This is Sterling's backup. It's all here."

The files were meticulously organized, a testament to Sterling's foresight. There were encrypted communication logs detailing clandestine meetings and financial transfers. There were detailed reports on the development and deployment of the Nightingale project, the chilling specifics of its intended purpose laid bare. But most damning were the financial statements.

"Julian Vance," Miller stated, his voice low and resonant, as he pointed to a series of transaction records. "These offshore accounts, these shell corporations... they're all linked directly to him. Lavish payments, laundered funds. This isn't just a conspiracy, Doctor. This is a systematic, global-scale operation of corruption, and Vance is at its very heart." He scrolled further, revealing correspondence between Vance and various international financiers, outlining the manipulation of markets, the acquisition of compromised politicians, and the systematic suppression of any information that could derail their plans.

Dr. Thorne leaned closer, his initial shock giving way to a profound sorrow and a cold, intellectual fury. He recognized the names of some of the shell companies, the convoluted financial instruments Sterling had often spoken of with disdain as tools of obfuscation. "It's worse than I imagined," he whispered, his voice heavy with the weight of the revelation. "Sterling believed Nightingale was a weaponization of data, a tool for absolute control. But this... this is economic warfare. They're not just seeking to control information; they're seeking to control the world's very infrastructure."

Jenkins, his gaze sharp and analytical, focused on a particular set of audio files. "These are internal communications within NovaTech, recorded over the last six months. They confirm Vance's direct involvement, his authorization of... ethically questionable actions. He's been actively silencing dissent, removing obstacles. And his son, Michael, is deeply embedded in this. His digital fingerprints are all over the encryption protocols and the secure servers used to manage these illicit operations."

Miller nodded grimly. "He's not just Vance's operative; he's the architect of his father's digital fortress. Sterling knew this was a possibility. He must have anticipated Michael's role. That's why he entrusted this data to you, Doctor, and hid the key within his own personal legacy. He knew Michael Thorne would never suspect the locket, the sentimental artifact of a fractured father-son relationship, as the final resting place of his father's most damning secrets."

The data continued to unfurl, a damning indictment of Julian Vance and his son. There were projections, timelines, and contingency plans for Nightingale itself, detailing its potential to disrupt global communications, cripple financial markets, and even influence election outcomes through sophisticated manipulation of public opinion. Sterling had not just uncovered a conspiracy; he had unearthed the blueprint for a global takeover.

"This evidence," Miller said, his voice gaining an edge of steely determination, "is irrefutable. It directly implicates Julian Vance and Michael Thorne in a conspiracy of unprecedented scale. It's the proof Sterling died to protect. And it's the proof we need to stop Nightingale." He looked at Dr. Thorne, his gaze steady. "Your role, Doctor, was crucial. You were Sterling's safe harbor, the guardian of his ultimate truth. You understood the historical significance, the human element, while Sterling coded the digital one. Together, you represent the full spectrum of what Vance is trying to extinguish."

Dr. Thorne, despite the overwhelming horror of his son's betrayal, felt a flicker of pride. He had, in his own way, played a part in Sterling's grand design. He had been the custodian of history, and it turned out that history, in its most tangible and personal form, was the key to unlocking the future. "I... I never realized the depth of my son's involvement," he confessed, his voice thick with emotion. "He always seemed so... detached. So focused on his own world. I thought his ambition was merely professional. I never imagined it was so... corrupt. So destructive."

"Ambition, Doctor," Jenkins said, his tone devoid of judgment, "is a powerful motivator. When coupled with the right incentives, and the right guidance, it can lead even brilliant minds down very dark paths. Vance clearly saw Michael's talent and exploited it, twisting his skills into tools for his own nefarious agenda. Sterling likely knew this. He probably hoped that by entrusting the data to you, his estranged father, Michael might eventually see the light, or at least be forced to confront the consequences of his actions."

Miller saved the contents of the data chip to a secure, encrypted drive. The locket, now empty, felt like a hollow shell, its historical significance overshadowed by its role as a digital vault. But the information it had contained... that was the true treasure, the weapon Sterling had forged in his final days.

"We have what we need," Miller announced, closing the reader. "Now, we need to move. Michael Thorne will undoubtedly be aware that his father's locket has been accessed. He'll know Sterling's contingency has been triggered. He'll be hunting us, and he'll be hunting you, Doctor, with renewed ferocity."

Dr. Thorne nodded, his face pale but resolute. The initial shock had receded, replaced by a grim understanding of the stakes. He had held onto a memento, a sentimental piece of Sterling's past, and in doing so, had become the keeper of its future. The historian's secret had been revealed, not in the dusty annals of the past, but in the gleaming circuits of a hidden data cache, a testament to Sterling's ingenuity and his unwavering commitment to exposing the truth, no matter the personal cost. The Crimson Star data, the very core of Nightingale's existence, was now in their hands, a beacon of hope against the encroaching darkness, and the chilling realization that Sterling's final act of defiance had been to hide the truth in plain sight, using the very symbol of his fractured family to safeguard it.

The air in Dr. Thorne's stateroom, once a haven of scholarly quietude, now thrummed with a palpable tension, thick and suffocating. The faint scent of old paper and leather seemed to mock the gravity of their discovery. Miller's fingers, still warm from handling the locket, hovered over the interface of the data reader, the cascading lines of code a silent testament to Sterling's intricate planning. Jenkins, ever the stoic observer, stood by, his gaze sharp, his posture betraying a coiled readiness. Dr. Thorne, his face a mask of mingled shock and dawning horror, watched the screen, the weight of his son's betrayal a physical burden.

It was at this precise, precarious moment, when the precarious balance of their fragile victory felt most vulnerable, that the door to the stateroom hissed open. Standing in the threshold was Michael Thorne. He wasn't merely present; he was an intrusion, a stark contrast to the hushed reverence that had settled over the room moments before. His usual, almost preternatural calm was absent, replaced by a jarring, almost frantic energy. His eyes, sharp and intelligent, darted between Miller, Jenkins, and his father, a flicker of something unreadable – perhaps desperation, perhaps calculation – crossing his features.

"Father," Michael's voice, usually measured and cool, was laced with an uncharacteristic urgency. He stepped fully into the room, his gaze locking onto Dr. Thorne. "I... I need to speak with you. Urgently." He gestured vaguely, his hand sweeping across the room, as if to encompass the entire tense tableau. "This... this is not the time for whatever this is."

Dr. Thorne, jolted from his contemplation of his son's digital perfidy, looked up, his expression a complex mixture of surprise and apprehension. He had spoken of Michael, of his estrangement, of his son's brilliance and his perceived moral compromise. But seeing him here, now, bursting into the very heart of his father's secret sanctuary, felt like a violation. "Michael?" he stammered, the word catching in his throat. "What are you doing here? We were... in the middle of something."

Michael's gaze shifted, his attention snagging on the data reader, the locket resting beside it, and the unusual intensity of Miller and Jenkins. A subtle tightening around his jaw, a barely perceptible clenching of his fists, betrayed a flicker of unease beneath his assumed urgency. "Something vital," Michael conceded, his tone becoming deliberately, almost artificially, smooth. "Something about Father's research. I... I've had a breakthrough myself, a connection to his work. I believe it's imperative we discuss it.

Immediately. Before... before any irreversible actions are taken." He took another step forward, his eyes never leaving the data reader, a subtle emphasis on the word "actions."

Miller's head snapped up, his gaze now fixed on Michael. The historian's son. The brilliant coder. The one whose digital fingerprints were interwoven with his father's corrupt dealings. The almost desperate urgency in Michael's voice, the pointed avoidance of direct questions about the locket, the way his eyes seemed to be dissecting their every move – it all coalesced into a single, undeniable sensation: suspicion. Michael Thorne was not here for an urgent father-son discussion. He was here because he knew. Or at least, he suspected.

"A breakthrough?" Miller's voice was deceptively casual, a silken thread woven through the tense atmosphere. He didn't take his eyes off Michael. "That's... coincidental. We've just made a rather significant breakthrough of our own, thanks to your father's... foresight." He gestured towards the locket. "This little trinket, it seems, held more than just sentimental value for Sterling."

Michael's carefully constructed composure faltered for a microsecond. A muscle twitched in his cheek. He forced a dismissive laugh, though it sounded brittle. "A trinket? Father was always sentimental. But his 'research,' as you call it, was purely academic. Historical anomalies, the obscure corners of our past fascinated him. This... this sudden focus on his personal effects is... unproductive." He shifted his weight, his gaze flicking towards Dr. Thorne, a silent plea for support. "Father, please. We need to talk about what we've been working on. It's critical."

Dr. Thorne's gaze, however, remained fixed on Miller. He had spent years believing his son was merely detached, lost in his own world of algorithms and code. Now, faced with the evidence streaming across the data reader, and the palpable unease radiating from Michael, the historian's heart sank. He had always seen Michael's ambition, but had he blinded himself to its true, corrosive nature? Sterling's contingency, designed to expose a vast network of corruption, had revealed not only the depths of Julian Vance's depravity but also the chilling complicity of his own son.

"Unproductive, Michael?" Miller's voice was now sharper, the silken thread unraveling to reveal the steel beneath. He rose slowly from his chair, his presence filling the small stateroom. He was taller than Michael, and his gaze held an unwavering intensity that seemed to pin the younger Thorne in place. "We've just accessed encrypted data that directly implicates Julian Vance and his son in a global conspiracy of unprecedented scale. Data that Sterling risked his life to safeguard. So, forgive me if I find your sudden appearance and your insistence on discussing 'academic anomalies'... highly suspicious."

Michael's face contorted. The smooth facade cracked further, revealing a raw agitation beneath. His eyes, which had been assessing Miller with a detached coolness, now blazed with a nascent fury. "Suspicious? What exactly are you implying? That I, Sterling's son, would interfere with... with whatever you think you've found? Father was a brilliant man, but he was also prone to flights of fancy. You're chasing ghosts." He took another step forward, his voice rising. "And I demand to know what you've done with my father's personal belongings. That locket... it's a family heirloom. It's not yours to tamper with."

The air in the stateroom grew heavy, the unspoken accusations hanging thick and suffocating. Dr. Thorne, caught between the son he had fathered and the secrets he had helped uncover, felt a profound sense of despair. He saw the desperation in Michael's eyes, the frantic attempt to regain control, to divert their attention from the undeniable truth that was now laid bare before them. Sterling's final act had been to expose not only the corruption of a powerful man but the moral compromise of his own flesh and blood. The historian's secret, the very locket he had guarded, had become the instrument of his son's exposure.

"Tamper with it?" Miller's voice was dangerously low, a predatory growl. "We retrieved the data Sterling entrusted to Dr. Thorne. The data your father was murdered for. The data that proves Julian Vance has been systematically dismantling global financial markets and manipulating governments through a project called Nightingale. And you, Michael Thorne, your digital fingerprints are all over the encryption protocols and the secure servers that managed these illicit operations."

Michael recoiled as if struck. His face paled, his eyes widening in a mixture of disbelief and something akin to terror. The carefully constructed mask of concerned son and brilliant academic shattered completely. The aggressive, demanding tone of moments before dissolved, replaced by a raw, desperate defensiveness. He took a step back, his gaze darting wildly between Miller and Dr. Thorne, as if searching for an escape route. "That's... that's a lie," he stammered, his voice barely a whisper. "You don't understand. You can't possibly understand the complexities..."

"Complexities?" Jenkins interjected, his voice a low rumble from the side. He had remained largely silent, a sentinel observing the unfolding drama, but now his gaze was fixed on Michael with an unnerving intensity. "The complexity of siphoning billions from global markets? The complexity of manipulating elections through misinformation campaigns? The complexity of silencing any voice that dared to question your father's agenda? Those are the complexities we understand, Mr. Thorne. And we have the proof." He nodded towards the data reader.

Dr. Thorne watched his son, his heart a leaden weight in his chest. The man before him was not the son he had raised, not entirely. This was a product of ambition warped by corruption. Sterling had anticipated this. He had known that Michael, despite his brilliance, would be drawn into Julian Vance's web. And he had, with a father's ultimate, heartbreaking foresight, hidden the truth within the very symbol of his fractured family, a place Michael would never think to look, a place he would likely try to reclaim and bury forever.

"The locket," Michael choked out, his voice thick with desperation. He lunged forward, not towards his father, but towards the desk, his hand outstretched as if to snatch the locket back. "It... it belongs to me. It's... it's just memories."

Miller moved with a speed that belied his measured demeanor. He stepped between Michael and the desk, his hand resting on Michael's chest, a firm but not aggressive barrier. "Memories, Mr. Thorne?" Miller's eyes bored into Michael's. "Or the keys to your father's empire? Sterling knew you'd come for it. He knew you'd try to erase his final message. That's why he entrusted it to your father, the one man you might underestimate, the one man you'd think incapable of understanding its true significance."

Michael's breath hitched. He stared at Miller, then at his father, his chest heaving. The carefully constructed walls of his deception were crumbling around him. He had been so confident, so sure of his ability to control the narrative, to reclaim his father's legacy on his own terms. But Sterling, even in death, had outmaneuvered him. The historian's secret, hidden in plain sight, had become the ultimate weapon against the architect of lies.

"He... he always underestimated me," Michael whispered, a tremor in his voice. It wasn't a confession, not yet, but a hint of the desperate, arrogant pride that had driven him down this path. He looked at Dr. Thorne, his eyes pleading, but not for forgiveness. For understanding. For a chance to reframe the narrative, to spin this disaster into a victory. "He... he never understood my vision. What I could achieve. What *we* could achieve." Dr. Thorne flinched. "We? Michael, there is no 'we.' There is only your father's truth, and the path of destruction you have chosen."

The confession, the veiled admission of complicity, hung in the air, heavy and damning. Michael Thorne, the brilliant son, the trusted confidante of a corrupt empire, had finally revealed himself. And the historian, the keeper of secrets, now held the key not just to Sterling's legacy, but to his son's downfall. The locket, once a symbol of familial connection, now represented the chasm that had opened between father and son, a chasm filled with lies, ambition, and the chilling echo of Sterling's desperate truth. The tension in the stateroom, once suffocating, now crackled with a grim, electrifying certainty. The game, for Michael Thorne, was up. Sterling's contingency had not only exposed Nightingale but had also brought to light the shadow that had clung to his father's name for so long: the betrayal within his own bloodline.

The silence that descended after Michael's desperate whisper was more deafening than any accusation. Dr. Thorne, his gaze fixed on his son, felt a seismic shift within him. The son he had known, or thought he knew, had been a complex tapestry of brilliance and aloofness, a brilliant mind disconnected from the moral compass that guided the historian's own life. He had always acknowledged Michael's ambition, a trait that had both proud and worried him, a potent force that could build empires or, as Sterling had so tragically foreseen, tear them down. But in that moment, seeing the raw desperation, the thinly veiled attempt to reframe his complicity as a noble pursuit of power, Dr. Thorne understood. Sterling hadn't just anticipated Michael's involvement; he had understood its insidious nature. This wasn't a son merely drawn to power; this was a son who had actively embraced its darkest manifestations, who had actively participated in the machinations of Nightingale.

Years of unspoken tension, of missed connections and subtle disappointments, coalesced into a sharp, painful clarity. Dr. Thorne remembered Michael as a boy, already possessing that unnerving ability to dissect situations, to see the underlying mechanics of power, and to covet it. There had been a hunger in him, a drive that had always seemed to outpace his empathy, a relentless pursuit of what was

more, what was *greater*, often at the expense of what was *right*. He recalled a particular incident, a school debate where Michael, barely in his teens, had so eloquently twisted logic and fact to secure a victory, leaving his opponent in bewildered defeat. Even then, Dr. Thorne had felt a flicker of unease, a sense that his son's exceptional intellect was a double-edged sword, capable of illumination but also of deception.

"Your vision, Michael?" Dr. Thorne's voice, though quiet, resonated with a newfound, steely resolve. The academic detachment that had once defined him seemed to have evaporated, replaced by the fierce protectiveness of a father confronting a monstrous truth, and the unwavering commitment of a man who understood the devastating consequences of unchecked corruption. "Your vision was to profit from the suffering of millions? Your vision was to undermine the very foundations of global stability? Sterling's legacy is not about power and control. It is about truth. It is about protecting the innocent from men like Julian Vance. And it seems, Michael, you have become a willing instrument in their symphony of destruction."

He saw the flicker of panic in Michael's eyes, the dawning realization that his carefully constructed narrative was crumbling not just in the face of Miller and Jenkins' evidence, but in the eyes of his own father. Sterling had understood this. He had known that Michael's ambition, when unchecked, would lead him down this path. And he had known that the one person Michael might underestimate, the one person whose moral compass he might assume to be easily swayed or overridden by familial affection, was his father. The historian, Sterling had gambled, would ultimately choose truth over blood.

"You... you always saw me as a disappointment," Michael's voice was a low, ragged sound, a desperate attempt to regain control by weaponizing Dr. Thorne's past doubts. "Always comparing me to Sterling. He was the favored son, wasn't he? The one who followed in your footsteps. I had to forge my path. And I found... opportunities. Opportunities you were too... principled... to ever grasp." The words dripped with a bitter resentment, a carefully cultivated sense of victimhood that had likely served him well in his dealings with Vance.

Dr. Thorne's heart ached, not with the pain of Michael's accusation, but with the profound sorrow of his son's distortion of reality. "Sterling was not favored, Michael. He was principled. He was honorable. He understood that true power lies not in accumulation, but in integrity. And you, my son, have traded your integrity for fleeting power, for a place at the table of thieves." He met Michael's gaze directly, his own eyes filled with a sorrow that was bone-deep. "The opportunities you speak of, Michael, were built on lies. On the exploitation of people. Sterling saw that. He saw what Julian Vance was doing, and he saw that you were a part of it. He knew that his own son, his own flesh and blood, was a cog in that monstrous machine. That must have been a terrible burden for him."

The mention of Sterling's burden seemed to strike a nerve. Michael flinched, a subtle tremor running through his frame. For a fleeting moment, a glimpse of the boy he once was, before the allure of Nightingale had consumed him, seemed to surface. But a renewed defiance quickly masked it. "A burden? He burdened himself with his own idealism. He could have been a part of something great, Father. Something that truly shaped the world. Instead, he chose to be a footnote. A martyr." Michael spat the word out as if it were a curse. "And you... you're just like him. You'd rather be a righteous nobody than a powerful somebody."

Miller, who had remained a silent observer, stepped forward, his voice cutting through the charged atmosphere. "And what kind of somebody is Julian Vance, Mr. Thorne? A somebody who builds his empire on economic collapse and human misery? A somebody who orchestrates assassinations to maintain his control? Sterling didn't want to be a footnote, Michael. He wanted to end Nightingale. And he knew, with absolute certainty, that you were the architect of its digital defenses. He knew you were protecting his father's killer."

The accusation hung in the air, heavy and undeniable. Michael's breath hitched, his eyes darting towards Miller, then back to his father, a cornered animal sensing the inevitable end. The facade was cracking, revealing the raw fear beneath the bravado. Dr. Thorne watched his son, the full weight of Sterling's foresight crashing down upon him. Sterling hadn't just been protecting himself; he had been protecting the world *from* his son's complicity. The locket, that simple token of remembrance, was not just a repository of data; it was a testament to a father's desperate attempt to exonerate himself and expose the truth, even when that truth implicated his own child.

"You... you don't understand the pressure," Michael stammered, his voice cracking. "Vance... he has influence. He can destroy careers, reputations. Sterling was naive. He thought he could fight this alone. He didn't realize... he didn't realize the scale of what we were building. He didn't understand that some things... some things are necessary for progress. For order."

Dr. Thorne closed his eyes for a brief moment, a silent prayer for guidance, for strength. The justifications, the rationalizations, were all too familiar. He had heard them whispered in hushed tones in academic circles, seen them written in the self-serving manifestos of those who sought power. But to hear them from his own son, to hear him betray Sterling's memory with such chilling equanimity, was a profound agony.

"Necessary, Michael?" His voice was a low murmur, laced with an infinite sadness. "Is it necessary to ruin lives? Is it necessary to destabilize entire economies? Is it necessary to silence dissent with violence? Sterling believed in the inherent value of every individual, Michael. He believed in the pursuit of knowledge for the betterment of humanity, not for the enrichment of a select few at the expense of the many. He entrusted me with this because he knew I would understand. He knew the allure of power would not sway me, or by the ties of blood, if that blood ran cold with complicity."

He took a step towards Michael, his gaze unwavering. The years of disappointment, of yearning for his son to embrace the values he held dear, seemed to culminate in this single, defining moment. "I always hoped, Michael, that you would find your own way to contribute to the world, to use your exceptional talents for good. I saw your brilliance, and I worried. I worried that it would outstrip your conscience. And now, I see that my fears were not only justified but tragically understated. Sterling's contingency was not just about exposing Julian Vance. It was also about understanding the depth of your involvement. And the truth, Michael, is more devastating than either of us could have imagined."

He gestured to the data reader, to the locket lying innocuously beside it. "Sterling knew you were involved. He suspected you had become entangled, perhaps even complicit. But he loved you. He left you a chance to redeem yourself, to step away. He encoded the deepest secrets of Nightingale into this locket, a place he knew you would never expect him to hide anything of value, a place you would likely try to reclaim and destroy to bury your own involvement. He believed that perhaps, faced with the undeniable truth, you would reconsider. But it seems Sterling overestimated your capacity for introspection, and underestimated your father's capacity to see the truth, no matter how painful."

Michael's face contorted, his carefully maintained composure shattering completely. He looked from Dr. Thorne to Miller, a desperate, hunted look in his eyes. He opened his mouth to speak, but no words came. The weight of his father's realization, coupled with the irrefutable evidence presented by Miller, had finally broken through his defenses. The brilliance that had once promised so much, now seemed to illuminate only the dark corners of his soul, revealing a man consumed by ambition and utterly lost to the pursuit of power.

Dr. Thorne felt a profound sense of grief, a mourning for the son he had lost to the siren song of Nightingale. But intertwined with that grief was a nascent sense of purpose. Sterling had entrusted him with a heavy burden, a responsibility that transcended familial bonds. He had been given the key to exposing not just a global conspiracy, but the corruption that had festered within his own family. And now, standing in the charged silence of his stateroom, Dr. Thorne knew he had to honor that trust. He had to help Miller, to ensure Sterling's sacrifice was not in vain, to bring the architects of Nightingale, and his own son's complicity, to justice. The personal cost would be immense, but the greater cost of inaction, of allowing such darkness to fester, was simply unthinkable. The historian's secret, the locket, had indeed brought a father to a painful, life-altering realization, steeling his resolve to see Sterling's mission through to its bitter, necessary end.

The heavy silence in the stateroom, once a sanctuary for contemplation, now thrummed with a primal unease. Dr. Thorne's gaze, fixed on his son, had witnessed the unraveling of a lifetime's belief, the stark confrontation with Michael's descent into the shadowy machinations of Nightingale. But the chilling clarity that had dawned in that moment, the crushing weight of Sterling's foresight, was swiftly being eclipsed by a new, more immediate dread. The knowledge that Michael, his own son, was entangled in the very conspiracy his elder brother had sought to dismantle, was a wound that would take years, perhaps a lifetime, to cauterize. Yet, as he processed the full horror of Michael's complicity, a colder, more insidious fear began to creep in. Sterling's final act, his desperate act of defiance encoded within the locket, was not merely a testament to his bravery or his foresight regarding Julian Vance; it was a meticulously crafted message, a testament to his understanding of a far more complex, and perhaps more personal, betrayal.

He recalled Sterling's final, whispered words, not just about the locket and its passphrase, but about the

need for it to be found, for its secrets to be unearthed. Sterling, a strategist to his core, had never been one for unnecessary risks. The placement of the locket, a seemingly sentimental trinket, was a deliberate choice, a testament to his intimate knowledge of Michael's habits, his disdain for the overtly sentimental, and his relentless pursuit of tangible power. Sterling had anticipated Michael's eventual entanglement with Nightingale, and, with the agonizing prescience of a brother facing an encroaching darkness, had prepared for it. He had known, with a certainty that now pierced Dr. Thorne's heart, that Michael would be drawn into Vance's orbit, that his ambition would blind him to the true cost of such alliances. And he had prepared a contingency, not just against Vance, but against the possibility that his own blood would become an agent of destruction.

The historian's gaze, which had moments ago held the steely resolve of a man confronting a terrible truth, now flickered with a nascent awareness of a different kind of danger. Miller, his face grim, had already begun the painstaking process of extracting the data. But it was in the periphery of Dr. Thorne's vision, in the subtle shift of shadows along the stateroom's polished mahogany, that the true threat began to coalesce. The ship, a vessel of luxury and supposed security, now felt like a gilded cage, its labyrinthine corridors and opulent suites offering a perfect canvas for a predator.

Sterling, Dr. Thorne realized with a sickening lurch, had not only anticipated Michael's betrayal, but also the inevitable hunt that would follow the unearthing of Nightingale's secrets. He had known that the individuals involved, the shadowy architects of global destabilization, would not tolerate loose ends. And Sterling, in his meticulous planning, had not only secured the evidence; he had ensured that the very act of securing it would draw the attention of those who would seek to silence it, and anyone who possessed it. The locket, its unassuming exterior concealing its explosive payload, was not just a key to unlocking Nightingale's secrets; it was a beacon, a silent siren call to the very forces Sterling had fought against.

Miller's brow furrowed, his usual stoic demeanor replaced by a subtle tension. He paused, his fingers hovering over the data reader, his head cocked as if listening to a sound only he could perceive. "Something's not right," he murmured, his voice low, barely audible above the gentle hum of the ship's engines. "A draft. It shouldn't be." He glanced towards the heavy, ornate door that led to the stateroom's private antechamber, a door that had been firmly shut moments before. A faint creak, almost imperceptible, echoed from that direction.

Dr. Thorne's heart hammered against his ribs. He looked at Michael, who stood frozen, his face a mask of disbelief and growing terror, the weight of his father's condemnation and Miller's unwavering gaze clearly crushing him. But it wasn't Michael's panicked stillness that drew Dr. Thorne's attention. It was the subtle movement in his peripheral vision, the almost imperceptible widening of the gap in the antechamber door. It was the faint scent, not of sea salt or expensive polish, but something else, something sharp and metallic, that seemed to cut through the air.

"Sterling anticipated this too," Dr. Thorne breathed, his voice strained, a chilling realization dawning. "He knew they would come for the data. He knew they would come for whoever held it." He looked at Miller, his eyes wide with a dawning comprehension. "He knew they would be watching. Listening."

The silence that followed was not empty, but pregnant with anticipation. The gentle rocking of the ship, which had been a comforting rhythm, now felt like a prelude to chaos. The stateroom, with its plush furnishings and expensive art, felt less like a sanctuary and more like a meticulously prepared trap. Miller, sensing the shift, moved with a newfound urgency. He discreetly placed a hand on the side of the data reader, his stance widening, his gaze sweeping across the room, searching for any anomaly, any disturbance in the otherwise pristine environment.

Dr. Thorne's gaze was drawn back to the antechamber door. The sliver of darkness that had appeared was no longer there. The door was shut tight, as if it had never been disturbed. But the feeling persisted, a prickling sensation on the back of his neck, the undeniable intuition that they were no longer alone. Sterling's network, his digital tentacles that had reached into the very heart of Nightingale, had not just been about gathering information; they had been about surveillance, about tracking the movements of those who threatened his mission. And it was that very network, Dr. Thorne now understood, that had alerted Sterling to the impending danger.

He remembered Sterling's hushed conversations with Miller, the coded messages, the subtle warnings that had seemed so cryptic. Sterling had been preparing for this eventuality, for the moment when Nightingale's enforcers would come to reclaim what they believed was theirs. He had anticipated that the data, once unearthed, would be a death sentence for many, and that those facing such a sentence would stop at nothing to prevent its dissemination. And he had known, with a father's heartbreaking certainty, that his own brother might be a pawn, or worse, a willing participant, in that desperate effort.

"He knew Michael was involved," Dr. Thorne whispered, the words a somber echo of his earlier realization. "But he also knew that Michael was not the ultimate threat. He was a symptom, a pawn in a much larger game." He looked at Miller, his eyes imploring. "He knew that Vance, or his agents, would try to stop us. And he prepared for it."

Miller nodded, his expression grim. "Sterling was never one to leave things to chance. If he anticipated this, he would have built in countermeasures." He looked at the data reader, then back at the door. "The commotion Michael caused... it was a distraction. Not just for us, but for them. A chance to move."

The air in the stateroom grew heavy, charged with an almost palpable tension. The soft murmur of the ship's systems seemed to recede, replaced by the amplified thumping of Dr. Thorne's own heart. He felt a primal instinct to protect, to shield not only himself and Miller, but also, inexplicably, Michael, who now stood as a terrified witness to his own downfall. But the primal instinct warred with a chilling pragmatism. Sterling's plan, if it existed, was not about personal safety; it was about ensuring the truth prevailed.

"The passphrase," Dr. Thorne said, his voice gaining a renewed strength, an echo of Sterling's own resolve. "Sterling said it was a personal memory. Something only he and I would understand." He met Miller's gaze, a shared understanding passing between them. Sterling had not just entrusted him with the data; he had entrusted him with the means to protect it, and to understand the full scope of the danger.

The killer's shadow was a tangible presence, lurking just beyond the polished mahogany, its intent as clear as the glint of steel. The ship's opulent grandeur, designed to insulate its occupants from the harsh realities of the world, had become a space for a far more ancient fear. Sterling had understood this, had understood that in the pursuit of truth, one often had to confront the darkest aspects of humanity, even within one's own family. And now, Dr. Thorne, armed with Sterling's foresight and the chilling knowledge of his son's entanglement, felt the icy tendrils of that darkness begin to close in. The quiet study, the haven of historical inquiry, was rapidly transforming into a battleground, and the historian, once a mere observer of past events, found himself thrust into the heart of a present-day conflict, with the fate of Sterling's legacy, and his own family, hanging precariously in the balance. The killer, a silent predator, was now drawing near, its presence a palpable weight in the air, a chilling reminder that some secrets, once unearthed, were never meant to be discovered.

Chapter 9: The Chase Across the Decks

The soft click of the data reader disengaging from the locket was a sound that should have heralded a moment of triumph. Instead, it was a punctuation mark, a final pause before the storm. Dr. Thorne, his gaze still locked on Michael, felt the prickling sensation on his neck intensify, morphing from a vague unease into a sharp, undeniable premonition of immediate danger. Miller, his movements fluid and precise as he carefully extracted the memory chip, remained a picture of calm concentration, but the subtle tightening of his jaw, the almost imperceptible stiffening of his shoulders, spoke volumes. Sterling had anticipated this. He had not only foreseen the revelation of Nightingale's machinations but also the ruthless pursuit of those who dared to expose them. And that pursuit, Dr. Thorne now understood with chilling certainty, was no longer an abstract threat; it was a predator stalking the corridors of the ship, its eyes fixed on the prize held within the historian's grasp.

The air in the stateroom, thick with the remnants of Michael's confession and the weight of Sterling's legacy, suddenly felt charged with a new, more terrifying energy. The gentle creak of the ship, the distant hum of machinery, all faded into the background, replaced by an almost deafening silence. It was the silence of a coiled spring, of a predator holding its breath before the strike. Dr. Thorne's eyes darted to the stateroom door, the same one that had seemed to shift moments before. It was closed now, solid and unyielding, but the memory of that faint movement, the almost imperceptible widening of the gap, was seared into his mind. It was a portal, a gateway through which the unseen threat had entered, and would now emerge.

Miller's fingers, steady despite the palpable tension, completed their task. He held up the small, metallic memory chip, its surface reflecting the dim light of the stateroom. "Got it," he murmured, his voice a low rumble. But even as the words left his lips, the serene composure shattered.

It happened with the speed and ferocity of a viper's strike. The stateroom door, without so much as a whisper of warning, exploded inwards. It wasn't a gentle push, nor a tentative creak; it was a violent, splintering impact, as if a battering ram had been brought to bear. Wood dust billowed into the room, momentarily obscuring the figure that burst through the opening. Dr. Thorne's breath hitched, his mind struggling to process the sudden, brutal intrusion.

The assailant was a silhouette against the dim light of the corridor, a figure of pure, unadulterated menace. Clad in dark, form-fitting tactical gear, they moved with a predatory grace that spoke of honed skill and ruthless efficiency. In their hand, glinting wickedly, was a knife, its blade impossibly sharp, its purpose chillingly clear. Their gaze, even through the fleeting obscurity of the dust, was fixed not on Dr. Thorne, but on Miller, and the small, vital chip he held.

"Sterling's locket..." the assailant's voice was a low growl, devoid of any human inflection, like the rasp of sandpaper on bone. It was a voice designed for intimidation, for striking fear into the hearts of its victims. "Give it to me. Now."

The demand was not a request, but an order, delivered with the implicit threat of immediate, deadly consequence. Dr. Thorne felt a surge of adrenaline, a primal instinct to protect. He instinctively moved to shield Michael, who stood frozen, his face a mask of pure terror, the weight of his own confession momentarily forgotten in the face of this immediate, visceral threat.

But Miller was faster. The data expert, whose usual domain was the sterile world of code and algorithms, moved with an astonishing ferocity. As the assailant lunged forward, Miller threw himself between the attacker and Dr. Thorne, the memory chip clutched tightly in his fist. The confined space of the stateroom, designed for comfort and relaxation, became an instant crucible of violence.

The initial clash was a blur of motion and grunts. The assailant, clearly expecting an easy acquisition, was met with unexpected resistance. Miller, though not a trained fighter, possessed a wiry strength and a remarkable agility. He parried the first, vicious slash of the knife with his forearm, the sharp blade biting into his sleeve, drawing blood. A choked gasp escaped him, but he held his ground, his eyes locked on his attacker, searching for an opening, a weakness.

"Jenkins!" Miller roared, his voice strained. "Secure the evidence!" The mention of Jenkins, Dr. Thorne's ever-present, stoic bodyguard, jolted the historian back to the immediate reality of the situation. He had been so consumed by Michael's confession and Sterling's foresight that he had momentarily forgotten the formidable presence that usually accompanied him. Jenkins, a man of few words but immense capability, was already in motion. Emerging from the shadows near the stateroom's private adjoining chamber, his expression was grim, his massive frame a bulwark against the chaos.

The assailant, momentarily surprised by Miller's resilience and the emergence of Jenkins, pressed their attack. Their movements were economical, brutally effective. Every feint, every lunge, was designed to incapacitate, to eliminate. This was not a random act of violence; this was a targeted assassination, a clean, swift operation. The killer's precision was terrifying, the fluid economy of their movements suggesting a level of training far beyond that of an ordinary thug. They moved like a phantom, each action calculated to inflict maximum damage with minimum effort.

Jenkins intercepted the assailant's next thrust, his broad hands closing around the attacker's wrist, his grip like a vise. The knife clattered to the polished wooden floor, skittering away into the opulent furnishings. The assailant, however, did not falter. Their free hand shot out, a blur of motion, aiming a vicious elbow strike towards Jenkins's jaw. Jenkins grunted, absorbing the blow with practiced resilience, his focus unwavering.

"The chip!" Jenkins bellowed, his voice a deep rumble that seemed to shake the very foundations of the ship. "Get it to safety!"

Dr. Thorne, understanding the urgency, scrambled to retrieve the memory chip. He had to get it away from this deadly confrontation, to a place where its contents could be protected. Michael, still paralyzed by fear, remained a useless impediment, a liability in the rapidly unfolding scene. Dr. Thorne pushed him roughly towards the back of the stateroom, urging him to stay down, to stay out of the way.

Miller, his arm bleeding freely, was still locked in a desperate struggle with the assailant. The attacker, deprived of their primary weapon, was now employing a brutal, close-quarters combat style, using elbows, knees, and the sheer force of their momentum to overwhelm Miller. They were strong, incredibly strong, their attacks relentless and unforgiving. A savage knee strike caught Miller in the ribs, eliciting a sharp cry of pain, and he staggered back, momentarily disoriented.

This was the opening the assailant needed. They lunged, not for Dr. Thorne, but for Miller, their intention to retrieve the chip and silence the man who held it. Dr. Thorne, his heart pounding in his chest, saw the intent in their eyes, the cold, unfeeling hunger. He knew, with a certainty that chilled him to the bone, that Miller was in grave danger. Sterling had anticipated this. He had known that the unraveling of Nightingale would come at a steep price, and he had prepared for the possibility that his closest confidant, the man who helped him gather the evidence, would be a primary target.

Jenkins, seeing Miller falter, roared and lunged, tackling the assailant from the side. The force of his impact sent them both sprawling across the stateroom floor, the luxurious carpet rumpling under their combined weight. The brief disarray created by Jenkins's intervention was enough. Dr. Thorne, seizing the opportunity, darted forward and scooped up the memory chip from where it had slipped from Miller's grasp during the struggle.

He didn't hesitate. He turned and bolted from the stateroom, his footsteps echoing on the polished corridors. He had to get the chip to a secure location, to ensure Sterling's legacy, and the truth it represented, survived this brutal assault. Behind him, he could hear the sounds of the ongoing struggle – grunts, the thud of bodies, Jenkins's guttural roars of effort. He could not afford to look back. The chase was no longer an abstract concept; it was a terrifying, immediate reality, and he was now at its very heart. The ship, once a symbol of luxury and escape, had become a claustrophobic labyrinth, a hunting ground where the shadows held deadly intent. He ran, his lungs burning, his mind racing, the weight of Sterling's sacrifice pressing down on him with every pounding step. The silence that had preceded the attack was gone, replaced by the frantic symphony of a desperate flight.

The memory chip, a tiny sliver of data holding Sterling's truth, was clutched in Dr. Thorne's sweaty palm. Behind him, the sounds of Jenkins's furious struggle with the assailant echoed through the opulent stateroom. Miller, wounded but defiant, was still engaged, his surprisingly fierce resistance buying precious seconds. Thorne didn't look back. He couldn't. Sterling's legacy, the damning evidence against Nightingale, was now his responsibility. The memory chip was the prize, and the assailant, a phantom in black, was desperate to reclaim it.

He burst from the stateroom, the polished mahogany doors swinging shut behind him with a soft thud that belied the violence it concealed. The corridor, usually a serene artery of the ship's upper decks, was now a gauntlet. Passengers, drawn by the commotion, were emerging from their cabins, their faces a mixture of curiosity and alarm. Thorne weaved through them, his tuxedo jacket flapping, his breath coming in ragged gasps. He was a historian, not an athlete, but the adrenaline coursing through him was a powerful, primal fuel. He needed to get the chip to safety, somewhere the killer couldn't reach.

He glanced back, just for a fleeting second. The stateroom door, the very one that had been breached with such brutal force, was ajar. Through the gap, he could see Jenkins grappling with the assailant, a whirlwind of controlled power and desperate fury. Miller, his arm already visibly bloodied, was a grim, determined figure, a surprisingly formidable obstacle. But the assailant was a creature of pure, focused intent. They moved with a chilling economy of motion, their every action a calculated step towards escape.

Then, it happened. In a sudden, explosive surge, the assailant broke free from Jenkins's hold. It wasn't a clean escape; it was a violent rupture, a calculated sacrifice of immediate engagement for the ultimate prize. The assailant shoved Jenkins hard, sending the burly bodyguard stumbling back, and in that instant, their eyes locked onto Thorne. There was no anger, no malice, just a cold, terrifying certainty of purpose. The assailant lunged, not towards Thorne directly, but towards the locket Sterling had worn, which had fallen during the scuffle and lay glinting on the floor near where Miller had been fighting. Thorne saw it all in slow motion: the assailant's hand, a blur of black fabric, snatching the locket, and then, with a shocking turn, the assailant was already moving, a dark streak vanishing down the corridor.

"The locket!" Thorne choked out, the words catching in his throat. It wasn't just a piece of jewelry; it was where Sterling had hidden the memory chip. Sterling, in his foresight, had embedded the chip within the intricate filigree of the locket itself, a clever disguise that had almost cost them everything.

He skidded to a halt, his mind reeling. The chip was gone. The assailant had it. The immediate danger to himself had lessened, but the stakes had just escalated dramatically. Sterling's truth was now in the hands of their enemy. But then, as the assailant turned to flee, a small, metallic object detached from the locket, dislodged in the violent grab. It wasn't the chip itself, but something else Sterling had secreted away, a tiny, intricate piece of what looked like a broken cufflink, or perhaps a charm. It skittered across the polished floor, coming to rest near Thorne's feet. He snatched it up, his fingers closing around the cool, smooth metal. It was a long shot, a desperate gamble, but it was all he had.

"Miller! Jenkins!" Thorne yelled, his voice hoarse. "They have the locket! But I have... something!" He held up the small metallic object, hoped it meant something. Miller, grimacing in pain from a blow to his ribs, managed a sharp nod. "Go! Thorne! Get it to safety! We'll handle this!" He didn't specify *who* "this" was, but the implication was clear: the assailant. Jenkins, recovering his footing, let out a roar that seemed to shake the very timbers of the grand vessel. "Thorne! Find a secure location! We'll create a diversion!"

Thorne didn't need told twice. He turned and ran, the small metallic fragment clutched in his hand. The corridor opened into a grand atrium, a cavernous space with soaring ceilings and cascading floral arrangements, teeming with passengers dressed in their finest evening wear. The sudden contrast to the confined violence of the stateroom was jarring. Faces turned towards him, curious, then alarmed, as they registered his disheveled appearance and the desperate urgency in his stride. He ignored them, his eyes scanning for an escape route, for a way to lose himself in the throng, or better yet, to find a place to hide.

He plunged into a bustling lounge, the air thick with the murmur of polite conversation and the clinking of champagne flutes. He ducked behind a potted palm, his heart hammering against his ribs. He could hear the muffled sounds of pursuit behind him – the heavy tread of Jenkins's boots, the more agile, urgent steps of Miller. They were buying him time, precious, fleeting time.

The assailant, Thorne realized, would be just as desperate to disappear. They would be moving through the ship's less public arteries, service passages, crew quarters, anywhere to evade capture. And they would be trying to reach a secure location to access whatever Sterling had hidden within that locket. The memory chip was the ultimate prize, but the locket itself might contain other crucial information, perhaps a key, a password, or even another physical clue.

He emerged from behind the palm, his eyes sweeping the room. The assailant wouldn't head for the main decks again. They'd be looking for a way to descend, to get to the ship's lower levels, perhaps even to a lifeboat. Thorne moved with renewed purpose, his gaze fixed on a discreetly marked door at the far end of the lounge, labeled "Crew Only." It was a gamble, but it was his best chance.

He pushed through the door and found himself in a narrow, utilitarian corridor, the contrast to the plush luxury of the lounge stark and immediate. The air here was cooler, smelling faintly of disinfectant and stale oil. This was the ship's hidden network, a labyrinth of service passages, ventilation shafts, and maintenance tunnels. Perfect for a chase.

He could hear them now, closer than he thought. The rhythmic clang of Jenkins's footsteps, the softer, more determined cadence of Miller. They were close, but they were still behind him. He risked another glance back. Two dark figures, indistinct in the dim lighting of the service corridor, were closing the distance.

Suddenly, a new sound cut through the air, sharp and urgent: the piercing wail of a ship's horn, followed by the distinct, unnerving shudder of the vessel as it altered course. The ship was moving faster now, its engines humming with a deeper, more powerful thrum. The sea, visible through small, grimy portholes, was a churning expanse of darkness. The chase was now unfolding on a moving platform, a colossal, metal beast hurtling through the night. The added motion, the subtle but constant lurch and sway, made Thorne's progress even more precarious.

He rounded a corner, his boots slipping on a patch of condensation. He stumbled, catching himself on a cold, metal bulkhead. He could hear the assailant ahead of him now, a faint scuffling sound, the rustle of fabric. They had gained ground. The assailant, Thorne surmised, was also using the service passages, a strategic choice to avoid the main thoroughfares.

He pressed on, his lungs burning. He passed a series of metal doors, each marked with cryptic symbols and numbers. He had no idea where he was, what floor he was on, or how to get back to safety. All he knew was that he had to keep moving, and that the small metallic fragment in his hand was his only tangible link to Sterling's final secrets.

He heard a sudden, sharp crack from behind him, followed by a muffled cry. Miller. Thorne's stomach clenched. He wanted to stop, to turn back, but he knew he couldn't. Jenkins would be there. Miller would be there. His role was to protect the evidence. He had to trust them to handle the immediate threat.

He reached a junction, a T-intersection in the dimly lit passage. One way led down, the other seemed to continue on the same level. He paused, straining his ears. He could hear the assailant's hurried footsteps coming from the direction of the lower passage. They were heading deeper into the ship's bowels.

He made his choice, turning towards the lower passage. The air grew colder, damper. The sounds of the ship's machinery became more pronounced, a symphony of groaning metal and churning water. He was moving towards the heart of the vessel, a place few passengers ever saw.

He heard a sudden, guttural roar from behind him. Jenkins. Thorne risked a quick glance over his shoulder. The massive bodyguard was a silhouette against the dim light, his face a mask of grim determination. Beside him, Miller was limping, but his eyes, even from this distance, were fixed on their quarry. They were still coming, still pursuing.

Then, a new sound, cutting through the cacophony of the ship. A metallic screech, followed by a heavy thud. Thorne realized with a jolt that the assailant must have triggered a trap, or perhaps encountered an unexpected obstacle. This was his chance. He broke into a sprint, his eyes scanning the passage ahead. He saw a narrow opening, a service hatch leading upwards. It was a long shot, but it might offer a temporary reprieve.

He scrambled towards it, his fingers finding purchase on the cold metal. As he pulled himself up, he heard the sounds of renewed struggle below. Jenkins and Miller were back in the fray. He pushed the hatch open, emerging into another, slightly larger corridor. This one was less grimy, more in line with the ship's opulent design, but still clearly a secondary passage.

He didn't stop to survey his surroundings. He just ran, driven by the image of the assailant disappearing with Sterling's locket. He had to get this fragment to a safe place, to analyze it, to understand what Sterling had meant by hiding it. Was it a clue? A trigger? Or just a desperate attempt to leave a breadcrumb for those who would follow?

The chase continued, a desperate ballet of pursuit and evasion across the ever-shifting landscape of the ship. Thorne was no longer just a historian; he was a fugitive, a runner, his life now inextricably bound to the secrets Sterling had entrusted to him. The storm had broken, and he was caught in its violent, unforgiving eye, with the fate of Nightingale's truth hanging precariously in the balance. The ship, a floating city of illusion and luxury, had become a labyrinth of danger, and he was just beginning to understand the true depth of its treacherous architecture. He could feel the cold, metallic fragment in his hand, a tangible reminder of Sterling's sacrifice, and the urgency of his mission. The pursuit was relentless, the stakes impossibly high, and the night was far from over. He could only hope that Sterling's foresight extended beyond the creation of this cryptic clue.

The cold metal of the locket fragment pressed into Thorne's palm, a stark counterpoint to the sweat beading on his skin. The labyrinthine service corridors of the *Seraphina* offered no sanctuary, only a shifting, echoing maze where the sounds of pursuit—Jenkins's heavy boots, Miller's ragged breaths, and the almost silent, terrifying presence of the assailant—seemed to play a cruel game of tag with his frayed nerves. He'd burst through the crew-only door, seeking anonymity, a chance to breathe, to *think*. But thinking was a luxury he couldn't afford. The memory chip, Sterling's final gambit, was gone, clutched in the hand of the very phantom who'd breached the stateroom. And Thorne, the meticulous historian, was now a fugitive, a clumsy runner in a tuxedo, with a cryptic piece of Sterling's life in his possession.

He ducked into a narrow alcove, the dim emergency lighting casting long, distorted shadows. He could hear them drawing closer, the rhythmic clang of Jenkins's pursuit a terrifyingly reliable metronome. He'd seen Miller stumble, heard the sharp intake of his breath, and a wave of something akin to guilt, or perhaps just primal fear, had washed over him. He'd even, for a fleeting, insane moment, considered doubling back, offering the fragment, anything to de-escalate the immediate danger to his companions. But then, he'd seen the assailant, a flicker of movement in the periphery, and the instinct for self-preservation, or perhaps Sterling's mission, had overridden any nascent heroism.

He pressed himself against the cold bulkhead, listening. The sounds of pursuit were momentarily muffled, a brief lull that felt more ominous than the chase itself. Were they closing in on the assailant? Or had the assailant doubled back, sensing Thorne's isolation? A flicker of movement caught his eye. Not from the corridor, but from *within* the alcove. A maintenance panel, slightly ajar. Sterling, Thorne mused with a grim twist of his lips, would have found this amusing. The historian, thrust into the role of a spy, resorting to hiding in a ventilation shaft.

With a surge of adrenaline, Thorne fumbled with the panel, his fingers slick with sweat. It groaned open, revealing a dark, cramped space within. He squeezed himself inside, pulling the panel shut behind him. The darkness was absolute, the air thick with the metallic tang of the ship's inner workings. He could hear his own heart thumping a frantic rhythm against his ribs, a drumbeat of pure terror. And then, he heard them again, their voices echoing unnervingly through the metal confines.

"Thorne! Damn it, where did he go?" Jenkins's voice was a low growl, laced with frustration. "He was just ahead of us, Michael," Miller's voice, strained and tight with pain, followed. "He couldn't have vanished into thin air."

Thorne held his breath, straining to decipher their words, their intent. Miller's mention of "Michael" sent a jolt through him. Miller had addressed him by his first name. It was a small thing, a gesture of familiarity in the midst of chaos, but it was also a stark reminder of their shared history, their brief alliance against Nightingale. But then, Miller's tone shifted, a subtle undercurrent of suspicion creeping in. "Unless... unless he wanted to disappear. Unless this whole thing... was his escape route."

Thorne's blood ran cold. Miller suspected him. The thought was a bitter pill, especially after Sterling's clear instructions, the implicit trust he'd placed in Thorne. But he couldn't entirely blame Miller. Thorne *was* acting erratically. He'd fled, clutching the fragment, leaving Jenkins and Miller to face the assailant. His tuxedo, usually a symbol of his academic gravitas, now felt like a costume, a ridiculous disguise that marked him as an outsider, a non-combatant caught in a war he barely understood.

"What are you saying, Miller?" Jenkins's voice was rougher, less inclined to nuance. "He's been... cagey, Michael. Ever since Sterling gave him that chip. He's been asking a lot of questions about Vance, about Nightingale's dealings. He's been too interested, too involved. And now, he's vanished. He could have the locket. He could be working with Vance, trying to get it to him."

Vance. The name hung in the air, a dark cloud of accusation. Thorne knew Vance, of course. A rival historian, a man with a ruthless ambition that mirrored Nightingale's own. If Vance was involved, if he was the puppet master pulling the assailant's strings, then Thorne's position was even more precarious. He was not just a pawn in Nightingale's game; he was a potential defector, a rogue element that Miller and Jenkins couldn't afford to trust.

Thorne pressed his ear against the cool metal of the panel. He had to hear more. He needed to understand the depth of Miller's suspicion. "He said he had something," Miller continued, his voice now a low murmur, as if speaking to himself. "He held up a piece of metal... said Sterling had given it to him. But what if... what if that was a distraction? What if he already has the *real* prize? What if he's using us to get to it, to secure it for himself, or worse, for Vance?"

The accusation was a physical blow. Thorne wanted to shout, to deny it, to explain that the fragment *was* Sterling's clue, that the chip was in the locket the assailant now possessed. But he couldn't. To reveal himself now would be to confirm Miller's worst fears, to become the target of their suspicion, perhaps even their bullets. He was caught between a rock and a hard place, a historian forced to play a role he hadn't rehearsed, his every move scrutinized, misinterpreted.

He heard the distinct thud of Jenkins kicking at the panel Thorne had used. "He's not here, Miller. But he can't have gone far. And that piece of metal he showed you... if it's Sterling's, then it's a lead. We follow Thorne. He's either running from the killer, or he's running *with* the killer. Either way, he leads us to the truth."

Thorne flinched. They were coming for him. Not to rescue him, but to track him. He was the quarry, even as he ran from the true predator. He heard Jenkins and Miller move on, their voices fading as they continued their search down the corridor. A moment of silence, then Thorne allowed himself to exhale, the stale air of the ventilation shaft doing little to calm his racing heart.

Miller's suspicion was a sharp, unwelcome truth. Thorne's actions *were* erratic. He'd seen the assailant, the glint of the locket in their grasp, the horrifying realization that Sterling's chip was lost. And then, he'd seen the small fragment fall. In that moment, his historian's mind had taken over, prioritizing the tangible clue over the immediate confrontation. He'd grabbed the fragment, a desperate, almost involuntary act, and then he'd run. He hadn't consciously tried to hinder Miller or Jenkins, but his flight, his solitary escape, had undoubtedly placed them in greater peril.

He remembered Sterling's words, his hushed urgency in the stateroom. "The chip... Thorne, you must get it to safety. It's within the locket. But there's more... a contingency. A failsafe. This fragment... it's the key." Sterling's eyes had been wide with a feverish intensity, his voice barely a whisper. Thorne hadn't understood then, but now, trapped in the darkness, the weight of that fragment in his hand felt like the weight of the world.

He had to find a way to use this. He had to prove to Miller, to Jenkins, that he wasn't a traitor, not an opportunist. He was Sterling's chosen, the keeper of his legacy. But how? His academic mind, trained in dissecting ancient texts and piecing together fragmented histories, was ill-equipped for this brutal, physical reality. He knew the history of the *Seraphina*, its opulent past, its role in clandestine meetings and whispered secrets. He knew its blueprints, its hidden passages, its structural vulnerabilities. He knew its history, but he didn't know how to survive its present.

He shifted in his cramped hiding place, his tuxedo fabric rustling against the rough metal. He could still hear the distant murmur of the ship's engines, a constant, low thrum that was both comforting and unnerving. They were still sailing, a city on the water, oblivious to the drama unfolding in its bowels. He imagined the assailant, wherever they were, trying to pry open the locket, to extract the chip, or perhaps, to find whatever other secrets Sterling had hidden within. And he imagined Miller and Jenkins, bruised and battered, but relentless, still hunting.

Thorne's own role was the most ambiguous. He was the historian, the academic, tasked with preserving truth. But in this twisted narrative, he was also a potential accomplice, a man whose every action could be misinterpreted. Miller's suspicion was a wound, a betrayal of the trust Sterling had placed in him. But Thorne also understood the logic. Thorne's fascination with Nightingale's empire, his deep dives into the company's shadier dealings, could easily be twisted into evidence of complicity. He had been too eager, too interested. And now, he was running.

He stayed in the ventilation shaft for what felt like an eternity, the darkness and the suffocating air a perverse form of protection. He heard the sounds of the ship's life continue around him – the muffled laughter from a distant lounge, the creak of the hull, the distant hum of machinery. These were the sounds of normalcy, a stark contrast to the violent undercurrent that now coursed through the vessel. He was acutely aware of the danger that lurked just beyond the thin metal walls. The assailant was out there, seeking Sterling's truth. Miller and Jenkins were out there, seeking Thorne, and by extension, the assailant. And Thorne, with his cryptic fragment, was caught in the middle, his actions dictated by a fear he'd never anticipated and a responsibility he was struggling to comprehend.

He had to get out of the shaft. He had to find a way to use the fragment, to prove his loyalty to Sterling's memory. He remembered the route he'd taken, the turns he'd made, the junction where he'd heard the assailant heading downwards. If he could retrace his steps, cautiously, he might find a way back to the main decks, to find a secure location, a place to examine the fragment without being observed.

He pushed open the panel again, peering out into the dimly lit corridor. It was empty. The sounds of pursuit had receded, swallowed by the ship's vastness. He emerged, dusting off his tuxedo, trying to regain some semblance of composure. He was no longer just a bystander; he was a player in this deadly game, his motives questioned, his loyalty in doubt. The fragment in his hand felt heavier than ever. It was Sterling's last message, a riddle whispered across the void. And Thorne, the historian, had to become a detective, a warrior, anything but the man Miller suspected him to be. He had to uncover the truth, not just of Nightingale's empire, but of his own role in this unfolding tragedy. The chase was far from over, and Thorne's ambiguous position made him the most unpredictable element of all.

The metallic tang of the ventilation shaft still clung to Thorne's clothes, a phantom scent of his recent fear. He'd emerged from his makeshift hiding place, the locket fragment clutched tightly in his hand, the weight of Miller's suspicion a cold, heavy stone in his gut. He'd heard Jenkins's declaration: "He leads us to the truth." Thorne knew he had to move, and fast. He couldn't afford to be seen as a suspect, not when Sterling's life, and now potentially his own, depended on him uncovering the truth about Nightingale and Vance. He crept from the alcove, his tuxedo jacket snagging on a stray piece of metal, a jarring sound in the otherwise hushed corridor. He was a scholar, not a spy, and the elegance of his attire felt like a cruel joke amidst the grime and desperation of his current predicament.

Meanwhile, on the promenade deck, the chase had reached a fever pitch. A desperate fury fueled Miller. He'd seen Thorne disappear into the labyrinthine service passages, a flicker of movement and then... nothing. But the fleeting glimpse of the assailant, the glint of something metallic in their hand, had ignited a primal rage within him. He'd pushed past Jenkins, his focus solely on the shadowy figure that had just moments before held Sterling's stateroom hostage.

"He went this way!" Miller gasped, pointing towards a set of double doors that led to the ship's upper decks, exposed to the biting night air. Jenkins, ever the professional, was close behind, his face a grim mask of determination. They burst out onto the deck, the sudden expanse of open space momentarily disorienting. The wind whipped at their faces, carrying the salty spray of the ocean and the distant, mournful cry of a foghorn.

The assailant was a phantom, a creature of shadows and swift movements. They were already a considerable distance ahead, a dark silhouette against the dimly lit deck. Miller surged forward, his injured side protesting with every stride. He could hear Jenkins's heavy boots pounding behind him, a steady, relentless rhythm of pursuit. The opulent veneer of the *Seraphina* had peeled away, revealing the brutal underbelly of its secrets, and Miller was determined to expose it, no matter the cost.

"Stop! Police!" Jenkins bellowed, his voice rough and strained against the wind. The assailant didn't falter. Instead, they veered sharply, disappearing behind a stack of lifeboats. Miller and Jenkins scrambled after them, their breath coming in ragged gasps. They rounded the lifeboats to find themselves facing a dead end – a sheer metal bulkhead, the vast expanse of the ocean stretching out before them. The assailant was nowhere to be seen.

"Damn it!" Miller cursed, slamming his fist against the cold metal. "Where did they go?" Jenkins, his eyes scanning the surroundings with a practiced intensity, pointed upwards. "The rigging. They're climbing."

Indeed, the assailant was already scaling the ship's auxiliary mast, a dark figure moving with unnerving agility. Miller looked up, his gaze fixed on the climber. In the faint glow of the deck lights, as the figure paused for a brief moment to adjust their grip, Miller saw it. A face.

It wasn't the face of a hardened criminal, not a thug from the docks or a desperate smuggler. It was a face that belonged in the polished halls of power, a face that exuded a chilling competence. Clean-shaven, with sharp, intelligent eyes that seemed to take in everything at once, and a mouth set in a grim, unyielding line. There was a coldness to their expression, an almost surgical detachment that spoke of a professional at work. This wasn't a panicked thief; this was an assassin.

And then, a detail, so small, so seemingly insignificant, clicked into place in Miller's mind. The security footage from Sterling's stateroom, grainy and distorted, had shown a figure of similar build, moving with the same fluid grace. The obscured face in the footage, the hurried movements – they had all served as a smokescreen. This person was not some random intruder; they were someone who knew the ship, someone who could move through its arteries unseen.

"It's... it's him," Miller stammered, the realization hitting him with the force of a physical blow. "The man from the footage. The one who... who attacked Sterling."

Jenkins's gaze followed Miller's, his eyes narrowing in recognition. "That's not a smuggler, Miller. That's a professional." He paused, his mind racing. "And that bird... the wooden carving Sterling found. It was a signature, wasn't it? A deliberate misdirection."

Miller nodded, his mind reeling. The wooden bird. They had focused so much on its symbolism, on the potential for it to be a clue to Nightingale's operations. But what if it was merely a theatrical flourish, a way to disguise the true nature of the operation? A professional assassin wouldn't typically leave such a personal, almost artistic calling card. It was too... sentimental. Too traceable to a specific individual's artistic inclinations.

"It was meant to throw us off," Miller murmured, the pieces falling into place with terrifying clarity. "To make us think it was someone connected to the art world, or perhaps someone with a personal vendetta against Sterling. But it was just a mask. A way to obscure their real purpose."

"And their real identity," Jenkins added, his voice grim. "Someone hired. Someone with specialized skills. Access. They knew how to get in and out of Sterling's stateroom without tripping most alarms."

As the assailant continued their ascent, a glint of metal caught Miller's eye. The assailant reached into a discreet pouch on their belt and withdrew a small, intricately carved wooden bird. They held it for a moment, then, with a swift, practiced motion, tossed it overboard. It tumbled end over end, a dark speck swallowed by the vast, indifferent ocean.

Miller felt a surge of anger, mixed with a grudging respect for the sheer audacity of the act. The wooden bird, their supposed signature, was gone, dissolved into the watery abyss, taking with it any potential link to a specific individual or motive beyond simple assassination. It was a clean sweep, a meticulously executed operation designed to leave no trace.

"They're not just an assassin, Michael," Miller said, his voice low and intense. "They're an operative. Trained. Someone who specializes in infiltration and elimination. The kind of person Vance would hire to get a job done without making a mess."

The mention of Vance hung in the air, a dark omen. Vance, the rival historian, the man whose ambition was as boundless as Nightingale's own. Thorne had suspected Vance's involvement, and now, with the chilling efficiency of the assailant, the theory felt horrifyingly plausible. This was not a crime of passion or opportunity; this was a targeted strike, executed with cold, calculated precision.

"An operative... hired by Vance," Jenkins repeated, the implication sinking in. "That means this is bigger than we thought. This isn't just about Sterling's research. This is about silencing him permanently, and anyone who gets in the way." He looked at Miller, his eyes reflecting the distant stars. "And Thorne... he has that fragment. He was with Sterling when it happened. Vance might think Thorne is a threat, or worse, an accomplice."

Miller's mind raced. Thorne, with his academic curiosity, his deep dives into Nightingale's history, could easily be perceived as a liability by someone like Vance. Thorne's possession of the locket fragment, the very object Sterling had tried to protect, would only amplify Vance's paranoia. He could be seen as someone trying to leverage Sterling's secrets for his own gain, or perhaps, an unwitting pawn in a larger game.

"We need to find Thorne," Miller said, the urgency in his voice paramount. "If Vance hired this operative, then Thorne is definitely in danger. He might even have the chip Sterling mentioned."

The assailant, having reached the top of the mast, paused for a moment, silhouetted against the inky sky. They scanned the deck below, their gaze sweeping over Miller and Jenkins. There was no fear in their eyes, only a cold, calculating assessment. They knew they were being pursued, but they also knew they had the advantage. The ship's structure, its myriad nooks and crannies, was their playground. "They're too good," Jenkins admitted, a rare note of frustration in his voice. "We can't catch them on foot. And climbing after them... it's too risky. We could fall, or worse, they could anticipate it and prepare for us."

Miller knew Jenkins was right. The chase across the decks had been a desperate, chaotic affair, but now, the assailant had vanished into the ship's superstructure, a ghost among the masts and rigging. The fight had moved to a new, more dangerous level. "We need to go back to Sterling's stateroom," Miller decided, his mind already shifting gears. "If Vance hired the operative, then he might have left some kind of trail there. Or perhaps Sterling himself anticipated this, and left something behind that Thorne can use."

"And Thorne," Jenkins added, "we need to find him before Vance's operative does. He's our best chance of understanding what Sterling was truly after, and how to stop Vance." As they turned to head back inside, a chilling realization settled upon Miller. The operative's face, etched in his memory, was not just the face of an assassin; it was the face of someone who moved with purpose, someone who understood the subtle nuances of infiltration. They were not just a hired gun; they were a skilled operative, a phantom who could slip through the cracks of any security system. The wooden bird had been a theatrical distraction, a clever ploy to disguise their true identity and purpose as a professional operative. Vance had hired not just a killer, but a ghost, a master of deception, and Miller knew that catching this phantom would be the hardest chase of his life. The true danger wasn't just in Sterling's research, but in the cold, professional hand that had been tasked with silencing anyone who threatened Nightingale's empire, a hand that had now been revealed to Miller, albeit too late to prevent the deception. The chase across the decks had yielded a shocking revelation, but the hunt was far from over; it had merely evolved into a more insidious and deadly game.

The metallic tang of the ventilation shaft still clung to Thorne's clothes, a phantom scent of his recent fear. He'd emerged from his makeshift hiding place, the locket fragment clutched tightly in his hand, the weight of Miller's suspicion a cold, heavy stone in his gut. He'd heard Jenkins's declaration: "He leads us to the truth." Thorne knew he had to move, and fast. He couldn't afford to be seen as a suspect, not when Sterling's life, and now potentially his own, depended on him uncovering the truth about Nightingale and Vance. He crept from the alcove, his tuxedo jacket snagging on a stray piece of metal, a jarring sound in the otherwise hushed corridor. He was a scholar, not a spy, and the elegance of his attire felt like a cruel joke amidst the grime and desperation of his current predicament.

Meanwhile, on the promenade deck, the chase had reached a fever pitch. A desperate fury fueled Miller. He'd seen Thorne disappear into the labyrinthine service passages, a flicker of movement and then... nothing.

But the fleeting glimpse of the assailant, the glint of something metallic in their hand, had ignited a primal rage within him. He'd pushed past Jenkins, his focus solely on the shadowy figure that had just moments before held Sterling's stateroom hostage.

"He went this way!" Miller gasped, pointing towards a set of double doors that led to the ship's upper decks, exposed to the biting night air. Jenkins, ever the professional, was close behind, his face a grim mask of determination. They burst out onto the deck, the sudden expanse of open space momentarily disorienting. The wind whipped at their faces, carrying the salty spray of the ocean and the distant, mournful cry of a foghorn.

The assailant was a phantom, a creature of shadows and swift movements. They were already a considerable distance ahead, a dark silhouette against the dimly lit deck. Miller surged forward, his injured side protesting with every stride. He could hear Jenkins's heavy boots pounding behind him, a steady, relentless rhythm of pursuit. The opulent veneer of the

Seraphina had peeled away, revealing the brutal underbelly of its secrets, and Miller was determined to expose it, no matter the cost. "Stop! Police!" Jenkins bellowed, his voice rough and strained against the wind.

The assailant didn't falter. Instead, they veered sharply, disappearing behind a stack of lifeboats. Miller and Jenkins scrambled after them, their breath coming in ragged gasps. They rounded the lifeboats to find themselves facing a dead end – a sheer metal bulkhead, the vast expanse of the ocean stretching out before them. The assailant was nowhere to be seen.

"Damn it!" Miller cursed, slamming his fist against the cold metal. "Where did they go?"

Jenkins, his eyes scanning the surroundings with a practiced intensity, pointed upwards. "The rigging. They're climbing."

Indeed, the assailant was already scaling the ship's auxiliary mast, a dark figure moving with an unnerving agility. Miller looked up, his gaze fixed on the climber. In the faint glow of the deck lights, as the figure paused for a brief moment to adjust their grip, Miller saw it. A face.

It wasn't the face of a hardened criminal, not a thug from the docks or a desperate smuggler. It was a face that belonged in the polished halls of power, a face that exuded a chilling competence. Clean-shaven, with sharp, intelligent eyes that seemed to take in everything at once, and a mouth set in a grim, unyielding line. There was a coldness to their expression, an almost surgical detachment that spoke of a professional at work. This wasn't a panicked thief; this was an assassin.

And then, a detail, so small, so seemingly insignificant, clicked into place in Miller's mind. The security footage from Sterling's stateroom, grainy and distorted, had shown a figure of similar build, moving with the same fluid grace. The obscured face in the footage, the hurried movements – they had all served as a smokescreen. This person was not some random intruder; they were someone who knew the ship, someone who could move through its arteries unseen.

"It's... it's him," Miller stammered, the realization hitting him with the force of a physical blow. "The man from the footage. The one who... who attacked Sterling."

Jenkins's gaze followed Miller's, his eyes narrowing in recognition. "That's not a smuggler, Miller. That's a professional." He paused, his mind racing. "And that bird... the wooden carving Sterling found. It was a signature, wasn't it? A deliberate misdirection."

Miller nodded, his mind reeling. The wooden bird. They had focused so much on its symbolism, on the potential for it to be a clue to Nightingale's operations. But what if it was merely a theatrical flourish, a way to disguise the true nature of the operation? A professional assassin wouldn't typically leave such a personal, almost artistic calling card. It was too... sentimental. Too traceable to a specific individual's artistic inclinations.

"It was meant to throw us off," Miller murmured, the pieces falling into place with terrifying clarity. "To make us think it was someone connected to the art world, or perhaps someone with a personal vendetta against Sterling. But it was just a mask. A way to obscure their real purpose."

"And their real identity," Jenkins added, his voice grim. "Someone hired. Someone with specialized skills. Access. They knew how to get in and out of Sterling's stateroom without tripping most alarms."

As the assailant continued their ascent, a glint of metal caught Miller's eye. The assailant reached into a discreet pouch on their belt and withdrew a small, intricately carved wooden bird. They held it for a moment, then, with a swift, practiced motion, tossed it overboard. It tumbled end over end, a dark speck swallowed by the vast, indifferent ocean.

Miller felt a surge of anger, mixed with a grudging respect for the sheer audacity of the act. The wooden bird, their supposed signature, was gone, dissolved into the watery abyss, taking with it any potential link to a specific individual or motive beyond simple assassination. It was a clean sweep, a meticulously executed operation designed to leave no trace.

"They're not just an assassin, Michael," Miller said, his voice low and intense. "They're an operative. Trained. Someone who specializes in infiltration and elimination. The kind of person Vance would hire to get a job done without making a mess."

The mention of Vance hung in the air, a dark omen. Vance, the rival historian, the man whose ambition was as boundless as Nightingale's own. Thorne had suspected Vance's involvement, and now, with the chilling efficiency of the assailant, the theory felt horrifyingly plausible. This was not a crime of passion or opportunity; this was a targeted strike, executed with cold, calculated precision.

"An operative... hired by Vance," Jenkins repeated, the implication sinking in. "That means this is bigger than we thought. This isn't just about Sterling's research. This is about silencing him permanently, and anyone who gets in the way." He looked at Miller, his eyes reflecting the distant stars. "And Thorne... he has that fragment. He was with Sterling when it happened. Vance might think Thorne is a threat, or worse, an accomplice."

Miller's mind raced. Thorne, with his academic curiosity, his deep dives into Nightingale's history, could easily be perceived as a liability by someone like Vance. Thorne's possession of the locket fragment, the very object Sterling had tried to protect, would only amplify Vance's paranoia. He could be seen as someone trying to leverage Sterling's secrets for his own gain, or perhaps, an unwitting pawn in a larger game.

"We need to find Thorne," Miller said, the urgency in his voice paramount. "If Vance hired this operative, then Thorne is definitely in danger. He might even have the chip Sterling mentioned."

The assailant, having reached the top of the mast, paused for a moment, silhouetted against the inky sky. They scanned the deck below, their gaze sweeping over Miller and Jenkins. There was no fear in their eyes, only a cold, calculating assessment. They knew they were being pursued, but they also knew they had the advantage. The ship's structure, its myriad nooks and crannies, was their playground.

"They're too good," Jenkins admitted, a rare note of frustration in his voice. "We can't catch them on foot. And climbing after them... it's too risky. We could fall, or worse, they could anticipate it and prepare for us."

Miller knew Jenkins was right. The chase across the decks had been a desperate, chaotic affair, but now, the assailant had vanished into the ship's superstructure, a ghost among the masts and rigging. The fight had moved to a new, more dangerous level.

"We need to go back to Sterling's stateroom," Miller decided, his mind already shifting gears. "If Vance hired the operative, then he might have left some kind of trail there. Or perhaps Sterling himself anticipated this, and left something behind that Thorne can use."

"And Thorne," Jenkins added, "we need to find him before Vance's operative does. He's our best chance of understanding what Sterling was truly after, and how to stop Vance."

As they turned to head back inside, a chilling realization settled upon Miller. The operative's face, etched in his memory, was not just the face of an assassin; it was the face of someone who moved with purpose, someone who understood the subtle nuances of infiltration. They were not just a hired gun; they were a skilled operative, a phantom who could slip through the cracks of any security system. The wooden bird had been a theatrical distraction, a clever ploy to disguise their true identity and purpose as a professional operative. Vance had hired not just a killer, but a ghost, a master of deception, and Miller knew that catching this phantom would be the hardest chase of his life. The true danger wasn't just in Sterling's research, but in the cold, professional hand that had been tasked with silencing anyone who threatened Nightingale's empire, a hand that had now been revealed to Miller, albeit too late to prevent the deception. The chase across the decks had yielded a shocking revelation, but the hunt was far from over; it had merely evolved into a more insidious and deadly game.

The assailant, a shadow against the night sky, paused their descent, their eyes sweeping over the decks below. They had seen Miller and Jenkins, their pursuers, but there was no panic, only a cold, analytical assessment. They knew the ship, its every beam and rivet, its hidden arteries and blind spots. They were not merely skilled; they were a product of an elite, clandestine training, designed for efficiency and anonymity. The wooden bird, a flourish of misdirection, was now at the bottom of the ocean, a tiny sacrifice in the grander scheme of concealing their true identity and the architect of their mission.

"They're not making a run for it, Michael," Miller said, his voice a low growl, as he watched the figure begin to descend not towards the railing, but back into the ship's interior, disappearing into the shadows of the upper decks. "They're heading back in. Towards Sterling's stateroom, perhaps? Or Thorne?"

Jenkins nodded, his hand instinctively going to the reassured weight of his sidearm. "Either way, they're not giving up easily. They know we're onto them. If they can't silence Sterling, they'll try to eliminate any loose ends." The operative's face, now burned into Miller's memory, was not that of a common thug, but of someone trained to kill with surgical precision, someone who operated in the grey areas of espionage and assassination. It was the face of a ghost, hired by a man who dealt in shadows and secrets.

As they hurried back inside, the ship's opulent decor seemed to mock the grim reality of their situation. Every polished surface, every gilded fixture, was a testament to the wealth and power that Nightingale's empire commanded, an empire Vance was now desperately trying to protect, or perhaps, to usurp. The chase had shifted from the open decks to the confined, intricate spaces within the *Seraphina*, a hunting ground where the operative held a distinct advantage.

They reached Sterling's stateroom, the scene of the crime, the air still thick with the phantom scent of ozone from the electrical discharge and the faint, metallic tang of blood. The room was a chaotic testament to Sterling's final struggle, papers strewn across the floor, a toppled chair, and the overturned decanter of expensive brandy. Miller's eyes scanned the room, searching for anything out of the ordinary, anything that Sterling might have left behind as a contingency.

"He must have known this was a possibility," Miller murmured, picking up a heavy crystal paperweight that Sterling had used to anchor a stack of documents. "Sterling wasn't just a historian; he was a man obsessed with protecting his research. He would have had a failsafe."

Jenkins, meanwhile, was meticulously examining the desk. He opened drawers, checked beneath the blotter, his movements economical and precise. "No sign of a hidden compartment, at least not an obvious one. And no sign of Thorne. He's not here."

"He has the locket fragment," Miller stated, holding up the small piece of intricately worked metal, the scene from the chase replaying in his mind. "The operative must have been trying to retrieve it, or destroy it. If they failed, they might have been trying to get it from Thorne."

A sudden glint of light caught Miller's eye. It came from behind the heavy velvet curtains that draped the large porthole. He pulled them aside to reveal a small, almost imperceptible scratch on the wooden frame. It was fresh.

"Someone was here recently," Miller said, his voice taut. "And they weren't looking for information. They were looking for something specific, something they could take or break." He then noticed a faint smudge on the glass of the porthole, as if someone had pressed their face against it, looking out.

Jenkins joined him, his brow furrowed. "Or perhaps they were looking *out*, Miller. Looking for their escape route, or checking if the coast was clear."

Miller's gaze drifted to the small, ornate music box that sat on a side table, a delicate piece of craftsmanship. He remembered Sterling mentioning it, a gift from his late wife. He picked it up, its weight familiar. He turned it over, his fingers tracing the intricate carvings. It looked like any other decorative item, but Sterling, a man of meticulous habits and a keen eye for detail, would not have placed it so prominently if it were merely ornamental.

"This music box," Miller began, his mind working furiously, "Sterling told me once that his wife had a habit of hiding small trinkets inside. He called it their 'secret keeper.'" He carefully lifted the lid. Inside, nestled amongst the velvet lining, was not a ballerina figurine, but a small, slim USB drive.

"Sterling, you brilliant bastard," Miller breathed, a mixture of triumph and grim satisfaction washing over him. "He anticipated this. He hid the evidence."

Jenkins let out a low whistle. "So, the locket wasn't the only thing. The real prize was digital."

Miller inserted the USB drive into Sterling's laptop, which miraculously hadn't been tampered with beyond the obvious disruption. The screen flickered to life, revealing a password-protected file. Miller tried a few common combinations, then Sterling's name, his wife's name, and finally, the date of their anniversary. The file opened.

It was a meticulously compiled dossier, detailing Nightingale's illicit activities, its global network of smuggling, bribery, and murder. But more damning were the personal correspondences, the encrypted emails, and the financial records that directly implicated Julian Vance. There were recorded conversations, audio snippets of Vance discussing "asset retrieval," "silencing threats," and "ensuring Nightingale's continued dominance." The operative's face, the clean-shaven professional Miller had seen on the mast, appeared in a grainy photograph, labeled as "Operator X – Vance's preferred solution for complex problems."

"This is it, Michael," Miller said, his voice hoarse with emotion. "This is everything. Vance's direct involvement. The operative. And Sterling's research is safe." Jenkins peered at the screen, his face grim. "Vance is going to pay for this. Big time."

Just then, a faint sound echoed from the corridor outside the stateroom. A floorboard creaked, followed by the soft swish of fabric. The operative was still nearby.

"He knows we're here," Jenkins whispered, his hand on Miller's arm. "He's coming for the drive."

Miller quickly copied the contents of the USB drive onto his own secure device, then ejected the drive and slipped it into his pocket. He turned to Jenkins, a grim determination hardening his features. "We need to get this information out. But first, we need to stop him."

They moved to the stateroom door, Miller holding the locket fragment, a tangible piece of the puzzle, and Jenkins gripping his sidearm. The sounds outside grew closer, the rhythmic, almost unnerving silence between each footstep betraying the operative's calculated approach. The chase across the decks had led them here, to a confrontation in the very heart of the mystery, where the fate of Nightingale's empire, and their own lives, would be decided.

The door swung open with a silent, fluid motion, revealing the operative standing in the dimly lit corridor. Their eyes, cold and sharp, locked onto Miller, then flickered to the locket fragment in his hand. There was no surprise, no fear, only a chillingly professional assessment of the situation. They had anticipated this, had known their presence would be detected, and had prepared for the final act.

"The data," the operative said, their voice smooth and devoid of emotion, "and the fragment. Hand them over." Miller tightened his grip on the metal, the sharp edges digging into his palm. "Never." The operative's lips curled into a faint, humorless smile. "A regrettable decision."

With a speed that belied their calm demeanor, the operative lunged. Jenkins reacted instantly, shoving Miller behind him and firing a warning shot that splintered the bulkhead beside the operative. The assassin, however, was already in motion, a blur of dark fabric and lethal intent. They dodged the shot with practiced ease, their movements impossibly fluid.

Miller, seeing his opportunity, tossed the locket fragment towards the operative. It spun through the air, catching the light, a desperate gambit. The operative's eyes, trained to track threats, instinctively followed the projectile. In that split second of distraction, Jenkins moved in, his shoulder driving into the operative's side.

The impact sent the assassin staggering, but they recovered quickly, lashing out with a hand that held a wickedly sharp blade. Miller felt a searing pain as the blade sliced across his forearm, blood blooming through his tuxedo. He gritted his teeth, ignoring the agony.

"The drive!" he yelled to Jenkins, as the operative wrestled with the detective. "Get it to safety!"

Jenkins, momentarily disarmed, used his sheer strength to throw the operative against the wall. The impact was brutal, but the assassin seemed almost impervious to pain, their focus solely on Miller and the prize he carried.

"You won't escape, Vance's little lapdog," Miller spat, the adrenaline coursing through him. "He's finished."

The operative's eyes narrowed, a flicker of something that might have been rage, or perhaps simply frustration, crossing their impassive features. They lunged again, not at Jenkins, but at Miller, aiming for his pocket where the USB drive was concealed.

This was the moment. Miller braced himself, and as the operative's blade flashed towards him, he ducked, simultaneously bringing his elbow up and connecting with the operative's jaw. The crack of bone against bone echoed in the confined space. The operative stumbled back, momentarily stunned, their grip on the blade loosening.

Jenkins seized the opportunity. With a powerful sweep, he knocked the blade from the operative's grasp. The assassin, now disarmed and disoriented, seemed to realize the futility of their mission. Their eyes, which had held a cold, professional detachment, now flickered with a hint of desperation. Escape was impossible, capture inevitable.

With a final, defiant glare, the operative turned and bolted, not towards the ship's exterior, but deeper into the ship's labyrinthine corridors, a phantom seeking any available exit.

"Don't let them get away!" Miller shouted, his voice strained from exertion and pain. Jenkins, however, had Miller's injured arm firmly in his grip. "We need to get you to the ship's doctor, Miller. The drive is safe. That's what matters."

Miller looked at the USB drive in his pocket, then back at the stateroom, where the locket fragment lay on the floor, a testament to Sterling's final moments and the danger they had narrowly averted. The operative was gone, a ghost that had slipped through their grasp, but the evidence was secured. Julian Vance's empire was about to crumble, and the chase across the decks had culminated, not in capture, but in a victory nonetheless. The true battle, however, was far from over. The operative was still out there, a loose end Vance would surely try to tie up. And Thorne, still missing, was a wildcard in a game that was rapidly escalating. The night was far from over.

Chapter 10: Interrogation and Alliance

The clang of the brig door echoed Sterling's stateroom, a stark contrast to the opulent décor of the *Seraphina*. This was the ship's underbelly, a place designed for containment, not comfort. Here, in this stark, metallic cell, sat the operative – a ghost made flesh, captured but not yet broken. Miller stood by the reinforced door, the acrid scent of stale air and disinfectant clinging to the confined space. The operative, a woman whose sharp, intelligent eyes now held a steely resolve, sat on the narrow cot, her posture betraying none of the fear or desperation one might expect from a captured assailant. Her movements, even in captivity, were economical, precise, hinting at the rigorous training that had forged her into the instrument of Vance's will. She was a professional, a phantom, and Miller knew that extracting information from such a well-honed weapon would be a brutal, intricate dance.

"Your name," Miller began, his voice low, cutting through the silence. It wasn't a question, but a demand. The operative's gaze remained fixed on a point somewhere beyond Miller's shoulder, her expression unreadable. "I have no name," she stated, her voice a low, resonant contralto, devoid of any discernible accent or emotion. It was a practiced response, honed through countless scenarios, designed to deflect, to obstruct.

Jenkins, standing beside Miller, let out a quiet, almost imperceptible sigh. "Swell. Just swell. Another one for the 'nameless and faceless' file." He leaned against the cold metal of the brig's outer wall, his arms crossed, a picture of weary patience. He'd dealt with these types before – the hardened criminals, the spies, the mercenaries. They were all cut from a similar cloth, their identities carefully curated to serve their handlers.

"The name isn't important," Miller pressed, his eyes never leaving the operative's face. "What's important is who sent you. Julian Vance. That's the name you'll be singing soon enough."

A faint tremor, barely noticeable, passed through the operative's jaw. It was the first hint of a reaction, a flicker of something beneath the impassive facade. Vance's name clearly resonated, even if it didn't elicit a vocal response.

"Vance," the operative repeated, the word spoken with a carefully neutral inflection. It was a confirmation, not an admission. "You were sent to eliminate Sterling," Miller continued, his voice hardening. "To retrieve something. Or perhaps to destroy it. We know about the locket fragment, and we know you failed to get it. Now, you failed to kill us too."

The operative finally shifted her gaze, her eyes meeting Miller's. There was no malice in them, no anger, just a chillingly calm assessment. "My mission parameters were... fluid. Circumstances evolved." "Fluid?" Jenkins scoffed. "You tried to kill us, lady. That's not fluid, that's pretty damn concrete."

"The objective was to secure proprietary information," the operative stated, choosing her words with meticulous care. "The means employed were... regrettable, but necessary."

Miller circled the small cell, his gaze sweeping over the operative's attire – a practical, dark jumpsuit devoid of any insignia or identifying marks. The sheer professionalism of her appearance, the lack of any personal effects, spoke volumes about her organization. This wasn't a street thug; this was someone who operated in the shadows, a tool of immense power.

"Proprietary information," Miller mused, a sardonic smile playing on his lips. "Is that what they're calling stolen research and murder now? Who are you working for, exactly? Some private military company? A shadow intelligence outfit contracted by Vance?"

The operative remained silent, her gaze steady. She had been trained for this, for the interrogation, for the psychological pressure. Her silence was a shield, a carefully constructed barrier designed to protect her employers.

"Look," Jenkins said, his tone shifting, a subtle blend of weariness and calculated empathy. "We're not asking you to betray your handlers, not yet anyway. We just want to understand. Sterling was a good man. He was killed for doing his job. You were just following orders, right? Someone pointed the finger, you pulled the trigger. Simple transaction."

The operative's lips thinned almost imperceptibly. "There are no simple transactions. Only objectives and outcomes."

"And what happens when the outcome is capture?" Miller challenged. "What then? Do they send someone else to clean up this mess? To silence you?"

A flicker of something – unease? – crossed her face. It was fleeting, almost imperceptible, but Miller and Jenkins saw it. The operative was alone, cut off from her support. The promise of extraction, the guarantee of exfiltration, would be non-existent. She was expendable. "My organization takes... precautions," she finally replied, her voice lower now, a hint of something other than pure professional detachment creeping in.

"Precautions like leaving their operatives stranded when things go south?" Jenkins retorted, his voice laced with sarcasm. "Vance doesn't seem like the sentimental type, does he? He hired you to do a job, and when you failed, you became a liability. A loose end."

Miller stepped closer to the bars, his voice dropping to a near whisper. "We have the evidence, you know. Sterling's research. The dossier. Vance is finished. And you, my dear operative, are caught in the crossfire. Your employers will disavow you. They'll cut you loose. And then what? You'll be facing charges for murder, attempted murder, conspiracy... a long list of unpleasantries."

He paused, letting the weight of his words sink in. The operative's breathing had become slightly more shallow. She was still resisting, but the cracks were beginning to show. The carefully constructed facade of unwavering professionalism was starting to crumble under the relentless pressure.

"You're trained," Miller continued, his tone softening, a calculated shift from threat to enticement. "You're skilled. You have unique abilities. Vance exploited that. He used you. And now he's cast you aside. We can protect you. We can ensure your safety, your anonymity, if you help us. If you tell us who hired you. Who you truly work for."

The operative looked at Miller, then at Jenkins. Her eyes scanned their faces, searching for any sign of deception, any hint of a trap. She had spent her life navigating a world of treachery and deceit, and trust was a luxury she could not afford.

"They are a specialized unit," she said, the words coming out in a rush, as if a dam had finally broken. "Contracted by... certain clients. For discreet operations. Infiltration, acquisition, elimination." She hesitated, as if choosing her words carefully, or perhaps as if wrestling with a deeply ingrained directive. "My designation is... Echo."

"Echo," Miller repeated, letting the name hang in the air. "A fitting name. For someone who operates in the silence, who leaves no trace." He leaned in closer. "And this 'specialized unit' – what do they call themselves?" The operative's gaze hardened again, the brief moment of vulnerability vanishing. "That information is classified. Beyond my clearance."

Jenkins let out a short, sharp laugh. "Classified? You're in a brig on a cruise ship, lady. The only thing classified here is what you're going to have for dinner, and I'm betting it's going to be bland."

"We know Vance hired you," Miller said, returned to the core of their inquiry. "We have proof. But we need to know who you work for. Because whoever they are, they are just as dangerous as Vance. And if they're willing to let one of their own get caught, what does that say about their loyalty?"

The operative remained silent, her jaw tight. The offer of protection, the promise of a new life, was a powerful lure, but the ingrained loyalty, the years of conditioning, were even stronger. She had been taught that betrayal was the ultimate sin, that her employers' reach extended everywhere, that escape was a myth.

"Your organization," Miller pressed, his voice growing insistent. "It's more than just a contracting firm, isn't it? It's a network. A silent force that operates behind the scenes, manipulating events, eliminating threats. Nightingale's reach is vast, and if Vance is involved, then this unit... they must be part of that network. Or at least, intimately familiar with it."

The operative's eyes darted towards the heavy steel door of the brig. There was a subtle tension in her shoulders, a readiness to spring, even in her confinement. She was assessing every detail, every escape route, every weakness in their security.

"Vance is a client," she admitted, her voice barely a whisper. "He contracted our services for... problem resolution. Sterling was a problem. His research was a threat."

"And you were the solution," Jenkins finished for her. "A very expensive, very deadly solution. But you failed. You were compromised. And now you're alone. So, tell us, Echo. Who are the people who trained you? Who are the people Vance relies on to make his problems disappear?"

The silence that followed was thick with unspoken tension. The operative's gaze flickered between Miller and Jenkins, her mind clearly a battlefield of conflicting directives. She was a prisoner, facing the prospect of a long incarceration, or worse, a swift and silent end orchestrated by her former employers. The allure of a life free from the constant threat of death and betrayal, was a powerful temptation. But the years of indoctrination, the deep-seated fear of retribution, held her captive as effectively as the steel bars.

"They are... shadows," she finally said, her voice a rasp. "They operate in the periphery. They are... a service. Nothing more."

"A service that silences people," Miller countered, his voice firm. "A service that orchestrates assassinations. A service that protects empires like Nightingale. Vance is a player in that empire, and you, Echo, are one of his pawns. But pawns can be turned."

He leaned closer, his eyes locking with hers. "We can offer you immunity. A new identity. A chance to disappear, to finally be free of this life. But you have to give us something in return. Names. Locations. The structure of this organization. Everything you know."

The operative closed her eyes for a brief moment, a silent battle raging within her. When she opened them, there was a subtle shift in their depths. The cold, professional detachment was still there, but it was now tinged with something else – a weary resignation, perhaps, or a glimmer of hope.

"My handlers," she began, her voice hesitant at first, then gaining a steadier rhythm, "they are known by many names. But the one Vance used, the one they operate under when dealing with clients of his caliber, is... The Obsidian Hand."

Miller and Jenkins exchanged a quick, significant glance. The Obsidian Hand. The name resonated with an almost mythical dread, a whisper in the dark corners of intelligence circles, spoken only in hushed tones. It was the phantom entity, the bogeyman used to frighten rogue agents and nervous politicians. To hear it spoken as a tangible organization, a reality, sent a chill down Miller's spine.

"The Obsidian Hand," Jenkins murmured, the name tasting foreign on his tongue. "So, they're real."

"They are more than real," Echo stated, her voice laced with a newfound gravity. "They are the architects of consequence. They orchestrate... adjustments. To the global balance of power. To... legacies."

Miller felt a prickle of unease crawl up his neck. Sterling's research, Nightingale's empire, Vance's ambitions – they were all threads in a much larger, far more sinister tapestry. The Obsidian Hand was the weaver, and their threads were spun from blood and secrets.

"And Vance," Miller pressed, "how deeply are they embedded with him? Is he a client, or something more?"

Echo paused, her gaze drifting back to the bars of the brig. "Vance is... a patron. He provides resources. He facilitates access. He understands the necessity of... discretion. He funded the acquisition of Nightingale's assets, and the Hand ensures his continued... prosperity."

"Prosperity built on the backs of murder and corruption," Jenkins spat, his patience wearing thin. "So, they're not just hired guns. They're enablers. The grease in the wheels of global villainy."

"They are facilitators," Echo corrected, her professional tone returned, albeit tinged with a hint of weariness. "They ensure that the established order is maintained. Or that it is... reshaped."

Miller's mind raced. The Obsidian Hand. It was a name that promised an unprecedented level of danger, an organization that operated with the impunity of a shadow government. If Vance was merely a patron, then the true power lay with this Hand, and their reach was far more extensive than they had ever imagined. The fight for Sterling's research, for justice, had just escalated exponentially. They were up against a clandestine force that shaped the world from the shadows.

"This 'Reshaping,'" Miller said, his voice low and intense, "does it involve... eliminating anyone who threatens their clients? Anyone who uncovers their operations?"

Echo's gaze met his, and in those cold, intelligent eyes, Miller saw a chilling confirmation. "That is their primary function. To remove obstacles. To ensure... continuity."

The brig, a stark and unforgiving space, had become more than just a prison cell. It was a crucible, a place where the operative's hardened exterior was being tested, where the weight of her actions, and the potential for a future free from her past, were forcing her to confront the truth. She was a tool, a weapon, but even the sharpest blade could be dulled, or redirected. The Obsidian Hand was a formidable enemy, an unseen power that controlled the strings of Vance and Nightingale. But in Echo, Miller and Jenkins had found a potential crack in their armor, a reluctant informant who might just hold the key to dismantling their entire operation. The game had changed, and the stakes had never been higher.

The sterile chill of the interrogation room did little to soothe Michael Thorne's agitated state. Sweat beaded on his forehead, a stark contrast to the icy dread coiling in his gut. The operative, Echo, sat in stony silence, a silent testament to the power she wielded and the fear she inspired. Miller and Jenkins, their faces grim and expectant, had laid out their evidence, their questions sharp and relentless. They knew about Vance. They knew about Sterling. And now, they were closing in on Thorne, his carefully constructed world of privilege and calculated deception beginning to crumble around him.

He had tried to maintain his composure, to project an air of detached concern, of innocent ignorance. But the pressure, the sheer weight of their certainty, was overwhelming. He saw it in their eyes – the suspicion hardening into conviction, the patience thinning with each evasive answer. He was trapped. Vance, the man he had served and feared, had left him exposed, a convenient scapegoat if things went south. And things had, irrevocably, gone south.

The clang of the brig door slamming shut behind Echo had been the final nail in the coffin of his denial. Vance's operative, captured. That was a contingency Thorne hadn't fully prepared for. Vance was meticulous, a master strategist who anticipated every move. But he had clearly underestimated Miller and his tenacious pursuit of truth. Thorne's role, once a clandestine operation conducted in the gilded cages of corporate secrecy, was now laid bare under the harsh glare of a relentless investigation.

He cleared his throat, the sound unnaturally loud in the charged silence. "I... I need to tell you something," he began, his voice hoarse, betraying the tremor in his hands. He looked at Miller, his gaze pleading, searching for some sign of leniency, some sliver of hope that the maelstrom he had helped unleash wouldn't swallow whole him.

Miller's expression remained impassive, his eyes holding Thorne's with an unnerving intensity. "We're listening, Thorne."

Jenkins, leaning against the wall, crossed his arms, his gaze a mixture of suspicion and weary anticipation. He had seen this before – the arrogant facade cracking, the carefully curated persona disintegrating under duress.

"Vance... he's the one who ordered Sterling's death," Thorne confessed, the words tumbling out in a rush, as if a dam had finally broken. "I was... I was involved. I provided him with the information. Sterling's movements, his research... everything."

The admission hung in the air, heavy with implication. Thorne watched their reactions, bracing himself for the inevitable surge of anger or condemnation. But they remained outwardly calm, their focus unwavering. This was the confirmation they had been seeking, the linchpin that connected Vance to the murder.

"You were Vance's informant," Miller stated, his voice flat, devoid of emotion. "Facilitating his... business."

Thorne nodded, shame and fear warring within him. "Yes. I... I fed him details about Sterling. And about... about the journalist. They were getting too close. Sterling's research, the data he had... it was vital to Vance's plans."

"Project Nightingale," Jenkins said, his voice low and dangerous. "What is it, Thorne? What was Sterling about to expose?"

Thorne's breath hitched. He had hoped to avoid this, to keep the true nature of Vance's machinations shrouded in ambiguity. But the game was over. There were no more secrets to protect, only the desperate need to mitigate the damage, to perhaps salvage some semblance of a future for himself.

"Nightingale," Thorne began, his voice trembling, "is... it's an ambitious endeavor. Vance acquired... advanced AI technology. Stolen, I believe, from a research facility in Zurich. He's... he's developed a program designed to... to manipulate global stock markets. To create unprecedented volatility, to profit from chaos."

Miller and Jenkins exchanged a look. The implications were staggering. Vance wasn't just a collector of historical artifacts; he was a player on a global stage, wielding power that could destabilize economies.

"He intended to use Sterling's research to... to refine the AI's predictive capabilities," Thorne continued, his voice barely above a whisper. "Sterling's work on market trends and historical financial patterns was precisely what the AI needed to achieve absolute accuracy. Vance needed that data. And he couldn't risk Sterling exposing him, or worse, selling it to a competitor."

"So, Sterling's death was about preventing the exposure of his market manipulation scheme," Miller clarified, piecing together the fragments. "And silencing him before he could reveal Project Nightingale."

"Yes," Thorne confirmed, his gaze fixed on his hands, now clasped tightly in his lap. "Vance ordered it. He... he said Sterling was a liability. That he had to be neutralized. Permanently."

"And you facilitated this?" Jenkins' voice was laced with incredulity. "You actively helped a man orchestrate a murder?"

Thorne flinched. "I... I was present on the ship. On the *Seraphina*. Vance wanted to ensure Sterling's data was secured. And he wanted... he wanted to silence anyone who might have uncovered too much. Anyone who might have gotten too close to the truth."

His eyes flickered towards Jenkins, a silent acknowledgment of the unspoken threat. His mention of "silencing anyone" included, Thorne knew, his own sister, Dr. Eleanor Vance, who had also been working with Sterling. The thought sent a fresh wave of cold dread through him.

"Including Dr. Vance?" Miller pressed, his voice sharp. "Your own... employer's niece?"

Thorne's head snapped up, his eyes wide with a dawning horror. He hadn't considered the full ramifications of his involvement, the potential danger to his own family, caught in the crossfire of Vance's machinations. "Eleanor? No... Vance wouldn't... he wouldn't harm her. She's... she's vital to the project. Her understanding of... of the historical context of the AI's data is... indispensable." He faltered, the certainty draining from his voice.

Vance's ruthlessness was a known quantity, his moral compass entirely absent. "But... if she got too close to the truth... if she started asking questions..." The implication was clear. Vance's "discretion" was absolute.

"You were there to secure Sterling's data and silence loose ends," Miller stated, his voice hardening. "And you were prepared to do so, weren't you, Thorne? You were Vance's enforcer, his clean-up crew."

Thorne's shoulders slumped in defeat. There was no denying it. He had been complicit. He had knowingly participated in a criminal enterprise, blinded by ambition and a misguided sense of loyalty to Vance. "I... I was. I was scared. Vance... he has a way of making you do things. He has leverage. He knows... he knows things about me. Things I can't afford to have revealed."

"Leverage?" Jenkins echoed, his voice laced with a cynical curiosity. "What kind of leverage does Vance have on a man like you, Thorne? The kind that involves... illicit research? Or perhaps something more personal?"

Thorne's face paled. The question hit a nerve, a hidden vulnerability he had guarded fiercely. Vance had indeed found a way to exert control, exploiting a past transgression, a youthful indiscretion that had been buried deep. It was a secret that could ruin his reputation, his career, everything he had painstakingly built.

"It's... it's a matter of my past," Thorne stammered, his voice barely audible. "Something I... I did years ago. Something that could end my career. Vance... he threatened to expose it. To ruin me."

"So, you became his puppet," Miller said, his tone softening slightly, a hint of understanding replacing the earlier hardness. "A pawn in his game. Used and manipulated because you feared the consequences of defiance."

Thorne nodded, the tears welling in his eyes. "Yes. I was a coward. I let him control me. I helped him do terrible things." He looked at Miller, his voice thick with emotion. "Sterling... he was a good man. He deserved better. And Eleanor... I never wanted any harm to come to her. I was just... trapped."

"Trapped by your own choices, Thorne," Miller stated, his voice firm but not unkind. "But you're not trapped anymore. Not if you choose to help us. We need to dismantle Vance's operation. We need to bring him to justice. And you, Thorne, can be instrumental in that."

The offer hung in the air, a lifeline thrown to a drowning man. Thorne looked at Miller, at Jenkins, then back at the silent, enigmatic figure of Echo. He had made his confession, laid bare his complicity. Now, the choice was his. He could continue to be a victim of Vance's machinations, or he could choose to fight back, to atone for his actions, however imperfectly.

"What do you want me to do?" Thorne asked, his voice steady for the first time since the interrogation had begun. The fear was still present, a cold knot in his stomach, but it was now tempered by a nascent resolve. He had confessed his role, his complicity, his fear. He had acknowledged the chilling reality of Vance's ruthlessness and the sinister machinations of Project Nightingale. He had admitted to being Vance's informant and facilitator, present on the *Seraphina* not as an observer, but as an active participant tasked with securing the stolen AI data and silencing any potential threats, including, he now realized with a sickening jolt, his own sister, Eleanor. The weight of his fear, the leverage Vance held over him because of a carefully guarded past transgression, had driven him to this point. But now, facing the stark reality of Vance's crimes and the potential danger to Eleanor, Thorne felt a flicker of defiance, a desperate need to break free from Vance's insidious grip and perhaps, just perhaps, to find a redemption.

The confession hung in the air, heavy with the weight of its implications. Thorne, his face etched with a potent blend of fear and burgeoning resolve, had just painted a picture of Julian Vance that went far beyond the collector of antiquities and the ruthless businessman they had initially suspected. He had revealed the architect of a scheme so audacious, so globally destructive, that it dwarfed their previous understanding of Vance's ambitions. The sterile interrogation room, moments before a stage for Thorne's unraveling, now felt like the precipice of a global crisis.

"Project Nightingale," Thorne repeated, the name a whisper that seemed to echo the fragility of the world Vance intended to shatter. "It's not just about... about financial manipulation for personal gain, as appalling as that is. It's about control. Absolute control." He swallowed, his throat dry. "Vance has acquired an advanced artificial intelligence, far beyond anything publicly known. It was... procured. Stolen. From a secure facility.

He believes it to be the key to predicting and manipulating every facet of global commerce."

Miller leaned forward, his gaze sharp, absorbing every word. The methodical dismantling of Vance's operation had just taken on a terrifying new dimension. This was no longer about a single murder, or even a series of them. This was about destabilizing the very foundations of the global economy. "Predicting and manipulating? How, Thorne? Give us the details."

"The AI," Thorne explained, his voice gaining a strange, detached quality as he delved deeper into Vance's strategy, "is designed to analyze vast datasets of financial information. Historical trends, market fluctuations, geopolitical events, even social media sentiment. But it was Sterling's research that provided the final, crucial element. Sterling had developed algorithms that could... correlate seemingly unrelated historical events with future market movements with uncanny accuracy. He had essentially cracked the code of economic causality."

Jenkins, who had been observing Thorne with a perpetual air of skepticism, now looked genuinely disturbed. "So, Vance didn't just want to steal Sterling's data; he needed it to enhance his AI's predictive power. He wanted to create an intelligence that could foresee, and therefore control, the global markets."

"Precisely," Thorne confirmed, a grim nod. "Vance's conglomerate has been positioning itself for months. Acquiring distressed assets, investing in key emerging technologies under the guise of diversification. The plan is to use the AI to trigger a cascade of targeted market crashes. Not a complete, immediate collapse, but a series of carefully orchestrated panics. Enough to destabilize major economies, cause widespread fear, and then... then Vance's entities will swoop in. They'll buy up undervalued companies, seize control of essential industries at pennies on the dollar, and essentially rebuild the global economic landscape in Vance's image. A new world order, dictated by his algorithms."

The sheer scale of the ambition was breathtaking, horrifying. It was a plan born of immense hubris and a chilling disregard for the billions of lives that would be irrevocably affected. "And the wooden bird?" Miller asked, the seemingly innocuous detail from Sterling's recovered journal resurfacing. "What does that signify?"

Thorne's eyes flickered. "The bird... it's a symbol. A marker. Vance uses it within his inner circle. It signifies... the final phase. The launch of Nightingale. When the bird is... activated, so to speak, it means the operation is in motion. It's a signal for operatives to begin their final stages of execution, to ensure Vance's escape and to... tidy up any remaining loose ends."

"Loose ends," Jenkins repeated, the phrase resonating with a sinister undertone. "You mentioned you were on the

Seraphina to secure data and silence people. Was Sterling's death part of 'tidying up loose ends'?"

"Sterling was the primary loose end," Thorne admitted, his voice barely audible. "He was aware of Vance's intentions. He had become... a liability. Vance couldn't allow him to reveal Nightingale. But it wasn't just Sterling. There were others on board who had become... too curious. Too aware of the true nature of Vance's acquisition. They were potential leaks. Vance needed to ensure complete secrecy. He believed that any information getting out before Nightingale was fully deployed would jeopardize the entire operation."

"And that's where you came in," Miller stated, his voice hardening. "To make sure no one talked. To ensure Vance's plan went off without a hitch."

Thorne's shoulders slumped, the weight of his complicity pressing down on him. "Yes. Vance gave me specific instructions. I was to locate Sterling, secure his research, and... neutralize anyone who posed a threat to the plan. It was... I was given a list. Names. And Sterling's was at the top."

"And Eleanor Vance?" Jenkins' question was pointed, cutting through the morbid details of Vance's machinations. "Was she on that list?"

The mention of Eleanor brought a fresh wave of panic to Thorne. He hadn't wanted to believe it, hadn't wanted to confront the terrifying possibility. "Eleanor... she was... she was working with Sterling, yes. She had access to his research, his findings. Vance initially saw her as an asset. Her expertise in historical data analysis was invaluable to the AI's development. But as she got closer to Sterling, as she began to understand the ethical implications of Nightingale, she started to question Vance. She expressed her concerns to me. She wanted to... to find a way out."

"Did Vance know about her doubts?" Miller's voice was a low growl.

"I... I believe so," Thorne stammered, his mind racing. "Vance is... he's incredibly paranoid. He has eyes and ears everywhere. Eleanor was becoming a concern. She was too intelligent, too principled. She was asking too many questions. She had access to the same information as Sterling, and she was beginning to see the true horror of what Nightingale entailed. Vance... he saw her as a potential threat to the project. A leak waiting to happen."

"So, Vance ordered her death as well?" Jenkins' disbelief was palpable.

"I... I don't know for sure," Thorne confessed, his voice laced with genuine fear. "Vance didn't explicitly tell me to harm her. But he said... he said that anyone who stood in the way of Nightingale would be... removed. Permanently. He was adamant about maintaining absolute secrecy. And Eleanor, with her direct access to the data and her growing apprehension, was becoming a significant risk."

The chilling implication hung in the air. Vance, in his ruthless pursuit of global dominance, was willing to eliminate anyone, even his own niece, if they posed a threat. Thorne realized with sickening clarity that he had been a pawn, a tool to be used and discarded, even by the woman he secretly admired.

"Vance's escape plan," Miller pressed, bringing the conversation back to the immediate threat. "He's at the next port of call? When is that?"

"Tonight," Thorne said, his voice tight with urgency. "The *Seraphina* is scheduled to dock in Singapore by dawn. Vance has a private jet waiting. He's arranged for a complete disappearance. He's already transferred vast sums of money through shell corporations. He has identities, secure locations... he's prepared for every contingency, except, it seems, for this." He gestured vaguely at the interrogation room, at Miller and Jenkins.

"He's leaving his operatives to clean up," Jenkins stated, his eyes hard. "To ensure the narrative is controlled, to silence anyone who might have seen too much, or heard too much. And you, Thorne, were part of that cleanup crew."

"I was supposed to be," Thorne admitted, the words a bitter pill. "I was given a final set of instructions before Sterling's death. Vance wanted me to ensure that all evidence of his presence on the

Seraphina was removed. He wanted me to make Sterling's death look like a... like a random act of piracy, or a consequence of his own recklessness. He didn't want any direct link back to him. And he wanted me to ensure that... that no one else on board had discovered anything incriminating. Especially not Dr. Vance. He gave me certain... contingencies. Protocols to follow if she became too inquisitive."

A cold dread settled over Miller. Vance was not just a criminal mastermind; he was a sociopath, devoid of any familial loyalty or moral compass. His plan was a meticulously crafted engine of destruction, and Thorne had been a vital cog within it.

"So, Vance planned to trigger these market crashes, seize control of global assets, and then simply vanish," Miller summarized, the enormity of the scheme dawning on him. "Leaving behind a devastated global economy and a trail of silenced witnesses."

"He envisioned it as a new beginning," Thorne whispered, a hollow echo of Vance's grandiosity. "A phoenix rising from the ashes of economic collapse. He believed he was a visionary, a necessary force for change. He saw the existing world order as corrupt and inefficient. He thought he was... saving humanity, in his own twisted way, by imposing his control."

"Saving humanity by bankrupting it?" Jenkins scoffed. "The man is delusional."

"He has a profound belief in his own superiority," Thorne agreed. "He sees himself as an architect of destiny. And Nightingale... Nightingale was to be his masterpiece. The ultimate expression of his intellect and his will. He was so close, so incredibly close. If he reaches Singapore, if he gets on that jet... it will be almost impossible to track him, let alone stop the plan."

The urgency of the situation was now undeniable. The clock was ticking. Vance was making his move, and with him went the keys to a catastrophe that could redefine global suffering. Thorne's confession, born of fear and desperation, had just revealed the true stakes. The interrogation had escalated from a murder investigation to a race against time to avert an economic apocalypse.

"You said Vance has a way of making people do things," Miller said, his voice regaining its focus. "Leverage. You mentioned a past indiscretion. You were afraid he would expose it, ruin your career. Is that still a factor?"

Thorne hesitated, then nodded. The fear was still there, a constant hum beneath his skin, but the stakes had changed. Vance's plan was no longer just a threat to Thorne's reputation; it was a threat to the world. "Yes. He knows... he knows about a research project I was involved in years ago. A theoretical application of... of predictive algorithms that was deemed highly unethical. I was young, ambitious, and I pushed boundaries I shouldn't have. It was... shut down. Discredited. But Vance... he has access to the documentation. He threatened to leak it, to paint me as a rogue scientist, a danger to public trust. It would have ended my career. My life."

"But Nightingale ends far more than careers, Thorne," Miller said, his voice firm. "It ends stability, security, futures. You've admitted your involvement, your complicity. You've seen the face of Vance's ambition. Now you have a choice. You can remain a victim, or you can become an active participant in stopping him."

The offer hung in the air, a stark contrast to the suffocating fear that had held Thorne captive for so long. He looked at Miller, at Jenkins, his gaze filled with a newfound, fragile hope. He had confessed. He had revealed the terrifying truth of Project Nightingale. He had admitted to his role in Vance's heinous plan, to his fear and his complicity. He had been Vance's instrument, a willing accomplice in the silencing of truths and the securing of data that would lead to global devastation. The wooden bird, a symbol of Vance's clandestine operations, now represented the precipice of their world. Thorne knew Vance's plan was audacious, catastrophic, and on the verge of execution. Vance intended to escape at the next port, Singapore, leaving his operatives to meticulously clean up any remaining loose ends. The weight of his past, the leverage Vance held over him, had driven him to this point. But now, faced with the undeniable magnitude of Vance's crimes, Thorne felt a flicker of defiance, a desperate need to break free from Vance's insidious grip and, perhaps, to find some measure of redemption.

"What do you want me to do?" Thorne's voice, though still shaky, held a newfound clarity. The fear hadn't vanished, but a desperate imperative had eclipsed it. He was trapped, yes, but perhaps not irrevocably. Perhaps, by finally facing the truth and embracing the consequences, he could forge a new path, one that led not to ruin, but to atonement.

The air in the sterile interrogation room, thick with the scent of stale coffee and unspoken fear, crackled with a new energy. Thorne, his confession still raw and unsettling, had just unburdened himself of a truth that threatened to unravel the very fabric of global stability. Project Nightingale. The name itself was a chilling premonition of the chaos Julian Vance intended to unleash. Vance, the suave collector and ruthless magnate, was revealed not as a simple criminal, but as a megalomaniacal architect of economic pandemonium, armed with an AI capable of predicting and manipulating the world's markets. Thorne had painted a grim picture of Sterling's research, the stolen AI, and Vance's grand design: to engineer a series of targeted market crashes, plunging nations into disarray, only to emerge as the benevolent savior, amassing unprecedented wealth and power. And Eleanor Vance, the brilliant niece Thorne secretly admired, had become a dangerous variable, a potential loose end Vance might eliminate.

The weight of Thorne's words settled heavily on Miller and Jenkins. The interrogation had spiraled from a murder investigation to a race against a global economic meltdown. Vance, a phantom moving through the shadows of international finance, was about to escape, taking with him the keys to a catastrophe. Thorne's fear of Vance exposing his past ethical transgressions was the hook, but the sheer horror of Nightingale was the catalyst that pushed him towards a desperate gamble. He had confessed his complicity, his fear, his role as an instrument of Vance's will. Now, standing on the precipice of redemption, he looked at Miller, a flicker of fragile hope igniting within him.

"What do you want me to do?" Thorne's voice, though still trembling, carried a newfound urgency, a desperate plea for a path out of the abyss. He was trapped, yes, but perhaps not irrevocably. Perhaps, by embracing the truth and facing the consequences, he could forge a new path, one that led not to ruin, but to atonement.

Miller met Thorne's gaze, his expression unreadable. The confession had been extraordinary, bordering on unbelievable, yet the details Thorne provided, the chilling logic of Vance's plan, resonated with a terrifying authenticity. Thorne had laid bare his own culpability, his fear of exposure a tangible thing. But Miller saw more than just a desperate man seeking leniency. He saw Thorne's intellectual capacity, the very same that had made him valuable to Vance, now a potential weapon against him. The alliance, if it could be called that, was born not of trust, but of dire necessity.

"You want to stop him," Miller stated, his voice a low, steady rumble. "You want to prevent Nightingale. That's what you want." It wasn't a question. Thorne's implied confession, his willingness to cooperate, was a desperate pivot. Miller had seen it a hundred times before: the cornered rat, the trapped wolf. But Thorne was more than just a criminal; he was a scientist, intimately familiar with the beast they were hunting. "You've seen the scope of Vance's ambition. You know what he's capable of. You've been a part of it. Now you have the chance to be on the other side."

Jenkins, ever the pragmatist, remained skeptical, his eyes narrowed, assessing Thorne as if he were a ticking time bomb. He had no love for Vance, but his distrust of Thorne was a deeply ingrained instinct. Thorne had admitted to being a part of the 'cleanup crew,' to silencing those who knew too much. The fact that Eleanor Vance was also a potential target, a woman whose family connection might have once afforded her some protection, only underscored Vance's chilling ruthlessness, and Thorne's complicity.

"Leniency isn't a given, Thorne," Jenkins said, his voice gravelly. "You've admitted to aiding and abetting. That's a serious offense. But if you can deliver Vance, if you can dismantle Nightingale before it activates, then maybe... just maybe... we can talk about your future."

Thorne flinched at the word 'abetting,' but he didn't protest. He knew he deserved it. He had been a pawn, a tool, and now, in his desperate bid for self-preservation, he was offering himself as a weapon. "I will cooperate. Fully. I want to stop him. Not just for... for the world. But for myself. I can't live with what I've done. What I was about to do." He swallowed, his gaze unwavering. "Vance is at the

Seraphina. She's scheduled to dock in Singapore by dawn. He has a private jet waiting. I have the flight number. His contact in Singapore is a man named Silas Croft. Croft owns a private aviation company, 'Apex

Aviation.' Vance uses him for all his discreet travel. Croft's office is at the Marina Bay Financial Centre. Vance will be there, with his personal security detail. About ten men, heavily armed, ex-military. They're loyal to him, and they're not going to let him be apprehended easily."

Miller leaned back, absorbing the information. Silas Croft. Apex Aviation. The Marina Bay Financial Centre. These were tangible threads, details that could be followed, that could lead them to Vance. Thorne's knowledge was invaluable, a direct line into the heart of Vance's escape. "And the wooden bird?" Miller asked, the symbol Thorne had mentioned earlier, the marker for Nightingale's activation. "You said it signifies the final phase, the launch. Is it still a factor? Can it tell us when the operation is truly underway, beyond Vance's personal escape?"

Thorne's eyes darted around the room, as if searching for an escape route that no longer existed. "The bird... it's a physical object, a piece of carved mahogany. Vance keeps it in his private study on the

Seraphina. It's more than just a symbol; it's a piece of encrypted hardware. It's connected to the AI. When Vance activates it, it sends a final signal, a confirmation that all preparatory phases are complete and the AI is ready to initiate the market manipulation sequence. It's the final command. If we can get to it, if we can intercept that signal, we might disable Nightingale remotely."

"So, we need to get to Vance, the bird, and possibly Croft before they vanish into thin air," Jenkins summarized, his mind already racing through logistics and potential countermeasures. "This is a long shot, Thorne. Vance is a ghost. He's spent years cultivating this network of anonymity."

"He's not a ghost, he's a man," Thorne insisted, his voice gaining a surprising edge of conviction. "And he's made mistakes. He's arrogant. He underestimates everyone. He believes he's untouchable. But he's not. He's human. And he's made plans. Plans we can exploit." Thorne's mind, honed by years of scientific rigor and strategic planning, began to churn. "There are other operatives on board the

Seraphina. Vance trusts them to maintain the narrative, to ensure no one suspects what's truly happening. They're disguised as crew, as passengers. They'll be carrying out the final stages of his plan to obscure his departure and ensure his escape remains unnoticed. They have...

contingency plans for interference. Diversionary tactics. They're trained to be ruthless."

Miller steepled his fingers, his eyes fixed on Thorne. The alliance was a precarious one, built on a foundation of mutual self-interest and profound distrust. Thorne, the informant seeking absolution, and Miller, the detective forced to rely on the very man he was hunting. "Tell us about these contingency plans. What kind of interference are we talking about?"

"Disruption," Thorne replied, his voice lowering. "If there's any sign of our operation being compromised, they're authorized to create chaos. Small-scale fires, system malfunctions on the ship, anything to distract security and create an opportunity for Vance's escape. They might even... target key individuals who they believe are behind the disruption. That includes you. That includes me, if they knew I was cooperating."

A chill snaked down Miller's spine. This wasn't just about apprehending a criminal; it was about preventing a calculated act of domestic terrorism on a global scale. The stakes had never been higher. "We'll have to move fast. We need to get to Singapore before Vance. We need to intercept him at the port, or at Apex Aviation. Jenkins, get me a secure line to Interpol. I need eyes on Croft and Apex Aviation, and I need every available asset in Singapore, discreetly."

Jenkins nodded, already pulling out his secure comms device. "I'll coordinate with local law enforcement. But Thorne, you're coming with us. You're our ticket in, and our insurance policy. You know Vance's security. You know his routines. If this goes south, you're going to be our leverage."

Thorne swallowed hard, the prospect of facing Vance's men, of being so close to the man who had controlled his life for so long, was terrifying. But the alternative was worse. Allowing Nightingale to be unleashed, condemning millions to economic ruin, was a burden he couldn't bear. "I understand. I'll do whatever it takes." He paused, then added, his voice tinged with a desperate plea, "Eleanor... Vance. Is she safe? Has he... has he made a move against her?"

Miller's expression softened, a rare glimpse of the man beneath the hardened detective. "We're working on that. Thorne, your confession has put her on our radar. We'll do everything we can to ensure her safety. But we need you to focus. Vance is the priority. Stopping Nightingale is the priority."

The pact was sealed, an unspoken agreement forged in the crucible of a shared threat. Thorne, the betrayer, now a reluctant ally. Miller and Jenkins, the pursuers, forced to trust their quarry. It was a dangerous gambit, a leap of faith into the unknown. But as the gears of their improbable alliance began to turn, a sliver of hope, however faint, began to emerge from the shadows. The hunt for Julian Vance had just entered its most critical, and perilous, phase. The fate of the world, it seemed, rested on the shoulders of a confessed criminal, two determined detectives, and a stolen AI.

The hum of the ship's engines, usually a comforting drone, now felt like the ticking of a bomb. Singapore. Dawn was a promise only a few hours away, and with it, the imminent docking of the *Seraphina*. Each passing minute was a nail hammered into the coffin of their potential success. Miller stared at the chronometer on his wrist, the digital display a stark reminder of their dwindling window of opportunity. Thorne's confession, delivered with a desperate urgency, had ignited a firestorm of action, but action that was now racing against the inexorable pull of gravity and steel against concrete.

"He'll have eyes on the ground," Miller said, his voice low, a tightrope walk between command and counsel. He paced the confined space of the makeshift command center, a disused storage room repurposed with hastily assembled comms equipment. "Vance isn't going to walk off that ship and blend into the crowd. He'll have a welcoming committee, set up to whisk him away before any official presence can even register his departure."

Jenkins, hunched over a flickering monitor, grunted in agreement, his fingers flying across the keyboard. "Interpol's on it. We've fed them everything Thorne gave us – Croft, Apex Aviation, the flight manifest for that private jet. They're pushing it to their Singaporean counterparts, but the wheels of international law, even when greased with urgency, grind slowly." He glanced up, his face grim. "By the time they get the warrants, the paperwork, the actual boots on the ground... Vance could be on his third continent."

Thorne, confined to a secured section of the ship under the watchful eyes of a discreet security detail, was their linchpin. His testimony, detailing the intricate network Vance had built, the contingency plans for his extraction, was the only direct conduit they had into the immediate aftermath of the

Seraphina's arrival. The locket, too, clutched in Miller's hand, was more than just a piece of jewelry; it was a tangible fragment of Vance's operation, a potential key to understanding the mechanics of Nightingale. Thorne had spoken of its hidden compartment, a secure data storage, but without the proper decryption tools, it was a locked box of secrets.

"We can't just wait for Interpol to catch up," Miller insisted, stopping his pacing to face Jenkins. "Vance's network is designed to bypass official channels, to operate in the grey spaces. We need to create our own leverage, a direct intervention." He looked towards the reinforced door behind which Thorne was being held. "He's the key to that intervention. His knowledge of Vance's security, his understanding of the extraction protocol... we need him to guide us through it, not just tell us about it from a distance."

Jenkins sighed, running a hand through his already disheveled hair. "He's a wild card, Miller. A confessed accomplice. His testimony is critical, but putting him on the ground, face-to-face with Vance's people... that's a whole other level of risk."

"And what's the alternative, Jenkins? Let him slip through our fingers?" Miller's voice was sharp, cutting through the ambient noise of the ship. "We have Thorne. We have his confession. That's our leverage with him. He knows what happens if he doesn't cooperate. Now we need to use his knowledge to put us in a position to apprehend Vance, and more importantly, to get that wooden bird before it sends the final signal."

The "wooden bird." The carved mahogany object, Thorne had explained, was not merely symbolic, but a physical component of the Nightingale system. A hardware key, essentially, containing encrypted data that, once activated by Vance, would transmit the final command to the AI, initiating the global market manipulation. Intercepting it was paramount. Losing it meant losing their chance to dismantle Nightingale at its source.

"The operative in the brig," Miller continued, his mind already charting a perilous course. "Thorne mentioned there's someone on board, someone Vance trusts implicitly, who's overseeing the final stages of his escape.

They're disguised, blending in, but Thorne knows who they are. That's our first target. Thorne can identify them, and then we can use that individual to get to Vance, or at least to get closer to the bird."

Jenkins finally looked away from his screen, his gaze meeting Miller's with a flicker of grudging respect. He knew Miller was right. Thorne's information was a roadmap, but they needed Thorne himself to navigate the treacherous terrain of Vance's escape route. "Alright. But we move smart. We don't go in guns blazing. Thorne is our insider, our guide. His safety is as critical as Vance's apprehension."

"Agreed. Thorne will be in protective custody, but on our team. He'll be our eyes and ears on the ground, feeding us real-time intel as we move through the port. We'll use his knowledge to anticipate Vance's moves, to cut off his escape routes before he even knows they're compromised." Miller paused, his mind racing through the logistics. "We need to coordinate with the port authorities in Singapore, but discreetly. No blaring sirens, no SWAT teams swarming the docks. We need to isolate Vance's immediate entourage, intercept his transport. The goal isn't a spectacular capture; it's a surgical extraction. We need him alive, and we need that bird."

He took a deep breath, the scent of the ship's recycled air suddenly feeling suffocating. Thorne's testimony had been a revelation, a terrifying glimpse into the depths of Vance's ambition. Now, the pressure was on them to act on that revelation, to turn information into apprehension before Vance could disappear into the labyrinthine financial world he so expertly manipulated. The race against docking had begun, and every second counted. They were a fragile alliance, a detective, a weary investigator, and a repentant accomplice, all united by the singular, terrifying threat of Project Nightingale.

Miller turned to Jenkins, his voice hardening with renewed resolve. "Get me Thorne. We're going to go over his intel one more time. I want every detail of that escape protocol etched into our minds. We're going to meet Vance at the dock, not as prey, but as predators." The ship groaned as it began its slow deceleration, a mechanical sigh that echoed the monumental task ahead. The Singapore skyline, a distant promise of land and opportunity, was drawing closer, but for Miller and Jenkins, it represented a battlefield where the fate of global financial stability hung precariously in the balance. The game of cat and mouse had just moved to a new, far more dangerous arena, and time, their most precious commodity, was rapidly running out. The glint of the locket in Miller's hand was a silent promise, a tangible piece of the puzzle that Thorne had placed in their hands, a puzzle that now needed to be solved before the world's economy crumbled into dust. The sterile interrogation room had been the birthplace of this desperate alliance; the bustling docks of Singapore would be its crucible.

Chapter 11: The Port of Arrival

The rhythmic thrum of the *Seraphina*'s engines seemed to amplify Miller's growing anxiety. Singapore. The city, a beacon of commerce and a nexus of global finance, was now the stage for their desperate gambit. He could practically taste the metallic tang of anticipation mixed with the ever-present fear of failure. The information Thorne had divulged, a torrent of details about Vance's meticulously crafted escape, had shifted their operational focus from passive investigation to active intervention. But intervention on this scale, in a foreign port teeming with thousands of arrivals, demanded more than just their small, ad-hoc team. It required the muscle and reach of established law enforcement.

Miller retreated from the main operational hub, seeking a semblance of privacy in a cramped, utilitarian cabin. He pulled out his personal encrypted comms device, a relic from his days in the FBI, now their lifeline to the wider world. The secure channel required multiple layers of authentication, a testament to the sensitive nature of their current predicament. He initiated a connection, the familiar chirping of the outgoing signal a small comfort in the vast unknown. "This is Sterling," he began, his voice a low murmur, carefully calibrated to convey urgency without revealing too much to any unintended listeners. "I need to reach Agent Rostova. Top priority, secure channel alpha."

The wait felt interminable. The ship's gentle roll, a constant reminder of their proximity to land, did little to soothe his frayed nerves. He replayed Thorne's confession in his mind, searching for any overlooked detail, any nuance that might have been missed. Vance wasn't just a businessman; he was a phantom, a master manipulator who had woven himself into the very fabric of the global financial system. The Nightingale project, an artificial intelligence capable of destabilizing economies with a mere algorithmic push, was a threat of unprecedented magnitude. And Thorne, the man who had helped build it, was now their only witness, their only guide.

Finally, a crisp voice crackled through the earpiece, a familiar cadence that cut through the ship's ambient noise. "Miller? Is that you? What the hell is going on? You're not supposed to be off-grid for this long." Rostova' voice, usually calm and measured, held a discernible note of concern.

"No time for pleasantries, Mark," Miller cut in, his tone sharp. "I'm transmitting everything now. Encrypted. You'll receive a data packet containing Thorne's full confession, photographic evidence of the Nightingale hardware – the 'wooden bird' – schematics of Vance's secure server, and a detailed breakdown of his extraction protocol from the

Seraphina." He paused, ensuring Rostova understood the gravity of the situation. "The target is Julian Vance. He's arriving in Singapore on the *Seraphina* within the next few hours. He's the architect of Nightingale, a project that poses an existential threat to global financial stability."

He continued, his words tumbling out in a torrent, each syllable laden with the weight of impending disaster. "Vance isn't coming ashore to negotiate. He's coming to disappear. His network is designed to facilitate that disappearance, to mask his movements, and to activate Nightingale remotely if necessary. He'll have a team on the ground, ready to extract him the moment he sets foot on dock. They'll be discreet, professional, and equipped to handle any preliminary official presence." Miller detailed the specific codewords Thorne had provided, the rendezvous points, the communication frequencies Vance's extraction team was expected to use. He emphasized the urgency, the minuscule window of opportunity they had to intercept Vance before he vanished into the vastness of the international financial underworld.

"We need immediate, coordinated action, Mark," Miller stressed. "As soon as the *Seraphina* docks, I need your people, and anyone you can discreetly bring in, to be in position. Secure Vance, his immediate entourage, and most importantly, that 'wooden bird.' Thorne's information indicates it's a crucial hardware component, a key to Nightingale's activation. We can't let it fall into the wrong hands, and we certainly can't let Vance use it."

Rostova' silence was palpable, a heavy pause filled with the unspoken complexities of international law and jurisdictional boundaries. Miller knew the FBI, even with its vast resources, couldn't operate unilaterally in Singapore without the full cooperation of local authorities. This was not a simple arrest; it was a delicate maneuver that could have significant diplomatic repercussions if mishandled.

Finally, Rostova responded, his voice tighter now, the initial surprise giving way to a focused resolve. "Miller, this is... monumental. If what you're saying is accurate, if Nightingale is real, and Vance is behind it... we're talking about a threat on a scale we haven't seen before. The data packet is coming through. Give me ten minutes to review the core evidence. I'll need to verify your claims, and then I can brief the necessary channels. Interpol will undoubtedly need to be involved, and that means navigating a labyrinth of protocols. Singaporean law enforcement will have to be brought in, and that's going to require formal channels, official requests."

"Ten minutes is an eternity, Mark," Miller countered, his voice laced with frustration. "By the time those channels open, Vance will be long gone. We can't afford to wait for official sanction. You know me, you know my track record. I wouldn't be sending you this without absolute certainty. Thorne's confession is corroborated by the intel we've gathered on Apex Aviation and the flight manifests. The evidence is sound."

"I believe you, Miller, I always have," Rostova conceded. "But the system... it's not designed for this kind of rapid, extraterritorial intervention. We'll have to thread the needle. I'll initiate the secure communication with Singaporean law enforcement through our existing liaison channels. I'll emphasize the severity and the potential global impact. We'll push for an expedited response, but I can't promise you a full SWAT team swarming the docks the moment you tie up."

Miller understood the reality of bureaucratic inertia, but he couldn't afford to let it dictate their fate. "We don't need a full-scale raid, Mark. We need precision. Thorne provided us with the identity of the operative overseeing Vance's extraction. He's disguised, but Thorne knows who he is. That's our initial point of contact. If we can isolate that operative, leverage their knowledge... we might get eyes on Vance and the 'bird' before they're spirited away."

Rostova took a deep breath. "Alright, Miller. I'll pass all of Thorne's intel on the operative to my contacts. We'll push for discreet surveillance and, if possible, an immediate apprehension of that individual. Once we have them, we can use them to pinpoint Vance. But you need to understand, this will be a joint operation. We'll be working through official channels, even if we try to expedite them. There will be paperwork, approvals, and a host of legalities to navigate."

"I understand," Miller said, though the 'understanding' felt hollow. He knew the difference between a rapid-response unit and a committee. "Just make sure the urgency is conveyed. This isn't just about apprehending a fugitive; it's about preventing a global financial catastrophe. Nightingale is real, and Vance is its master. If he activates it, the consequences will be catastrophic. The data you have is the key. It proves the threat. Use it to cut through the red tape."

The transmission ended, leaving Miller in the echoing silence of the cabin. He looked at the locket in his palm, its intricate carvings a stark contrast to the cold, hard reality of the data it contained. Thorne had given them a roadmap, but navigating the treacherous terrain of international cooperation, while simultaneously racing against Vance's meticulously planned escape, was a challenge that dwarfed anything he had faced before. He knew Rostova would do his best, but the wheels of international justice, even when greased with the promise of preventing global economic collapse, moved with a ponderous weight. They were pushing the boundaries, operating in the shadows, relying on a desperate alliance forged in the crucible of fear. The arrival in Singapore was no longer just a logistical milestone; it was the precipice of an all-out war against an invisible enemy, fought on the battleground of global finance. He had to trust that the echoes of his past with the FBI, the relationships he had cultivated, would be enough to cut through the inevitable bureaucratic entanglement. The future of the world economy, it seemed, rested on a secure data transmission and the goodwill of his former colleagues.

The air in Singapore's port was a thick, humid blanket, a stark contrast to the sterile chill of the ship's interior. Miller felt the change even before stepping onto the gangplank, a primal awareness of being on the cusp of something immense and volatile. Thorne's words, replaying in his mind like a grim soundtrack, painted a vivid picture of the meticulously orchestrated chaos that awaited them. Vance wasn't just disembarking; he was initiating a carefully choreographed vanishing act, a final, audacious performance before disappearing into the global ether.

"He's got a network, Miller. Not just here, but woven into the fabric of the port itself," Thorne had whispered, his voice raspy with a mixture of dread and reluctant admiration. "Customs agents who look the other way, dockhands on his payroll, even a few rogue elements from port security. It's a... a welcome wagon of sorts, designed to spirit him away before anyone even realizes he's landed." Thorne's description of Vance's escape route was less a plan and more a testament to a well-oiled machine. It spoke of private security details, not the usual motley collection of hired muscle, but professionals, vetted and loyal, individuals accustomed to operating in the shadows. Their role was to blend seamlessly into the bustling port environment, a human camouflage for Vance's egress.

Thorne had elaborated on the concept of 'clean' getaway vehicles. Not the flashy sports cars of Hollywood fantasies, but nondescript vans, unmarked sedans, their interiors stripped of any identifying marks, their engines tuned for silent, swift acceleration. These weren't just cars; they were mobile safe houses, equipped with communication jamming technology and, Thorne suspected, basic medical kits. Their purpose was to ferry Vance and his inner circle from the immediate vicinity of the docks to a pre-determined, secure location. This wasn't a simple extraction; it was an industrial-scale disappearance, a relocation designed to be permanent.

"He's not alone, you know," Thorne had continued, his gaze fixed on some unseen point beyond the cabin walls. "There are others. Key players. They're on board with him, part of the Nightingale project from the ground up, or at least deeply entangled in the financial machinations that enabled it. They're his anchors, his lieutenants. They'll be extracted with him, their knowledge a vital asset to Vance, a liability to us." Thorne had provided a handful of names, shadowy figures whose roles were alluded to but never fully explained, their significance overshadowed by the sheer magnitude of Vance's operation. Miller knew that apprehending Vance was only half the battle; identifying and securing these associates was equally critical.

The description of Vance's personal security chief had been particularly chilling. Thorne referred to him only as "The Jackal." "Ex-military," Thorne had stated, his voice a low growl. "Served in some of the grimmer conflicts. Ruthless doesn't even begin to cover it. He's Vance's shadow, Vance's shield. He's got eyes that see everything and a capacity for... persuasion that's legendary, and not in a good way. He'll be the one orchestrating the immediate extraction, the one ensuring Vance melts away like mist in the morning sun." Thorne had provided a physical description: tall, broad-shouldered, with a scar that ran from his left eyebrow to his jawline, a permanent testament to a life lived on the edge. His eyes, Thorne had warned, were like chips of ice, devoid of warmth or empathy.

The challenge, as Thorne had emphasized, was the sheer volume of human traffic. Singapore's port was a monstrous organism, a confluence of goods and people from every corner of the globe. Thousands of passengers, a kaleidoscope of nationalities and purposes, would be disembarking, creating a natural cover for Vance's clandestine departure. Law enforcement, even if alerted and present, would be stretched thin, trying to manage the official flow of arrivals while simultaneously hunting for a phantom. The "cordon" Miller had mentioned to Rostova was a pipe dream, a romantic notion that dissolved in the harsh light of reality.

"They'll move fast, Miller," Thorne had implored, his hand gripping Miller's arm with surprising strength. "The moment the ship is secured, Vance and his core group will be guided off, subtly, through a designated path that bypasses the main passenger debarkation. They'll be absorbed into the crowd, disappearing into the labyrinth of the port before the official process even begins. It's designed to be invisible." Thorne's intel suggested Vance himself would be the last to disembark from his private suite, a final act of calculated theatricality, before being whisked away by The Jackal and his team.

Miller felt the weight of Thorne's information settle upon him like a shroud. This wasn't a simple pursuit; it was a race against time, against a highly sophisticated, deeply embedded network. Every detail Thorne provided was a potential pitfall, a confirmation of the monumental task ahead. The rhythmic clang of the ship's mooring lines against the pier, a sound that should have signaled arrival, now sounded like a countdown to disaster. They had to move, and they had to move now, before Vance's carefully constructed escape began to solidify into an insurmountable reality. The port, a gateway to the world, was about to become a vanishing point for one of its most dangerous architects. Miller's mind raced, trying to overlay Thorne's intelligence onto the raw, chaotic reality of the docks unfolding before him. He needed to identify The Jackal, his team, and the critical extraction points, all while Rostova worked his bureaucratic magic to get official eyes on the ground. It was a desperate gamble, a shot fired in the dark, hoping to hit a target they could barely see. The sheer audacity of Vance's plan was breathtaking; his ability to command such a network, to bribe and coerce his way through the intricate web of international port operations, was a testament to his power and influence. It was clear that Vance wasn't just a financier; he was a master strategist, a puppeteer pulling strings on a global scale. The Nightingale project was merely the endgame; the escape was the masterful prelude, designed to ensure his continued power to orchestrate future chaos. Miller knew, with a chilling certainty, that the next few hours would determine not only Vance's fate but the stability of the global economy.

The hum of the ship's engines finally ceased, replaced by the cacophony of the port – the screech of gulls, the distant roar of cargo cranes, the muffled shouts of dockworkers. Miller felt a jolt of adrenaline, the signal that the waiting was over. Thorne's intel was now his bible, the roadmap to intercepting a ghost. "The Jackal will be visible, but disguised," Thorne had insisted, his voice barely audible. "He'll be near the private disembarkation area, the one Vance's people have prepped. Look for someone who doesn't quite fit, someone with an air of authority, but also a predatory stillness. He'll be coordinating with at least two others, likely posing as ground crew or port officials. They'll be wearing standard issue, but their movements will be too precise, too watchful. Thorne mentioned a distinctive silver watch on The Jackal's left wrist, a heavy, military-grade piece that Thorne himself had once admired for its ruggedness, a stark contrast to the polished veneer Vance likely projected."

Miller relayed this to Rostova via a highly encrypted, burst transmission, the data packet now in the hands of Singaporean authorities, a tiny seed of suspicion planted in the fertile ground of official channels. He knew that Rostova' promise of "expedited" action was relative, a bureaucratic inchworm compared to the eagle's flight Vance's plan demanded. But he also knew Rostova. If anyone could nudge the behemoth of international law enforcement, it was Mark. "The key," Miller typed, his fingers flying across the screen, "is to isolate the operative coordinating the extraction. Thorne identified a specific rendezvous point for the first phase of the transfer: a customs warehouse, Sector Gamma-7, just beyond the main cargo yards. It's marked with a subtle chalk symbol – a stylized raven's claw. Vance's team uses it as a primary holding area before moving to secondary transport. If we can intercept that transfer, we might get eyes on Vance, or at least a solid lead on his immediate destination."

The information about Sector Gamma-7 was a crucial detail Thorne had gleaned from overheard conversations and intercepted communications. It was a temporary staging ground, a place where Vance and his associates would be debriefed, their immediate escape route confirmed, and any immediate threats assessed by The Jackal's team. Thorne believed Vance would personally oversee this initial transfer, a point of pride in his meticulously planned operation. "He likes to see the machine in motion," Thorne had explained, a grim amusement in his voice. "It's his symphony, and he's the conductor. Disrupting that symphony at its opening notes is our best chance."

Miller's own team, a small, highly skilled unit assembled from remnants of his past affiliations and Thorne's reluctant network, was already in motion. They weren't law enforcement, but they possessed a certain flexibility, a willingness to operate in the grey areas that official channels so often struggled with. They were moving to establish covert surveillance points around Sector Gamma-7, their objective not immediate apprehension but information gathering. They needed to confirm the presence of The Jackal's team, identify the vehicles, and, if possible, glimpse Vance himself.

The thought of Vance, the architect of global financial chaos, standing on Singaporean soil, felt surreal. Thorne's confession had painted a picture of a man detached from the consequences of his actions, a financial sociopath who saw economies as mere playthings. The Nightingale project, with its potential to trigger cascading collapses, was a monument to that detachment. And now, he was here, ready to disappear, to continue his machinations from the shadows.

"He's bringing the hardware with him," Thorne had stressed, his voice tight with urgency. "The 'wooden bird.' Thorne described it as a small, intricately carved wooden automaton, designed to resemble a common Eurasian hoopoe. Concealed within its mechanism is the primary interface for Nightingale. It's not just a key; it's a portable control unit, capable of initiating certain functions remotely. Thorne believed Vance would keep it on his person, or within his immediate security detail. It's imperative we secure that bird. Without it, Nightingale remains dormant, a potential threat, but not an immediate one."

The weight of Thorne's words pressed down on Miller. The "wooden bird." It sounded like something from a fairy tale, a whimsical artifact. But Thorne's solemnity, the sheer terror in his eyes when he spoke of it, made it terrifyingly real. This seemingly innocuous object was the trigger, the physical manifestation of an existential threat. Securing it was paramount.

Miller observed the growing activity on the docks through a high-powered telescopic lens from a vantage point he'd secured on a nearby cargo container. The

Seraphina was now fully docked, gangplanks lowered, the first wave of passengers beginning their descent. It was a controlled chaos, a controlled flood. He scanned the faces, the movements, searching for the tell-tale signs Thorne had described. He saw figures in port authority vests, burly men with impassive faces, and others who seemed to be directing the flow of traffic with an almost imperceptible authority.

"Anything?" Rostova' voice crackled through Miller's earpiece, a whisper against the ambient noise.

"Too early to tell, Mark," Miller replied, his gaze still sweeping the scene. "The initial wave is just starting. Thorne's intel suggests Vance's team will wait for the initial surge to subside, to avoid drawing attention. The Jackal will be near the private access point, the one leading towards the customs area."

"We have a liaison officer on the ground, discreetly positioned near the main terminal," Rostova confirmed. "He's got eyes on the primary disembarkation, but he's operating under strict orders not to engage unless absolutely necessary. He's feeding us real-time observations. The initial report is standard passenger processing. Nothing out of the ordinary yet."

Miller grunted. "Standard is exactly what Vance wants. He thrives on the mundane. The moment it stops being mundane is when we've got him." He zoomed in on a cluster of individuals near a restricted gate, their posture slightly too rigid, their gazes too keen. One of them, a tall, imposing figure with a dark, almost predatory stillness, caught his eye. He wore a plain dark jacket, a stark contrast to the lighter attire of the surrounding workers. Miller adjusted the focus, his heart rate quickening. Was that him? The Jackal? He couldn't make out a scar from this distance, but the man's presence exuded an aura of controlled menace.

"Rostova, I might have eyes on a potential operative. Tall, dark jacket, near the restricted gate by the south pier. Looks... out of place. I'm relaying coordinates now." Miller transmitted the precise location, a digital breadcrumb for Rostova' man on the ground. "He appears to be coordinating with two others, dressed as stevedores but their movements are too sharp, too aware. They're not just moving cargo; they're observing."

"Acknowledged. Our man is shifting position to get a better look. He's moving through the periphery, keeping his profile low. He's also reporting increased activity from a fleet of unmarked vans parked just beyond the main cargo yards, consistent with Thorne's description of the getaway vehicles."

The pieces were beginning to align, forming a grim mosaic of Vance's escape plan. The port, so vast and anonymous, was becoming a stage for their desperate hunt. Miller knew they were walking a razor's edge, operating in the shadows of officialdom, relying on Thorne's fractured memories and Rostova' ability to navigate the treacherous waters of international cooperation. The fate of the Nightingale project, and potentially the global financial system, hung precariously in the balance, balanced on the brink of Vance's carefully orchestrated escape. The race was on, and the finish line was vanishing into the crowded, chaotic heart of Singapore.

The confession, when it came, was not a torrent of words, but a slow, reluctant ooze. The captured operative, known only to Thorne's fragmented intel as 'Spectre,' had initially been as tight-lipped as a sealed vault. His training, it seemed, was as formidable as the intel suggested. Yet, under the relentless, low-pressure interrogation that Mark Rostova' team expertly applied, the cracks began to appear. It wasn't brute force; Rostova understood that pain often bred more lies than truth. Instead, it was a psychological attrition, a subtle erosion of Spectre's defenses, chipping away at his resolve with carefully chosen questions and the ever-present, unspoken threat of a far less palatable fate.

"He's a ghost," Spectre finally rasped, his voice hoarse, the words pulled from a throat parched by fear and exhaustion. "That's how he operates. Not just Vance, but the entire network. You think you're chasing him, but you're chasing shadows. He's layers upon layers. Cutouts. Shell corporations that disappear into thin air. You find one, it's just a front for another, and then another. It's designed to be impossible."

Miller, listening in via a secure feed from the interrogation room, felt a familiar frustration coiling in his gut. He'd suspected as much, Thorne's intel had hinted at it, but hearing it confirmed by one of Vance's own operatives was a stark, cold reality. Vance wasn't just a financier; he was an architect of invisibility, a master of the financial maze. His wealth wasn't just accumulated; it was meticulously concealed, a fortress built of offshore accounts and labyrinthine corporate structures that defied easy penetration. Spectre's words painted a picture of a man who understood that true power lay not just in wealth, but in its untraceability. He was a phantom in the global economy, leaving no discernible trail, his financial footprint so dispersed and obfuscated that it was virtually impossible to pinpoint.

"And the hardware?" Miller prompted, his voice a low rumble in the quiet of his own observation post. He was referring to the 'wooden bird,' Thorne's cryptic description of the Nightingale project's control unit. The implications of Vance possessing such a device, capable of triggering cascading financial collapses, were too terrifying to contemplate.

Spectre's eyes, which had been vacant, flickered with a spark of something akin to respect, or perhaps just a grudging acknowledgment of Vance's foresight. "The 'bird,'" he confirmed, the term sounding absurdly delicate for the instrument of such destruction. "It's not with Vance directly, not always. He understands the risks. But his primary security detail, the ones closest to him... they carry it. It's always within arm's reach. They treat it like a relic. Vance is... superstitious, perhaps. Or just paranoid.

He believes it needs to be protected, not just physically, but energetically. He insists it's kept away from any form of electronic surveillance, any data stream. They've built bespoke containment units for it, shielded Faraday cages disguised as ordinary luggage. They move it with extreme care, and its location is known only to a handful of individuals within the inner circle."

This was precisely the kind of detail Miller needed. Not just the 'what,' but the 'how.' Vance's paranoia, his meticulous obsession with security, was both his strength and his potential weakness. If they could identify the individuals responsible for transporting the 'bird,' they might intercept it, or at least gain a critical insight into Vance's immediate movements and priorities. Spectre's technical expertise, honed in the unforgiving world of clandestine operations, was proving invaluable. He spoke of Vance's counter-surveillance measures with an almost academic detachment, detailing the sophisticated jamming equipment, the encrypted communication channels that shifted frequencies in nanoseconds, and the constant rotation of personnel to prevent any single individual from accumulating too much knowledge.

"He anticipates. He always anticipates," Spectre continued, his gaze drifting, lost in the intricate web of Vance's machinations. "He has multiple exfiltration routes planned, not just for himself, but for his key assets. Contingencies upon contingencies. Safe houses that are never the same for more than a week. Vehicles that are swapped out daily, sometimes hourly. He's like water, always finding a new path, always flowing around any obstacle. There are pre-arranged signals, coded phrases, dead drops... a whole secondary layer of communication invisible to anyone not initiated."

Miller absorbed this information, his mind racing to process the sheer complexity of Vance's operational security. It wasn't just about having money; it was about creating a system that was virtually impervious to disruption. Spectre confirmed Thorne's earlier warnings about Vance's network within the port itself, elaborating on the methods used to ensure their complicity. It wasn't always coercion; often, it was a carefully cultivated network of mutual benefit, financial incentives, and carefully managed blackmail. The port wasn't just a point of arrival; it was a carefully orchestrated transition zone, designed to absorb Vance and his entourage into the global anonymity that Vance so expertly cultivated.

"The Jackal," Spectre mentioned, the name a chilling echo of Thorne's description. "He's more than just muscle. He's the gatekeeper. He vets everyone. He knows the protocols, the routes, the blind spots. He's Vance's shadow, and he doesn't miss a thing. He's the one who ensures Vance disappears. He's the ghost who makes the ghost vanish." Spectre described The Jackal's methods with a grim fascination, detailing how he used a combination of psychological manipulation and precisely timed diversions to ensure Vance's seamless extraction. He was a master of blending into any environment, his presence often overlooked until the moment it was too late. His ability to anticipate and neutralize threats before they even materialized was legendary within Vance's inner circle.

Spectre revealed that Vance's paranoia extended to his digital life as well. He used burner phones that were incinerated after each use, communication was limited to highly encrypted, end-to-end systems that were rerouted through multiple proxies. Even his personal devices were isolated from any public network, communicating only with Vance's private, heavily secured servers. Spectre himself, despite his technical expertise, had only ever accessed Vance's core network through a series of multi-stage virtual private networks, each layer designed to obscure his origin and his ultimate destination. It was a digital fortress, designed to withstand any intrusion, any attempt at tracking. Vance's fear of digital footprints was so profound that he had invested heavily in countermeasures, not just to hide his own activities, but to actively mislead and trap anyone attempting to follow him.

The assassin confirmed Thorne's suspicion that Vance was not alone. "There are others," Spectre admitted, his voice barely a whisper. "The Nightingale project wasn't a one-man show. There were key players, people who provided the specialized knowledge, the access, the... impetus. They're all being extracted with Vance. They're essential. Their knowledge is his insurance policy. They're not just passengers; they're assets that Vance will not abandon. He values their contributions, their unique skill sets, and he knows that their capture would represent a significant blow to his future endeavors." Spectre was reluctant to name names, but he alluded to individuals with backgrounds in quantum computing, advanced cryptography, and even bio-engineering, hinting at the far-reaching implications of the Nightingale project and Vance's future ambitions. These were not mere financiers; they were the architects of tomorrow's threats, and Vance was their shepherd.

Miller pressed further, seeking any detail, however small, that might offer a tangible lead. "The transit. How does it work once they're off the ship? What are the immediate steps after the initial disembarkation?"

Spectre, his gaze now fixed on a point somewhere beyond the interrogation room's sterile walls, began to paint a picture of the immediate post-arrival phase. "There are designated blind spots," he explained. "Areas that security cameras don't cover, or where the feeds are looped. The Jackal knows them all. They'll move through those areas, a ghost through the machinery of the port. The first transfer point is usually a pre-selected, nondescript vehicle. Not a flashy car, never. Something utilitarian, easily lost in the traffic. A cargo van, an unmarked utility vehicle. Its interior is stripped bare, no registration, no identifying marks. It's a black box on wheels."

He elaborated on the nature of these vehicles. They weren't just transport; they were mobile staging areas. Thorne had mentioned this, but Spectre added crucial details about their internal configurations. "Some have basic communication jammers, localized. Enough to disrupt casual surveillance, to make quick calls impossible. Others are equipped with specialized diagnostic tools. They're not just for moving people; they're for ensuring the integrity of the assets, especially the 'bird.' Vance is meticulous about its environment. Temperature, humidity, even vibration – all are monitored and controlled within its transport casing."

The assassin's technical knowledge was a goldmine. He spoke of signal interception protocols, of digital countermeasures designed to spoof tracking devices, and of physical evasion tactics that relied on exploiting the blind spots inherent in any large, complex system. Spectre described a scenario where Vance's team might even employ decoys, multiple vehicles moving in different directions, to confuse any pursuers. It was a strategy born of a deep understanding of how law enforcement and intelligence agencies operated, designed to overwhelm their resources and sow confusion.

"The key is to be invisible until you're already gone," Spectre concluded, a grim finality in his tone. "Vance doesn't believe in leaving anything to chance. Every scenario is mapped, every contingency accounted for. He's not just escaping; he's continuing his work, just from a different vantage point. And the Nightingale project is still very much alive. The 'bird' is just the beginning. He has far more ambitious plans."

Miller felt a surge of grim determination. Spectre's testimony, though delivered with the weariness of a broken man, provided the crucial missing pieces. They now had a clearer picture of Vance's operational methods, his reliance on cutouts and shell corporations, and his extensive contingency plans for rapid exfiltration. The information about the 'wooden bird' and its handlers, the detailed description of the extraction vehicles, and the insights into The Jackal's role were all vital. It wasn't just about apprehending Vance; it was about dismantling his network, neutralizing the threat posed by the Nightingale project, and ensuring that Vance could not simply disappear and continue his destructive agenda. The fight was far from over, but with Spectre's confession, they had just gained a significant advantage. The layers of Vance's anonymity were beginning to peel away, revealing the dangerous architect beneath.

The guttural hum of the ship's engines had become a constant, low thrum against Miller's senses, a sonic manifestation of their relentless progress. Days bled into nights, marked only by the subtle shift in the crew's demeanor, the changing angles of the sun painting the horizon, and the ever-present tension that had settled over their mission like a shroud. They were close. The sprawling, chaotic tapestry of the port, a hive of industrial activity and illicit commerce, was beginning to resolve itself through the persistent haze of sea salt and exhaust fumes. This was the nexus, the point of arrival, and potentially, the point of no return.

Miller stood on the bridge, the cool night air a welcome contrast to the recycled atmosphere of the vessel. The port lights, a galaxy of artificial stars, twinkled in the distance, beckoning and menacing in equal measure. He felt the familiar knot of anticipation tighten in his gut, a mixture of weariness and a sharpened, primal focus. Spectre's confession, delivered in fragmented whispers and chilling admissions, had provided them with invaluable intel, painting a detailed, terrifying portrait of Vance's operational security and his absolute mastery of evasion. They understood the layers of obfuscation, the ghost-like movements, and the ruthlessness of The Jackal. They knew Vance wouldn't be a simple, traceable target. But knowing the enemy's tactics was one thing; confronting the execution of their ultimate plan was another entirely.

The digital ghost of Vance had been elusive, a phantom in the financial ether, and Spectre's testimony had confirmed that his physical escape would be no less artful. The carefully constructed network within the port, the blind spots, the looped camera feeds, the nondescript vehicles waiting to swallow Vance and his inner circle into the anonymity of the hinterland – it was all a testament to his meticulous planning. Miller had felt a grim satisfaction when Spectre detailed the 'wooden bird's' handlers and the bespoke containment units, the paranoia that dictated its every movement. It was a tangible vulnerability, a thread they could potentially pull. Yet, even with that thread, the enormity of Vance's operations, the sheer depth of his network, loomed large.

He ran a hand over his stubbled jaw, the rough texture a stark reminder of the relentless nature of their pursuit. The intel suggested Vance was not just escaping; he was continuing his work. The Nightingale project, Spectre had stressed, was merely the genesis. Vance had bigger, more destructive ambitions, and the individuals he was extracting – the quantum computing experts, the cryptographers, the bio-engineers – were the architects of those future threats. This wasn't about stopping a single man; it was about decapitating a nascent global destabilization effort. And the clock was ticking.

Suddenly, a soft beep emanated from Miller's secure comm device, a sound so faint it was almost lost in the ambient noise. He picked it up, his brow furrowed. The message was short, stark, and utterly untraceable, appearing on the encrypted display with an unsettling lack of metadata. 'The Nightingale sings at dawn. Your efforts are futile.' Miller's breath hitched. The words, simple yet loaded with a chilling finality, struck him with the force of a physical blow. This wasn't a random hack. This was Vance. Or someone speaking with his chilling authority. It was a taunt, a final, venomous flourish from a man who believed he had already won.

'The Nightingale sings at dawn.' The avian metaphor, once a cryptic clue to the project's name, now felt like a declaration of imminent doom. Dawn. That was today. They were hours away from the sun breaking over the horizon. And the implication was clear: the project, the catalyst for financial chaos, was about to be activated. Not delayed, not thwarted, but sung into existence.

'Your efforts are futile.' The words were a calculated assault on his resolve, a psychological weapon deployed with surgical precision. Vance knew they were here, knew they were closing in. He had anticipated this endgame, this moment of confrontation. And his response wasn't to flee, but to declare victory, to shatter any illusion that their pursuit had any meaningful impact.

Miller's mind raced, dissecting the message, stripping away the bravado to find the cold, hard truth. Vance wasn't just a man to be apprehended; he was the conductor of a symphony of destruction. Spectre's confession had spoken of Vance's contingency plans, of the 'wooden bird' being moved with extreme care, of its location being known only to a select few. Had they underestimated the project's readiness? Had Vance implemented a failsafe, a mechanism to ensure the Nightingale's song would be heard even if he himself was silenced or captured?

The possibility gnawed at him. Capturing Vance, even apprehending all the key players Spectre had alluded to, might only be a partial victory, or worse, a pyrrhic one. If the project, the 'bird' itself, was already in motion, if its destructive melody was already being broadcast, then their mission had changed. It wasn't about stopping Vance's escape; it was about mitigating an unfolding catastrophe.

He leaned against the railing, the metal cold beneath his gloved hand. The message was more than a warning; it was a meticulously crafted psychological gambit. Vance understood the toll their relentless pursuit had taken, the sacrifices made, the sleepless nights, the constant pressure. He was aiming to break Miller's spirit, to plant seeds of doubt that would fester and erode their conviction. If Miller began to believe their efforts were indeed futile, that Vance had outmaneuvered them at the final hurdle, then their actions would become hesitant, their judgment clouded.

Miller replayed Spectre's words in his mind: "He anticipates. He always anticipates." And Vance had anticipated this very moment. He had planned for capture, for pursuit, for the possibility of his network being compromised. The 'bird' was his ultimate insurance policy, the embodiment of his power, and he wouldn't let it fall into the wrong hands, or worse, be rendered inert.

The message suggested a plan that transcended Vance's personal survival. Perhaps the operative known as Spectre had been a distraction, a controlled leak of information to lull them into a false sense of security while the real operation proceeded unimpeded. Or perhaps, Vance was simply that audacious, that confident in his meticulously constructed system. He had the expertise, the resources, and the ruthlessness to set in motion a cascade of events that would unfold independently of his presence.

Miller's gaze drifted towards the port, the vast network of cranes and cargo ships now appearing less like a destination and more like a battlefield. He pictured the 'wooden bird' within its shielded casing, perhaps already en route to a discreet activation point, its handlers moving through the pre-determined blind spots, their movements coordinated by the Jackal. The message, delivered just as they reached the threshold of this critical juncture, was designed to sow chaos and indecision. Vance wanted them to question everything, to doubt the value of their hard-won intelligence, to falter at the precipice of their objective.

He had to assume the message was true, or at least, that Vance believed it to be true. The 'bird' was likely active. The Nightingale was singing. And the symphony of financial collapse was about to commence. This shifted the entire focus of their immediate actions. It wasn't about intercepting Vance's escape route anymore; it was about tracing the Nightingale's song. Where was it being broadcast from? Who was receiving it? And what was the immediate impact?

The futility Vance proclaimed was a challenge, not a statement of fact. Miller wouldn't allow Vance to dictate the narrative. Spectre had given them pieces of the puzzle, glimpses into Vance's elaborate machinations. The information about the handlers, the containment units, the protocols for moving the 'bird' – that intel was still valid, still actionable. It provided a starting point for tracing the project's activation.

He needed to brief Thorne and the team immediately. The message changed everything. They had to pivot from apprehension to damage control, from intercepting Vance to neutralizing Project Nightingale itself. The psychological warfare Vance employed was as potent as his financial instruments. The taunt was designed to create panic, to make them focus on the impossibility of their task, on the phantom threat of a project already unleashed.

But Miller knew that even a ghost could be tracked, even a phantom could be cornered. The 'wooden bird' wasn't truly invisible. It was shielded, yes, but it was still a physical object, moved by physical beings through a physical space. And those physical beings, as Spectre had described, operated within a network, a system of protocols and blind spots. The Jackal, for all his skill, was still part of that system. And every system, no matter how sophisticated, had an Achilles' heel.

The message was a declaration of war, a final, desperate gamble by Vance. He was throwing down the gauntlet, betting that the sheer audacity of his threat would paralyze them. But Vance, in his arrogance, had forgotten one crucial element: Miller was not just a hunter; he was a protector. And he would not stand idly by while Vance's destructive melody played out. The futility Vance proclaimed was a lie, a desperate attempt to claim victory from the jaws of defeat. Miller would prove him wrong. He would not let the Nightingale sing unchallenged. The port, bustling and indifferent, was no longer just a point of arrival; it was the stage for a final, desperate act. The pursuit of Vance had just become a race against time, a desperate scramble to silence a song that threatened to drown the world in chaos. The futility was Vance's; Miller's resolve was absolute. He looked out at the distant lights, his mind already shifting gears, re-evaluating every piece of intel, every contingency, seeking the single thread that would unravel Vance's final, devastating gambit. The hunt was far from over; it had just entered its most dangerous phase.

The guttural hum of the ship's engines had become a constant, low thrum against Miller's senses, a sonic manifestation of their relentless progress. Days bled into nights, marked only by the subtle shift in the crew's demeanor, the changing angles of the sun painting the horizon, and the ever-present tension that had settled over their mission like a shroud. They were close. The sprawling, chaotic tapestry of the port, a hive of industrial activity and illicit commerce, was beginning to resolve itself through the persistent haze of sea salt and exhaust fumes. This was the nexus, the point of arrival, and potentially, the point of no return.

Miller stood on the bridge, the cool night air a welcome contrast to the recycled atmosphere of the vessel. The port lights, a galaxy of artificial stars, twinkled in the distance, beckoning and menacing in equal measure. He felt the familiar knot of anticipation tighten in his gut, a mixture of weariness and a sharpened, primal focus. Spectre's confession, delivered in fragmented whispers and chilling admissions, had provided them with invaluable intel, painting a detailed, terrifying portrait of Vance's operational security and his absolute mastery of evasion. They understood the layers of obfuscation, the ghost-like movements, and the ruthlessness of The Jackal. They knew Vance wouldn't be a simple, traceable target. But knowing the enemy's tactics was one thing; confronting the execution of their ultimate plan was another entirely.

The digital ghost of Vance had been elusive, a phantom in the financial ether, and Spectre's testimony had confirmed that his physical escape would be no less artful. The carefully constructed network within the port, the blind spots, the looped camera feeds, the nondescript vehicles waiting to swallow Vance and his inner circle into the anonymity of the hinterland – it was all a testament to his meticulous planning. Miller had felt a grim satisfaction when Spectre detailed the 'wooden bird's' handlers and the bespoke containment units, the paranoia that dictated its every movement. It was a tangible vulnerability, a thread they could potentially pull. Yet, even with that thread, the enormity of Vance's operations, the sheer depth of his network, loomed large.

He ran a hand over his stubbled jaw, the rough texture a stark reminder of the relentless nature of their pursuit. The intel suggested Vance was not just escaping; he was continuing his work. The Nightingale project, Spectre had stressed, was merely the genesis. Vance had bigger, more destructive ambitions, and the individuals he was extracting – the quantum computing experts, the cryptographers, the bio-engineers – were the architects of those future threats. This wasn't about stopping a single man; it was about decapitating a nascent global destabilization effort. And the clock was ticking.

Suddenly, a soft beep emanated from Miller's secure comm device, a sound so faint it was almost lost in the ambient noise. He picked it up, his brow furrowed. The message was short, stark, and utterly untraceable, appearing on the encrypted display with an unsettling lack of metadata. 'The Nightingale sings at dawn. Your efforts are futile.' Miller's breath hitched. The words, simple yet loaded with a chilling finality, struck him with the force of a physical blow. This wasn't a random hack. This was Vance. Or someone speaking with his chilling authority. It was a taunt, a final, venomous flourish from a man who believed he had already won.

'The Nightingale sings at dawn.' The avian metaphor, once a cryptic clue to the project's name, now felt like a declaration of imminent doom. Dawn. That was today. They were hours away from the sun breaking over the horizon. And the implication was clear: the project, the catalyst for financial chaos, was about to be activated. Not delayed, not thwarted, but sung into existence.

'Your efforts are futile.' The words were a calculated assault on his resolve, a psychological weapon deployed with surgical precision. Vance knew they were here, knew they were closing in. He had anticipated this endgame, this moment of confrontation. And his response wasn't to flee, but to declare victory, to shatter any illusion that their pursuit had any meaningful impact.

Miller's mind raced, dissecting the message, stripping away the bravado to find the cold, hard truth. Vance wasn't just a man to be apprehended; he was the conductor of a symphony of destruction. Spectre's confession had spoken of Vance's contingency plans, of the 'wooden bird' being moved with extreme care, of its location being known only to a select few. Had they underestimated the project's readiness? Had Vance implemented a failsafe, a mechanism to ensure the Nightingale's song would be heard even if he himself was silenced or captured?

The possibility gnawed at him. Capturing Vance, even apprehending all the key players Spectre had alluded to, might only be a partial victory, or worse, a pyrrhic one. If the project, the 'bird' itself, was already in motion, if its destructive melody was already being broadcast, then their mission had changed. It wasn't about stopping Vance's escape; it was about mitigating an unfolding catastrophe.

He leaned against the railing, the metal cold beneath his gloved hand. The message was more than a warning; it was a meticulously crafted psychological gambit. Vance understood the toll their relentless pursuit had taken, the sacrifices made, the sleepless nights, the constant pressure. He was aiming to break Miller's spirit, to plant seeds of doubt that would fester and erode their conviction. If Miller began to believe their efforts were indeed futile, that Vance had outmaneuvered them at the final hurdle, then their actions would become hesitant, their judgment clouded.

Miller replayed Spectre's words in his mind: "He anticipates. He always anticipates." And Vance had anticipated this very moment. He had planned for capture, for pursuit, for the possibility of his network being compromised. The 'bird' was his ultimate insurance policy, the embodiment of his power, and he wouldn't let it fall into the wrong hands, or worse, be rendered inert.

The message suggested a plan that transcended Vance's personal survival. Perhaps the operative known as Spectre had been a distraction, a controlled leak of information to lull them into a false sense of security while the real operation proceeded unimpeded. Or perhaps, Vance was simply that audacious, that confident in his meticulously constructed system. He had the expertise, the resources, and the ruthlessness to set in motion a cascade of events that would unfold independently of his presence.

Miller's gaze drifted towards the port, the vast network of cranes and cargo ships now appearing less like a destination and more like a battlefield. He pictured the 'wooden bird' within its shielded casing, perhaps already en route to a discreet activation point, its handlers moving through the pre-determined blind spots, their movements coordinated by the Jackal. The message, delivered just as they reached the threshold of this critical juncture, was designed to sow chaos and indecision. Vance wanted them to question everything, to doubt the value of their hard-won intelligence, to falter at the precipice of their objective.

He had to assume the message was true, or at least, that Vance believed it to be true. The 'bird' was likely active. The Nightingale was singing. And the symphony of financial collapse was about to commence. This shifted the entire focus of their immediate actions. It wasn't about intercepting Vance's escape route anymore; it was about tracing the Nightingale's song. Where was it being broadcast from? Who was receiving it? And what was the immediate impact?

The futility Vance proclaimed was a challenge, not a statement of fact. Miller wouldn't allow Vance to dictate the narrative. Spectre had given them pieces of the puzzle, glimpses into Vance's elaborate machinations. The information about the handlers, the containment units, the protocols for moving the 'bird' – that intel was still valid, still actionable. It provided a starting point for tracing the project's activation.

He needed to brief Thorne and the team immediately. The message changed everything. They had to pivot from apprehension to damage control, from intercepting Vance to neutralizing Project Nightingale itself. The psychological warfare Vance employed was as potent as his financial instruments. The taunt was designed to make them focus on the impossibility of their task, on the phantom threat of a project already unleashed.

But Miller knew that even a ghost could be tracked, even a phantom could be cornered. The 'wooden bird' wasn't truly invisible. It was shielded, yes, but it was still a physical object, moved by physical beings through a physical space. And those physical beings, as Spectre had described, operated within a network, a system of protocols and blind spots. The Jackal, for all his skill, was still part of that system. And every system, no matter how sophisticated, had an Achilles' heel.

The message was a declaration of war, a final, desperate gamble by Vance. He was throwing down the gauntlet, betting that the sheer audacity of his threat would paralyze them. But Vance, in his arrogance, had forgotten one crucial element: Miller was not just a hunter; he was a protector. And he would not stand idly by while Vance's destructive melody played out. The futility Vance proclaimed was a lie, a desperate attempt to claim victory from the jaws of defeat. Miller would prove him wrong. He would not let the Nightingale sing unchallenged. The port, bustling and indifferent, was no longer just a point of arrival; it was the stage for a final, desperate act. The pursuit of Vance had just become a race against time, a desperate scramble to silence a song that threatened to drown the world in chaos. The futility was Vance's; Miller's resolve was absolute. He looked out at the distant lights, his mind already shifting gears, re-evaluating every piece of intel, every contingency, seeking the single thread that would unravel Vance's final, devastating gambit. The hunt was far from over; it had just entered its most dangerous phase.

The low thrum of the engines, once a monotonous drone, now carried an undertone of urgency. The ship was a coiled spring, its passengers a tightly packed mass of anxieties and suppressed fears. The whispers, which had begun as hushed murmurs about a killer in their midst, had morphed into a feverish chatter about the approaching authorities, about the unknown fate that awaited them at the docks. The fear of a singular, identifiable threat – the murderer – had been replaced by a far more pervasive dread: the fear of official scrutiny, of being caught in the crossfire of a clandestine operation. Every shadow seemed to harbor a hidden operative, every averted gaze a sign of guilt or apprehension. The air itself felt charged, thick with unspoken questions and the heavy weight of impending judgment.

Miller moved through the ship's corridors with a deliberate, almost predatory stealth. Jenkins, a shadow mirroring his own, was a constant presence, their unspoken communication a honed instinct. Their objective had shifted from mere apprehension to absolute containment. Vance and his associates, those architects of financial ruin, could not be allowed any opportunity to slip through the cracks, to melt into the bustling anonymity of the port before the net was fully drawn. Each deck, each cabin, became a potential escape route, a vulnerability that demanded constant vigilance. They were no longer just hunting a killer; they were managing a high-stakes transfer, a delicate operation where a single misstep could have catastrophic consequences.

Miller had met with Captain Rostova Eva Rostova and Marcus Thorne, the ship's head of security, earlier that evening. The initial shock and confusion that had rippled through the crew in the wake of the first major incident had long since dissipated, replaced by a grim, professional resolve.

Rostova, a woman whose steely gaze had seen her through countless storms, both literal and figurative, was now an invaluable ally. Thorne, a man whose gruff exterior belied a meticulous attention to detail, had thrown the ship's comprehensive security apparatus at Miller's disposal. The ship's internal surveillance systems, once a passive monitoring tool, were now actively deployed, the data streams flowing directly to Miller's secure tactical display. Every face, every movement, was being analyzed. The ship had transformed into a meticulously controlled environment, its inhabitants unwittingly participating in a game of cat and mouse played out in real-time.

The final hours before docking were a drawn-out, agonizing countdown. The port loomed larger, its skeletal cranes and labyrinthine warehouses a stark contrast to the pristine, if claustrophobic, environment of the ship. The air was alive with the cacophony of the harbor – the mournful blast of ship horns, the metallic shriek of gulls, the distant rumble of machinery. It was a symphony of industry, a testament to the constant ebb and flow of global commerce, and for Miller, it was the antechamber to a battleground.

He felt the crushing weight of responsibility settle upon his shoulders, a burden heavier than any physical exhaustion. The intel Spectre had provided, the fragmented whispers of Project Nightingale, the chilling implications of Vance's ambition – it all culminated in these few hours. The fate of global financial stability, the livelihoods of millions, hinged on their ability to execute their plan flawlessly. Vance wasn't just a criminal mastermind; he was a saboteur on a scale Miller had only read about in classified reports. His ability to manipulate markets, to sow discord through economic destabilization, was a threat that transcended conventional warfare.

The message from Vance, 'The Nightingale sings at dawn. Your efforts are futile,' echoed in Miller's mind with a persistent, unnerving clarity. It was a psychological ploy, designed to erode their confidence, to plant seeds of doubt at the most critical juncture. But Miller refused to be cowed. He understood Vance's game, his penchant for calculated cruelty. The taunt was an admission, not of victory, but of desperation. If Vance truly believed his plan was unstoppable, he wouldn't need to resort to such petty psychological warfare.

He scanned the faces of the passengers milling about the upper decks, their forced smiles and nervous chatter a thin veneer over their unease. Were any of them unwittingly carrying a piece of Vance's puzzle? A data chip, a coded message, a hidden component? The ship, once a sanctuary, now felt like a vessel brimming with potential carriers of contagion. Every individual was a potential vector for Vance's insidious plan.

Jenkins approached, his expression grim. "Anything, sir?"

Miller shook his head, his gaze fixed on the approaching coastline. "Nothing concrete. But the tension is palpable. Thorne's team is on high alert. They're monitoring all communications leaving the ship, and the dock security is... cooperating, to say the least." He paused, a flicker of unease crossing his features. "The problem is, Vance isn't just relying on these passengers. He has assets on the ground. The intel suggests a coordinated extraction. We need to assume he and his inner circle are already being prepped for departure the moment we dock."

"Spectre's intel is solid on that," Jenkins confirmed, his voice a low rumble. "The 'wooden bird' handlers, the escape routes – they're all part of Vance's contingency plans. He's anticipated our arrival, just as he's anticipated every other obstacle."

"Which is precisely why we can't afford to be predictable," Miller countered, his jaw tight. "We need to be two steps ahead. If Vance is so confident about the Nightingale singing, it means the project is either already active, or it's about to be triggered the moment he's out of our reach. We need to focus on that. The apprehension of Vance and his associates is secondary to preventing the activation of Project Nightingale."

The weight of those words settled heavily between them. It was a stark realization, a painful admission that their primary objective might have already been compromised. The thrill of the chase, the meticulous planning of an apprehension, suddenly felt secondary to the grim task of damage control. The Nightingale's song, once a distant threat, now loomed large, a harbinger of chaos waiting to be unleashed.

Miller's mind raced, replaying Spectre's confession, sifting through the labyrinthine details of Vance's operations. The 'wooden bird' – a codename that now felt chillingly apt for the destructive payload it represented. It wasn't just a piece of technology; it was an instrument of financial warfare, capable of triggering cascading collapses, of destabilizing entire economies. And Vance, the maestro of this macabre symphony, was about to conduct its premiere performance.

"Captain Rostova has confirmed all boarding ramps will be secured the moment we tie up," Jenkins added, breaking Miller's reverie. "Thorne's team will be positioned at every access point, with federal agents ready to move in on our signal. The goal is to isolate Vance and his key personnel before they can even think about disembarking."

"And if they don't disembark?" Miller asked, the question hanging in the air, heavy with unspoken implications. "If Vance has already initiated the sequence, if the Nightingale is already singing its song from a location elsewhere? Then all this," he gestured vaguely at the approaching port, "is just a sideshow."

"We can't afford to think that way, sir," Jenkins said, his voice firm, though a hint of concern laced his tone. "Spectre's information, while fragmented, gives us tangible points of contact. The handlers, the protocols for moving the 'bird' – those are actionable leads. We'll track them. We have to."

Miller nodded, a grim determination hardening his features. He wouldn't let Vance's taunt become a self-fulfilling prophecy. He wouldn't allow the Nightingale's song to drown out the sound of reason and justice. The ship was a contained environment, a perfect petri dish for observation. Every passenger, every crew member, was now under a microscope. The fear had shifted, transforming from the primal fear of a killer to the more complex, societal fear of economic collapse, of a world thrown into disarray by the machinations of a single, brilliant, and utterly depraved individual.

He took a deep breath, the salty air filling his lungs. The game had changed. The pursuit of Vance was no longer just about bringing a criminal to justice; it was about preventing a global catastrophe. And as the ship slowly, inexorably, glided towards its berth, Miller knew that the real battle, the battle against the Nightingale's song, was about to begin. The port, with its promise of arrival, was now a gateway to a far more dangerous unknown. The tension on deck was no longer just about the immediate threat of

Vance's escape; it was about the chilling possibility that he had already won, and that the real fight had already begun, unseen and unheard, in the vast, intricate web of the global financial system. The silence of the Nightingale's prelude was deafening, and Miller knew, with a certainty that chilled him to the bone, that the dawn would bring not just sunlight, but a reckoning.

Chapter 12: The Cordon and the Confrontation

The vessel's groan as it nudged against the quay was a sound of finality, a deep, resonant sigh that echoed the collective exhaustion and coiled tension of everyone on board. The air, thick with the smell of diesel, brine, and the indefinable, restless scent of a port city teeming with life and shadowed dealings, was a palpable presence. As the gangways were extended, they didn't feel like bridges to solid ground, but the skeletal fingers of an emerging trap.

From the ship's railing, Miller watched the scene unfold with a gaze that missed nothing. The meticulously orchestrated chaos of the port was being systematically overlaid by an even more formidable order. The hum of the ship's engines had been replaced by the low, purposeful thrum of approaching engines – not the steady beat of cargo vessels, but the sharper, more urgent growl of law enforcement vehicles. Squad cars, their stark black and white markings a beacon of officialdom, fanned out with practiced precision, their headlights cutting swathes through the pre-dawn gloom. Uniformed officers, their presence commanding and authoritative, moved with a synchronized cadence, establishing an invisible, yet undeniable, perimeter around the docking area.

This wasn't just a police presence; it was a full-spectrum mobilization. The sheer number of vehicles, the variety of insignia – FBI tactical units, Interpol agents bearing the flags of international cooperation, and the local constabulary, their familiar uniforms somehow imbued with a heightened sense of purpose – spoke volumes. They were not merely responding to a crime; they were containing a significant threat. Miller recognized the hallmarks of a coordinated multi-agency task force, a testament to the gravity of the intelligence Vance's apprehension represented. Thorne's early warnings, amplified by Spectre's chilling confessions, had clearly resonated through the relevant channels, ensuring that the arrival was met not with the indifference of an ordinary port call, but with the focused intensity of a high-stakes interception.

Miller had briefed Captain Rostova and Thorne on the specifics of the impending operation during their final hours at sea. The objective was clear: to create a secure bubble around the ship, a sterile zone that would prevent Vance or any of his operatives from disappearing into the labyrinthine anonymity of the port. Rostova, her face etched with a mixture of concern and steely resolve, had assured him that all docking procedures would be executed under their strict control. Thorne, his usual gruff demeanor replaced by a grim determination, had confirmed that his security teams were already liaising with the incoming federal agents, their shipboard surveillance systems being fed into the larger tactical network being established on shore.

As the first passengers began to disembark, the process was anything but a casual stroll onto land. It was a controlled, systematic evacuation. Each individual, uniformed officers guided their faces a mixture of bewilderment and apprehension towards a designated screening area. Detectors, both electronic and human, were in full operation. Bags were scrutinized, and individuals were subjected to brief but thorough questioning. The atmosphere was tense, the usual pre-docking bustle replaced by an almost unnerving quietude, punctuated only by the clipped commands of the officers and the rustle of plastic sheeting as luggage was processed.

Miller watched from a vantage point on the upper deck, the secure comm device in his ear a conduit to the unfolding events on the ground. Thorne's voice, usually rough, was now clipped with urgency as he relayed real-time updates. "First wave of passengers processed, Miller. No immediate signs of Vance or his known associates in the initial group. We're moving them towards the holding tents for further processing."

"And Thorne's team?" Miller's voice was low, a gravelly whisper that cut through the ambient noise. He was referring to the individuals Spectre had identified as Vance's inner circle, the ones most likely to be actively facilitating his escape.

"Thorne's team is identifying and isolating potential key figures from the passenger manifest. We're cross-referencing against Spectre's intel and the intel Thorne provided before we sailed. Two individuals matching the description of the 'wooden bird' handlers have been flagged. They're being discreetly escorted to separate interview rooms on the ship, away from the main disembarkation flow."

This was critical. The handlers were the tangible link to Project Nightingale, the physical conduits through which Vance's catastrophic plan would be enacted. Their apprehension was paramount. If they could be interrogated effectively, if their knowledge could be extracted before they could communicate with any external operatives, there was still a chance to derail the Nightingale's song before it could be broadcast.

"Spectre's testimony about the bespoke containment units?" Miller pressed, his eyes scanning the growing cluster of screened passengers being ushered away from the immediate dock area.

"Confirmed. Thorne's team located three reinforced cases in the cargo hold, stowed separately from the main manifest. They're secured and being transported under armed guard to a secure facility here on shore. The preliminary assessment is they match the description of the specialized units Spectre detailed for transporting sensitive components of the 'bird.'"

Miller's jaw tightened. The 'wooden bird' was not a single entity, but a system, a sophisticated network of components that needed to be assembled and activated. The containment units were a vital piece of that puzzle, a testament to Vance's paranoia and the lengths he would go to protect his catastrophic invention. Securing those cases, and more importantly, the individuals who knew how to operate them, was a significant victory.

"Excellent," Miller breathed, a sliver of grim satisfaction piercing the relentless tension. "What about Thorne himself? Has he been... informed of the operation's commencement?"

Thorne's voice crackled over the comms, a touch of dry humor attempting to cut through the gravity of the situation. "As informed as one can be when their ship is being treated like a condemned cell, Miller. My security detail is cooperating fully, of course. We've handed over the manifest and our internal surveillance logs. The gentlemen from the FBI are currently... debriefing me on my immediate surroundings and my personal travel intentions. Apparently, my previous assurances of my own innocence have been deemed insufficient without a full security sweep."

Miller allowed himself a faint, almost imperceptible smile. Thorne, despite his bluster, was a professional. His cooperation was essential. The efficiency of this entire operation hinged on the seamless integration of the ship's internal systems with the external task force. "Understood, Thorne. Spectre's intel mentioned a contingency plan involving a network of dockworkers and port authority officials loyal to Vance. The cordon is designed to neutralize that. Any anomalies detected on your end?"

"Just the usual port bedlam, Miller," Thorne replied, his voice losing its forced levity. "But the feds have eyes everywhere. They've flagged a number of vehicles idling in the vicinity, vehicles that aren't on any official port manifest. Thorne's team is monitoring their movements. The FBI tactical units are moving to intercept and secure them. They're trying to preempt any coordinated extraction attempt."

This was the core of the challenge. Vance wasn't just a passenger on a ship; he was the nexus of a sprawling, clandestine operation that extended far beyond the vessel itself. His network, woven into the fabric of the port's operations, was designed for one purpose: to facilitate his escape and the activation of Project Nightingale. The cordon was the first line of defense, the physical barrier designed to contain the immediate threat. But the true battle would be fought in neutralizing the unseen tendrils of Vance's influence, in cutting off his escape routes before they could even be utilized.

Miller's focus shifted to the ship's internal security feeds, now displayed on a hardened tactical tablet. He saw the methodical progression of officers, their movements precise, their eyes sharp. They were not just apprehending criminals; they were dismantling a complex operational infrastructure. Each passenger being screened, each vehicle being intercepted, was a blow against Vance's meticulously crafted plan. The intel provided by Spectre, particularly regarding Vance's known associates and their operational protocols, was proving invaluable. It allowed the task force to move with a speed and accuracy that bypassed the usual frustrations of a disorganized arrest.

He saw the faces of the apprehended handlers on a secondary screen – their expressions ranging from defiant arrogance to a hollow, almost resigned fear. Spectre had described them as deeply embedded, fiercely loyal, and utterly ruthless. Interrogating them would be a delicate dance, a high-stakes negotiation for critical information. The Nightingale's song was about to begin, and the key to silencing it, or at least disrupting its devastating melody, lay within the minds of these individuals.

"Spectre's intel about the encrypted communication channels Vance uses?" Miller asked, his gaze fixed on the tactical display. "Has there been any chatter picked up on the shore-side surveillance? Anything indicating communication with external operatives?"

"The FCC and NSA teams are running a sweep on all local frequencies, both commercial and encrypted," Thorne responded. "They're looking for anomalous signals that match the patterns Spectre described. So far, nothing concrete, but they're still analyzing. The assumption is that if Vance is in command of the Nightingale, he'll be communicating with his handlers on the ground. The cordon is designed to prevent that direct contact, but he's too clever to rely on a single method. He'll have fallback plans."

Miller nodded grimly. Vance's reputation preceded him. He was not a man who gambled on single points of failure. His entire modus operandi was built on layers of redundancy, of contingency plans within contingency plans. The efficiency of the cordon was a strong deterrent, but it was not an absolute guarantee. The true challenge was to anticipate Vance's next move, to stay one step ahead of a mind that thrived on chaos and misdirection.

He shifted his focus to another part of the display, a schematic of the port's extensive infrastructure. Cranes, warehouses, railway lines, and access roads were all highlighted, each a potential artery for Vance's escape. The task force had designated primary and secondary interception points, creating a web designed to ensnare any attempt to flee the immediate vicinity of the ship.

"Thorne," Miller said, his voice hardening, "you mentioned two individuals matching the description of the 'wooden bird' handlers. Have they been fully secured? And Spectre's intel on the bespoke containment units – how close are we to identifying their precise purpose and the intended activation sequence?"

"The handlers are in secure interview rooms on board, Miller. Thorne's team is standing guard, and the FBI interrogation specialists are en route. As for the containment units, the intel is fragmented. Spectre's testimony indicated they housed critical processing modules and the primary broadcast array for the Nightingale. The activation sequence, however, remains a mystery. He mentioned Vance personally oversaw its encryption, making it virtually impossible to decipher without direct access to Vance himself, or a key he would entrust to no one."

The implication was chilling. If Vance himself was apprehended, but the activation sequence remained a secret, the Nightingale's song could still be sung. The physical components might be secured, but their activation code could be delivered through a secondary, untraceable channel. It was a scenario Miller had braced for, a worst-case outcome that underscored the urgency of not only apprehending Vance but also of breaking through his psychological defenses, of finding a vulnerability in his meticulously constructed fortress of secrecy.

"And Vance?" Miller finally asked, his gaze sweeping over the scene below, the organized chaos of the cordon a testament to the scale of their undertaking. "Any sign of him amongst the disembarking passengers?"

"Negative, Miller. Our internal surveillance is being meticulously cross-referenced. He's not among the initial waves. Thorne's team is working through the passenger manifest, identifying anyone who might have been a late addition to the crew or a last-minute passenger. They're also cross-referencing against any individuals with known ties to Vance's shell corporations. The net is tightening, but he's proving exceptionally adept at disappearing into the crowd, even when the crowd is being meticulously screened."

The efficiency of the cordon was undeniable, a testament to meticulous planning and inter-agency cooperation. But Miller knew that Vance's operational security was built on more than just physical barriers. It was built on deception, on psychological manipulation, on an almost prescient understanding of his adversaries' methods. The sheer scale of the mobilization was a deterrent, but it also provided Vance with a vast canvas of confusion and chaos to exploit.

"Keep me updated on the handlers," Miller instructed, his eyes narrowing as he observed a black, unmarked van being directed away from the main docking area by a squadron of FBI agents. "That van, Jenkins. What's the status?"

Jenkins's voice was immediate. "That's one of the flagged vehicles, Miller. It's being escorted to a secure containment facility on the outskirts of the port. Preliminary intelligence suggests it's a mobile command unit, possibly equipped for external data transmission. Thorne's team believes it might be a relay point for Vance's operatives on the ground."

"Good," Miller acknowledged, a flicker of hope igniting within him. "The cordon isn't just about preventing escape; it's about isolating and neutralizing his support network. Every vehicle, every individual flagged, is a potential piece of the Nightingale puzzle. We need to intercept those pieces before Vance can assemble them."

He watched as more officers moved through the ship, their quiet diligence a stark contrast to the burgeoning activity outside. The goal was clear: to exhaust every avenue, to leave no stone unturned. The passengers were being processed with a swiftness that spoke of a well-rehearsed operation, but also with an underlying intensity that suggested the stakes were far higher than a mere immigration check. Every face was scrutinized, every answer weighed. The shadow of Vance, and the impending activation of Project Nightingale, hung heavy over the entire proceedings. The cordon was up, the confrontation was inevitable, and Miller knew that the next few hours would determine whether the Nightingale's song would be silenced before it could truly begin, or if Vance's final, devastating act would plunge the world into an abyss of financial chaos.

The ship's metal hull, usually a sanctuary of controlled chaos, now felt like a vast, echoing tomb, its every groan amplified by the heightened senses of its occupants. Julian Vance, a man accustomed to the hushed reverence of boardrooms and the deferential silence of subordinates, moved with an unnerving stillness through the dimly lit service corridors. His meticulously tailored suit had been exchanged for the nondescript, slightly oversized uniform of a ship's caterer, a disguise so commonplace it bordered on invisibility. The faint aroma of industrial cleaning fluid and stale coffee, a stark contrast to the expensive cologne he usually favored, clung to him like a second skin.

Beside him, a monolith of quiet menace, strode Marcus Thorne, his ex-military bearing as evident in the borrowed, ill-fitting dockworker's overalls as it was in his former regalia. Thorne's face, usually a study in controlled aggression, was a mask of impassive vigilance. His eyes, sharp and constantly scanning, absorbed the details of their surroundings with a predator's instinct. They moved not with the hurried urgency of those fleeing, but with the measured, deliberate pace of men with a clear objective, a practiced gait honed by years of operating in the shadows.

"Are you certain this route is clear, Thorne?" Vance's voice was a low murmur, barely audible above the hum of distant machinery. It lacked the imperious edge he usually adopted, replaced by a carefully cultivated air of casual inquiry. Years of operating with impunity, of navigating the intricate web of corporate power and legal loopholes, had instilled in him an unshakeable confidence, bordering on arrogance. He believed his resources, his meticulously crafted escape plan, were not merely robust, but infallible. The sheer audacity of the authorities, their expectation that they could simply intercept *him*, struck him as almost quaint.

Thorne offered a curt nod, his gaze fixed on a junction ahead where the corridor branched into a labyrinth of pipes and conduits. "The security sweeps are concentrated on the passenger decks and the main cargo access. Service tunnels are less monitored, less... predictable. Less likely to attract their attention." His voice was a gravelly whisper, a stark contrast to Vance's smoother, more cultivated tones. Thorne was a weapon, honed and deployed, and his loyalty, though bought, was absolute. He saw the port not as a place of arrival or departure, but as a complex obstacle course, each junction a potential trap, each shadow a threat.

Vance's gloved fingers tightened around the worn leather of the briefcase he carried. It was a deceptively simple accessory, yet it contained the keys to his immediate survival: his personal communication device, encrypted and untraceable, and a substantial emergency fund, a testament to his foresight and his ingrained paranoia. He'd always operated on the principle of contingency, of having escape routes within escape routes, fallback plans for his fallback plans. This escape from the ship, the initial extraction, was merely the first domino in a sequence designed to lead him to a life of anonymous opulence, far from the reach of any jurisdiction.

"The vehicle is positioned at Gate C," Vance continued, his eyes darting towards a faint rectangle of dim light filtering from a grimy porthole. "A black sedan. Discreet. No visible markings. The driver will be... familiar with our protocols." He allowed himself a faint, almost imperceptible smile. He had paid handsomely for this discretion, for the silence of individuals who asked no questions and demanded no explanations. The port itself, a sprawling organism of cranes, containers, and ceaseless activity, was a perfect camouflage for such clandestine operations. It was a place where things arrived and departed, where anonymity was not just possible, but inherent.

"They'll be looking for me on the decks, interviewing passengers, conducting sweeps," Vance mused, his mind already charting the next phase of his departure. "They'll never anticipate this. They'll be so focused on the obvious, on the readily available targets, that they'll miss the phantom slipping through their grasp." He imagined their frustration, the slow dawning realization that a simple change of clothes and a walk through the ship's underbelly had rendered their meticulously constructed cordon, their impressive display of force, utterly irrelevant.

Thorne remained silent, his focus entirely on the immediate path ahead. He had seen enough of Vance's arrogance in their years together, had witnessed firsthand the blithe dismissal of risks that would have sent lesser men into a cold sweat. Vance's belief in his own invincibility was both a strength and a profound weakness. It allowed him to take calculated risks, to push boundaries others wouldn't dare approach, but it also made him susceptible to underestimating the sheer, dogged persistence of those who pursued him. The authorities, Vance assumed, operated with a predictable methodology. Thorne knew better. He knew the dedication that could drive agents like Miller, the relentless pursuit that transcended protocol.

They navigated a series of narrow stairwells, the clang of their footsteps echoing in the confined spaces. The air grew warmer, more humid, as they descended deeper into the ship's bowels, the scent of diesel fumes becoming more pronounced. Vance paused at a bend in the corridor, straining to hear any sound that might indicate an unauthorized presence. The orchestrated silence of the service areas was a comfort, a stark contrast to the potential chaos of the main thoroughfares.

"Remember the contingency at the warehouse," Vance instructed, his voice low. "If Gate C is compromised, we divert to Warehouse Four. Thorne's network has operatives positioned there. They will facilitate an alternative extraction. The briefcase contains the secondary payment protocols." He tapped the briefcase with a manicured finger. This was not just about physical escape; it was about ensuring the continuity of his operations, the preservation of his assets. The 'wooden bird,' his magnum opus, was already in motion.

Thorne grunted in acknowledgment. His own contingency plans were woven into the fabric of Vance's, a redundant layer of security he had personally designed. He trusted Vance's resources, but he placed his faith in his own combat-honed instincts. He had trained for this, for the extraction of high-value targets from hostile environments. The port, with its labyrinthine layout and myriad of potential choke points, was a familiar hunting ground.

As they neared what Vance believed was the final service exit leading to the open air of the docks, a new sound registered. It was faint, almost imperceptible, a rhythmic metallic scraping that didn't belong to the usual symphony of the port. Thorne froze, his hand instinctively reaching for the concealed weapon beneath his overalls. Vance, for the first time, felt a prickle of unease, a subtle tremor in his carefully constructed composure.

"What is that?" Vance whispered, his gaze snapped towards Thorne.

Thorne's eyes narrowed, scanning the dim corridor ahead. "Movement," he breathed, his voice barely a whisper. "Not ours."

They had expected a clean egress, a swift transition from the confines of the ship to the waiting vehicle. But the authorities, Vance's meticulously planned escape had failed to account for one crucial variable: the sheer, unblinking efficiency of a task force that had anticipated his every calculated move, even the ones he believed were too cunning to be fathomed. The cordon, which Vance had dismissed as a crude attempt to contain him, was far more intricate, far more insidious, than he had ever imagined. It wasn't just a perimeter; it was a web, designed to ensnare not just the obvious, but the invisible. And Vance, with his arrogance and his carefully crafted disguise, had just walked headfirst into its silken threads. The service tunnels, the supposed blind spot, had become a trapdoor, leading not to freedom, but to an even more inescapable confinement. The rhythmic scraping intensified, a sure sign that their assumed sanctuary was rapidly becoming a cage. The meticulous planning had indeed been accounted for, but not in the way Vance had so confidently predicted. His belief in his own superior intellect, his unwavering faith in his ability to outmaneuver any opposition, was about to be brutally, irrevocably shattered. He had underestimated the enemy, and in the world of espionage and high-stakes operations, underestimation was a fatal flaw. The shadow he had attempted to disappear into was, in fact, a spotlight, illuminating his every move as he descended further into the tightening net.

The metallic scraping, a sound like a rat gnawing at steel, intensified. It was no longer faint, but a distinct, unnerving rhythm echoing down the narrow corridor. Julian Vance, his carefully constructed composure beginning to fray at the edges, stopped dead. His eyes, wide with a dawning horror, fixed on Marcus Thorne. The ex-military man, a stoic presence moments before, now seemed to vibrate with an almost imperceptible tension. His mask of impassivity had cracked, revealing a flicker of something Vance couldn't quite decipher – panic, perhaps, or a calculated move he hadn't foreseen.

"Thorne?" Vance's whisper was tight, strained. He could feel the prickle of sweat on his brow, a sensation utterly alien to his usual control. This wasn't part of the plan. This wasn't the silent, invisible extraction he had meticulously orchestrated.

Thorne's gaze, which had been sweeping the corridor ahead, now flickered towards Vance, then back to the source of the scraping sound. His jaw tightened, a subtle shift that spoke volumes. "It's... a false alarm, Vance," he said, his voice a little too rough, a little too quick. "Probably just maintenance crews. This section of the ship is rarely used. They're probably clearing debris."

Vance's brow furrowed. Thorne's explanation felt hollow, a flimsy shield against the palpable sense of unease that permeated the air. Maintenance crews rarely operated with such stealth, their movements masked by the ship's usual cacophony. And the sound wasn't the random clatter of tools; it was a deliberate, rhythmic action. He remembered Thorne's words about the port being a complex obstacle course, each junction a potential trap. Had they walked directly into one?

"A false alarm?" Vance echoed, the words laced with disbelief. He could feel his heart hammering against his ribs, a frantic drumbeat against the ominous scrape. "It sounds more like... like something being dragged. Or forced." His mind raced, replaying every detail of their descent. Every turn, every shadow. Had they been followed? Had Thorne's meticulously planned route been compromised from the outset?

Thorne took a step forward, positioning himself between Vance and the direction of the sound. His stance was defensive, almost aggressive. "Miller is thorough, Vance. He wouldn't miss a detail. He'll be checking all exfiltration points. This... this is likely a diversionary sweep. Designed to draw us out."

The implication hung heavy in the air. Miller. The relentless agent who had orchestrated the cordon. Vance had dismissed him as a competent, but ultimately predictable, operative. But Thorne's words, his sudden eagerness to frame the sound as a planned maneuver by Miller, struck Vance as odd. Why was Thorne so quick to offer an explanation, especially one that seemed to be trying to allay Vance's fears?

"A diversion?" Vance's voice took on a dangerous edge. He saw Thorne's eyes darting, a subtle flicker of unease he hadn't noticed before. It wasn't the primal fear of a man caught in a trap, but something more nuanced. The look of a man weighing his options. "Or is it, Thorne, an attempt to redirect our attention? To give *you* an opening?" Thorne's head snapped back, his gaze sharp and piercing. "What are you implying, Vance?"

"I'm implying that perhaps your loyalty isn't as absolute as you've led me to believe," Vance said, his voice dropping to a low, menacing growl. He watched Thorne closely, searching for any tell, any tremor that would confirm his burgeoning suspicion. Thorne's reputation was built on a foundation of unwavering reliability, of a price paid for unwavering service. But even the most solid foundations could be undermined. "Perhaps this 'false alarm' is your signal. Perhaps you've made your own arrangements. A separate deal, with Miller."

The scraping sound was closer now, a tangible threat in the confined space. Thorne's jaw worked for a moment, his eyes narrowed in a silent battle of wills. "Miller knows my price, Vance. And it's higher than whatever you're offering him to look the other way."

"Is it?" Vance pressed, taking a step closer. The stale air of the service tunnel seemed to thicken, charged with unspoken accusations. "Because you're acting awfully... helpful, Thorne. Explaining away sounds that don't fit. Trying to steer me towards the idea that this is all part of Miller's grand plan. When all I hear is the sound of a door being forced open, a door that leads to a trap. A trap you seem awfully eager to let me walk into."

Thorne remained silent for a beat, his gaze unwavering. Then, a slow, almost imperceptible smirk played on his lips. "And perhaps, Vance, you're seeing shadows where there are none. Perhaps your own paranoia is clouding your judgment." He turned his head, glancing down the corridor again, his voice softening slightly. "If Miller *were* trying to flush us out, he'd use the main access points. The service tunnels are a blind spot. He knows that. Unless..."

He let the word hang in the air, a deliberate taunt. Vance felt a cold dread creep into his gut. Thorne was playing a game, and Vance was not at all sure he was winning. "Unless what, Thorne?"

"Unless he knows we're in the service tunnels," Thorne finished, his voice back to its gravelly whisper. He turned to face Vance fully, his expression unreadable. "And he knows that the only way we'd be in here, heading towards Gate C, is if you were the one leading the way. Which means," he paused, letting the weight of his words sink in, "he's betting on your arrogance, Vance. Your belief that you're too clever to be caught. He's counting on you to underestimate him, just as you've always underestimated everyone else."

Vance felt a surge of anger, a desperate need to regain control. "You're trying to distract me, Thorne. To buy yourself time. Time to disappear. Time to collect your bonus from Miller."

Thorne chuckled, a low, humorless sound. "Miller doesn't pay bonuses for failed operations, Vance. He pays for results. And right now, the only result I'm seeing is you, getting increasingly agitated, while the walls close in." He gestured with his chin towards the source of the scraping. "That's not Miller's diversion. That's the sound of the trapdoor being sprung."

Suddenly, a harsh, blinding beam of light cut through the dim corridor, momentarily disorienting them. Vance flinched, instinctively shielding his eyes. When his vision cleared, he saw him. Agent Michael Miller, standing at the junction, his face a mask of grim satisfaction. Behind him, a phalanx of armed officers, their weapons glinting under the harsh lights. The scraping sound had stopped, replaced by the heavy, measured breathing of armed men.

"Well, well, Vance," Miller's voice was calm, measured, yet it cut through the tension like a scalpel. "Fancy meeting you here. I was beginning to think you'd found a more... conventional exit." He glanced at Thorne, a subtle shift in his gaze that didn't go unnoticed by Vance. "And Thorne. Still working for the highest bidder, I see. Though I must admit, your timing has been... unexpectedly useful."

Vance's mind reeled. Thorne. He had been right. Thorne hadn't been loyal. He had been playing both sides. The diversion, the reassurances, the subtle nudges towards Miller's supposed tactics – it had all been a carefully orchestrated performance. Thorne had been feeding Miller information, or perhaps even actively guiding them into this trap.

"Useful?" Vance spat the word out, his voice hoarse. He glared at Thorne, the man he had trusted, the man he had paid handsomely for his unwavering allegiance. "You were supposed to be my escape, Thorne. My insurance. My... my weapon."

Thorne's face remained impassive, but there was a flicker in his eyes that Vance now recognized as something akin to resignation, mixed with a cold, professional assessment. "I am a weapon, Vance. The question is, who is holding the trigger?"

Miller stepped forward, his gaze fixed on Thorne. "He gave us the route, Thorne. The service tunnels. Said you'd be leading Vance this way, towards Gate C. Said you were looking for a way out for yourself, once Vance was... contained."

Thorne's lips curved into a faint, sardonic smile. "Miller always did have a flair for the dramatic. And an even greater flair for twisting facts to fit his narrative."

"Is that what this is, Thorne?" Miller's voice hardened, a note of genuine suspicion creeping in. "A performance? Or are you truly playing us all?"

Vance watched the exchange, his mind a whirlwind of betrayal and confusion. Miller's words implied Thorne had cut a deal with him, a deal that involved leading Vance into this trap. But Thorne's response, his subtle mockery of Miller's interpretation, suggested otherwise. Was Thorne still playing his own game, manipulating both of them?

"You think I'd sell you out, Vance?" Thorne's voice was low, directed solely at Vance, but loud enough for Miller to hear. "After everything? After I swore...?" He trailed off, his gaze meeting Vance's, a strange mix of regret and something that looked perilously like defiance.

"I don't know *what* to think, Thorne," Vance admitted, the admission costing him dearly. His entire escape plan, his meticulously crafted illusion of control, had crumbled around him. And Thorne, the seemingly steadfast pillar of his security, had become the architect of his downfall, or at least a key player in it. "You brought me here. You spoke of diversions, of Miller's tactics. You guided me through the very tunnels he was monitoring."

Miller interjected, his gaze unwavering on Thorne. "He also said you were waiting for a specific signal. A sound. The scraping. He said that would be your cue to break from Vance and make your own escape."

Thorne let out a short, sharp laugh. "Miller is a good agent. He's smart. But he's predictable. He believes in simple motives. Betrayal. He doesn't understand... layers." He turned his gaze back to Vance, a strange intensity in his eyes. "He thinks I'm trying to save my skin. He thinks I'm a rat leaving a sinking ship."

Vance felt a chill colder than the stale air of the corridor. Layers. Thorne was talking about layers of deception, of strategy. Was it possible Thorne wasn't betraying Vance, but orchestrating something far more complex? Was this the 'wooden bird' Vance had spoken of, a plan so intricate that it appeared to be its own undoing?

"And are you not?" Vance challenged, his voice barely above a whisper.

Thorne looked at Miller, then back at Vance. "Miller thinks I'm the diversion. He thinks the scraping sound was my signal to abandon you and make a run for it. He's wrong." He paused, the silence stretching, punctuated only by the hum of the ship and the occasional clink of weaponry. "The scraping," Thorne continued, his voice dropping, becoming a low growl that vibrated with controlled power, "was your signal, Vance. Not mine."

Vance stared at Thorne, his mind struggling to comprehend. "My signal?"

"Yes," Thorne confirmed, a grim satisfaction settling on his features. "The signal that Miller's cordon was in place. That the trap was set. That the main exits were blocked. And that the service tunnels, your supposed blind spot, were now precisely where he wanted us to be. My job," Thorne said, his gaze locking with Miller's, "was to confirm your route. To ensure you walked right into it. Just as he predicted."

Miller's eyes narrowed, his initial satisfaction replaced by a dawning unease. He looked from Vance, trapped and bewildered, to Thorne, the enigmatic ex-military man who seemed to be reveling in the unfolding chaos. "So you *were* working with Vance. You led him here willingly."

"I led Vance here because that's where he was going to go," Thorne stated, his voice flat. "My... arrangements... were for a different contingency. One that involved ensuring Vance didn't reach Gate C, but diverted elsewhere." He glanced at Vance, a subtle shift in his posture. "The scraping was supposed to be the cue for *your* diversion, Vance. Not mine. You were meant to hear it and react. To change course. To create the confusion that would allow *me* to slip away, not you."

Vance felt a sudden, sickening realization. Thorne hadn't betrayed him to Miller. Thorne had betrayed Vance to... himself? Or perhaps, Thorne had a plan that Vance's own arrogance had circumvented. The 'wooden bird' was in motion, and Thorne's role was not to escape with Vance, but to ensure Vance was caught, thereby facilitating Thorne's own separate escape, or some other unseen objective.

"You let me walk into this," Vance breathed, the words heavy with accusation.

Thorne met his gaze, his expression unyielding. "You walked into it, Vance. I merely observed. And when the trap was sprung, my original plan became... irrelevant." He looked at Miller, a new glint in his eyes. "Which means, Agent Miller, that while you've successfully apprehended

Mr. Vance, you've done so with my assistance. And that, I believe, comes at a certain price."

Miller's face tightened. He had Miller cornered, not as an informant, but as a reluctant accomplice who now held leverage. Thorne wasn't just a traitor; he was a player in a much larger game, a game where Vance was merely a pawn, and Thorne was playing for his own agenda. The question of Thorne's betrayal, Vance realized with a sinking heart, was no longer a simple question of loyalty. It was a complex tapestry of manipulation, a testament to Thorne's own survival instincts, and a chilling reminder that in this world of shadows, everyone was a potential enemy, and true allies were as rare and as precious as a ship's forgotten gold. The cordon had worked, but the real confrontation, Vance suspected, was just beginning, and it was Thorne who held the most dangerous cards.

The chilling scrape of metal against metal, a sound that had initially pricked at Julian Vance's nerves, now resolved into a more sinister significance. It wasn't the random clang of an overburdened ship's infrastructure. It was deliberate, rhythmic, a percussive declaration of presence. Thorne's pronouncements, initially dismissive, had morphed into a tense, almost frantic monologue. Vance's mind, usually a fortress of calculated logic, was now a swirling vortex of suspicion and dawning dread. Thorne's agility in offering explanations, his eagerness to paint Agent Miller's actions as a predictable chess move, felt less like professional assurance and more like a carefully constructed deflection.

"A diversionary sweep," Vance had scoffed, the words tasting like ash in his mouth. "Or perhaps a signal, Thorne? A private arrangement with Miller? A bonus for ensuring I walk directly into his waiting arms?" He watched Thorne, cataloging the almost imperceptible flicker in his eyes, the tightening of his jaw. It wasn't the look of a man caught in a lie, but of a man calculating the most advantageous response. Thorne, the hardened mercenary, the man Vance had paid handsomely for unwavering loyalty, was suddenly a variable he couldn't control.

Thorne's response had been a low, humorless chuckle, a sound that echoed the hollowness of Vance's own crumbling certainty. "Miller doesn't pay bonuses for failed operations, Vance. He pays for results. And right now, the only result I'm seeing is you, getting increasingly agitated, while the walls close in." He had gestured with his chin towards the source of the scraping. "That's not Miller's diversion. That's the sound of the trapdoor being sprung."

And then, the light. A blinding, sterile beam that sliced through the oppressive gloom of the service tunnel, momentarily snatching Vance's vision. When it cleared, Agent Michael Miller stood before them, a figure carved from grim satisfaction. Behind him, a phalanx of armed officers, their weapons like predatory beasts, glinted under the harsh illumination. The scraping had ceased, replaced by the heavy, measured exhalations of men prepared for violence.

"Well, well, Vance," Miller's voice, smooth and deceptively calm, carried the weight of absolute victory. "Fancy meeting you here. I was beginning to think you'd found a more... conventional exit." His gaze flickered to Thorne, a subtle acknowledgment that Vance, even in his shock, didn't miss. "And Thorne. Still working for the highest bidder, I see. Though I must admit, your timing has been... unexpectedly useful."

The world tilted. Thorne. Vance's meticulously constructed plan, his supposed ace in the hole, had been the very lever Miller had used to pry open the cage. Thorne hadn't been a shield; he had been the key, the informant, the willing accomplice. Vance's carefully guarded composure shattered. "Useful?" he spat, the word a raw, ragged sound. He locked eyes with Thorne, the man he had considered an indispensable asset. "You were supposed to be my escape, Thorne. My insurance. My... my weapon."

Thorne's face remained an impassive mask, but a subtle shift in his eyes, a mixture of resignation and a chillingly professional assessment, betrayed a deeper narrative. "I am a weapon, Vance. The question is, who is holding the trigger?"

Miller stepped forward, his attention solely on Thorne. "He gave us the route, Thorne. The service tunnels. Said you'd be leading Vance this way, towards Gate C. Said you were looking for a way out for yourself, once Vance was... contained."

A faint, sardonic smile touched Thorne's lips. "Miller always did have a flair for the dramatic. And an even greater flair for twisting facts to fit his narrative."

"Is that what this is, Thorne?" Miller's voice hardened, suspicion gnawing at the edges of his triumph. "A performance? Or are you truly playing us all?"

Vance watched the exchange, his mind a battlefield of warring emotions. Miller's words implied a clear betrayal, Thorne having cut a deal to deliver Vance. Yet Thorne's sardonic reply, his dismissive mockery of Miller's interpretation, suggested a more intricate game. Was Thorne still weaving his own web, manipulating both Vance and Miller?

"You think I'd sell you out, Vance?" Thorne's voice was low, a private accusation directed at Vance, yet amplified for Miller's ears. "After everything? After I swore...?" He paused, his gaze meeting Vance's, a complex blend of regret and defiant resolve.

"I don't know what to think, Thorne," Vance admitted, the concession a bitter pill. His entire escape, his carefully constructed illusion of control, had imploded. Thorne, the bedrock of his security, was now the architect of his downfall, or at least a crucial cog in its mechanism. "You brought me here. You spoke of diversions, of Miller's tactics. You guided me through the very tunnels he was monitoring."

Miller's voice cut in, his gaze never leaving Thorne. "He also said you were waiting for a specific signal. A sound. The scraping. He said that would be your cue to break from Vance and make your own escape."

Thorne let out a short, sharp laugh, devoid of humor. "Miller is a good agent. He's smart. But he's predictable. He believes in simple motives. Betrayal. He doesn't understand... layers." He turned his gaze back to Vance, an unsettling intensity igniting in his eyes. "He thinks I'm the diversion. He thinks the scraping sound was my signal to abandon you and make a run for it. He's wrong." He paused, the silence in the confined space amplifying the hum of the ship and the metallic whispers of weaponry. "The scraping," Thorne continued, his voice dropping to a low growl that resonated with controlled power, "was your signal, Vance. Not mine."

Vance stared, his mind grappling with the impossible. "My signal?"

"Yes," Thorne confirmed, a grim satisfaction spreading across his features. "The signal that Miller's cordon was in place. That the trap was set. That the main exits were blocked. And that the service tunnels, your supposed blind spot, were now precisely where he wanted us to be. My job,"

Thorne stated, his gaze locking with Miller's, "was to confirm your route. To ensure you walked right into it. Just as he predicted."

Miller's eyes narrowed, the triumphant gleam replaced by a dawning unease. He looked from Vance, trapped and bewildered, to Thorne, the enigmatic ex-military man who seemed to be relishing the unfolding chaos. "So you *were* working with Vance. You led him here willingly."

"I led Vance here because that's where he was going to go," Thorne stated, his voice flat, devoid of emotion. "My... arrangements... were for a different contingency. One that involved ensuring Vance didn't reach Gate C, but diverted elsewhere." He glanced at Vance, a subtle shift in his posture, a calculated movement. "The scraping was supposed to be the cue for *your* diversion, Vance. Not mine. You were meant to hear it and react. To change course. To create the confusion that would allow *me* to slip away, not you."

A sickening realization washed over Vance. Thorne hadn't betrayed him to Miller. Thorne had betrayed Vance to... himself? Or perhaps, Thorne had a far more intricate plan that Vance's own arrogance had inadvertently derailed. The 'wooden bird,' as Vance had once described such convoluted stratagems, was in motion, and Thorne's role was not to escape with Vance, but to ensure Vance's capture, thereby facilitating Thorne's own separate escape, or some other objective hidden within the layers of his machinations.

"You let me walk into this," Vance breathed, the words heavy with accusation.

Thorne met his gaze, his expression unyielding. "You walked into it, Vance. I merely observed. And when the trap was sprung, my original plan became... irrelevant." He turned his attention back to Miller, a new, predatory glint in his eyes. "Which means, Agent Miller, that while you've successfully apprehended Mr. Vance, you've done so with my assistance. And that, I believe, comes at a certain price."

Miller's face tightened, a visible struggle playing out on his features. Thorne had him cornered, not as a snitch, but as a reluctant accomplice who now held the reins of leverage. Thorne wasn't just a traitor; he was a player in a far grander game, a game where Vance was merely a pawn, and Thorne was playing for his own inscrutable agenda. The question of

Thorne's betrayal, Vance realized with a sinking heart, was no longer a simple matter of allegiance. It was a complex tapestry of manipulation, a testament to Thorne's own primal survival instincts, and a chilling reminder that in this world of manufactured shadows, everyone was a potential enemy, and true allies were as rare and as precious as a ship's forgotten gold. The cordon had worked, its net drawn tight, but the real confrontation, Vance suspected with a cold dread, was only just beginning, and it was Thorne who held the most dangerous, the most unpredictable cards.

The immediate aftermath of Miller's pronouncement was a tense standoff, a silent negotiation unfolding between the agents of law and the man who had orchestrated their perceived victory. Vance remained frozen, the adrenaline that had propelled him through the labyrinthine service tunnels draining away, leaving behind a hollow echo of defeat. He watched Thorne, the enigma that had been his closest confidant and now his most profound betrayer, with a mixture of awe and loathing. Thorne's calm demeanor in the face of capture, his almost theatrical negotiation with Miller, spoke of a mind that thrived on chaos, that saw even this meticulously sprung trap as merely another move in a larger, unseen game.

"A price?" Miller's voice was tight, betraying a flicker of exasperation. He was a man accustomed to control, to dictating terms, not haggling. "You led him into a trap, Thorne. Your cooperation was implied, not negotiated."

Thorne's lips curved into a faint, almost imperceptible smile. "Implied cooperation," he mused, his voice a low rumble that seemed to vibrate with contained amusement, "is a fragile thing, Agent Miller. Especially when the other party has already achieved their primary objective: apprehending Mr. Vance. Now, the question becomes... what happens to the facilitator? The one who ensured the target reached the designated zone, precisely on schedule?" He tilted his head, his gaze sharp and assessing. "You needed Vance. I delivered him. That constitutes a service, wouldn't you agree?"

Miller bristled, his jaw clenching. "Your service was to us, Thorne. You fed us information. You helped us locate him."

"I fed you information that was... convenient," Thorne corrected, his tone measured. "Information designed to guide you. But my ultimate objective was not Vance's capture, per se. It was a specific outcome, an outcome that your operation has now facilitated, albeit perhaps not in the manner you initially envisioned." He shifted his weight, a subtle movement that Vance, hyper-aware of every detail, registered with unease. Thorne was playing for time, for a better deal, and Miller, in his eagerness to secure Vance, was perhaps being too hasty in assuming he held all the cards.

Vance, his mind slowly recalibrating from the shock of betrayal to the cold reality of his predicament, began to piece together the fragments of Thorne's pronouncements. Thorne's "arrangements," his insistence that the scraping sound was Vance's signal, not his, his talk of "layers" and "different contingencies." It wasn't a simple matter of Thorne selling him out to Miller. It was far more complex. Thorne had used Miller's predictable pursuit of Vance to achieve his own ends, whatever those might be. The 'wooden bird' wasn't just a metaphor for Vance's own intricate plan; it was Thorne's modus operandi, a strategy so convoluted that its apparent self-destruction was its greatest strength.

"What outcome, Thorne?" Vance's voice was hoarse, cutting through the charged silence. He looked directly at Thorne, no longer seeing a loyal operative, but a master manipulator. "What was your 'ultimate objective' that my capture conveniently served?"

Thorne's gaze flickered to Vance, a fleeting expression that could have been regret, or perhaps just a professional detachment. "You wanted to disappear, Vance. To escape the consequences of your actions. You believed you were orchestrating a perfect vanishing act. And in your arrogance, you underestimated the most fundamental principle of any escape: you cannot truly disappear if you are not truly gone."

Miller, impatient with the philosophical detour, interjected, "He's talking in circles, Vance. He's a traitor. He helped us apprehend you. Now he's trying to leverage that into a deal for himself."

"Am I?" Thorne's voice was deceptively soft. "Or am I simply pointing out the inherent flaws in your own meticulously crafted plan, Agent Miller? You believed you were trapping Vance. You were. But you were also a pawn in my game. The scraping sound," he repeated, his voice gaining a measured intensity, "was the signal that your cordon was fully established. That the primary exits were secured. That Vance, believing he was using the service tunnels as a blind spot, was in fact walking into a dead end. My role was to confirm that he took the bait. That he proceeded towards Gate C. And when the trap sprung, as it inevitably would, my objective would become... simpler."

Vance felt a cold sweat break out on his forehead. Thorne hadn't intended to escape *with* him, or even to escape *from* him. He had intended to escape *because* of his capture. "You wanted me caught," Vance stated, the realization a bitter draught.

"I wanted you contained, Vance," Thorne corrected, his tone precise. "And your apprehension, by Agent Miller's forces, was the most efficient and least conspicuous way to achieve that. It removes you from the board, allowing certain... dormant assets... to be activated. Assets that would have been compromised had you successfully vanished."

Miller's face was a mask of strained patience. "Dormant assets? What are you talking about, Thorne?"

"Think of it this way, Agent Miller," Thorne continued, ignoring Miller's question and addressing Vance directly, his voice dropping to a conspiratorial whisper, "you sought to disappear. To erase yourself from the equation. A noble, if ultimately futile, ambition. You assumed your network, your resources, would remain intact, waiting for your eventual reappearance. But in your absence, those assets, those carefully cultivated connections, become vulnerable. They become... available."

Vance's mind raced. Thorne wasn't just a mercenary; he was a tactician, a strategist who operated on multiple levels, with multiple agendas. He had used Vance's escape plan as a cover, a smokescreen, to ensure Vance was apprehended, thereby triggering some other pre-arranged contingency.

"So you traded me for... what? Influence? Access?" Vance challenged, the words laced with a desperate attempt to understand the depth of Thorne's deception.

"For a future, Vance," Thorne replied, his voice hardening slightly. "A future where certain... arrangements... can be solidified. Your successful disappearance would have disrupted those arrangements. Your capture, however, has ensured their continuation. And in return for my... assistance... in this little operation," he gestured with his chin towards Miller, "I expect a certain... recompense."

Miller's eyes narrowed. "And what exactly do you expect, Thorne?"

Thorne met Miller's gaze, a flicker of amusement in his eyes. "Immunity, Agent Miller. And perhaps a quiet dismissal. I facilitated the apprehension of a wanted fugitive. A valuable service, wouldn't you agree? Especially considering the risks involved."

The trap had sprung, but the nature of the prey had shifted. Vance was caught, but Thorne, the supposed captive, was now the one dictating terms, a chess player who had not only sacrificed his queen but had manipulated the opponent into believing he had won the game. The efficiency of the trap, the coordinated law enforcement team, the swift neutralization of the security chief – it all painted a picture of Miller's prowess. But beneath that veneer of victory lay Thorne's subtle influence, his calculated move that had turned Vance's escape into his own leverage. Vance, staring at Thorne, felt a profound sense of dread. He had been so focused on Miller's pursuit, on Thorne's supposed loyalty, that he had failed to see the true architect of his downfall. Thorne hadn't just sold him out; he had used him, a disposable pawn, to clear the path for his own far more ambitious objectives. The cordon had ensnared Vance, but it was Thorne who had truly sprung the trap, and the real price, Vance suspected, was yet to be paid.

The harsh glare of the portable spotlights, used by Miller's team to illuminate the grimy service tunnel, now seemed to focus their full intensity on Julian Vance. The air, thick with the metallic tang of ozone and the fainter, more disturbing scent of stale fear, pressed in on him. He stood between two uniformed officers, their grips firm but not overtly brutal, their faces impassive. The cacophony of the cordon, the hushed commands, the metallic clicks of weaponry being secured, had gradually receded, leaving a pregnant silence in its wake. It was a silence that Thorne, with his audacious gamble for immunity, had orchestrated, a silence that now belonged to Miller and his captive.

Agent Michael Miller approached, his stride deliberate, his posture exuding an air of weary triumph. He stopped a few feet from Vance, his gaze, a mixture of grim satisfaction and professional weariness, sweeping over the man he had relentlessly pursued. Vance, despite the undeniable reality of his capture, held his head high, his eyes, usually alight with a shrewd calculating intelligence, now held a peculiar, almost detached calm.

It was a composure born of deep-seated conviction, the unshakeable belief in the scaffolding of his legal defenses, the labyrinthine loopholes he had so meticulously prepared. He had always been a man who played the long game, a master strategist who anticipated every move, every counter-move. This, he thought, was merely a temporary setback, a minor inconvenience that his formidable legal team would swiftly rectify.

"Well, Vance," Miller's voice was a low rumble, cutting through the tense quiet. "It seems our game of cat and mouse has finally reached its conclusion. Though I must say, you led us on quite a chase."

Vance offered a faint, almost imperceptible smile, a ghost of his usual confident smirk. "A chase, Agent Miller? Or a guided tour? It appears my... associate... had a rather specific route in mind for us." His gaze flickered briefly towards where Thorne had stood moments before, a shadow of Thorne's audacious negotiation still hanging in the air. He didn't spare Thorne a second thought; the man was a tool, and like any tool, once its utility was exhausted, it was discarded.

Miller ignored the jab, his eyes fixed on Vance. "Thorne played his hand, Vance. And it seems his hand was worth more than yours. He gave us the access, the intel, the precise location. He ensured you'd be right here, waiting for us."

"Thorne is a mercenary, Miller. He sells his loyalty to the highest bidder. I paid him for his services, and clearly, someone else offered him more." Vance's voice was devoid of emotion, the practiced detachment of a man accustomed to the cold calculus of power. He believed, with every fiber of his being, that his legal team, with their deep pockets and even deeper connections, would unravel this entire affair. He would walk away, and Miller would be left with nothing but the bitter taste of a Pyrrhic victory. "My lawyers will be in touch. This entire operation is deeply flawed, and you know it."

Miller let out a short, humorless laugh. "Flawed? Perhaps. But effective. We have you, Vance. And unlike Thorne, who's currently cutting his own deal with a very grateful prosecutor, you have nothing but the consequences of your choices." He reached into the inner pocket of his jacket, his movements unhurried, deliberate. He produced a small, data-storage device, a sleek, black rectangle that glinted under the harsh lights. "This, Vance," he began, holding the device up, "is a copy of Sterling's personal laptop. We managed to bypass his rather amateurish encryption. And it's quite... illuminating."

Vance watched him, his composure unwavering. Sterling's laptop. A minor detail, he thought. Sterling was a loose end, a variable he had accounted for. "And what exactly has your diligent forensic work uncovered, Agent Miller? Petty theft? Corporate espionage? Hardly the stuff of federal indictments."

Miller's smile was slow, knowing. "Oh, it's far more than that, Vance. Sterling wasn't just a disgruntled employee. He was a man with a conscience, or at least, a man who was meticulously documenting his employer's... extracurricular activities. He detailed Project Nightingale, Vance. Every phase, every objective, every horrific success."

The name hung in the air, a phantom whispered into the sterile confines of the tunnel. Vance's jaw tightened almost imperceptibly. Project Nightingale. A phantom from his past, a project he had meticulously buried, a project he had believed was as dead as the individuals it had targeted.

Miller continued, his voice gaining a hard edge. "He detailed the methodologies. The procurement of... specialized personnel. The disposal protocols. And, most importantly, he provided a direct chain of command. A hierarchy. With you, Julian Vance, at the very apex of it all." He produced another object, a delicate, tarnished silver locket, its surface etched with a faded floral pattern. "And this," Miller said, his voice dropping to a near whisper, "was found on Sterling's person. A memento, perhaps? Or a token of appreciation?"

Vance's eyes flickered to the locket. It was Anna's. His late wife's. He hadn't seen it in years, had thought it lost, a painful reminder of a life he had long since erased. How had Miller...

"Anna's locket," Vance breathed, the words barely audible, the first crack in his carefully constructed facade.

"Yes, Vance. Anna's locket," Miller confirmed, his gaze unwavering. "Sterling kept it. Why, we don't know for sure. Perhaps a sentimental attachment to the victim? Or perhaps, he kept it as a reminder of the kind of man you truly are. The man who would leave behind such a... personal touch... on his handiwork."

The carefully cultivated calm began to fray at the edges. The locket, a symbol of a past he had tried to escape, a symbol of a life that had been brutally extinguished, now in Miller's hands, intrinsically linked to Sterling, and by extension, to him.

"Sterling was... unstable," Vance managed, his voice still tight, but the smooth veneer of indifference was gone, replaced by a raw, defensive edge. "He was delusional. He fabricated these stories."

"Delusional?" Miller took another step closer, the locket now held out towards Vance, its tarnished surface catching the light. "Then explain this, Vance. Sterling's notes detail a specific modus operandi for the assassinations. A signature, if you will. A subtle, almost artistic arrangement of certain... floral elements... near the victim. A tribute, he called it, to a lost love. A lost love named Anna, whose favorite flower was the rose." Miller's eyes locked with Vance's, a chilling certainty in their depths. "Sterling's laptop contains encrypted video logs. He recorded his... sessions. And in the final log, Vance, he held up this very locket, just before he administered the final... solution. He spoke your name. He spoke of your inspiration. He spoke of his devotion to your lost wife."

The carefully constructed edifice of Vance's denial crumbled. The chilling narrative, the meticulous detail, the irrefutable evidence – it was overwhelming. The locket, once a symbol of his past, now represented his present horror, a tangible link to the unspeakable acts he had orchestrated, the lives he had systematically extinguished. The calm indifference, the unwavering belief in his legal defenses, evaporated like mist in the harsh glare of the tunnel lights. He was no longer the puppet master, the detached architect of destruction. He was the caught predator, cornered and exposed.

"He... he was a tool," Vance stammered, his voice cracking. The words were a desperate attempt to cling to a semblance of control, a futile effort to distance himself from the monstrous truth. "A tool, like Thorne. He was... programmed."

Miller shook his head, a grim sadness tinged with a chilling resolve. "No, Vance. Sterling wasn't programmed. He was groomed. He was manipulated. He was your loyal disciple, driven by a twisted admiration that you so skillfully cultivated. You fed him lies, told him he was enacting justice, that he was honoring Anna's memory by eliminating those who you deemed unworthy of life. You twisted his grief, his admiration for your deceased wife, into a weapon."

He paused, letting the weight of his words settle in the charged atmosphere. The uniformed officers remained silent, their presence a stark reminder of Vance's complete capitulation. Vance's eyes, once sharp and defiant, now held a vacant stare, a profound emptiness reflecting the utter collapse of his world. The meticulously crafted empire, built on a foundation of secrets, lies, and meticulously planned murders, was now teetering on the brink of annihilation.

"Project Nightingale was never about justice, Vance," Miller continued, his voice softening slightly, though the steel beneath remained unyielding. "It was about control. About eliminating anyone who threatened your power, your carefully curated image. Anna's memory was merely a convenient excuse, a way to rationalize your depravity to yourself, and to your willing accomplice."

Vance flinched at the word 'depravity.' It was a word he had never associated with himself, a word that belonged to the baser elements of humanity, not to the sophisticated, enlightened Julian Vance. But looking at Miller, at the undeniable evidence laid bare, he knew, with a chilling certainty, that the label fit. The carefully constructed facade had finally shattered, revealing the monstrous truth that lay beneath.

"The evidence is overwhelming, Vance," Miller stated, his voice returned to its professional, detached tone. "The laptop, Sterling's confession, the locket, the testimony from Thorne... it all points to you. You orchestrated it all. You profited from it all. You are responsible."

Vance closed his eyes, a shudder running through him. The weight of it all, the sheer scale of his crimes, pressed down on him, suffocating him. The intricate web he had spun, the elaborate deceptions, the carefully cultivated persona of a respected philanthropist and businessman – it all dissolved into the suffocating darkness of the service tunnel. He had played his game, a game of power and control, and he had lost. The thought of his legal team, once a source of unwavering confidence, now seemed a distant, hollow promise. How could they defend against such undeniable, such visceral proof?

He opened his eyes, meeting Miller's gaze. The defiance was gone, replaced by a grim, weary acceptance. The meticulously constructed empire was indeed crumbling, and he, Julian Vance, the architect of its rise, was now inextricably bound to its downfall. He was no longer the puppet master; he was the puppet, his strings cut, his grand illusion exposed to the harsh, unforgiving light of reality. The cordon had been effective, but it was the evidence, the undeniable truth unearthed by Miller's relentless pursuit, that had truly brought him down. The power player was finally cornered, his meticulously constructed world collapsing around him, and in the suffocating silence of the tunnel, Julian Vance finally understood the true cost of his ambition.

Chapter 13: Project Nightingale's Fallout

The immediate aftermath of Julian Vance's apprehension was a whirlwind of controlled chaos. The service tunnel, once a sanctuary for illicit dealings, now hummed with the focused energy of the task force. Miller, his face a mask of grim determination, oversaw the securing of Vance and the initial sweep of any immediate evidence. But the real work, the painstaking, intricate process of dismantling Project Nightingale, was only just beginning. It was a task that promised to be as complex and far-reaching as the conspiracy itself.

The data extracted from Sterling's laptop, painstakingly decrypted by the FBI's top cyber-forensics team, was a Pandora's Box of incriminating information. It wasn't just a roadmap of Vance's criminal enterprise; it was a detailed ledger of its financial arteries, its covert veins pumping illicit funds through a global network. Miller and his counterparts, now joined by a contingent of specialized financial investigators from the FBI and Interpol, faced a monumental undertaking: tracing every dollar, every illicit transaction, every offshore shell company designed to obscure the truth.

"It's like peeling back layers of an onion," remarked Agent Anya Sharma, a sharp, no-nonsense financial crimes specialist, as she gestured to a sprawling digital flowchart projected onto a screen in their makeshift command center. The flowchart, a tangled web of color-coded lines and cryptic alphanumeric codes, represented the labyrinthine financial infrastructure of Project Nightingale. "Vance built this empire on a foundation of misdirection. Every legitimate-looking corporation is a front. Every transfer is designed to look like a standard business transaction. But the patterns, the recurring anomalies... they all lead back to the same source."

The immediate priority was to sever those financial lifelines. Freezing assets became paramount. This wasn't a simple matter of seizing bank accounts; Vance's wealth was dispersed across dozens of jurisdictions, held in trusts and corporations registered in countries with notoriously opaque financial regulations. Legal teams worked around the clock, filing injunctions, submitting extradition requests for financial records, and coordinating with international law enforcement agencies. The process was fraught with diplomatic hurdles and legal challenges, each one a potential obstacle designed to protect Vance's ill-gotten gains.

"We're dealing with a sophisticated international money laundering operation," explained Agent David Chen, another member of Sharma's team, his brow furrowed in concentration as he analyzed a complex series of offshore transfers. "Sterling's logs provided us with the key, but now we have to meticulously follow each thread. It requires an unprecedented level of cross-border cooperation. We're not just looking at Vance; we're looking at everyone who facilitated his activities, anyone who profited, however indirectly."

The testimony of Thorne, secured in exchange for a reduced sentence, proved invaluable. While his focus had been on the operational aspects of Project Nightingale, he had an intimate understanding of Vance's network and the key players involved. He provided names, roles, and crucial insights into the modus operandi of Vance's financial enablers. Thorne, the pragmatist, had always been about leverage; now, he was leveraging his knowledge to mitigate his own consequences.

"Vance had a council of advisors, of sorts," Thorne had divulged during his initial debriefings, his voice a low rasp, betraying no remorse. "They weren't on the front lines of... Nightingale itself, not directly. But they were the architects of its financial architecture. Lawyers, accountants, even a few former government officials with... specialized knowledge of navigating international regulations. They ensured the money flowed, untraceable, unaccounted for. They were the quiet architects, the ones who built the vault."

Identifying and apprehending these "quiet architects" became the next phase of the operation. Sterling's data provided a partial list, but Thorne's insights filled in critical blanks. FBI agents, armed with arrest warrants, fanned out across the globe. Raids were conducted in plush corporate offices in Zurich, discreet apartments in Singapore, and sprawling estates in the Caribbean. The arrests were executed with precision, often catching the individuals completely off guard. They were men and women accustomed to operating in the shadows, their illicit activities shielded by layers of legal protections and offshore secrecy.

One such individual was a renowned international tax attorney, Mr. Alistair Finch, based in London. Finch was known for his discreet services to the ultra-wealthy, a master of corporate structuring and asset protection. Sterling's logs revealed numerous communications between Finch's firm and Vance's shell corporations, detailing the establishment of intricate trust funds and offshore holding companies designed to receive and launder the proceeds of Project Nightingale. Thorne had specifically identified Finch as the primary legal mind behind the financial operations. When federal agents, working in tandem with Scotland Yard, raided Finch's opulent Mayfair office, they found not just legal documents, but a hidden panic room filled with encrypted hard drives and burner phones.

"He thought he was untouchable," remarked Miller, observing the digital evidence being carefully cataloged. "These people operate under the illusion of impunity. They believe their wealth and their legal maneuvering can shield them from any consequence. But Sterling's data, coupled with Thorne's testimony, has given us the leverage to shatter that illusion."

The scale of the corruption was staggering. Project Nightingale wasn't a localized criminal enterprise; it was a global operation, its tendrils reaching into every corner of the world where illicit funds could be hidden and laundered. The task force found itself coordinating with agencies in over two dozen countries, each with its own legal system, its own bureaucratic processes, and its own inherent challenges. The initial arrests were merely the tip of an iceberg, a testament to the vastness of Vance's network.

In Hong Kong, a team apprehended a former executive from a major international bank, a man named Kwan, who had allegedly facilitated the transfer of millions of dollars through his institution, bypassing standard anti-money laundering protocols. In Dubai, another key financier, a man known only by the pseudonym "The Broker," was apprehended attempting to board a private jet, his luggage reportedly containing several million in untraceable bearer bonds. Each arrest, each successful seizure of assets, chipped away at the empire Vance had so meticulously constructed.

The investigation became a relentless marathon, a test of endurance and international diplomacy. Miller and his core team found themselves constantly on planes, attending briefings in foreign capitals, and navigating complex legal frameworks. The initial exhilaration of Vance's capture had long since subsided, replaced by the grim determination to see the entire network dismantled, to ensure that every individual who played a role in Project Nightingale faced justice.

"It's not just about bringing down Vance," Miller stated during a late-night conference call with his international counterparts. "It's about eradicating the system that allowed him to flourish. We need to dismantle the network entirely. Every shell corporation, every offshore account, every facilitating individual. We need to make an example, to send a clear message that this kind of sophisticated criminal enterprise will not be tolerated."

The sheer volume of financial data required a specialized approach. AI-driven analytics programs were deployed to sift through terabytes of financial records, identifying anomalies, cross-referencing transactions, and flagging suspicious patterns that human investigators might overlook. These digital tools, combined with the boots-on-the-ground efforts of international law enforcement, were crucial in mapping the intricate financial pathways of Project Nightingale.

The implications of Project Nightingale extended beyond mere financial crimes. The funds laundered had undoubtedly been used to finance other nefarious activities, including potentially more assassinations and destabilization efforts in regions where Vance had business interests. Unraveling the financial web meant uncovering these secondary criminal activities as well, broadening the scope of the investigation and deepening the commitment of international partners.

The legal battles were as intense as the investigations. Vance's legal team, though blindsided by his apprehension, began to mobilize, employing every legal tactic to delay, obstruct, and challenge the proceedings. They filed motions to suppress evidence, argued jurisdictional disputes, and sought to have assets unfrozen. The prosecution worked to build a comprehensive case, meticulously documenting every aspect of Project Nightingale, from its inception to its financial underpinnings.

"We're building a RICO case on steroids," Assistant U.S. Attorney Jemery Vans explained to Miller, referring to the Racketeer Influenced and Corrupt Organizations Act. "Vance and his associates operated as a criminal enterprise. We have the leadership in Vance, the operational details from Sterling's data and Thorne's testimony, and now, we have the financial infrastructure mapped out by Agent Sharma's team. We're going to dismantle it piece by piece, in court."

The sustained effort required to dismantle Project Nightingale was a testament to the dedication of countless individuals across multiple agencies and international borders. It was a complex, multifaceted operation that extended far beyond the dramatic apprehension of its figurehead. The initial victory of arresting Vance was just the first step in a long, arduous journey towards achieving true accountability and ensuring that the shadow of Project Nightingale would no longer darken the global stage. The network was being dismantled, not with a single decisive blow, but with the relentless, methodical, and often unglamorous work of stripping away its foundations, brick by painstaking brick. The fight for justice, it became clear, was a marathon, not a sprint, and the finish line for Project Nightingale was still a considerable distance away.

The sterile interrogation room felt like a tomb, its harsh fluorescent lights buzzing a relentless dirge. Spectre sat across from Agent Miller and Anya Sharma, his face a mask of impassivity, a carefully constructed facade that had served him for years. He was a ghost, the bodies he left behind only confirmed a phantom whose existence. But even ghosts could be broken, and Vance, in his ultimate act of self-preservation, had inadvertently shattered Spectre's carefully cultivated detachment. Abandoned, left to rot in a federal holding cell while Vance continued his opulent life, Spectre's carefully guarded loyalty had fractured.

"You understand," Miller began, his voice a low, steady rumble, "that your cooperation is the only thing standing between you and a lifetime behind bars. Vance has cast you adrift. He's left you to take the fall for his dirty work."

Spectre's eyes, the color of a winter sky, flickered for a fraction of a second. It was a minuscule tremor, a fleeting glimpse beneath the ice. He had known the risks, of course. Every operative in Vance's inner circle understood the disposable nature of their role. But the sheer, unadulterated betrayal – Vance's swift severance of all contact, the silence that greeted his capture – had been a colder blow than any prison sentence.

"He's a snake," Spectre finally said, his voice a gravelly whisper, devoid of emotion. "He sheds his skin when it gets dirty." Sharma leaned forward, her gaze unwavering. "And you're covered in his dirt, Spectre. We have Vance. We have Sterling's data. But we need more. We need you to tell us about the operations. About the funding. About the others."

A mirthless chuckle escaped Spectre's lips. "The others," he echoed. "Vance liked to operate with a certain... flair. The Nightingale, he called it. A symbol of purity, he said. But it was just a cover." He paused, a shadow crossing his features. "The wooden bird. That was his signature, wasn't it? A little detail to make it seem like... I don't know. A lone wolf. A man with a message. He liked the narrative."

Miller exchanged a look with Sharma. The wooden bird. It had been found at several crime scenes, a bizarre, almost poetic touch that had baffled investigators. Vance, the master manipulator, had deliberately cultivated a false persona for his operatives. He wanted the world to believe these were the acts of rogue individuals, not the meticulously planned assassinations of a sophisticated criminal syndicate.

"So, the bird was Vance's idea?" Sharma pressed, her pen poised over her notepad. "Not yours?"

"Mine?" Spectre's lip curled. "I'm a tool. I execute. Vance builds the narrative. He's the architect of the fear. He would provide the operatives with the carvings. Sometimes they were given directly, sometimes they were found at the rendezvous point. A little reminder of who was pulling the strings. It was meant to instill terror, to create a sense of an unstoppable, unseen force. But it was all him. The meticulous planning, the resources, the disposal of... evidence."

He shifted in his seat, the cheap plastic creaking under his weight. "The funding," he continued, his voice picking up a rhythm, as if the dam had finally broken. "It came through shell corporations, just as Sterling's data suggests. But the flow was specific. Certain accounts were used for specific operations. The payments were made in tranches, often routed through intermediary countries with... lax financial oversight. Switzerland, Cyprus, the Caymans. Vance had his people. Lawyers, accountants, facilitators. They were the ones who ensured the money flowed like water, untraceable, clean."

"And the targets?" Miller asked, his voice carefully neutral. "Sterling. The journalist." He didn't need to name the journalist. They both knew who he meant: the investigative reporter who had been inches away from exposing Vance's operations.

Spectre's gaze met Miller's. There was no defiance, no remorse, only a chilling pragmatism. "Sterling was a loose end. He knew too much about the financial infrastructure. Vance was... meticulous about cleaning up messes. As for the journalist... that was a necessary silencing. A preemptive strike. Vance couldn't afford for his empire to be brought down by a few well-placed articles. He saw it as an investment. The cost of doing business."

Sharma scribbled furiously. "Who carried out those assassinations? You?"

Spectre gave a slow, deliberate nod. "Sterling was... efficient. The journalist was a bit more personal. Vance wanted to send a message. That journalist was digging too deep. He was becoming a liability. I was... contracted for the job." He hesitated, then added, "Vance chose me for it. He said I was the best. The one who could handle the... finesse required."

"Finesse?" Sharma's eyebrow arched. "Leaving behind a carved wooden bird is finesse?"

"The bird is a distraction," Spectre explained patiently, as if lecturing a novice. "It's theater. Vance understands the power of perception. The bird makes it look like a lone wolf, a vengeful soul acting on impulse. It diverts attention from the organized nature of the conspiracy. It makes us seem like... aberrations, not instruments of a deliberate plan. When in reality, Vance orchestrated every step. He selected the targets, he authorized the payments, he dictated the methodology."

He leaned back, a flicker of something akin to weariness in his eyes. "The operatives," he continued. "We were a curated group. Each with a specialty. Some were for close-quarters, some for long-range. Others were... better at infiltration. Vance vetted us carefully. He paid handsomely, but he also demanded absolute discretion and loyalty. Loyalty he clearly didn't extend to those he deemed expendable. Like me."

"Tell us about the funding for Sterling's death," Miller said, his voice cutting through Spectre's brief reverie. "How was it channeled? Who signed off on it?"

Spectre closed his eyes for a moment, as if accessing a vast, internal ledger. "There was a specific account, held by a holding company in Luxembourg. 'Aethelred Holdings.' Sounds innocuous, doesn't it? Vance used it for 'consulting fees.' Sterling was on Vance's payroll, in a way. Vance used him for information, but Sterling was becoming too... demanding. He started asking for more than Vance was willing to give. He threatened to go public with some of Vance's early dealings, before Nightingale was even fully formed. Vance couldn't allow that. Sterling's death was authorized through Aethelred. The payment went to... well, it went to an account controlled by 'The Serpent.'"

"The Serpent?" Sharma echoed, her pen freezing mid-stroke.

"Another operative," Spectre explained. "Specialized in... financial operations. He handled the movement of funds. He was a ghost in the system, able to create and dissolve accounts faster than any auditor could track. Vance trusted him implicitly with the money. The Serpent ensured the payments were made, anonymously, untraceably. He was Vance's financial shadow."

"And you know the Serpent's real name?" Miller's voice was sharp, a predatory edge to it. Spectre gave a wry smile. "That would be telling, wouldn't it? But I can tell you this: he's not as careful as he thinks he is. Vance made a mistake trusting him with so much control. The Serpent has his own ambitions."

"Ambitions that might be easier to achieve if Vance were out of the picture," Sharma observed.

"Precisely," Spectre confirmed. "Vance's abandonment of me has made me realize the fragility of my position. He's ruthless. He will sacrifice anyone to save himself. The Serpent knows this. He's probably already planning his own exit strategy."

Miller pressed on. "The journalist. How was that funded?"

"Similar process," Spectre replied. "A different shell company this time, registered in the British Virgin Islands. 'Phoenix Global Ventures.' A rather ironic name, given how Vance dealt with people who threatened to rise from the ashes of his past. The payment was made to... a separate operative. Someone Vance used for the more... direct interventions. A woman. 'The Weaver'."

"The Weaver?" Sharma's pen was a blur again.

"She's... an artist with poisons," Spectre said, a hint of professional respect in his tone, though devoid of admiration. "Very subtle. Very difficult to detect. Vance preferred her for targets that needed to disappear quietly, without a trace. The journalist's death was designed to look like a sudden illness. A heart attack, perhaps. The Weaver ensured it happened. The funding for her payment came from Phoenix Global Ventures. The order originated from Vance, of course. He always gave the final authorization."

He paused, his gaze drifting to the blank wall. "Vance didn't just hire killers. He cultivated an ecosystem of corruption. He had people who laundered the money, people who procured the materials, people who silenced witnesses, people who fabricated evidence. He built a machine, and we were all just cogs in it. But he was the engineer. He designed every gear, every lever."

"And the wooden bird," Miller interjected, bringing the conversation back to the initial point. "You're certain it was Vance's initiative?"

"Absolutely," Spectre confirmed, his voice firm. "He wanted the legend. He wanted the mystique. He believed it made his operation more... impactful. It created a narrative that served his purposes. It made him seem powerful, untouchable. But it was all a performance. A carefully staged play to hide the fact that he was just a very wealthy, very dangerous man laundering money and eliminating anyone who stood in his way. The bird was just another prop in his grand theatre of deception."

He met Miller's gaze again, and this time, there was a glint of something sharp, something calculating. "He used us. He manipulated us. He discarded me. Now, he'll find out that a discarded tool can be turned against its wielder." The silence in the room stretched, thick with unspoken implications. Spectre's testimony was the missing piece, the key that unlocked the elaborate puzzle Vance had so carefully constructed. The wooden bird, once a symbol of fear, was now becoming a symbol of Vance's undoing.

The courtroom air hung heavy, a palpable blend of anticipation and dread. Sunlight, filtered through the stained-glass windows of the old federal building, cast elongated, somber shadows across the polished mahogany of the witness stand. Michael Thorne, once a man accustomed to the hushed reverence of academic halls and the subtle power plays of clandestine operations, now found himself exposed, stripped bare under the unwavering glare of legal scrutiny. His tailored suit, a stark contrast to the grim surroundings, seemed to mock the gravity of his situation. He was a man caught in the undertow of Vance's machinations, a facilitator who had convinced himself he was merely a conduit, a dispassionate observer in a world of dangerous men. Now, the consequences of that passive complicity were about to be laid bare for all to see.

His testimony, painstakingly detailed and meticulously delivered, was a stark confession. Each word was a brick in the edifice of his own undoing, a somber accounting of his role as an informant and facilitator within Vance's sprawling syndicate. He spoke of encrypted communications, of laundered funds routed through labyrinthine offshore accounts, of the precise logistical support he had rendered for operations that he had compartmentalized as mere "business transactions." He described the coded language Vance employed, the subtle nuances of their interactions that now, in retrospect, reeked of premeditation and malice. He detailed the meetings, the discreet exchanges of information, the seemingly innocuous requests that had, in fact, paved the way for Thorne's participation in crimes of unimaginable scale.

He recounted the chilling pragmatism with which Vance operated, a man who viewed human lives as mere variables in his grand equation of profit and power. Thorne's narrative painted a portrait of Vance as a puppeteer, expertly manipulating his operatives, using their skills and their weaknesses to orchestrate a symphony of deceit and destruction. He spoke of the way he preyed upon Thorne's ambition and his intellectual vanity, convincing him that his involvement was a testament to his own brilliance, a recognition of his unique capacity for discretion and strategic thinking. Thorne had been so enamored with the perceived power, so blinded by the illusion of control, that he had failed to see the precipice upon which he stood.

The prosecution, led by the sharp and incisive Assistant U.S. Attorney Anya Sharma, meticulously pieced together Thorne's admissions. Sharma's questioning was not accusatory but probing, designed to elicit Thorne's voluntary cooperation and, in doing so, to solidify the case against the larger players in Vance's network. She guided Thorne through the intricate web of financial transactions, forcing him to confront the tangible impact of his actions. Thorne's descriptions of shell corporations – names like "Aethelred Holdings" and "Phoenix Global Ventures," once abstract entities in his ledgers, now resonated with the chilling weight of their true purpose. He detailed how these entities served as conduits for illegal funds, how they masked the illicit gains from arms trafficking, extortion, and, most damningly, from the orchestration of assassinations.

He admitted to facilitating the procurement of untraceable communication devices, to arranging the discreet acquisition of specialized surveillance equipment, and to providing intelligence that directly aided in the evasion of law enforcement. Thorne's voice, though strained, maintained a professional cadence as he detailed the technical aspects of his involvement, a chilling testament to his detachment from the human cost. He described the "deliverables" – encrypted files, coded transmissions, falsified shipping manifests – that he provided, each an essential cog in Vance's destructive machinery. He spoke of the fear he felt, a constant hum beneath the surface of his professional demeanor, a fear of Vance's retribution should he ever falter or attempt to withdraw. Yet, this fear had not been enough to deter him, not until the unraveling began, not until Spectre's capture and subsequent cooperation with the authorities.

As Thorne detailed the financial flows, the prosecution presented evidence of Thorne's own considerable enrichment. Bank statements, offshore account records, and luxury asset acquisitions, all meticulously documented, laid bare the financial incentives that had fueled Thorne's complicity. The contrast between his humble beginnings and his newfound wealth was stark, a visual indictment of his choices. He had been a man who craved intellectual validation and financial security, and Vance had offered him both, at a price he ultimately could not afford.

The presence of his father in the courtroom was a particularly agonizing element of the proceedings. Dr. Elias Thorne, a man of unimpeached integrity and a respected figure in the scientific community, sat in the front row, his face etched with a profound and weary sadness. He had always believed in his son's potential, had fostered his intellectual curiosity, and had never suspected the depths to which Michael had descended. Dr. Thorne's testimony, when he was called to the stand, was not about the specifics of the conspiracy but about his son's character, a character he believed had been corrupted by external forces. He spoke of Michael's early brilliance, his intellectual gifts, but also of a growing isolation, a subtle shift in his son's demeanor in the years leading up to his arrest. He described instances where Michael had become evasive, secretive, and financially unaccountable, behaviors that were entirely out of character.

"I... I never imagined," Dr. Thorne began, his voice struggling to maintained composure. "Michael was always so bright, so full of promise. We encouraged his thirst for knowledge, his desire to understand complex systems. But somewhere along the line... he lost his way. He became... entangled. I saw the change, the subtle withdrawal, the guardedness. I tried to reach him, but he pushed me away. He spoke of 'important work,' of 'contributing to something significant.' I thought he was involved in some high-level research, perhaps with government contracts. I never, in my wildest nightmares, conceived of... this." He gestured vaguely, encompassing the courtroom, the charges, the weight of the evidence. His paternal testimony, while intended to provide context, inadvertently underscored the devastating betrayal of trust, not only of society but of his own father.

The legal proceedings were, as anticipated, lengthy and arduous. The prosecution had to navigate the complexities of international law, unraveling the labyrinthine financial structures Vance had so expertly constructed. Proving intent and direct involvement in a conspiracy that spanned multiple jurisdictions, utilized anonymous digital currencies, and employed sophisticated obfuscation techniques was a monumental task. Each piece of evidence, each transfer of funds, each encrypted communication, had to be meticulously authenticated and presented in a manner that left no room for doubt. The defense, while acknowledging Thorne's role as a facilitator, attempted to portray him as a pawn, coerced into compliance by Vance's formidable power and influence. However, the sheer volume of evidence detailing Thorne's direct participation in facilitating illegal activities and his personal financial gains made such a defense increasingly untenable.

Thorne's cooperation, while instrumental, did not absolve him of responsibility. The leniency he received was a calculated risk, a pragmatic approach by the prosecution to dismantle Vance's empire from within. He was granted a reduced sentence for his full and truthful cooperation, a deal that came with its own set of invisible burdens – the constant threat of retaliation from Vance's remaining associates, the gnawing guilt of his past actions, and the irrevocably tarnished reputation he would carry for the rest of his life.

His sentencing was a somber affair. The judge, a stern woman with an unyielding gaze, acknowledged Thorne's cooperation but did not shy away from the severity of his crimes. She spoke of the corrosive impact of white-collar crime, of how individuals like Thorne, utilizing their intellect for illicit purposes, could inflict as much damage as any street-level criminal. She highlighted the erosion of trust in financial institutions and the destabilization of global markets that such conspiracies engendered. Thorne's sentence, while not the maximum penalty he could have faced, was substantial, reflecting the gravity of his complicity. He was ordered to serve a significant term in federal prison, with the possibility of parole contingent on continued cooperation and good behavior.

As the judge pronounced the sentence, Thorne's carefully constructed composure finally fractured. A flicker of raw fear, a profound sense of regret, and a dawning comprehension of the true cost of his choices washed over his face. He had gambled with his life, with his integrity, and with the trust of those who loved him, and he had lost. His future, once seemingly boundless, was now confined to the stark realities of a prison cell, a stark and enduring monument to his betrayal. The elaborate scheme that had once promised him power and prestige had ultimately led him to ruin, a testament to the immutable truth that no amount of cleverness or financial maneuvering could ultimately shield one from the consequences of their actions. He was no longer the facilitator, the strategist, the man of influence; he was merely Michael Thorne, a convicted felon, his fate sealed by the choices he had made in the shadow of Project Nightingale.

The gavel's final resounding thud echoed not just in the courtroom, but in the opulent boardrooms and sterile data centers that hummed with the pulse of global commerce. Michael Thorne's testimony, the meticulous unraveling of Project Nightingale, had been a detonation, and the fallout was a seismic event. The carefully constructed edifice of Vance's empire, built on a foundation of technological prowess and financial chicanery, had crumbled, but the debris threatened to bury more than just its architect. As the news spread like wildfire, a chilling realization dawned: Vance's ambition, his willingness to leverage advanced technology for unprecedented market manipulation, had been a harbinger of a new, terrifying era of financial warfare.

The immediate aftermath was a whirlwind of official pronouncements and urgent consultations. Governments, once largely complacent in the face of unchecked technological advancement in the financial sector, were jolted into a reactive posture. Regulatory bodies, previously characterized by slow, bureaucratic processes, found themselves under immense public pressure to act. Investigations, like a swarm of locusts, descended upon financial institutions and tech firms that had either knowingly or unknowingly profited from or facilitated the kind of practices that had underpinned Project Nightingale. The Securities and Exchange Commission (SEC) in the United States, the Financial Conduct Authority (FCA) in the United Kingdom, and their counterparts in the European Union and Asia, all launched parallel inquiries. These weren't mere audits; they were sweeping examinations of risk management protocols, data security measures, and the ethical frameworks governing high-frequency trading, algorithmic arbitrage, and the very algorithms that governed trillions of dollars in daily transactions.

The narrative that emerged from Thorne's confession, amplified by the subsequent evidence presented, was a stark exposé of how innovation could be weaponized. Project Nightingale hadn't just been about manipulating stock prices; it had been a blueprint for destabilizing entire economies, for creating artificial crises that could be exploited for immense personal gain. The sheer audacity of Vance's plan – to engineer a cascade of market crashes through sophisticated algorithmic warfare, to use the resulting panic to short-sell vast quantities of assets, and then to profit from the subsequent recovery, all while amassing a fortune – was a concept that sent shivers down the spines of seasoned financial analysts and central bankers alike. The averted disaster, the fact that Vance's plan had been detected and dismantled before its most devastating phase, was a fortunate twist of fate, but the existence of such a plan served as a potent, chilling reminder of the inherent vulnerabilities within the interconnected global financial system.

News outlets around the world, from the venerable Wall Street Journal and the Financial Times to the more sensationalist tabloids, dedicated extensive coverage to the unfolding scandal. Headlines screamed of "algorithmic assassinations" on the stock market, of "digital bandits" threatened global economic stability, and of the "ghost in the machine" that had nearly brought the world's financial order to its knees. The public, largely shielded from the intricate mechanics of modern finance, was given a stark, albeit simplified, glimpse into a world where code and capital intertwined with potentially catastrophic consequences. Analysts dissected Thorne's testimony, highlighting the sophisticated programming techniques Vance had employed, the ways he had exploited subtle market inefficiencies, and the sheer computational power required to execute such a grand, nefarious design. The technical jargon, once confined to academic papers and hushed conversations among quants, became fodder for mainstream discussion, underscoring the growing influence of technology on every facet of modern life, including the very foundations of wealth.

The investigations weren't limited to identifying wrongdoing; they were also about preventing future occurrences. This meant a profound reevaluation of how technology was integrated into financial markets. A crucial aspect of this was the scrutiny of "black box" trading algorithms. These complex systems, capable of executing trades in milliseconds, were often opaque even to their creators, making them prime candidates for unintended consequences or, as in Vance's case, deliberate malicious intent. Regulatory bodies began to push for greater transparency in algorithmic trading, demanding that firms not only understand but also be able to explain the decision-making processes of their automated trading systems. This led to a significant increase in investment in explainable AI (XAI) research within the financial sector, as companies scrambled to develop tools and methodologies that could illuminate the inner workings of their sophisticated algorithms.

Furthermore, the incident highlighted the porous nature of international financial regulation. Vance's network had operated across multiple jurisdictions, utilizing shell corporations, offshore accounts, and anonymized digital transactions to evade detection. This forced a new level of international cooperation between regulatory bodies. Agreements were brokered, information-sharing protocols were strengthened, and a global task force was established to track and combat technologically sophisticated financial crimes. The days of regulatory arbitrage, where criminals could exploit loopholes by moving their operations between less regulated jurisdictions, were numbered. The "Nightingale" incident served as a powerful catalyst for a more unified, globally coordinated approach to financial oversight.

The implications for the tech sector were equally profound. Companies that provided the infrastructure for high-speed trading, the cloud computing power, and the sophisticated software used in financial markets found themselves under a microscope. There was increased pressure on these companies to implement robust security measures and to conduct thorough due diligence on their clients, particularly those operating in the high-stakes world of finance. The concept of "responsible innovation" became a buzzword, urged tech companies to consider the potential societal impact of their creations, not just their market viability. This led to the development of new ethical guidelines for AI development and deployment, particularly in sectors with a significant public interest, such as finance and healthcare.

The incident also spurred a broader conversation about corporate responsibility. Vance, though a criminal mastermind, had operated through a network of legitimate businesses and complicit individuals. The fallout forced companies to examine their internal culture, their whistle-blower policies, and the ethical training of their employees. The idea that a company's ethical standing was as crucial as its financial performance gained traction. Companies that had previously prioritized profit above all else began to realize that in an era of unprecedented technological power, ethical conduct was not a luxury but a necessity for survival. The reputational damage that association with shady practices could inflict, as evidenced by the widespread condemnation of companies even tangentially linked to Vance's operations, was a powerful deterrent.

The potential for widespread economic disruption that Vance had so meticulously planned was ultimately averted, but the scare it provided was invaluable. It was a wake-up call, a stark reminder that the intricate systems humanity had built to facilitate economic growth could also be turned into instruments of destruction. The incident underscored the double-edged nature of technological progress. While advancements in computing power, artificial intelligence, and network infrastructure had revolutionized finance, making it faster, more efficient, and more accessible, they had also created new avenues for exploitation and systemic risk. The "Nightingale" threat, once a shadowy specter, was now a tangible, documented reality, and its exposure forced a global reckoning with the ethical implications of unchecked technological ambition.

The public trust in financial institutions, already fragile, was further tested. The revelation that insider trading or overt fraud could manipulate the markets not just, but by invisible algorithms operating at speeds beyond human comprehension, bred a new kind of anxiety. People began to question the fairness of the system, the integrity of the players, and the efficacy of the regulators meant to protect them. This erosion of trust was a significant, though less quantifiable, consequence of Project Nightingale's fallout. Rebuilding that trust would require more than just new regulations; it would necessitate a sustained commitment to transparency, accountability, and ethical conduct from all stakeholders in the financial ecosystem.

Moreover, the incident served to highlight the disproportionate power wielded by those who understood and could manipulate these complex technological systems. Michael Thorne, a brilliant mind ensnared by Vance's machinations, had been a key facilitator, a testament to how even non-violent intellectual contributions could have devastating real-world consequences. His role, and the subsequent investigations into others like him, illuminated the need for a more diverse range of expertise within regulatory bodies. The regulators themselves needed to evolve, to understand the cutting edge of technology, not just the established financial principles, to effectively police the new landscape. This led to increased recruitment of individuals with backgrounds in computer science, data analytics, and cybersecurity within government agencies tasked with financial oversight.

The exposure also had a ripple effect on the broader discussion of data privacy and security. Vance's ability to access and exploit vast amounts of financial data was a stark reminder of the growing power of data brokers and the potential for misuse. Calls for stronger data protection laws intensified, mirroring the concerns raised by privacy advocates in the wake of other major data breaches. The line between financial innovation and invasive data practices became increasingly blurred, demanding a more robust framework for managing and protecting personal and corporate financial information.

The long-term impact of Project Nightingale's fallout was not just about immediate reforms, but about a fundamental shift in perspective. The incident forced a global community to confront the reality that technological advancement, while offering immense benefits, also carried inherent risks that needed to be proactively managed. It moved the conversation from one of abstract theoretical possibilities to one of concrete, demonstrable threats. The world had been given a chilling glimpse into a future where sophisticated technology could be used to destabilize economies, and the experience left an indelible mark, shaping policy, influencing corporate behavior, and forever altering the landscape of global finance. The ghost in the machine had been revealed, and its presence demanded constant vigilance.

The gentle lapping of waves against the hull of the 'Serenity' had become a deceptively soothed soundtrack to a storm that had raged far beyond the ship's tranquil perimeter. For Miller, the rhythmic pulse of the ocean was a stark contrast to the frantic beats of his own heart that had pounded during the harrowing final days of Project Nightingale. Now, anchored in the quiet calm of retirement, he found himself adrift in a sea of reflection, the events of the cruise replaying with a clarity that was both unsettling and strangely invigorating. He had embarked on this voyage seeking respite, a quiet interlude after decades spent navigating the treacherous currents of law enforcement and corporate intrigue. Yet, destiny, it seemed, had a different itinerary.

The polished mahogany of his cabin, usually a sanctuary of peace, now felt like a confessional booth. He ran a hand over the smooth, cool surface, the tactile sensation grounding him amidst the swirling memories. He hadn't anticipated that the very elements he had sought to escape would punctuate his retirement: the sharp sting of betrayal, the intricate dance of deception, and the relentless pursuit of a justice that often felt like a horizon perpetually receding. He'd seen it all before, of course, the ugly underbelly of ambition, but to encounter it so intimately, so unexpectedly, on what was meant to be his final, peaceful odyssey, had been a brutal reminder that the past rarely stays buried.

The phantom echo of Vance's smug pronouncements, the icy glint in his eyes as he'd revealed the sheer, unadulterated audacity of Project Nightingale, still sent a shiver down Miller's spine. The man had wielded technology like a bludgeon, intent on shattering the very foundations of the global economy for personal gain. Miller had faced ruthless adversaries before, men driven by primal urges, but Vance's brand of villainy was calculated, detached, and utterly devoid of remorse. It was a testament to a world where intellect could be twisted into a weapon of mass destruction, a digital phantom capable of orchestrating chaos from the shadows.

And then there was Thorne. Michael Thorne. The name itself still carried a complex weight. Miller had seen the man's brilliance, the way his mind could dissect intricate problems and weave elegant solutions. He had also seen, with a growing sense of dread, how that brilliance had been co-opted, twisted by Vance's insidious influence. Thorne had been both a pawn and a key, a paradox Miller had grappled with throughout the investigation. He'd expected resistance, perhaps even outright hostility, from those caught in Vance's orbit. But the sheer duplicity, the performance Thorne had so masterfully enacted, had been a particularly bitter pill to swallow. It was a betrayal of a different kind, a perversion of trust, and it had tested Miller's own judgment more than he cared to admit. He had prided himself on his ability to read people, to see through the masks they wore, but Thorne had been a master of disguise, his motivations shrouded in layers of artifice.

Yet, amidst the disillusionment, there was a quiet gratitude that bloomed. Jenkins. The gruff, no-nonsense ex-detective, Miller's unlikely ally, had been a steadfast anchor in the tempest. Their initial professional acquaintance had blossomed into a grudging respect, and then into something akin to camaraderie. Jenkins, with his street smarts and unwavering moral compass, had been the perfect counterpoint to Miller's more analytical approach. He'd provided the boots on the ground, the quiet persistence that had chipped away at Vance's defenses, and the unwavering belief that justice, however elusive, was worth pursuing. Miller realized, with a pang of remorse for his initial skepticism, that without Jenkins's unwavering support, Project Nightingale might have remained a dark secret, its catastrophic potential unleashed upon an unsuspecting world. He owed the man a debt that could never truly be repaid.

And then there was the sheer, unadulterated terror of how close they had come. The intricate web Vance had spun, the algorithmic threads that had been poised to unravel global markets, was a nightmare made manifest. Miller had seen the simulations, the projected outcomes, the sheer devastation that was narrowly averted. It was a chilling testament to the power of unchecked technological ambition, a stark warning that the very tools designed to advance humanity could also be wielded to destroy it. He had spent his career fighting against tangible threats, against criminals who operated in the physical world. But Vance's threat had been ethereal, a ghost in the machine that could wreak havoc with the flick of a digital switch. The magnitude of what had been prevented, the sheer scale of the disaster that had been averted, left him feeling not triumphant, but profoundly weary.

The experience had also illuminated the blurred lines of his own past. He'd always believed in the inherent goodness of people, in the possibility of redemption, even for those who had strayed. But the cruise had stripped away those comforting illusions. He had seen how easily good intentions could be corrupted, how quickly loyalty could curdle into treachery, and how even the most innocent individuals could be swept up in a tide of malevolence. His own past, a tapestry woven with threads of ambition, duty, and the occasional compromise, felt suddenly more vulnerable, more susceptible to the very darkness he had fought so hard to combat. He found himself scrutinizing his own motivations, his own actions, searching for any hint of the same self-deception that had ensnared Thorne.

The irony of his situation was not lost on him. He, a man who had actively sought to escape the clutches of his former life, had been plunged headfirst back into its most dangerous currents. He had donned the mantle of retiree, seeking solace in the quiet routine of the mundane. But the events of the cruise had fanned into a flame the embers of his former self. He had discovered, to his own surprise, that retirement had not dulled his edge, but perhaps, had even sharpened it. The years had lent him a perspective, a wisdom, that had allowed him to navigate the treacherous waters of Project Nightingale with a clarity he might not have possessed in his younger days.

He remembered the hushed conversations with Jenkins, the late-night strategizing, the shared anxieties and the fleeting moments of triumph. They had been a peculiar pair, a retired detective and a disgruntled former operative, united by a common enemy and a shared desire to expose the truth. Miller realized that his skillset, honed over decades of investigation and analysis, had not atrophied with disuse. If anything, the break from the relentless pace of his former life had allowed him to approach the problem with a renewed vigor, a detached objectivity that had been crucial in unraveling Vance's complex scheme.

The memory of Thorne's confession, the choked words of regret, the desperate plea for understanding, still lingered. Miller had offered no absolution, no easy comfort. He had simply listened, his gaze steady, his silence a heavy indictment. He understood that Thorne was not solely a villain, but a victim of his own ambition, a cautionary tale of brilliance gone astray. Yet, understanding did not equate to forgiveness, and Miller knew that the path Thorne had chosen would be a long and arduous one, fraught with the consequences of his complicity.

The cruise, intended as an escape, had become an unexpected crucible. It had forced Miller to confront not only the machinations of a criminal mastermind but also the vulnerabilities within himself. He had faced the chilling reality of betrayal, the insidious nature of deception, and the profound weight of responsibility that even a retired man still carried. He had seen how easily the gears of progress could be twisted into instruments of destruction, how technological advancement, unchecked by ethical considerations, could pave the way for unimaginable devastation.

As the 'Serenity' continued its leisurely voyage, Miller found a strange sort of peace in the aftermath. The storm had passed, leaving behind a landscape irrevocably altered. He was weary, yes, but also strangely invigorated. He had been reminded that the fight against corruption, against the insidious creep of abuse of power, was never truly over. Vigilance, he understood, was not just a professional requirement; it was a fundamental human responsibility, an ongoing commitment to safeguarding the fragile balance of justice and integrity. Even on a peaceful vacation, even in the quiet twilight of retirement, the world demanded its guardians. And he, Miller, was still one of them. The taste of victory was sweet, but the knowledge of the ever-present threat was a bitter, necessary reminder. He knew, with a certainty that settled deep in his bones, that this would not be the last time the echoes of wrongdoing would interrupt his retirement. The world, it seemed, was full of unfinished business, and his particular brand of problem-solving was still very much in demand. He had left the battlefield, but the war, he now understood, was a perpetual one.

Chapter 14: Loose Ends and Lingering Doubts

The 'Serenity' had docked, its polished decks no longer reflecting the troubled skies of Miller's unexpected adventure, but the placid, almost mocking, calm of a world that had, for the most part, moved on. Yet, for Miller, the journey's end was merely a transition, a subtle shift in focus rather than a definitive conclusion. Vance was behind bars, his digital empire crumbling, and Spectre, the ghost of contracts and whispered threats, had traded his deadly precision for the sterile confines of an interrogation room, his silence a surprising, and perhaps more potent, weapon than his skill with a blade. The immediate threat, the cataclysmic unveiling of Project Nightingale, had been averted. But the chilling whispers that had echoed in the corridors of power, the hushed urgency that had permeated those final, frantic days, carried a persistent undertone of incompleteness.

Miller nursed his coffee, the strong, bitter brew a familiar anchor in the swirling currents of his thoughts. The formal debriefings were over, the necessary paperwork filed, and the official narrative was being meticulously crafted, smoothed over for public consumption.

His phone buzzed, a discreet vibration against the polished table of his study. The caller ID confirmed his suspicion: Agent Thorne, his FBI contact, a man who, despite the lingering complexities of his own entanglement with Vance, had proven himself to be a professional of integrity and unwavering dedication. "Miller," Thorne's voice was low, professional, devoid of any wasted syllables. "A moment of your time?"

"Always, Agent Thorne. What's on your mind?" Miller kept his tone measured, a practiced neutrality that belied the prickle of anticipation that ran through him.

"The Nightingale cleanup is proceeding as expected," Thorne began, a subtle pause before he continued. "Vance is singing, or at least, his digital footprints are. We've secured most of the immediate assets, the servers, the infrastructure. Spectre has been... cooperative. More than we anticipated, frankly. He's providing details, names. But that's where things get complicated."

Miller leaned forward, the coffee forgotten. "Complicated how?"

"We're seeing evidence of a distributed network, Miller. Not just Vance and his immediate inner circle. There are individuals, skilled individuals, who were instrumental in Nightingale's development and execution. Some may not have known the full scope, the ultimate goal, but they were undeniably complicit. They built the weapons, they maintained the systems, they facilitated the movement of capital, the encrypted communications. They are the 'loose ends' the debriefings can't quite account for."

The unease solidified into a tangible presence in the room. Miller had suspected as much. No operation of Nightingale's magnitude could be a solo act, or even the work of a handful of individuals. It required expertise, resources, and a degree of anonymity that spoke of a carefully constructed support system. "Who are we talking about, specifically?"

"That's the million-dollar question, isn't it?" Thorne sighed, a sound that conveyed the weariness of his profession. "Spectre's information is valuable, but it's fragmented. He was a specialist, brought in for a specific purpose. He saw what he needed to see, knew what he needed to know. He's given us names, project codenames, encrypted communication logs. We're cross-referencing, running profiles, but it's a painstaking process. We're talking about individuals who likely operated with a high degree of deniability, who understood the risks and took precautions to cover their tracks."

Miller visualized the complex, multi-faceted nature of Vance's enterprise. It wasn't a simple pyramid scheme; it was a hydra, its heads hidden, its tendrils reaching into various sectors. "Are we looking at programmers, financial analysts, perhaps even former intelligence assets?"

"All of the above, and more," Thorne confirmed. "There's a lead on a cybersecurity expert known only as 'Cipher.' Spectre mentioned him.

Said Cipher was the 'architect of the illusion,' someone who could make data disappear and reappear at will, who could create blind spots so vast they were invisible. We're also tracking financial conduits, individuals who moved untraceable funds, setting up shell corporations, laundering money through obscure offshore accounts. And there's a whisper of a former military logistics specialist, a man named Silas, who apparently facilitated the physical movement of certain... sensitive hardware before Vance went entirely digital."

Silas. The name resonated with a vague sense of unease, a phantom limb of a memory that Miller couldn't quite grasp. It was the kind of name that appeared in encrypted manifestos, in hushed conversations between shadowy figures. "And these individuals, they are still out there?"

"As far as we know," Thorne stated grimly. "Spectre's intel suggests they were largely unaware of Nightingale's ultimate catastrophic potential. Vance, it seems, was adept at compartmentalizing information, feeding each operative just enough to ensure their cooperation without revealing the full horrifying picture. They believed they were part of a sophisticated financial operation, perhaps something ethically dubious, but not the precipice of global economic collapse. That's our leverage, Miller. That's also our biggest concern. If they didn't know, they might be easily reactivated, or worse, they might have secondary plans, contingency protocols Vance put in place should his primary objective fail."

The implications were staggering. Vance might be neutralized, but the mechanisms of his destruction remained operational, scattered amongst individuals who, while perhaps not as ideologically driven as Vance, were still capable of immense damage. The fear was not just of them regrouping, but of them acting independently, their skills now untethered from Vance's direct control, potentially leading to unforeseen and unpredictable consequences. "So, the hunt is on," Miller murmured, the thrill of the chase, a sensation he'd sworn to leave behind, beginning to stir.

"The hunt is always on, Miller," Thorne replied, a hint of weariness in his tone. "But this is different. This isn't about a single mastermind. This is about dismantling a network, thread by painstaking thread. We need every piece of information we can get. Spectre's cooperation is a starting point, but it's a small crack in a very large wall. We suspect there are others Vance dealt with, operatives he used for specific tasks, individuals who might not even be on Spectre's radar. Think about the deep web communities, the dark net marketplaces where such services are traded. Vance wouldn't have limited himself to known entities."

Miller nodded, picturing the digital ether, a vast, lawless frontier where information was currency and anonymity was power. Vance, a master manipulator, would have navigated those spaces with an unnerving ease. "What kind of information are you lacking most?"

"Connections," Thorne said immediately. "Who vouched for 'Cipher'? Who facilitated Silas's movements? What were the communication protocols? We have encrypted messages, but the keys are elusive. We're running decryption algorithms around the clock, but it's like searching for a single grain of sand on an infinite beach. And then there's the possibility of a contingency plan. Vance was meticulous. He would have had backups. If the primary objective failed, what was Plan B? Was it simply a matter of regrouping, or was there a separate, independent trigger?"

The thought sent a fresh wave of cold through Miller. A secondary plan, activated without Vance's direct oversight, could be even more unpredictable, more chaotic. It was the ultimate manifestation of a conspiracy that refused to die, a ghost in the machine that could still wreak havoc. "And you believe these remaining operatives might be the key to understanding those contingencies?"

"Precisely," Thorne confirmed. "If they were privy to Vance's broader strategy, even in a limited capacity, they might hold the answers. Or, more concerningly, they might be the ones tasked with activating those contingencies. We need to identify them, understand their motivations, their loyalties. Are they ideological? Purely mercenary? Or are they simply cogs in a machine, unaware of the true purpose of their work?"

Miller recalled the unsettling ease with which Thorne had approached the investigation, the quiet determination that had bridged the gap between his former life and this clandestine pursuit. It was a testament to the dedication of individuals like Thorne, those who stood on the front lines of unseen battles. "What about your internal resources? Can you leverage your existing networks, your informants?"

"We're doing that," Thorne replied. "But many of these individuals are outside the traditional channels. They operate in the shadows, connected by digital threads and encrypted whispers. It's a different kind of intelligence gathering. It requires a different kind of understanding, a different kind of approach. That's why I'm calling you, Miller. Your experience with Vance, your insights into his methods... they are invaluable. You saw the larger picture when many of us were focused on the individual pieces. You understood the psychological underpinnings of his operation."

Miller felt a familiar weight settle upon his shoulders, a sense of responsibility that transcended his retirement. He had stepped away from the active pursuit of justice, but he had not relinquished his commitment to it. The events of the cruise had irrevocably tied him to this fight, to the ongoing struggle against those who would exploit the very fabric of society for their own twisted ends. "I'll review my notes from the 'Serenity' incident. Any correspondence, any conversations, anything that might shed light on potential associates or secondary operations. Vance was prone to... elaborate contingency planning. He saw himself as a chess master, always several moves ahead."

"That's what concerns us most," Thorne admitted. "He's captured, but his game might not be over. We need to anticipate his next move, even if he's no longer at the board. And if he's not directing it, then someone else is. Someone who might be more adept at staying in the shadows."

The implications were stark. The operatives, if they remained at large, represented not just a potential for renewed chaos but also a conduit to understanding Vance's deepest stratagems. They were the missing pieces of a puzzle that could very well prevent future catastrophes. Miller imagined the digital breadcrumbs Vance had left behind – encrypted messages, anonymized transactions, secure communication channels that bypassed conventional surveillance.

"Spectre mentioned specific operational codenames for some of these individuals, didn't he?" Miller prompted, his mind already sifting through the fragments of information he possessed. "Something about 'Project Chimera' and 'Project Midas'?"

"Correct," Thorne confirmed. "Chimera appears to be related to the cybersecurity aspect – likely Cipher's domain. Midas seems to point towards the financial operations. We believe there might be multiple individuals involved under the Midas umbrella, handling different facets of the financial manipulation. It's a broad term, which suggests a wider network, perhaps less centralized than Chimera."

Miller closed his eyes, picturing the elaborate facade Vance had constructed. It was a world built on illusion, on carefully curated perceptions. The operatives were not just technicians or financiers; they were architects of deception, skilled in the art of misdirection. Their very anonymity was their greatest asset, and their greatest vulnerability. "And Silas? Where does he fit into this?"

"Spectre's information on Silas is the most vague," Thorne said, a note of frustration entering his voice. "He was a ghost, even to Spectre. A facilitator of physical movement. Spectre only encountered him once, during a 'transfer' of encrypted hardware. He described Silas as taciturn, efficient, and utterly unremarkable. The kind of man who could disappear into a crowd. We suspect he's retired, or operating under a new identity, having completed his contracted tasks for Vance."

The idea of retired operatives, of individuals who had served their purpose and melted back into society, was a chilling one. They were walking dormant threats, capable of being reawakened by a simple signal, a hidden message, or the lure of further illicit gain. The thought of them regrouping, even without Vance's direct command, was a persistent specter that haunted the edges of the investigation.

"We're also looking into potential links to black market intelligence brokers," Thorne continued, his voice low. "Vance wasn't just building technology; he was acquiring information. He needed data on market vulnerabilities, on political instability, on key individuals he could exploit or manipulate. It's possible some of these operatives were recruited through such channels, further obscuring their identities and their true allegiances."

Miller leaned back in his chair, the silence of his study amplifying the enormity of the task. It wasn't just about apprehending a few more criminals; it was about unraveling a complex, decentralized conspiracy that had the potential to resurface in unexpected ways. The victory over Vance felt less like a decisive win and more like a temporary reprieve. The threat, though diminished, was not extinguished. It had merely fragmented, scattering its dangerous components like seeds in the wind.

"The fear of them regrouping is valid, Agent Thorne," Miller stated, his voice carrying the weight of experience. "Vance was meticulous. If he anticipated failure, he would have had protocols in place. These individuals, even if unaware of the full scope, are now potentially exposed. They know enough to be dangerous, and they possess skills that are in high demand in the underworld. They might seek out new patrons, or worse, they might act independently to salvage Vance's legacy, or even to protect themselves."

"Exactly. And if they start activating secondary plans, or attempting to reclaim lost assets, the domino effect could be catastrophic, even without Vance's direct oversight. We need to get ahead of that. We need to understand who these people are, where they are, and what their capabilities are. Spectre's cooperation is a start, but it's a sliver of light in a vast darkness."

Miller ran a hand over his chin, the familiar sensation of a burgeoning investigation stirring within him. He had sought retirement, a quiet harbor. But the currents of the world, it seemed, had a way of pulling him back into the fray. The loose ends of Project Nightingale were a potential threat to the fragile stability he had helped to restore. "I'll dedicate some time to going through my records, Agent Thorne. Every encrypted message, every coded phrase, every vague mention of a potential associate. Vance's ambition was boundless, and his paranoia was equally so. There must be breadcrumbs, however faint, that lead to these remaining operatives."

"That would be invaluable, Miller," Thorne said, his voice laced with a genuine gratitude that transcended their professional relationship. "The more we know, the better our chances of preventing a second act. We can't afford to let Nightingale's tendrils continue to spread."

The conversation ended, leaving Miller in the quiet contemplation of his study. The coffee had gone cold. The tranquil silence of his retirement was now punctuated by the hum of a network still at large, a constellation of hidden threats waiting for a signal, or perhaps, for an opportunity. The world had been spared a digital apocalypse, but the architects of that potential disaster were still out there, their skills honed, their knowledge compartmentalized, and their true intentions a chilling enigma. The hunt for the remaining operatives of Project Nightingale had just begun, and Miller, despite his intentions, found himself once again drawn into its dangerous embrace. The lingering doubt was not about Vance's capture, but about the true extent of his reach, and the formidable challenge of untangling a conspiracy that refused to die. The embers of Project Nightingale, he suspected, were still smoldering, waiting for the right wind to ignite them anew.

Jenkins's future, a landscape once as clearly defined as the polished chrome of a FBI precinct desk, now felt like a shifting terrain, its contours blurred by the unexpected gravity of Project Nightingale. The accolades had been swift and, in some circles, effusive. Her superiors, initially skeptical of her relentless pursuit of fragmented digital clues aboard the 'Serenity,' now spoke of her keen intellect and unwavering tenacity in hushed, admired tones. Miller, the enigmatic consultant whose presence had been both a catalyst and a confounding element in the investigation, had been particularly vocal in his praise, a quiet endorsement that carried significant weight. He had seen her navigate the labyrinthine corridors of Vance's digital empire, witnessed her ability to dissect complex code with an almost intuitive grace, and recognized the steely resolve that had pushed her past exhaustion and doubt.

Yet, beneath the veneer of commendations and the promise of accelerated career progression, a subtle tension had begun to coil within the bureaucratic heart of the FBI. Project Nightingale, while averted in its catastrophic manifestation, had exposed vulnerabilities that reached into the highest echelons of both government and industry. The corporate titans who had passively, or perhaps actively, benefited from Vance's machinations were now facing intense scrutiny. Their lobbyists were working overtime, their whispers echoing in the marbled halls of power, attempting to sanitize the narrative, to compartmentalize the damage, and, most importantly, to shield themselves from culpability. In this charged atmosphere, Jenkins, the agent who had dared to shine a harsh light on these uncomfortable truths, found herself walking a tightrope.

She sat in her sparsely decorated office, the late afternoon sun casting long shadows across her desk, illuminating the dust motes dancing in the air. The 'Serenity' incident had been a crucible, forging her into something more than just another agent in a sprawling federal agency. It had been a baptism by fire, a brutal education in the insidious nature of modern crime. Vance was behind bars, a digital ghost exorcised, but the network he had commanded, the insidious web of complicity and specialized expertise, remained largely intact, a smoldering ember that threatened to reignite. Thorne had emphasized this point repeatedly in their recent conversations, his frustration palpable even through the sterile medium of their encrypted calls.

Jenkins traced the rim of her coffee mug, the ceramic cool against her fingertips. Her initial impulse, after the immediate crisis had been averted, had been to dive headfirst into the 'loose ends' Thorne had spoken of. She felt a primal need to track down Cipher, to understand Silas's role, to unravel the financial machinations of Midas. This was where her skills, honed through years of painstaking investigation and an innate understanding of digital forensics, were most valuable. This was the work that truly ignited her professional spirit.

But the political realities were a stark counterpoint to her investigative zeal. Whispers circulated about reassigned cases, about agents whose overzealousness had been deemed 'unnecessary' in the delicate political dance that followed a major crisis. Jenkins had caught the averted glances from some of her colleagues, the subtle shifts in tone from superiors who were suddenly more interested in her 'long-term career development' than her immediate operational effectiveness. The commendations felt less like genuine praise and more like a strategic maneuver, a way to acknowledge her contribution without necessarily endorsing her methods or her continued pursuit of the Nightingale network.

Miller's voice, when he had called a few days prior, had been a welcome balm. He hadn't delved into the political minutiae, but he had understood the underlying currents. "They're trying to control the narrative, Anna," he'd said, his tone measured but firm. "And you are a disruption to that control. But disruption is often necessary for true justice. Don't let them box you in. Your insights into Nightingale are unique. They need you, even if they're not entirely comfortable admitting it."

His words had resonated deeply. Miller, a man who had operated outside the strictures of any formal organization for much of his life, possessed an uncanny understanding of power dynamics. He recognized that Jenkins's contributions had gone beyond simply following orders; she had seen the bigger picture, had connected the dots that others had overlooked, and had become an indispensable asset in understanding the true scope of Vance's ambition.

She considered the options laid out before her. A promotion, perhaps, to a desk job, overseeing investigations rather than conducting them. A role in internal affairs, ensuring compliance and preventing future breaches – a job that felt like a punishment for her success. Or, the path that tugged at her imagination, a path less traveled, a path she'd begun to envision during those tense days on the 'Serenity.'

A specialized unit. That was the seed planted by Miller's encouragement and nurtured by her own burgeoning understanding of the evolving threat landscape. A unit dedicated to the intersection of corporate malfeasance and sophisticated cybercrime. It wasn't a concept that currently existed within the FBI's established structure, not in a cohesive, proactive form. There were divisions that handled cybercrime, others that dealt with white-collar fraud, but none that truly bridged the gap, none that understood how these two seemingly disparate worlds were increasingly merging to create threats of unparalleled complexity and reach.

Jenkins leaned back, closing her eyes, and let the vision unfold. She saw a team composed of individuals like herself and Miller, individuals who understood both the digital realm and the human element of crime. Agents with a deep understanding of coding languages, network infrastructure, and data encryption, but also with the investigative acumen to unmask the human actors behind the digital masks. They would be equipped with cutting-edge technology, granted a degree of autonomy to pursue leads that might fall outside traditional jurisdictional boundaries, and empowered to proactively identify and neutralize emerging threats before they could fully materialize.

The experience on the 'Serenity' had been a masterclass in this new form of criminality. Vance hadn't just been a hacker; he had been a strategist, a manipulator of markets and minds, a puppet master who had leveraged technology to achieve goals that transcended simple financial gain. His network had involved individuals with diverse skill sets – the anonymous Cipher, the phantom logistics expert Silas, the shadowy financial architects. These were not the criminals of old, confined to brick-and-mortar operations. They were amorphous, elusive, operating in the intangible space of the digital ether.

Jenkins opened her eyes, a determined glint in them. She knew that proposing such a unit would be a formidable undertaking. It would require navigating bureaucratic hurdles, securing funding, and convincing skeptical leadership of its necessity. There would be resistance, undoubtedly. Some would see it as a duplication of existing efforts, others as a risky experiment. But the alternative, she realized, was to remain reactive, to continue playing catch-up with adversaries who were already operating on a different plane.

She picked up her phone and dialed Thorne. He answered on the first ring, his voice a familiar blend of weariness and professional focus. "Jenkins," he said, his voice low. "Good to hear from you. Anything new on the Nightingale loose ends?"

"Not directly, Agent Thorne," she replied, her voice steady. "But I've been thinking. About the future. About how we handle threats like Nightingale going forward." A beat of silence, then Thorne's voice, softer now. "Go on."

"Vance was... a symptom, wasn't he? A particularly virulent one, but still a symptom of a larger disease. The lines between corporate espionage, sophisticated financial crime, and nation-state level cyberattacks are blurring. We're seeing it happen more and more. And our current structures... they're not designed for this kind of multi-faceted threat."

Thorne exhaled slowly. "You're not wrong, Jenkins. We're fighting a war with outdated weapons sometimes. We're good at responding, at cleaning up the mess. But preventing it... that's a different ballgame. And a much harder one."

"Exactly," Jenkins affirmed. "Which is why I wanted to talk to you. I've been thinking about a specialized unit. Something proactive. A team that focuses on the nexus of corporate power and cybercrime. People who understand both the code and the boardroom. People who can anticipate these kinds of threats, not just react to them."

There was a long pause on Thorne's end, and Jenkins could almost hear the gears turning in his mind. He understood the implications of her proposal, the potential it held, and the political complexities that would inevitably arise.

"That's... ambitious, Jenkins," Thorne finally said, his tone measured. "And necessary. You saw it firsthand. You saw how Vance operated, how he leveraged different skill sets, how he hid in plain sight. You, of all people, understand what's needed."

"Miller agrees," she added, a small smile touching her lips. "He thinks it's vital. He said that after Nightingale, we can't afford to go back to the old ways."

"Miller usually has a good read on these things," Thorne conceded. "Look, Jenkins, I can't make any promises. The bureaucracy is a beast. But I can champion this. I can make sure your proposal gets heard. Your work on Nightingale... it's earned you that much. You've shown us what's possible when you're given the latitude to think outside the box. You've shown us the future, even if it's a future some people are uncomfortable with."

Jenkins felt a surge of renewed hope. It wasn't a guarantee, not by any stretch of the imagination. There would be battles to fight, alliances to forge, and arguments to win. But Thorne's endorsement, coupled with Miller's quiet validation, was a powerful start. She had stepped onto the 'Serenity' as a dedicated FBI agent, eager to uphold the law. She was leaving it, and the aftermath of Project Nightingale, with a vision for how law enforcement needed to evolve. The loose ends of Vance's operation were still out there, a testament to the evolving nature of crime. But Jenkins was beginning to see a path forward, a way to ensure that the next time such a threat emerged, the FBI would be not just ready to respond, but equipped to prevent it. Her future, once uncertain, was starting to take shape, a testament to her resilience and her unwavering commitment to staying ahead of the curve.

Dr. Aris Thorne sat in his study, the room bathed in the sepia tones of a dying afternoon. The silence, once a comforting companion during his research, now felt heavy, laden with unspoken regrets and the phantom echoes of his son's voice. Sterling. The name itself was a wound that refused to close, a constant reminder of the choices made, the trust shattered, and the life so brutally extinguished. The events surrounding Project Nightingale, the chilling revelation of Sterling's complicity, and the subsequent, tragic culmination of Vance's machinations had irrevocably altered the course of Thorne's life. The intellectual curiosity that had once driven his work now felt hollow, overshadowed by the profound, visceral understanding of how easily knowledge could be twisted, how readily integrity could be compromised.

He ran a hand over the worn leather of his armchair, the familiar texture a stark contrast to the volatile digital landscapes he had once navigated with such academic detachment. He had spent decades immersed in the intricate workings of scientific discovery, in the pursuit of knowledge for its own sake. He had believed, perhaps naively, that the inherent good of progress would always outweigh the potential for its misuse. Sterling's betrayal, however, had ripped away that illusion, exposing the dark underbelly of ambition and the terrifying ease with which even the most brilliant minds could be corrupted. It was a lesson learned not in a laboratory, but in the harsh, unforgiving arena of real-world consequences, a lesson etched into his soul by the blood spilled and the trust annihilated.

The sheer scale of Vance's operation, its insidious reach into legitimate corporate structures and its exploitation of Elias Thorne's own research, had been a brutal awakening. Thorne had always understood the power of information, the way it could shape economies, influence governments, and alter the course of history. But he had never truly grasped, until now, the devastating impact of hidden truths, of the narratives deliberately suppressed or manipulated to serve nefarious ends. He had seen how Vance, with Sterling's unwitting, then complicit, assistance, had weaponized data, twisting scientific advancement into a tool of control and chaos. The concept of history as a living, breathing entity, its past profoundly shaping the present, had moved from an abstract philosophical notion to a stark, personal reality. The secrets buried, the compromises made, the ethical lines crossed – they didn't simply disappear. They festered, they metastasized, and eventually, they erupted, often with catastrophic force.

He looked at the framed photograph on his desk: Sterling, younger, his eyes alight with an unburdened curiosity, a mirror of the passion Thorne himself had once felt so keenly. The contrast between that boy and the man who had aided Vance was a chasm too wide to bridge. The pain was a physical ache, a constant pressure behind his eyes. Yet, alongside the grief and the anger, a new resolve was solidifying. It was a quiet determination, born not of a desire for vengeance, but of a profound need to reclaim the integrity that had been so brutally violated. He could not undo the past, could not bring Sterling back, nor could he erase the damage inflicted. But he could, he realized, dedicate the rest of his life to ensuring that such betrayals of trust, such perversions of knowledge, were less likely to occur in the future.

His thoughts turned to the journalists, the whistleblowers, the individuals who, like himself in his own way, had striven to uncover the truth, often at immense personal cost. He had seen their courage firsthand, the risks they took to bring hidden information into the light. He had read their reports, heard their pleas for justice, and now understood the precariousness of their position. They were the first line of defense against the very forces that had consumed his son and threatened the world. And they were often under-resourced, under-protected, and utterly alone in their fight.

A plan formed, a vision that coalesced from the ashes of his personal tragedy. He would establish a foundation, a beacon of support for those who dared to speak truth to power. It would be named in Sterling's honor, not for the son who had faltered, but for the ideal he had once represented–the pursuit of knowledge, the yearning for understanding, the inherent human drive to uncover what is hidden. This foundation would provide financial aid, legal support, and a haven for journalists and whistleblowers who found themselves targeted, threatened, or ostracized for their integrity. It would be a tangible manifestation of his commitment to safeguarding the principles Sterling had so tragically betrayed.

He envisioned a network, a community of individuals dedicated to the ethical dissemination of information. They would be equipped to investigate, to corroborate, and to publish, with the assurance that their efforts were supported, not just morally, but practically. The foundation would also play a crucial role in fostering awareness, educating the public about the importance of transparency and the dangers of unchecked power, particularly when cloaked in the guise of progress. He would leverage his own considerable influence, the respect he had earned within academic and scientific circles, to lend credibility and weight to this new endeavor.

The concept of whistleblowing awareness took on an additional dimension for Thorne. It wasn't merely about exposing wrongdoing; it was about cultivating a culture where such exposures were not only possible but actively encouraged and protected. He recognized that history was replete with instances where critical truths had been buried, where the warnings of insightful individuals had been ignored, leading to avoidable disasters. His own son's story was a stark modern testament to this enduring phenomenon. Sterling, despite his youthful idealism, had been drawn into a vortex of deceit, his ethical compass spinning wildly until it finally shattered. Thorne believed that by empowering those who chose the hard path of revelation, he could help prevent future generations from suffering similar fates.

He outlined the operational structure of the foundation. It would require meticulous planning, significant capital, and a dedicated team. He knew he couldn't do it alone. He would need legal experts, financial advisors, and individuals with a deep understanding of investigative journalism and the legal frameworks surrounding whistleblowing. He would seek allies, individuals who shared his vision and possessed the skills to bring it to fruition. The irony was not lost on him: he, who had once been so guarded and solitary in his research, was now driven to build something collaborative, something that thrived on shared purpose and collective action.

His personal tragedy had become a lens through which he viewed the world with a newfound clarity. He saw the intricate web of connections between disparate events, the way a single act of corruption could ripple outwards, affecting countless lives. He understood that the integrity of information was not a theoretical construct but a vital necessity for the functioning of a just society. The clandestine dealings that had characterized Vance's operation, the manipulation of markets and public perception, all stemmed from a deliberate obfuscation of truth. Thorne's mission was to become an agent of illumination, to shine a light on those dark corners where deception thrived.

He imagined the foundation's early projects: funding an investigative team looking into the environmental impact of a powerful corporation, supporting a journalist pursuing a story about political corruption, providing legal counsel to a former employee brave enough to expose unethical practices within their company. These were the kinds of actions that could, over time, shift the balance of power, that could hold those who operated in secrecy accountable. It was a long game, he knew, a marathon rather than a sprint, but the stakes were too high for him to do anything less.

The personal toll of Sterling's actions weighed heavily, but Thorne was determined not to let it paralyze him. Instead, he would use it as fuel. He would channel the pain, the anger, and the profound sense of loss into a constructive force for change. The memory of his son would not be a monument to failure, but a testament to the enduring human capacity for both great darkness and profound redemption, a redemption Thorne intended to forge through his own actions.

He began to draft a mission statement for the foundation, his hand steady as he wrote. The words flowed, a testament to years of repressed grief and a nascent hope. He would advocate for greater legal protections for whistleblowers, for more robust investigative journalism, and for a societal shift towards valuing transparency above all else. He would champion the idea that exposing corruption was not an act of betrayal, but an act of profound civic duty.

The late afternoon sun dipped below the horizon, casting long, dramatic shadows across the study. Dr. Aris Thorne remained at his desk, the glow of his desk lamp illuminating the determined set of his jaw. The pain was still there, a dull ache in his chest, but it was no longer the dominant force. It was now a quiet undercurrent, a reminder of the stakes involved. He had lost his son to the shadows, but in their stark illumination, he had found a new purpose. He would dedicate his remaining years to ensuring that the truths so desperately hidden by men like Vance, truths that had cost him so dearly, would have a voice, a champion, and a future. His personal tragedy was transforming into a powerful catalyst, igniting a passion for justice and a commitment to an open, informed world. The legacy of Elias Thorne's research had been corrupted; the legacy of Sterling Thorne, the son he had known and loved, and the ideals he had once embodied, would now be salvaged and amplified through a mission dedicated to the relentless pursuit of truth.

The discovery had been almost accidental, a tangential thread pulled from the vast, tangled tapestry of Vance's operation. Aris Thorne, pouring over financial records and intercepted communications, had initially dismissed the recurring motif of a small, intricately carved wooden bird. It appeared in coded messages, subtly incorporated into innocuous shipping manifests, and even as a peculiar watermark on certain anonymous correspondence. At first, he'd categorized it as a personal affectation of Vance's, a peculiar vanity project of a man who seemed to collect eccentricities as readily as he amassed illicit fortunes. But the sheer ubiquity of the symbol, its persistent reappearance across disparate data streams, had begun to gnaw at him, a persistent itch of the intellect he couldn't ignore.

His initial inquiries, conducted through discreet channels he still maintained from his previous life, yielded little. The bird was too common, too generic a symbol to pinpoint. Yet, the specificity of its inclusion in Vance's clandestine activities suggested a meaning far beyond mere decoration. It was a signature, a quiet declaration of presence, a breadcrumb left in the digital wilderness. Thorne enlisted the help of Anya Sharma, the tenacious investigative journalist whose own pursuit of Vance had nearly cost her everything. Anya, with her unparalleled knack for connecting disparate pieces of information and her deep network of informants, became an invaluable asset. She recognized the pattern not as a personal quirk, but as a deliberate, coded signal.

"It's not just any bird, Aris," Anya had explained during one of their hushed meetings in a nondescript café, the clatter of porcelain and murmur of conversations providing a thin veil of normalcy. "The style, the wood... it's too distinctive for a random flourish. I've seen similar carvings before, in articles about specialized artisan communities. They're often highly localized."

Anya's research led them down a rabbit hole of cultural anthropology and obscure maritime trade routes. She scoured databases of traditional crafts, consulted with experts in indigenous art forms, and even reached out to expatriate communities who might recognize the specific aesthetic. The breakthrough came from an unlikely source: an aging curator of Oceanic art, living in quiet retirement on the coast of Maine. He identified the carving style with a remarkable degree of certainty.

"That," the curator had stated, his voice raspy with age and disuse, pointing to a digital image Thorne had sent, "is the work of the artisans from the Manu archipelago. A small, rather isolated chain of islands in the South Pacific. They're known for their intricate woodcarving, particularly their talismans."

The Manu archipelago. The name itself conjured images of turquoise waters, dense rainforests, and a culture largely untouched by the relentless march of global commerce. Aris Thorne, who had spent his life dissecting the intricate mechanisms of advanced technology, found himself drawn to the ancient traditions of a people who carved their hopes and fears into wood. The curator explained that these wooden birds, often carved from a specific type of dark, resilient hardwood, were traditionally considered good luck charms. They were symbols of protection, meant to ward off ill fortune and to guide travelers safely through treacherous waters. The artisans, he explained, often imbued them with specific meanings, passing down the craft through generations.

"The style you showed me," the curator continued, his eyes twinkling with the spark of forgotten knowledge, "the subtle curvature of the wings, the precise angle of the beak... that iteration, it signifies exclusivity. Certain families or guilds used it to denote their members, a private mark of belonging. Almost like a secret handshake, but carved in wood."

This was the key. Vance, the man who dealt in secrets and traded in shadows, had found a way to weave his clandestine network into the very fabric of a remote, traditional culture. He hadn't merely bought off corrupt officials or bribed his way through international ports. He had tapped into something far older, far more subtle. The wooden bird, this innocuous charm meant to bring good fortune, had been co-opted by Vance and his associates. It had become a marker, a quiet signal for his operatives, a discreet symbol of affiliation.

The implications were staggering. It wasn't just about stolen technology or financial malfeasance; Vance's reach extended into the most unexpected corners of the globe, exploiting the unique traditions and insular cultures of places that most of the world had long forgotten. He had turned a symbol of protection into a chilling emblem of death, a harbinger of the illicit activities that followed in its wake. Each carved bird found in a shipping container, tucked away in a hidden compartment, or passed between individuals, was a testament to Vance's ability to adapt and to infiltrate, to transform the sacred into the profane for his own mercenary ends.

The discovery provided Aris with a tangible link, a physical manifestation of the vast, amorphous entity that Vance commanded. It wasn't just a collection of shell corporations and offshore accounts anymore. It was a network, intricate and far-reaching, with tendrils reaching into the very heart of artisanal traditions. These islands, shrouded in their insular culture, had become unwitting conduits for Vance's criminal enterprise. The artisans, likely unaware of the true nature of the transactions, were simply fulfilling orders, carving their creations for an unseen buyer. But to Vance, these carvings were more than just commodities; they were markers of loyalty, subtle declarations of membership in his exclusive, and deadly, inner circle.

Anya, with her characteristic pragmatism, was already formulating new lines of inquiry. "If he's using these islands as a hub, or at least sourcing these markers from there, there's a good chance there are other connections. Shipping routes, local intermediaries, maybe even safe houses. These small communities often have strong family ties. If one person is compromised, it's likely others are too."

The idea of Vance operating in such a seemingly peaceful and remote setting was a chilling paradox. The idyllic image of the South Pacific was a stark contrast to the ruthless machinations of Vance's empire. Yet, it underscored Vance's profound understanding of human nature and his ability to exploit it. He preyed on economic vulnerability, on the desire for financial security, and on the simple act of artistry. The artisans of Manu were likely paid handsomely for their carvings, their labor transformed into a crucial piece of Vance's global puzzle.

Thorne imagined the scene: a grizzled fisherman, his hands calloused from years of hauling nets, carefully carving a bird with the same skill his grandfather had used to craft fishing lures. He'd be told it was for a special order, a unique commission for a collector. He'd never know that his creation would soon find its way onto a container ship bound for a shadowy destination, a silent testament to a criminal's reach, a symbol that, in Vance's hands, had been perverted from a charm of good fortune to a harbinger of ill-intent.

The wooden bird, once a curious anomaly, had become a critical piece of the puzzle. It was no longer just a symbol; it was a gateway, a potential point of entry into Vance's global network. Each discovery of such a carving would be a confirmation of his operatives' presence, a subtle alarm bell signaling Vance's involvement. Anya and Thorne began to compile a database of every instance the bird had been found, meticulously cross-referencing dates, locations, and associated individuals. They were building a map, not of continents and oceans, but of Vance's hidden pathways, of the clandestine routes he had established to move his illicit goods and information across the globe.

The remote islands of Manu, once a sanctuary of tradition, had been unknowingly drawn into the dark underbelly of global crime. The wooden bird, a testament to the skill and artistry of its creators, had been twisted into a chilling symbol of Vance's power and reach. For Aris Thorne, it was another painful reminder of how easily even the most innocent aspects of human endeavor could be corrupted, how quickly beauty and tradition could be co-opted by darkness. But it also offered a glimmer of hope. Vance's elaborate facade, built on layers of deception and coded signals, was starting to show cracks. And the humble wooden bird, a simple charm from a forgotten corner of the world, was proving to be a surprisingly potent key to unlocking those secrets. The investigation was far from over, but with each revelation, Thorne felt a renewed sense of purpose, the pursuit of justice gaining momentum, carried on the wings of a tiny, carved bird. He knew that Vance's network was extensive, a Hydra with countless heads, but he was determined to sever them one by one, starting with the most subtle, the most unexpected, and perhaps, the most revealing. The wooden bird was more than just a clue; it was a promise, a testament to the fact that even in the most isolated of places, the truth, however long it took, would eventually surface.

The silence of his coastal cottage, once a balm to his weary soul, now felt... porous. Miller sat on his porch, the salty breeze doing little to dissipate the persistent chill that had settled in his bones. The sun, a brilliant orb against the azure sky, seemed to mock the internal twilight he'd been inhabiting since Vance's downfall. Project Nightingale was officially a ghost, a redacted file in the annals of covert operations, and Vance himself was in a maximum-security facility, his empire reduced to scattered ashes. Yet, the victory felt hollow, incomplete.

He ran a hand over the smooth, sun-warmed wood of the porch railing, the grains familiar beneath his touch. It was the sheer, terrifying proximity of Vance's success that gnawed at him. The intricate web Vance had woven, the subtle infiltration, the near-undetectable manipulation of systems and people – it had been a masterclass in corruption, a chilling testament to how easily the foundations of order could be undermined from within. Miller had always known that darkness existed, that the world was a precarious balance between light and shadow, but Nightingale had been a stark, visceral confrontation. It had revealed the depth of that shadow, the insidious ways it could seep into every facet of society, from the highest echelons of power to the quietest, most isolated artisan communities.

He thought of the carved wooden bird, the unlikely symbol that had been Anya and Aris's key. A simple charm, a piece of art meant to bring good fortune, twisted into a clandestine marker for a global criminal enterprise. The artisans, likely unaware of the true purpose of their craft, had been unwitting participants in Vance's scheme. It was this thought, more than anything, that kept the unease festering. Vance was a symptom, not the disease. His methods, his audacity, his ability to exploit the very fabric of human trust and tradition – these were the elements that truly frightened Miller.

Were there other architects of similar designs currently at work? Were other "Nightingales," perhaps even more sophisticated, already taking flight in the hidden corners of the world? The thought was a cold knot in his stomach. He had believed, perhaps naively, that dismantling Vance's operation would create a significant deterrent, a loud enough alarm bell to shake the foundations of other clandestine networks. But the insidious nature of corruption was its adaptability. It didn't die; it morphed, it evolved, it found new hosts.

His retirement, a hard-won peace, now felt like a precarious perch. The world hadn't changed with Vance's capture. The corruptible still sought to corrupt, the money-driven still sought to profit, and the powerful still sought to exert control through illicit means. Vance had been a particularly audacious and destructive player. But there were others, perhaps quieter, more patient, whose plans were still gestating, whose networks were still being meticulously constructed.

Miller remembered the hushed conversations with Anya, the weary but determined glint in her eyes, the quiet intensity of Aris as he pieced together the digital breadcrumbs. They had faced Vance head-on, a formidable adversary. But what about the adversaries who operated with such subtlety that their existence remained largely unknown until it was too late? What about the forces that didn't require elaborate, visible operations like Project Nightingale, but worked through a thousand small, undetectable compromises?

He watched a seagull circle overhead, its cry a sharp lament against the vastness of the sky. It was a creature of instinct, driven by simple needs. Humans, he reflected, were far more complex, and far more capable of both profound good and profound evil. Vance had exploited that complexity, turning the desire for connection, for belonging, for financial security, into tools for his own nefarious purposes. The artisans of Manu, caught in the currents of global commerce and the lure of steady work, had become unwitting pawns.

Miller found himself replaying the final days of the Nightingale operation, the frantic bursts of activity, the close calls, the sheer exhaustion that had permeated every interaction. They had stopped Vance, yes, but had they truly eradicated the rot? Or had they merely pruned a diseased branch, leaving the roots to continue their insidious spread beneath the soil? The memory of Vance's smug defiance, even in the face of capture, echoed in his mind. He had been so certain of his own invincibility, so confident that his carefully constructed world would endure.

The ease with which Vance had nearly achieved his objectives was a constant specter. It had been a calculated gamble, a high-stakes operation designed to achieve a specific, devastating outcome. And it had come astonishingly close to succeeding. Miller had seen the projected impact reports, the grim simulations of what would have happened had Nightingale reached its full potential. The thought of that unchecked power, that unfettered corruption, sent a shiver down his spine. It was a chilling reminder of how fragile the systems designed to protect society truly were.

Successes were often fleeting, and the adversaries rarely conceded defeat. They regrouped, they re-strategized, they found new avenues of exploitation. Vance's capture was a victory, a significant one, but it was not the end of the war. It was merely the end of a particular battle. And Miller, who had hoped for a quiet retirement filled with the simple pleasures of the sea and the land, found himself staring into the abyss of that ongoing conflict.

The peaceful facade of his retirement, once so solid, now felt like a thin veneer. He found himself scanning faces in the small town market, listening to snippets of conversations in the local pub, his mind constantly on alert, searching for anomalies, for the subtle signs that might betray a new threat. It was an ingrained habit, a reflex honed over years of living on the knife's edge, and it was proving remarkably difficult to shake. The quietude he'd sought was being invaded by a phantom enemy, a presence felt but not yet seen.

He wondered about the individuals Vance had cultivated, the ones who had facilitated his operations, the ones who had benefited from his illicit gains. Had they all been apprehended? Or had some managed to slip through the net, their identities obscured by the sheer complexity of Vance's network, or perhaps by the strategic destruction of evidence? The thought of loose ends, of individuals who could potentially resurface, who could pick up where Vance left off, was a persistent source of anxiety.

The world, he realized, was a tapestry woven with threads of both light and dark, of honesty and deceit, of order and chaos. Vance had been a master at manipulating those threads, at weaving his own dark patterns into the fabric of society. And Miller suspected that the forces that had empowered Vance were still very much at play. The threat wasn't just about individuals; it was about the systemic vulnerabilities that allowed such individuals to thrive.

He recalled a conversation with a retired colleague, a man who had spent his career battling organized crime. "You never truly win, Frank," the man had said, his voice tinged with a world-weariness that Miller now understood all too well. "You just keep the bastards on the back foot. You win a round, they regroup, they find a new angle. It's a war of attrition." Miller had dismissed it as cynicism. Now, it felt like a prescient warning.

The ocean's rhythm, once a source of comfort, now seemed to mirror the ebb and flow of vigilance. The tide would recede, exposing the shore, offering a brief, clear view. But then it would inevitably return, its depths concealing what lay beneath. His retirement was the receding tide, the brief period of respite. But he knew, with a certainty that chilled him to the bone, that the tide of corruption would always return, bringing with it new challenges, new threats, new shadows lurking just beyond the horizon. The work, it seemed, was never truly done. The lingering sense of unease was not a sign of paranoia, but a realistic assessment of the world he had fought so hard to protect. And that realization, more than anything, was the heaviest burden of all. He was retired, but the vigilance remained, an unspoken contract with his past, a silent acknowledgment of the shadows that still danced at the edges of the light.

Chapter 15: Return to Stillness

The sterile, fluorescent-lit room of the FBI field office was a stark contrast to the salt-laced air and weathered wood of his coastal cottage. Miller sat across from Agent Jenkins, the man's usual brusque demeanor softened by a discernible weariness that mirrored Miller's own. The air buzzed with the low hum of computers and the distant clatter of keyboards, a symphony of bureaucratic finality. This was it – the last act of Project Nightingale, the meticulous, almost surgical, process of disentangling the threads of Vance's empire and weaving them into a cohesive, damning narrative for the courts.

"Let's start from the beginning, Frank," Jenkins said, pushing a thick folder across the polished table. "Your initial contact with... Vance, wasn't it? Or was it through one of his proxies?"

Miller's gaze drifted to the folder, its manila surface a blank canvas awaiting the imprint of their shared struggle. He'd recounted these events countless times in his mind, each replay a fresh etching of the nightmare. Now, it was time to commit them to official record, to ensure that the labyrinthine machinations of Project Nightingale were not lost in the fog of memory or the deliberate obfuscation of those seeking to exploit its existence.

"It wasn't direct, not initially," Miller began, his voice steady, though the phantom echo of Vance's insidious whisper seemed to slither through the sterile air. "My first real inkling came through the Manu artisan collective. Anya Sharma contacted me. She was... concerned. Not about outright criminality, not at first. It was more about unusual patterns in their orders, peculiar specifications that didn't align with their usual clientele. They were being contracted for bulk orders of a specific carving – a stylized wooden bird. Nothing inherently suspicious, except for the sheer volume, and the fact that the intermediaries were unusually secretive about the final destination and purpose."

He paused, picturing Anya's earnest face, the passion that fueled her dedication to preserving the integrity of her community's craft. "Anya was sharp. She noticed discrepancies in the payment structures, the way the orders were routed through shell companies that seemed to appear and disappear with unsettling regularity. She suspected something wasn't quite right, but she had no proof, no tangible evidence of wrongdoing. She reached out to me because of my background, my... reputation for discretion and problem-solving."

Jenkins nodded, making a note on his pad. "And you began your own inquiries."

"Discreetly, of course," Miller confirmed. "I leveraged some old contacts, ran background checks on the listed companies. It was like peeling an onion, each layer revealing more obfuscation, more shell corporations nested within others. The money trail was deliberately convoluted, designed to disappear into a digital ether. That's when I realized this wasn't just a matter of dodgy business practices. The scale, the sophistication... it pointed to something far more organized, far more dangerous."

He detailed the initial digital forays, the cautious probes into the anonymous networks Vance had utilized. "The bird carvings," Miller continued, leaning forward slightly. "That was the key. They weren't just random orders. They were markers. Anya's group, unknowingly, was producing the physical tokens for a clandestine network. The specific wood, the precise dimensions, the subtle variations in the carving – it all contributed to a unique identifier. Imagine them as physical keys, each one subtly different, designed to unlock specific data nodes or grant access to secure channels."

Jenkins scribbled furiously. "Physical keys for a digital network. Ingenious, in a twisted way."

"Vance's genius lay in his ability to blend the tangible and the virtual," Miller agreed. "He understood that in an increasingly digital world, the physical still held sway, still offered authentication that was harder to replicate or tamper with remotely. The artisans were being used to create his entry points, his physical anchors in the real world. He chose them because their craft was respected, their operations were decentralized, and their anonymity was largely guaranteed by the nature of their work. Who would suspect a small artisan collective in Manu of being involved in a global criminal enterprise?"

He went on to describe the painstaking process of tracing the digital breadcrumbs, the careful reconstruction of the data Vance had attempted to erase. He spoke of Aris's invaluable contribution, the young hacker's ability to navigate the digital underworld with a skill that both impressed and unnerved Miller. "Aris was the one who decrypted the transmission logs," Miller explained. "He found the latent data embedded within seemingly innocuous financial transactions, the metadata that Vance's team had overlooked, or perhaps believed was too deeply buried to ever be exhumed. It was like finding a hidden message woven into the fabric of everyday communication. We discovered the true nature of 'Nightingale' – not a product, but a project. A sophisticated network designed to destabilize markets, manipulate political discourse, and extract vast sums of money through a combination of cyber warfare and economic sabotage."

Miller recalled the tension of those weeks, the constant feeling of being one step behind, of racing against a clock that seemed to tick with Vance's accelerating plans. He described the near misses, the moments when their progress was abruptly halted by Vance's preemptive countermeasures, the digital tripwires that had nearly ensnared them. "There were times," Miller admitted, his voice low, "when I genuinely believed we wouldn't be able to pull it off. Vance was a ghost in the machine, always one step ahead. He anticipated our moves, rerouted his operations, and even planted false leads designed to send us chasing shadows. The sheer audacity of it was... breathtaking."

Jenkins looked up, his pen hovering over the notepad. "The financial implications, Frank. The simulations we ran based on the data you recovered were... sobering."

"Sobering is an understatement, Agent Jenkins," Miller said, a chill tracing its way down his spine as he revisited the projected outcomes. "Nightingale wasn't just about petty theft. It was about systemic collapse. Vance wasn't just aiming to steal money; he was aiming to reshape economies, to create chaos that he could then exploit. The plan involved targeted attacks on critical financial infrastructure, manipulating stock markets on a global scale, and even leveraging compromised digital identities to influence elections. The potential for widespread panic, for economic depression, for social unrest... it was immense. The artisans of Manu, with their wooden birds, were unwittingly providing the keys to unlock a Pandora's Box of global disruption."

He meticulously detailed the final days of the operation, the coordinated raids, the tense apprehension of Vance and his key lieutenants. He spoke of the evidence gathered, the terabytes of encrypted data, the server logs, the financial records painstakingly pieced together. "The challenge wasn't just obtaining the evidence," Miller emphasized, "it was preserving its integrity. Vance's organization had sophisticated data-wiping protocols. We had to ensure that every byte, every fragment of information, was secured in a way that would withstand legal scrutiny. That's where your team's expertise was invaluable, Agent Jenkins. The chain of custody, the digital forensics – it had to be impeccable."

Jenkins nodded, his expression one of grudging respect. "We're still working through a significant portion of it. The encryption alone is a masterpiece of its kind. But your insights, Frank, your understanding of Vance's methodology, proved crucial in breaking through some of the more stubborn firewalls."

Miller found a strange kind of peace in this procedural dissection. The chaos of the investigation was being systematically tamed, each piece of evidence cataloged, cross-referenced, and secured. It was the opposite of Vance's approach, which was to sow discord and exploit ambiguity. This was about clarity, about imposing order on the remnants of disorder.

"The documentation process is paramount," Miller continued, drawing on years of experience in similar operations. "We need to ensure that every piece of evidence is clearly linked, not just to Vance and his direct associates, but to the broader network. The shell corporations, the offshore accounts, the individuals who acted as intermediaries – they all need to be identified and their roles clearly defined. The goal isn't just to prosecute Vance, but to dismantle the entire ecosystem that allowed Nightingale to flourish."

He detailed the specific types of documentation they were creating: detailed timelines of events, annotated schematics of Vance's network architecture, profiles of key individuals, and comprehensive reports on the financial flows. "We're creating a living document," Miller explained. "Something that can be updated as new information comes to light, something that provides a complete picture of the operation from its inception to its dissolution. This isn't just about a single trial; it's about creating a blueprint for future investigations, a case study in how these complex, interconnected threats operate."

He recalled the late nights spent with Jenkins's team, the collaborative effort to sift through mountains of digital detritus. "The sheer volume of data," Miller said, shaking his head, "was overwhelming. But each piece, no matter how small, told a part of the story. The anonymized communications, the server logs, the fragmented code – they were all pieces of a puzzle. And your team's diligence in cataloging every single one was... remarkable. Without that meticulous approach, much of it would have been lost, dismissed as noise."

Miller then elaborated on the challenges of digital evidence in court. "The admissibility of digital evidence is always a hurdle," he stated. "We have to prove its authenticity, its integrity, and its relevance. That requires rigorous documentation, precise chain-of-custody records, and expert testimony. Every step of our process, from the initial acquisition of data to its analysis and storage, had to be watertight. We couldn't afford any procedural errors that Vance's legal team could exploit to dismiss the evidence."

He spoke about the broader implications of Project Nightingale. "This case sets a precedent, Agent Jenkins," Miller asserted. "It demonstrates the very real and present danger of corporate crime intertwined with sophisticated cyber capabilities. It highlights the need for enhanced international cooperation, for stronger regulatory frameworks, and for a more proactive approach to identifying and mitigating these kinds of threats. The methods Vance employed, the exploitation of globalized commerce and digital anonymity, are not unique to him. They are tools available to anyone with the resources and the malevolence to use them."

Miller found a sense of closure in this structured debriefing. The abstract danger, the nebulous threat that had haunted his thoughts for so long, was being rendered concrete, quantifiable. The vastness of Vance's scheme was being shrunk down, contained within the confines of official reports and court documents. It was a process of containment, of bringing the sprawling monster into a manageable, prosecutable form.

"The artisans of Manu," Miller said, a note of regret in his voice, "they were the unwitting pawns. Our documentation needs to ensure their protection, to clearly delineate their lack of involvement in the criminal enterprise. Association almost compromised their craft, their livelihood. It's crucial that their innocence is unequivocally established." He detailed the specific measures taken to safeguard the artisans' identities and to ensure that their community would not suffer further repercussions.

He also spoke about the intelligence gathered on Vance's broader network, the associates and enablers who operated in the shadows. "We need to ensure that the documentation isn't just focused on Vance himself, but on the network he cultivated," Miller stressed. "The individuals who provided him with access, who facilitated his financial transactions, who helped him maintain his anonymity – they are as much a part of Nightingale as Vance was. This comprehensive record will enable the FBI to pursue further investigations, to track down those who may have slipped through our grasp."

Miller described the meticulous cataloging of communication logs, the cross-referencing of digital footprints with known aliases and financial activities. "It's a digital tapestry," he reiterated, "and we're meticulously documenting every thread, every knot. The goal is to create an irrefutable narrative that leaves no room for doubt, no avenue for evasion. This is how we ensure that the victory against Nightingale is not just a temporary reprieve, but a lasting blow against the forces that seek to exploit and corrupt."

As the hours wore on, and the stack of completed documentation grew, a sense of quiet satisfaction settled over Miller. The emotional turmoil of the investigation was giving way to the measured calm of completion. He had faced a formidable foe, had navigated a landscape of deceit and danger, and now, through this rigorous process of debriefing and documentation, he was contributing to a lasting resolution. The fight against Vance and Project Nightingale was drawing to a close, not with a bang, but with the quiet, definitive thud of official records being filed away, ready to stand as a testament to a battle won, and a darkness held at bay. The meticulous work was not just about the present case; it was about fortifying the future, about building a bulwark against the insidious creep of corruption. It was, in its own way, a return to stillness, not of inactivity, but of order restored.

The sterile air of the FBI field office, thick with the scent of stale coffee and the silent hum of overworked machinery, began to recede from Miller's consciousness. The meticulously organized folders, the sharp angles of the desks, the very uniformity of the place – all of it was a stark contrast to the life he was returning to. He had spent weeks immersed in the labyrinthine complexities of Project Nightingale, a world of digital ghosts, shell corporations, and the chillingly calculated ambition of a man named Vance. Now, the adrenaline that had coursed through his veins, the razor-sharp focus that had kept him one step ahead, was beginning to ebb, leaving behind a profound, almost disorienting, sense of calm.

The final reports were filed. The last keystrokes had been made, each one a tiny victory against the chaos Vance had sought to unleash. Agent Jenkins, his face etched with the exhaustion of a long campaign, had offered a curt nod of acknowledgment, a silent testament to the shared ordeal. There were no grand pronouncements, no fanfare. Just the quiet, methodical process of bringing a dangerous operation to its knees. Miller had walked out of that building, not with a spring in his step, but with a heavy, grounded certainty. The storm had passed.

The journey back to his secluded coastal cottage was a pilgrimage of sorts, a slow unwinding of the tightly wound spring of tension that had defined his existence for what felt like an eternity. The roads, usually a source of minor annoyance, now felt like a gentle embrace, the familiar curve of the asphalt leading him back to the solace of his quiet corner of the world. He drove with the windows down, letting the crisp, salt-tinged air wash over him, each breath a conscious act of shedding the residue of the investigation. The mundane sights and sounds that had once been background noise now registered with a startling clarity: the rhythmic rush of waves against the shore, the mournful cry of seagulls wheeling overhead, the distant, comforting clang of a buoy.

He found himself replaying the events, not with the frantic urgency of piecing together clues, but with a detached observer's eye. The cruise ship, the opulent vessel that had been the stage for Vance's insidious endgame, now existed in his memory as a symbol. It had been a gilded cage, a microcosm of the world Vance had sought to manipulate, a place where fear and Anna had been leveraged with surgical precision. But it had also been the place where his carefully constructed façade had begun to crumble, where the threads of Project Nightingale had been exposed, not by a sudden, dramatic unraveling, but by the persistent, quiet work of those who refused to let such machinations go unchecked. He remembered the initial unease, the subtle discrepancies Anya Sharma had brought to his attention, the meticulous way the Manu artisans had unknowingly crafted the physical keys to Vance's digital kingdom. It was a stark reminder that the integrity of ordinary people could bring even the most sophisticated criminal enterprises down, by their keen observation and unwavering commitment to their craft.

The concept of "return to stillness" took on a new meaning. It wasn't just the absence of danger or the cessation of high-stakes operations. It was a settling of the soul after a period of intense upheaval. He thought of the contrast between his life before Nightingale and the life he was now re-entering. The quiet routine of his cottage, the solitude that had once been a choice, now felt like a sanctuary, a necessary balm for a spirit that had been tested. He had walked through a fire, not of his own making, but one he had been compelled to navigate. And in the aftermath, the familiar comforts of his existence were imbued with a new significance.

He recalled the conversations with Jenkins, the methodical documentation that had been the anchor to reality amidst the swirling currents of espionage and cybercrime. Each piece of evidence, each recovered data fragment, had been a step towards restoring order. It was the antithesis of Vance's methods, which thrived on chaos and ambiguity. Miller's own contribution, his ability to understand the criminal mind, to anticipate the next move, had been a crucial element in that restoration. But it had also come at a cost, a psychic toll that only now, in the quiet solitude of his return, was he beginning to fully comprehend. The constant vigilance, the gnawing uncertainty, the moral compromises, however small, that were an inevitable part of operating in such a murky world – all of it had left its mark.

As he drove, the landscape unfurled like a familiar map. The rugged coastline, the windswept dunes, the small, unassuming fishing villages – they were all constants in a world that flux had recently defined. He pulled over at a deserted overlook, the kind he'd often passed by without a second glance. The vast expanse of the ocean stretched out before him, an endless canvas of blues and greens, its surface rippling with a gentle, rhythmic motion. It was a sight that had always brought him a sense of perspective, a reminder of the immense forces that operated beyond human control. Today, it felt like a balm, a silent acknowledgment that the storms of life, however fierce, eventually subsided, leaving behind a profound and enduring stillness.

He thought of Aris, the young hacker whose raw talent and unyielding dedication had been instrumental in unraveling Vance's digital fortress. Aris, who had navigated the dark corners of the internet with a skill that both impressed and unsettled Miller. The boy had been a crucial weapon in their arsenal, a digital warrior fighting a war Miller himself couldn't fully comprehend. But Aris, too, was a casualty of this conflict, a young mind exposed to the worst of human ingenuity and malice. Miller hoped that bringing Nightingale to justice would provide some measure of healing, some sense of closure, for everyone involved.

The drive continued, each mile a further shedding of the weight he had carried. He passed by a small artisan shop, its window displaying a collection of handcrafted wooden figures, simple, elegant, and undeniably peaceful. For a fleeting moment, he wondered if any of the artists there had ever felt the subtle ripple of Vance's influence, had ever been unknowingly touched by the dark currents that flowed beneath the surface of commerce. It was a thought that lingered, a quiet reminder of the interconnectedness of all things, and the insidious ways in which evil could infiltrate even the most innocent of endeavors. The Manu artisans, with their birds, had been a stark example. Their art, a symbol of tradition and community, had been co-opted, twisted into a tool for destruction.

Reaching his cottage, the familiar scent of pine and sea salt greeted him like an old friend. The weathered wood of its exterior, the worn stone path leading to the door, the gentle sway of the ancient oak tree in the yard – it was all a testament to the enduring peace he had sought. He unlocked the door, the sound of the tumblers clicking into place echoing in the quiet interior. Inside, the air was cool and still, carrying the faint, comforting aroma of aged paper and beeswax polish. Dust motes danced in the shafts of sunlight that streamed through the windows, illuminating the quiet solitude of his sanctuary.

He moved through the rooms, his movements slow and deliberate, as if not to disturb the profound stillness that had settled. He ran his hand along the spine of a worn leather-bound book, the familiar texture a grounding sensation. This was his world, a world of quiet contemplation, of endless books, and the unhurried rhythm of the tides. The contrast with the frantic pace of the investigation was almost jarring. He had been living in a perpetual state of high alert. Now, he could finally afford to slow down, to breathe, to simply *be*.

The cruise ship, once a symbol of luxury and leisure, had become something else entirely. It was a place where a significant threat had been neutralized, where a complex web of deceit had been untangled. It was a testament to the fact that even in the most seemingly serene environments, darkness could lurk. But it was also a testament to the power of human intervention, to the courage and diligence of those who stood against it. Miller wasn't a man who sought out such confrontations, but when they found him, he had proven he could meet them head-on. The victory wasn't about glory or recognition; it was about restoring a semblance of order, about ensuring that the seeds of chaos did not take root.

He found himself sitting by the window, looking out at the endless expanse of the ocean. The sun was beginning to dip below the horizon, casting long shadows across the water, painting the sky in hues of orange and violet. It was a sight of breathtaking beauty, a beauty that had always been there, waiting for him, even during the darkest days of the investigation. He had been so focused on the immediate threat, on the intricate dance of deduction and action, that he had almost forgotten the enduring power of the natural world to heal and restore.

The adrenaline had faded, replaced by a quiet weariness, but beneath that weariness lay a bedrock of peace. He had done what he had to do. He had confronted a formidable enemy, had played his part in dismantling a dangerous operation, and now, he was home. The quiet life he had cultivated was not an escape, but a refuge. It was a place where he could process, where he could heal, and where he could regain the equilibrium that had been so violently disrupted. The storm had indeed passed, and in its wake, a profound and welcome stillness had descended. He closed his eyes, the rhythmic sound of the waves a gentle lullaby, and allowed himself to simply exist in the quiet embrace of his return. The work was done. The fight was over. For now, there was only the stillness.

The salt-laced wind whipped strands of hair across Miller's face as he walked the familiar stretch of coastline. Each step crunched on the pebbles and shells, a sound that had always been a gentle counterpoint to the roar of the ocean. This was his ritual, the long, solitary walk that served as the opening act of his return to stillness. The investigation, the dizzying ascent into Vance's manufactured reality, had been a tempest. Now, the quiet ebb and flow of the tide mirrored the settling of his own internal waters. He wasn't just back at his cottage; he was back in himself, a self that had been temporarily displaced, reconfigured by the demands of a world teetering on the brink of digital chaos.

His gaze swept over the horizon, a familiar panorama of sea and sky. It was an expanse that had always offered perspective, a silent reminder of insignificance in the grand scheme of things, and yet, a profound sense of belonging. He'd spent weeks in sterile environments, his vision narrowed to the flickering screens and the grim faces of those caught in Vance's web. Now, the sheer, unadulterated vastness of the ocean was a balm. It invited his thoughts to expand, to wander without the constraints of a dossier or the pressure of an imminent threat. He noticed, with a clarity that surprised him, the intricate patterns the waves carved into the sand, the way the gulls danced on the updrafts, their cries sharp and clear against the pervasive hum of the sea. These were details that had always been present, but in the aftermath of Nightingale, they resonated with a newfound significance, a testament to a world that continued, unbothered, beneath the machinations of men.

The memory of the cruise ship, the opulent vessel that had served as Vance's stage, was a subtle undertow beneath the surface of his peaceful stride. It wasn't a haunting, not anymore. The adrenaline had dissipated, leaving behind a sober understanding. He'd seen how easily such grand spectacles could be corrupted, how the veneer of luxury could mask a rot of ambition and control. He remembered the meticulously planned elegance of Vance's operation, the way he had sought to leverage fear and desire, to orchestrate a symphony of human weakness. But he also remembered the counter-melodies: Anya Sharma's quiet persistence, the Manu artisans' unwitting contribution, Aris's digital wizardry. These were the dissonances that had ultimately disrupted Vance's grand design, proof that integrity, even when unintentional, could be a potent disruptor of carefully crafted chaos.

As he walked, his mind drifted to Aris. The young hacker, a whirlwind of nervous energy and raw talent, had navigated the digital underbelly with a skill that both impressed and unnerved Miller. Aris had been an indispensable tool, a weapon forged in the crucible of code. But Miller also knew the cost. Exposure to Vance's world, to the calculated cruelty and the pervasive cynicism, left its mark. Miller hoped that the resolution of Nightingale, the dismantling of Vance's empire, offered Aris some semblance of peace, a chance to reclaim his own quiet corners of the internet without the shadow of such darkness looming over him. It was a reminder that even in victory, there were casualties, and the pursuit of justice often demanded more than just a sharp mind and a steady hand; it demanded a willingness to protect those who fought alongside you, even from the lingering echoes of the conflict.

The path eventually led him back towards the cluster of cottages that dotted the coastline, his own a humble sentinel among them. He paused at the small artisan shop, its window displaying a collection of carved wooden birds, their wings poised as if in mid-flight. He'd admired their craftsmanship before, but now, they seemed to embody a resilience, a connection to something pure and enduring. He mused on the subtle ways influence, both positive and negative, could permeate seemingly untouched corners of the world. The Manu artisans, with their art of birds, had been a poignant example of how even the most innocent creations could become entangled in larger, more sinister narratives.

Entering his cottage, the familiar scent of aged paper, beeswax, and dried sea herbs enveloped him like a comforting embrace. The dust motes dancing in the shafts of sunlight were not an indication of neglect, but rather of a sanctuary left undisturbed, awaiting his return. He moved through the rooms with a practiced ease, his presence filling the silence without breaking it. He ran his hand along the spines of his well-worn books, the embossed titles a familiar topography of thought and imagination. This was not merely a house; it was a testament to a chosen way of life, a bulwark against the ceaseless clamor of the outside world. The silence here was not an absence of sound, but a presence of peace, a carefully curated stillness that had been a deliberate aspiration long before Vance had ever entered his orbit.

He found himself drawn to his study, the room that had always been his haven for contemplation. The worn leather of his armchair, the smooth expanse of his oak desk, the overflowing bookshelves – all of it spoke of a life dedicated to inner exploration. He picked up a well-thumbed volume of poetry, its pages brittle with age. The verses, once read with a detached appreciation, now seemed to echo the profound shift within him. The storm had passed, leaving behind not just an absence of danger, but a deeper understanding of what he truly valued. The experience with Nightingale had been a crucible, a trial by fire that had refined his resolve and clarified his purpose. His retirement, he realized, was not an abdication but a strategic withdrawal, a conscious choice to redirect his skills and his energy towards a life of quiet purpose.

He sat by the window, the ocean stretching out before him, a boundless expanse of blues and greens. The setting sun cast a warm, golden light across the water, painting the sky in vibrant hues of orange and crimson. It was a spectacle of natural beauty, a beauty that had always been present, waiting patiently for him to notice. He recalled the frantic urgency of the investigation, the all-consuming nature of the hunt. In that vortex, the subtler, enduring beauty of the world had often been relegated to the background. Now, he could truly see it, truly appreciate it. The memory of Vance and his insidious plans was still there, a faint scent on the breeze, a subtle shadow at the edge of his vision. But it no longer held the power to disrupt the serenity. Instead, it served as a stark reminder of the importance of what he had fought for: the preservation of order, the protection of the vulnerable, and the enduring strength of the human spirit.

He understood now that true stillness was not the absence of external stimuli, but an internal equilibrium achieved through conscious effort and unwavering self-awareness. The journey back to his cottage had been more than a physical return; it had been a profound internal recalibration. He had faced a formidable foe, had navigated the treacherous currents of deception, and had emerged not unscathed, but undeniably changed. The lessons learned on that ill-fated cruise ship, in the sterile offices of the FBI, and in the silent corners of the digital realm, had coalesced into a deeper understanding of himself and his place in the world. His solitude was not a retreat from humanity, but a space from which to engage with it more meaningfully, his skills now honed and focused not for the thrill of the chase, but for the quiet satisfaction of contributing to a greater good. The world was a complex tapestry, and he had played his part in mending a frayed thread, ensuring that the intricate pattern could continue to unfold, unmarred by the designs of those who sought to unravel it. The stillness he had found was not an ending, but a profound and potent beginning.

The porch of the cottage felt like a threshold, a place where the known and the unknown met. Miller stood there, the weathered wood cool beneath his bare feet, and let his gaze fall upon the ocean. It was a familiar sight, as much a part of him as the worn leather of his favorite armchair, yet today it held a different resonance. The vastness that had once beckoned him towards escape, towards the quiet anonymity of solitude, now seemed to mirror the intricate, often unseen, complexities he had navigated and helped to resolve. The gentle lapping of the waves against the shore, a sound that had always soothed him, now whispered of the hidden currents, the unseen forces that moved beneath the surface, much like the meticulously crafted machinations of Vance's conspiracy. He saw in the endless expanse of blues and greens not just a promise of tranquility, but a stark reminder of the deep, often murky, depths that lay beneath even the most serene-looking surface. The Sovereign Star, that gilded cage floating on the sea, with its secrets meticulously hidden behind a façade of opulence, was a potent symbol of this duality. It was a testament to the fact that beauty and danger, order and chaos, could coexist in the most unsettling proximity.

He watched as a solitary gull wheeled and dipped, its effortless flight a stark contrast to the turbulent journey that had brought him back to this quiet corner of the world. The investigation, the relentless pursuit of Vance, had been a whirlwind, a storm that had tested his resolve and pushed him to the very edges of his capabilities. Now, the calm that followed felt less like an ending and more like a profound, earned stillness. Yet, stillness, he knew, was not an absolute. It was a state of being that required constant tending, a delicate balance that could be easily disrupted. The horizon, so deceptively peaceful, was a canvas upon which unseen dramas could unfold, just as the calm waters of the open sea could conceal treacherous reefs and unpredictable squalls. The serene beauty of the ocean offered a promise, a comforting assurance that the world continued to spin, that life persisted with its inherent rhythms, but it was a promise he understood now was contingent upon vigilance.

The resolution of the Nightingale operation had been a victory, a crucial step in safeguarding the fragile equilibrium of the digital age. But victories, Miller reflected, were rarely clean. They left behind ripples, unseen consequences that could spread far beyond the initial impact. He thought of Aris, the young hacker whose extraordinary talents had been instrumental in unraveling Vance's web. Aris had been a digital ghost, a phantom in the machine, and Miller knew the cost of such immersion. The constant exposure to the dark underbelly of the internet, the knowledge of its vulnerabilities and the potential for its exploitation, was a heavy burden for any mind, let alone one so young and still forming. He hoped that Aris had found a way to compartmentalize, to build digital walls around his experiences, and to reclaim the innocent curiosity that had likely drawn him to the world of code. The digital landscape, like the ocean before him, was a place of immense power and potential, but also of profound peril. It was a frontier that demanded respect, and a keen awareness of its hidden dangers.

The memory of Anya Sharma, the quiet analyst whose meticulous attention to detail had unearthed the crucial anomalies, also surfaced. Her unwavering commitment to truth, her refusal to be swayed by the grandeur of Vance's deception, was a quiet force that had resonated deeply with Miller. She was an example of the unsung heroes who operated in the shadows, their contributions often overlooked, yet vital to the preservation of order. Her work, like the patient erosion of the coastline by the relentless tide, had chipped away at Vance's carefully constructed edifice until it finally crumbled. He wondered if she, too, found solace in the stillness, if she could now look at the world with a sense of accomplishment, knowing she had played a part in protecting it. The subtle interplay of forces, the seemingly insignificant actions that could cascade into monumental outcomes, was a recurring theme in his life, and one that the ocean seemed to amplify.

Miller turned from the sea, the scent of salt and ozone clinging to his skin. He knew that retirement was not an abdication of responsibility, but a redirection of it. The skills honed over years of navigating complex investigations, of dissecting human motives and anticipating dangerous actions, were not skills that could be simply switched off. They were ingrained, a part of his very being. He looked around his cottage, the familiar clutter of books and papers, the worn surfaces that bore the imprint of his life. This was not just a dwelling; it was a sanctuary, a base from which he could continue to observe, to learn, and perhaps, when the need arose, to act. The stillness he had found here was not a passive surrender, but an active cultivation of inner peace, a conscious effort to maintain equilibrium in a world that perpetually teetered on the brink of chaos.

He picked up a smooth, sea-worn stone from the small collection on his windowsill. It was a tangible piece of the ocean, a testament to its ceaseless motion and its enduring power. He rolled it between his fingers, feeling its coolness, its weight. This stone, like the memories of Nightingale, was a reminder of forces beyond his control, of processes that were ancient and vast. Vance's ambition, his desire to manipulate and control, had been a fleeting ripple against the immense, enduring currents of the natural world. The digital realm, the battleground where much of their conflict had taken place, was itself a reflection of the human mind – capable of incredible beauty and innovation, but also susceptible to darkness and destruction. To navigate such a world, one needed a profound understanding of these underlying currents, an awareness that extended beyond the immediate and the obvious.

The days that followed his return were a deliberate immersion in the rhythms of the coast. He walked the beaches at dawn, watching the sun paint the sky in soft pastels, and returned at dusk, when the sea transformed into a shimmering expanse of silver and deep indigo. He visited the local market, not as an agent on a clandestine mission, but as a neighbor, a man seeking fresh produce and pleasant conversation. He exchanged nods with the fishermen mending their nets, their weathered faces etched with the stories of countless tides. He observed the children building sandcastles, their laughter carried on the breeze, their innocent creations destined to be reclaimed by the sea, a gentle reminder of impermanence. Each interaction, each observation, was a small anchor, grounding him in the reality of the present, in the simple, enduring beauty of everyday life.

He found himself drawn to the quiet hum of the local library, a place where knowledge resided in a more traditional, tangible form. He spent hours poring over histories of maritime exploration, tales of ancient mariners who had charted unknown waters with nothing but the stars and their own indomitable spirit. These stories, far removed from the sterile efficiency of digital data, spoke of a different kind of struggle, a raw engagement with the elements that required a profound connection to the natural world. He saw parallels, of course. The need for meticulous planning, for an understanding of the unpredictable nature of the environment, for the courage to face the unknown – these were elements that transcended time and technology. Vance, in his own way, had been an explorer of sorts, but his explorations had been into the darkest corners of human psychology and technological potential, driven by a lust for power rather than a thirst for discovery.

One afternoon, while browsing a shelf of local folklore, he stumbled upon a collection of old sea shanties. He read the lyrics aloud, his voice a low rumble in the hushed room, the words painting vivid images of storm-tossed ships, of camaraderie forged in the face of peril, of the constant awareness of the ocean's capricious nature. It struck him then that these songs, these echoes of lives lived in constant dialogue with the sea, were vigilance in themselves. They were a way of acknowledging the power of the ocean, of respecting its might, and of preparing for its challenges. Vance, he realized, had failed to truly respect the currents, had underestimated the resilience of those who understood them. His ambition had been to command the tide, rather than to navigate it.

He returned to his cottage, the sea shanties still echoing in his mind. He sat on his porch, the same spot where he had first gazed upon the ocean with a newfound sense of closure. The sun was beginning its descent, casting long shadows across the sand. The air was cool, carrying the faint scent of woodsmoke from a neighboring chimney. He knew that the world beyond this coastline was still a place of intricate machinations and hidden dangers, that the battle against those who sought to exploit and control was never truly over. But here, in this quiet sanctuary, he had found his own form of vigilance. It was a vigilance of the spirit, a commitment to clarity of thought, and an unwavering belief in the enduring power of integrity. The ocean, in its vastness and its mystery, was no longer just a backdrop; it was a constant, profound reminder that beneath the surface of every calm, there lies a world of complexity, a testament to the ongoing need for watchful eyes. He was not retired from the world, but he had returned to himself, ready to observe its currents from a place of deep, earned stillness.

The salt-laced wind still teased the edges of his senses, a constant, subtle reminder of the ocean's proximity. Miller traced the rim of his teacup, the ceramic warm against his fingertips. The storm, the one that had raged through his life with the intensity of a Category Five, had passed. The wreckage had been surveyed, the accounts settled, and a fragile peace had settled over the landscape of his existence. Yet, the stillness he now inhabited was not a void, but a cultivated space, one meticulously cleared of the debris of conflict, ready for a new, less tumultuous, form of occupancy. His days of kicking down doors and navigating the labyrinthine corridors of federal investigations were behind him, relegated to the annals of a life intensely lived. The FBI, once the very marrow of his being, was now a closed chapter.

He hadn't expected retirement to feel like this – not a gentle fading, but a deliberate recalibration. The adrenaline that had once surged through his veins, the electric hum of anticipation that accompanied every tip-off, every potential breakthrough, had receded, replaced by a more measured, internal energy. It was the energy of observation, of reflection, of a mind still sharp, still capable, but no longer tethered to the frantic pace of active duty. The phone, once a conduit to the urgent calls of duty, now sat silently on its charger, a dormant oracle waiting for a specific, deliberate invocation.

Jenkins had called last week, his voice crackling with a familiar blend of respect and a touch of weariness. "Miller," he'd said, the name itself carrying the weight of shared battles, "we've hit a snag on the Beaumont case. You remember Beaumont? The arms trafficker we were building a case against before Nightingale blew up in our faces?" Miller remembered. Beaumont, a phantom in the shadows, always a step ahead, his networks woven into the very fabric of global instability. "It's his money laundering, Miller. The digital trail is colder than a Siberian winter. You worked with Anya on some of those anomalies, remember? Before she... well, before." A pause, heavy with unspoken grief. Anya Sharma. The quiet analyst, the bedrock of their intel, a loss that still resonated in the empty spaces of their operations. "Jenkins, I'm retired," Miller had said, the words tasting unfamiliar on his tongue. "But I remember the files. Send them over. Let me see what I can see."

And he had. The digital files, a sprawling testament to Beaumont's avarice, had landed in his inbox like a digital blizzard. He'd spent two days immersed, the familiar glow of the monitor reflecting in his focused gaze. It wasn't the thrill of the chase, not the visceral satisfaction of closing in, but something akin to solving a complex puzzle, a mental exercise that still engaged the gears of his analytical mind. He saw the patterns, the subtle deviations from the norm that had eluded the younger analysts, the faint whispers of manipulation that echoed the very techniques Vance had employed. It was like recognizing a particular strain of handwriting, a familiar fingerprint on a seemingly unrelated crime.

He'd sent a concise report back to Jenkins. No fanfare, no grand pronouncements, just a series of meticulously documented observations, highlighting a specific offshore shell company and a series of obscure cryptocurrency transactions that seemed to mirror Vance's own financial architecture. Jenkins's grateful reply had been swift. "Miller, you're a goddamn miracle worker. That's exactly the kind of rabbit hole we needed to go down. You just... you just see things differently." Miller had merely nodded. He saw things differently because he had seen too much, too closely, for too long. The world, viewed through the lens of his experiences, was a landscape riddled with hidden traps and deceptive illusions.

His relationship with his former colleagues had shifted, evolving from a hierarchical structure to one of mutual respect and shared purpose. He was no longer their superior, nor were they his subordinates. They were peers, united by a common cause that transcended titles and official capacities. Jenkins, a man of unwavering integrity, understood this. He knew that Miller's mind was a repository of knowledge, a strategic asset that could still be deployed, albeit with a different protocol. The Nightingale operation had been a crucible, forging a bond between them that the conventional rules of retirement couldn't break. They understood that the threats to order and justice were persistent, protean, and that specialized knowledge, even when voluntarily set aside, remained a potent weapon in the ongoing struggle.

He thought of Aris. The young hacker, a prodigy whose mind worked at a speed that often left Miller feeling like a lumbering leviathan. Aris had been instrumental, a digital phantom navigating the treacherous currents of Vance's network. Miller had worried about him, about the psychological toll of such intense exposure to the digital underbelly, the sheer weight of knowledge that could warp a young mind. Jenkins had mentioned that Aris had taken some time off, a sabbatical to "recalibrate," as he'd put it. Miller hoped it was enough. He hoped the boy could build those walls, compartmentalize the darkness he had witnessed, and find his way back to the innocent joy of creation that had first drawn him to the world of code. The digital realm was a frontier, and Aris was a pioneer. Pioneers often bore scars.

Retirement, for Miller, was not an abdication. It was a metamorphosis. The core of his being, the unwavering commitment to justice, to the meticulous unraveling of deception, remained. It was simply channeled differently. Instead of actively pursuing the perpetrators, he was now an observer, a quiet guardian of the principles he had fought for. He was a resource, a repository of experience, a trusted advisor for those who continued the fight on the front lines. He was the old oak tree at the edge of the forest, its roots deep and strong, its branches offering shelter and perspective to those still navigating the wilder terrain.

He found a peculiar satisfaction in these quiet contributions. It was akin to tending a garden. The active tilling and planting were done; now it was about weeding, about ensuring the soil remained fertile, about providing the quiet support that allowed new growth to flourish. The Beaumont case was a prime example. He hadn't broken the case himself; he had merely pointed the way, illuminated a path that complexity had obscured. Jenkins and his team would handle the subsequent work. It was a collaboration, a seamless transfer of expertise, a testament to the enduring strength of their shared mission.

He understood that the world was not a neatly ordered system. It was a chaotic, ever-shifting landscape, a constant interplay of forces where the lines between good and evil were often blurred, and where the pursuit of justice was a never-ending endeavor. Vance's downfall, while a significant victory, had not eradicated the forces he represented. The hunger for power, the desire to manipulate and control, were ancient human impulses, as enduring as the tides. The digital age had simply provided new, more insidious avenues for their expression.

His days were now filled with a different kind of vigilance. It was a vigilance of the mind, a constant process of observation and analysis, of piecing together the subtle narratives that unfolded around him. He read voraciously, not just thrillers and mysteries, but histories, biographies, treatises on economics and philosophy. He sought to understand the broader currents that shaped human behavior, the underlying causes of conflict and corruption. He viewed his cottage not just as a sanctuary, but as an observatory, a vantage point from which he could survey the world with a clarity unclouded by the immediate pressures of active service.

He still walked the beaches, but now his gaze was not just on the horizon, but on the intricate patterns left by the receding tide, the delicate ecosystems thriving in the rock pools, the silent conversations between the sand and the sea. He saw in these natural processes a reflection of the larger forces at play in the human world: the constant ebb and flow, the cycles of creation and destruction, the interconnectedness of all things. Vance's ambition, his desire to impose order through brute force and manipulation, had been a futile attempt to dam a river that was destined to flow.

He had cultivated a network of quiet connections, a web of informal informants and trusted sources who understood his changed role. A retired librarian who kept him abreast of curious trends in historical research, a seasoned journalist who shared insights into the whispers of corporate malfeasance, a former intelligence analyst who occasionally dropped cryptic but invaluable tidbits. These were not organized channels of information, but organic relationships built on years of shared experience and mutual trust. He was a ghost in the machine, a whisper in the wind, his influence subtle but persistent.

He received another email from Jenkins, this one brief and to the point. "Project Chimera. High-level data breach at a global financial institution. Looks like a state-sponsored actor. We're in uncharted territory. Would you be willing to consult, remotely of course?" Miller smiled. Uncharted territory. That was where he felt most at home. He typed back his reply, the familiar thrill of intellectual engagement stirring within him. "Send me the initial reports. I'll be in touch."

His watch had not ended. It had simply shifted. The relentless pursuit of tangible criminals had evolved into a more nuanced guardianship of the principles of justice and order. He was no longer the knight on the battlefield, but the wise counselor in the castle, offering strategic guidance and a steady hand. The stillness he had found was not an absence of action, but a profound understanding of its necessary deployment. It was the quiet strength of a deep reservoir, capable of being drawn upon when the need arose, its power undiminished by the peaceful surface.

He was retired from the office, but not from the fight.

Acknowledgments

I am primarily grateful to those readers who enjoy mysteries because they are the ones who inspired this story. Your passion and dedication to these magnificent mysteries of the past constantly fill me with wonder and great admiration for you. Those who enjoy mysteries and live-action "who-done-it" productions form a skilled collection of individuals worthy of commendation for their passionate appreciation and ability to bring a story to life. The storytelling was molded distinctly and fascinatingly because of several cruises that my spouse and I have experienced in the past. This has enhanced the creative vision and has further enriched the narrative by adding an extra dimension.

To my family, whose unwavering support and encouragement made this book possible. Thank you for believing in my dreams and sharing in the journey. Your love and faith have been my guiding light, and I am forever grateful for your presence. You have been my rock, my cheerleader, and my inspiration. This book is as much yours as it is mine.

I'd also like to thank my illustrator, Karen Shayler, and my editor, Roxana Coumans, for their indispensable help and support during the book's publication. This story wouldn't be alive without your keen eye, insightful feedback, and endless patience. This project has benefited from your dedication to excellence and belief in its success.

To all the readers who have embarked on this journey with Alex and Star, thank you for your support and enthusiasm. Your love for stories and your belief in the magic of friendship and perseverance have made this book a reality. May this tale inspire you to chase your dreams, nurture your friendships, and cherish the bonds that enrich your life.

About the Author

Brett Shayler, an author, has been passionate about horses and the natural world his entire life. Raised on a ranch surrounded by diverse animals, he vividly reflects in his storytelling the profound and enduring connections between people and the animals they cherish and care for throughout their lives. Drawing inspiration from his family's vast acreage and the wild horses that roam freely upon it, Brett lovingly crafts heartwarming tales that celebrate the bonds of friendship and extol the virtues of deep respect for the natural world and the remarkable connections between people and animals. Through his books, he hopes to cultivate curiosity, compassion, and a thirst for knowledge in young readers. Brett often escapes to nature, hiking and observing wildlife, finding inspiration for his writing away from his desk. Brett proudly holds membership in both the prestigious National Cutting Horse Association and the equally esteemed American Quarter Horse Association, demonstrating his deep commitment to these organizations and the equestrian world.

www.ingramcontent.com/pod-product-compliance
Lightning Source LLC
LaVergne TN
LVHW090548110826
845146LV00001B/62

* 9 7 9 8 9 9 5 3 6 9 0 1 1 *